THE UNSOLVABLE CASE

"You know anything about this case?" Ryan asked, taking one more drag before stubbing out his cigarette.

"Not much. Lady judge disappeared about six months ago. Discovered her body in a pond recently, stuffed in some kind of trunk. Never found her car anywhere. Shay made the incident into a campaign issue, saying it pointed to O'Hara's incompetence."

"You got it," Ryan said. "This case is colder than Chicago in January. No way we'll solve it. Ain't gonna happen." He hunched forward, so close that Leal could smell the booze on the other man's conspiratorial whisper. "But that's just it. They expect us to fall on our faces on this one. We're getting set up to get hung out to dry, Leal...."

Other *Leisure* books by Michael A. Black:

A KILLING FROST

MICHAEL A. BLACK

RANDOM VICTIM

LEISURE BOOKS NEW YORK CITY

To Len Jellema, one of the finest men I've ever known.

A LEISURE BOOK®

April 2008

Published by

Dorchester Publishing Co., Inc.
200 Madison Avenue
New York, NY 10016

ISBN 10: 0-8439-5986-X
ISBN 13: 978-0-8439-5986-4

Visit us on the web at www.dorchesterpub.com.

ACKNOWLEDGMENTS

Every writer has a list of people he wishes to acknowledge, and the problem is you can never thank them all. But, to name a few...

First, I'd like to thank Joseph Wambaugh. It was reading his book, *The New Centurions*, so many years ago that first steered me toward the Military Police and then into civilian law enforcement. I owe you one, Joe. Thanks.

My former teachers, from Miss Rehak ripping up my story in front of the class in sixth grade, to my undergrad days at NIU learning the basics from Mary Sue Scriber, James McNiece, and Orville Baker, to my second undergrad experience at Moraine Valley Community College refining my writing (and my Spanish) under Len Jellema and Rolando Arocha, to the final polishing in grad school at Columbia College studying under Patricia Pinianski, Shawn Shifflett, and Patty McNair...and all the rest who are too numerous to mention here, I humbly thank you all. As the saying goes, if you're reading this, thank a teacher.

And as the other saying goes, if you're reading it in English, thank our military. I'd like to extend that to all the protectors, civilian and military, who stand watch, whether in foreign lands or on our soil...Who stand together or walk alone...Who are out there on that thin line that separates civilization from chaos...Who do their best to keep evil away from innocence, thus allowing society to sleep blissfully at night...Who are ready to lay down their lives in the protection of others.

I can say that I've met some of the finest people I've ever known while spending the majority of my adult life in uniform (both civilian and military). I am honored to have stood beside them.

It is to all of these people, and so many more, that this book is truly dedicated.

RANDOM VICTIM

CHAPTER ONE
Meeting at a Rest Stop

Waves of heat rose from the tapering ribbon of expressway, and Martin Walker could hear the distant rumble of motorcycles. They appeared gradually on the horizon as three incremental dots shimmering in the midday sun. It had to be them. He studied the sight momentarily before forcing himself out of the air-conditioned comfort of his Mercedes-Benz. It was insufferably hot, even for early September. He flipped the alarm button on his remote and walked across the expanse of asphalt toward the solid-looking brick building housing the rest stop toilet facilities so graciously provided by the Illinois Department of Transportation. He could already feel himself starting to sweat.

As he got to the big metal door, scratched and painted with a myriad of graffiti, the stench caused his nostrils to flare. Where the hell do all our tax dollars go to that they can't at least keep these goddamn things cleaned? he thought. But the unmuffled roar of the three Harleys was growing steadily louder, and as Walker grabbed the metal handle and stepped inside he knew that the unpleasant smell wasn't really what was causing his anxiety.

Several urinals lined the far wall opposite a row of toilet stalls and twin sinks. It was even hotter in here than it was outside, and Walker continued to sweat profusely. So profusely he could feel the wetness of his collar and hoped it wouldn't seep through his shirt and into the jacket lining of his gray suit. Taking up a position at the urinal nearest the sink, he leaned on the rectangular metal privacy screen, making his best effort at nonchalance. The sound of the motorcycles outside ceased. Walker waited and moments later the door swung open, making a resounding thump as it hit the solid stone of the brick wall.

Nuke strode in, clad in his usual dirty blue jeans, sleeveless Levi's jacket, and engineer boots. Walker's nod was ignored and Nuke walked over to the far end of the enclosed stalls. One by one he kicked open each door, the metal making a sharp clinking sound that hurt Walker's ears, but he knew better than to say anything. Nuke's dark hair hung in a mangy, unkempt fashion, and reflective sunglasses masked his eyes. The huge, winged Harley Davidson emblem seemed stretched across the back of the jacket, pulled taut by the oversized muscles. After he'd checked the last stall, the big man turned and went to the urinal closest to Walker.

"How's it going?" Walker asked, trying to coax the slight tremor out of his voice. The other man ignored the greeting, but lowered the sunglasses on his nose.

"What the fuck you starin' at, Marty?" he said as he began to urinate.

Walker bristled at the use of the nickname he hated. But he knew Nuke loved to bait him, and dealing with this big cretin had become a necessary evil. Pursing his lips, he looked away.

Nuke shifted a wad of tobacco to the front of his mouth, just inside his lower lip. His head turned with the quickness of a large jungle cat, and a loping stream of spit shot out, landing on the floor next to Walker's shoe.

"Hey," Walker said. "Cut it out, would you?" Stepping back from the sinks, he reached inside the pocket of his suit coat and removed an envelope. He quickly laid it on the top of the metallic surface. "There it is."

Nuke finished urinating, gave Walker a sly sideways glance, and grabbed the envelope with his left hand. At the same time a huge buck knife suddenly appeared in his right. With a flick of his wrist he popped the blade open. Walker recoiled automatically. Nuke smirked and used the finely honed blade to slice through the paper seal. Walker felt the shiver travel down his spine, wishing Nuke would put the damn thing away. Knives disturbed him. Nuke disturbed him. He watched as the big man slipped the bills out and counted them. Satisfied, he rolled them into his pants pocket and slowly unbuttoned the Levi's jacket, providing Walker a glimpse of the sculptured muscularity of massive pectorals and upper abdomen along with the black rubber handle of a chrome pistol.

Nuke withdrew a plastic baggie of white powder and set it on the sink. Walker could see the bag was still wet with sweat. Damn, he hated to touch it, but what choice did he have? Every time Walker protested to Connors about dealing with this unsavory character, the other man would only laugh and make some facetious comment about how much Nuke liked Walker.

"Relax, Marty," Connors would say. "Nuke's spent enough time in the joint to be one of your kind of guys."

My kind of guys, Walker thought. Shit.

"Wanna taste it?" Nuke asked.

Walker shook his head.

"No, I . . . I trust you," he said, trying his best not to let his voice waver again. He knew that Nuke had probably diluted the shipment at least twice before today, but there was nothing he could do about it.

Nuke sent another stream of dark spit into the sink next to the baggie just as Walker began reaching for it. Walker stopped and looked at him, and Nuke raised the sunglasses from his eyes and winked. Then he moved with an easy stride toward the door. Walker stared after him and grabbed the baggie, wishing he had some paper towels to dry it off. But the stupid place had one of those electronic dryers. Good for the environment, the small metal tag on top said. What the hell do I care about how many trees it takes to make a goddamn towel, Walker thought as he pocketed the baggie. Fumbling with his keys, he went to the door in time to hear the percussive roaring of the motorcycles start up again. After a few intermittent bursts the sound grew progressively fainter.

Walker stepped outside in time to see Nuke and his two stooges zooming toward the northbound lanes of the expressway. Walking briskly, he went to his car, preferring to make a quick departure himself. It was then that he noticed it: a big smear of brown spit dribbling down the side window of the Mercedes and onto the chrome strip.

Damn that bastard Nuke, thought Walker, wishing like hell that he didn't have to put up with him. But he really knew better. After he'd arranged for them to take care of the "Miriam problem," what choice did he have?

He was in too deep now. And there was no turning back.

CHAPTER TWO
Twenty-sixth and California Avenue

Sharon Devain picked him out immediately from the description her supervisor, Steve Megally, had given her earlier that morning: half-Mexican/half-Irish, tall, rangy build, dark hair, mustache. It was customary for the state's attorneys to be randomly matched with the police officers coming in to testify before the Cook County grand jury at Twenty-sixth and California Avenue, but Sharon had been given specific orders to locate Sergeant Francisco Leal and prep him for his testimony.

"Lead him through it quickly, and make sure he doesn't blow up at anybody," Megally had told her. "I don't want any more problems."

The "problems" to which Megally had referred to were an allusion to Leal's previous testimony at the Sixth District criminal courts building in Markham during a combination bond and preliminary hearing. The incident, which had occurred three months ago, had become known as "The Dark Gable Incident." Leal, who had been recovering from a gunshot wound, testified at the warrant arrest bond hearing of Marcus LeRigg, suspected drug dealer. After reading the complaint and hearing LeRigg's prior arrest record (seventeen arrests but only one conviction for possession dating back five years), Judge Edward Charles

Gable issued LeRigg a fifty thousand dollar I-Bond, which meant no money had to be posted and LeRigg was free on his signature until trial.

LeRigg smiled mockingly as the pronouncement was made and scratched his nostril, looking directly at Leal. Leal complained to the state's attorney in a harsh whisper, and Judge Gable, seeing this, instructed Leal to repeat what he'd said for everyone's benefit. Leal, who later stated that he did not want to commit perjury, said that he understood now why the judge was often called "Dark Gable."

"And why is that?" Judge Gable asked.

"Because your head's so far up your ass it'd take a tractor to pull it out," Leal answered, the anger rising in his voice. "I'll bet it is dark up there."

After surveying the stunned silence of the courtroom, the judge held Leal in contempt and ordered him taken into immediate custody. The situation went from bad to worse as Leal, who was being escorted away by the deputies, commended the judge for freeing a drug dealer and locking up the police officer who had arrested him. "Can I at least have an I-Bond, Your Honor?" Leal yelled seconds before the door slammed shut.

The state's attorney requested to see Judge Gable in chambers and quickly apologized, claiming that Leal was still overwrought from being shot and the recent death of his partner. The wound, the state's attorney explained, was causing Leal to cough up blood in the downstairs lockup. The judge said he would reconsider if Leal apologized, but hizzoner did recommend an immediate psychological evaluation for the errant cop.

"To think that man is walking around with a gun is . . . troubling," the judge said.

The police psychologist subsequently noted that Leal was indeed suffering from delayed stress syndrome brought about by the recent traumas, both physical and emotional, and recommended a period of rest and relaxation while Leal recovered his full health. It was then decided that he would be granted a month's leave from duty, in addition to the two months medical leave for which he was already scheduled. He would also receive a letter of reprimand and a five-day suspension without pay for his improper conduct at the felony bond hearing. The entire incident, naturally, would go in his personnel file. At the end of the three months, Leal's present duty assignment, as an undercover drug enforcement agent with the Metropolitan Enforcement Group (MEG), would be reevaluated.

But now, instead of risking the volatile officer at a preliminary hearing, where LeRigg's high-priced lawyer might press the right buttons to create another incident, Leal was subpoenaed to testify before the grand jury. It would just be him, a state's attorney, and twenty-three civic-minded citizens who were on jury duty.

"Are you Sergeant Leal?" she asked tentatively.

He nodded.

"I'm Sharon Devain, with the State's Attorney's office." She extended her hand. "Let's sit over here and I'll prep you."

She led him over to a pair of chairs behind the counter and went through the sequence of questions she was going to ask him. She noticed that his expression never seemed to change, even though she smiled frequently at him, just trying to be pleasant. God, he looks so grim, she thought. Enough to scare the hell right out of those poor pissy jerks sitting in the next room. I hope to hell he holds it together.

"We should be pretty much set. I read the reports this morning," she said, gathering up the file and giving him one more high voltage smile to try and relax him. His eyes seemed to soften slightly, she noticed. But she also noticed that his gaze moved up and down her body with a surreptitious sweep, lingering slightly on her breasts.

Looks like his libido's fully recovered anyway, she thought.

Leal took time out from his brooding to assess her as she sat in front of him. He estimated her to be in her late twenties. The mane of blond hair cascaded down around her shoulders in soft waves, but was probably lightened a little, judging from her eyebrows. Her skin had a pale creaminess to it that told him she didn't spend too much time at the beach. Or in the tanning booth at the health club. But her figure looked pretty good. Softly feminine rather than angular. He wondered what she'd look like without the lightweight brown women's suit coat and matching skirt. The dainty gold serpentine chain bounced lightly on the front of her white blouse when she turned her head, explaining the questions that she'd be asking him in front of the grand jury. He wondered about the blouse, too, and what she'd look like without that.

She crossed her legs and he glanced at her knee as it protruded through the slit in her skirt.

"Like I said, it seems pretty clear cut," she said, pausing to take off her jacket and drape it on the back of a nearby chair. To Leal's delight her blouse was sleeveless and showed him a glimpse of her soft shoulder and smooth underarms.

"Everything's clear cut when you're testifying before the grand jury," he said, cracking a smile for the first time.

Sharon smiled back. He noticed a slight tobacco stain on her front teeth, but it was still an attractive smile. Too many cigarettes, too much coffee. Not enough time to relax in the sunshine. Sounded like him a few months back.

"Why don't you go wait in the anteroom and I'll call you when it's your time," she said. She hiked up her skirt in back as she turned to retrieve her jacket.

Leal went through the doorway and took a seat in one of the sturdily built oak chairs. They had armrests and the deep rich polished look that reminded him of the kind in his uncle's dining room when he was a kid. The floor was carpeted in a dark tan, but failed to hide the dirt from the shoes of all the police who came there to testify. The room itself was small, but filled with variations of the same theme: Chicago coppers in blue, suburban cops in darker blue, plainclothes policemen in polyester sport coats. Leal's own sports jacket was light brown. He owned better ones, but it wasn't smart going to court looking like you just stepped out of *Gentlemen's Quarterly*. Especially if you worked undercover narcotics. Sean O'Herlieghy had told him that when Leal was just a rookie and Sean had been breaking him in.

"It's too easy to plant seeds of doubt in a juror's mind if you come in looking like a million bucks," he had told him. "Then the sons of bitches start thinking that you look too damn good to be an honest copper."

Leal had internalized virtually everything Sean had told him, considering it a lesson from the master. O'Herlieghy had gone up the ladder and was now a captain. And Leal had received orders to report in to see him as soon as he was finished at the grand jury. He wondered what Sean would say about "The Dark Gable Incident." Leal figured he already knew the answer to that one. It was one meeting that he was not looking forward to.

The brown, leather-padded door to his left opened and Sharon Devain stepped partially in and glanced at him.

"Sergeant Leal," she said, giving him an encouraging little wink as he got up.

The grand jury room had three enormous windows against the rear wall that displayed the expanse of blue sky over the factory landscape to the east. The rest of the room seemed unnaturally dark by comparison. Three consecutively elevated rows of theaterlike chairs were set behind curving wooden tables, the fronts of which were skirted to the carpeted floor. The twenty-three people sequestered for the grand jury for this month sat in various sections of the arena, some in clusters, others off by themselves. Leal went to the wooden booth and sat in the chair. The clerk, a middle-aged black woman, approached him and said with rote precision, "Do you swear by the ever-living God that what you're about to say is the whole truth and nothing but?"

He replied in the affirmative.

"Officer, state your name and duty assignment," Sharon Devain said.

"Sergeant Francisco Leal, Cook County sheriff's police. My current assignment is with the Metropolitan Enforcement Group."

"That's also known as MEG?" Sharon said. "And what is your primary function in this unit?"

Keep it simple, he thought. "We buy illegal drugs in an undercover capacity."

"And in May of this year did you have occasion to be working on an investigation concerning the purchase of illegal drugs from one Marcus LeRigg?"

"Yes."

"Please, tell us, Sergeant Leal, in your own words how this investigation came about."

Leal began a cautious explanation of the tenuous process of buying drugs undercover: the arrest that leads to an informant, the informant who leads to a supplier, the controlled buys, building a relationship with the supplier, the arrest of the supplier, and then beginning the process all over again, trying to catch a bigger fish the next time. It was like working your way up the food chain. LeRigg exemplified a major step upward for his team of undercover agents, and maybe, although he didn't say it, that was why they got a little careless.

"And you spoke with Mr. LeRigg to set this deal up?" Sharon asked.

"Yes, ma'am," Leal said. Always be polite in testifying. Another O'Herlieghy maxim.

"So tell us, Sergeant, what exactly happened on the night of May nineteenth of this year?"

Leal took a deep breath. The darkened superstructure of the abandoned factory snapped into place in his memory as it had done so many times since that night.

Patches of misty fog obscured most of the surroundings except for a radius of about fifty feet. It was chilly for spring, and a dampness had seemed to settle over him. Two halos sprung around the headlights of LeRigg's Caddie as he flashed the lights twice. Leal's partner, Bobby Hilton, his long dark hair pulled back into a ponytail, returned the signal and drove forward slowly. They were off the radio, not wanting to risk getting picked up by an errant scanner. But Leal knew that Johnny De-Wayne and the rest of their backups would be spreading out through the factory now.

"We had just started the exchange of money for the two kilograms of cocaine," Leal said, his voice suddenly cracking slightly, "when we were interrupted."

Sharon appeared to notice this and paused to glance at him. "When you say 'interrupted,' what exactly do you mean, Sergeant?"

The darkly tinted rear window of LeRigg's Cadillac lowered with electronic precision, and he looked up at Leal.

"Ready to do the do?" LeRigg said.

LeRigg and two other men got out of the car, each wearing long leather coats that no doubt concealed heavy weaponry. Leal felt for the comfort of his own Beretta on his right hip.

"After we showed LeRigg the money, he was in the process of opening the trunk to allow us to sample the cocaine, and then we made the final exchange," Leal said, speaking slowly and clearly. He was hoping the accompanying tremor he felt in his voice wouldn't be audible.

"And then what happened?" Sharon asked.

"As we were in the process of placing the gym bag with the drugs in our trunk, we came under fire."

The screech of tires as another car seemed to come out of nowhere. Bobby had been watching LeRigg and the two flunkies, and Leal barely turned in time to see the huge gun flashes tearing through the night. You see the flash and then hear the sound, someone had always told him. But he felt the sound instead. Like a brick had smacked into the left side of his chest. This wasn't supposed to be a "buy-bust" and they weren't prepared. More gunshots . . . Or was it thunder? Leal didn't know as he felt his legs going weak, twisting underneath him, the strength pouring out of his body as the blood seeped between his fingers.

Gunfire again. Bobby running, firing, then abruptly stopping. Leal looked up and saw his partner's head jerk to the side as if recoiling from a massive punch, his eyes having that vacant, glassy look when his head snapped back . . .

"Officer Hilton was killed," he heard himself say. "And I was wounded."

The world retreated into a velvety silence. Leal's head lolled back, and he saw Bobby falling toward him. More flashes lit up the darkness. Suddenly Johnny DeWayne was kneeling next to them. Leal could see Johnny's lips moving, but couldn't understand the words. He followed the other man's gaze down toward his chest, seeing the bright red, bubbling froth expelling steam with each of his breaths. Each one feeling like someone was twisting a knife into his chest.

"So Officer Hilton was killed, and you were wounded?" Sharon said.

"That's correct," Leal answered.

"And did you happen to see Mr. LeRigg during this time?"

"Yes, he fled in his vehicle as soon as the gunfire started," Leal said. "Officer DeWayne and the others administered to Officer Hilton and myself. LeRigg got away."

"And Mr. LeRigg was subsequently picked up on a warrant?"

"Yes," Leal said. *And he came up with some bullshit about his car being stolen by two dudes.*

"Thank you, Sergeant," Sharon said. She turned to the arena of spectators. "Are there any questions?"

A middle-aged white guy in the third row raised his hand. A solitary one, and Leal figured the guy had probably been there for the past three weeks thinking he was hot shit.

"Why weren't there additional officers on the scene to arrest him?" the guy asked. His voice had an almost condescending twang to it. *Who the hell does this guy think he is?* Leal thought. *Because, asshole, we never have enough fucking people or time or money . . .*

"Well, sir," Leal said, clearing his throat and speaking as slowly as he could. "We were in the process of building a case and hadn't planned to make an arrest at this time."

"How long did you work on this particular investigation?" a woman asked from the second row.

"From the initial contact with our informant, it was approximately three months, ma'am."

"Why do you think Mr. LeRigg had the gunmen with him?" It was the son of a bitch in the third row again, and Leal mentally imagined going up to the seat and pimp-slapping the smug bastard.

"Oftentimes, when dealing with situations such as these," Leal paused to wring any condescension out of his voice, "when dealing with individuals who are trafficking illegal drugs, they may feel that there's an opportunity to keep the money and their product. We call it, in the vernacular of the street, a rip-off." He looked directly at the man now, keeping his expression totally neutral. He noticed Sharon staring at him. *Man, she looks nervous,* he thought. *Probably worried I'm gonna blow up any second.* That brought the trace of a smile to his lips.

After a few more clarifications, Leal was excused. He took his seat back in the anteroom and waited. He reached in his shirt pocket and pulled out some gum, his latest passion since he'd quit smoking. Unwrapping the gum, he couldn't believe how dry his mouth was.

Christ, he thought. A little bullshit session like this, and I'm a candidate for the funny farm. Better get it together before I hit the street again.

He found himself wishing he had a cigarette, despite not having smoked for over five and a half months, and was tempted to try and bum one from one of the other coppers sitting there. But he pushed the thought from his mind, knowing that he couldn't afford to smoke again. The bullet had ripped through the lower part of his lung on the left side. If Johnny DeWayne hadn't put that laminated card over the bubbling wound as it sucked in air . . .

But as Leal chomped on the gum the desire for nicotine began to fade, and he reflected on how good it felt to be alive. After three months of therapy, swimming every day at the YMCA, and drinking only three cups of coffee a day, he felt and looked better than he had in years. His animosity toward the civilians who had asked the inane questions in the grand jury even began to diminish.

I gotta stop hating everybody, he thought. Loosen up. But if only I could stop seeing Bobby's face when I have to talk about it . . .

Sharon Devain came out of the doorway and smiled at him.

"You've got a true bill, Sergeant," she said. "Number seven-oh-six." Stepping all the way out, she closed the door behind her. Leal rose to his feet. Sharon began walking toward the main office area, talking over her shoulder. "They only had a few questions about why LeRigg was picked up on a warrant instead of being arrested on the spot. I guess they've been watching too much TV."

Leal smiled and followed her.

"Coffee?" she asked.

"Sure," Leal said, appreciating the chance to talk with her some more.

They came to a small corner of offices down the hall. The walls, which were just tall drywall dividers, were painted a putrid shade of yellow and covered with bulletin boards. On one wall, near a section of desks, the boards had rows of cut-off neckties, each tacked above a card bearing a state's attorney's name. The cards also had an offense, a date, and a verdict. Printed on the one with Sharon's name was *Aggravated Battery*, along with a *Guilty* verdict, but instead of a necktie, the wispy nylon leg of pantyhose hung there.

"It's an old custom here," she said, nodding at the oddly decorated wall as she picked up a pot from under an electric coffeemaker. "Our first wins in a felony jury trial." She poured the hot liquid into two Styrofoam cups. "Cream? Sugar?"

Leal shook his head. "Black's fine, thanks."

He watched her load hers with sugar and creamer, then swirl a plastic stirrer around. She brought the cup to her lips and took a solid, but dainty sip. "I think it went pretty well in there," she said.

"You mean because I didn't blow up?" he said, grinning.

Sharon laughed. "Well, I must confess, I was wondering what the man was going to be like who took old Dark Gable down a peg."

Leal feigned a grimace. "Isn't there anybody in the whole court system who hasn't heard that story?" He liked the way she laughed. It was both musical and hearty at the same time.

"Oh, I've dealt with that man many times when I was out in the Sixth District," she said. "Don't think that I didn't think about dissing him." She smiled. "That's why this assignment here at the grand jury was so nice. I didn't have to deal with any judges or anything, for the most part."

"Sounds great," he said. He brought the coffee to his

lips as he assessed her some more. No wedding or engage-ment rings, he noticed. *I wonder what the chances of her going out with me are?*

"But this is my last day here, though," she said, taking another sip and looking at him over the rim of the cup. "I'm going to be working out of five in Felony Review."

"Is that good or bad?"

"It's different," she said. "You have to stay on call for twenty-four hours, and go out in the field to interview sus-pects and review cases. I even had to buy a new car in an-ticipation of getting beeped in the middle of the night." She smiled.

I'd like to beep you in the middle of the night, Leal thought. But he said, "Well, I have to get going." Mentally he danced with the question of asking for her phone num-ber. *Oh, hell, she's a lawyer, for Christ's sake,* he thought. *Lawyers and cops don't mix.* He took a final swig of his coffee and dropped the cup in the wastebasket. "I'm sup-posed to report to headquarters for reassignment."

"Oh, you're getting reassigned, too, huh? Where to?"

"Don't know yet," he said. "Back to uniform probably."

"Oh yeah? So, is that good?"

He raised his eyebrows and shrugged nonchalantly.

"Well," Sharon said, reaching out and shaking hands with him. "Maybe we'll bump into each other again some-time."

"Yeah, maybe," Leal said, feeling the squeeze of her hand, and wondering if their paths would cross again.

CHAPTER THREE

Return to Mecca

As Leal walked out of the Criminal Courts building and descended the pebbled series of cement steps he marveled at how nice the day had turned out. The bright sunshine he'd seen through the sixth floor windows of the grand jury room had burned off the low hanging clouds that had darkened the sky as he'd driven in earlier. Scattered groups of people milled about on the various flattened sections and stairs. A group of blacks, their hats all cocked the same way to signify gang unity, sat impassively on the cement bench. There seemed to be a constant stream of coppers going in and out.

I wonder how many people we'll indict today, Leal thought as he stopped to buy a Styrofoam cup of coffee from the "meat wagon" parked in front by the curb. The Dominican vendor always did a bang-up business there and Leal chatted with him in Spanish for a moment before moving across California Avenue toward the grassy island of trees that separated the avenue from the boulevard. A young woman had her canteen truck parked there, but she seemed more intent on soaking up the sun in her red halter top than selling anything.

"The business is better right there in front," Leal said, holding up his cup.

"Yeah, I know, babe," she said, smiling at him. "But what ya gonna do? Carlos got here first." She cocked a thumb at the parking garage behind her and said, "I'll get the next wave when he runs out."

Leal nodded approvingly, fishing for the keys to his Chevy Monte Carlo. The car had been red once, but it had clearly seen better days. As he got in he glanced around to see the young woman still checking him out. Then she tilted her head and grinned.

"I know," she called out. "Your other car's a Mercedes, right?"

Stung by her remark, Leal snorted as he got in and slammed the door.

Screw her, he thought. Like she's the queen of Sheba working a vending truck in front of the county jail, for Christ's sake. Then he reflected that the Chevy did look like a wreck. It hadn't seemed an issue when he was in MEG because of the endless supply of pristine, confiscated cars that he always used. He seldom even drove his old Chevy. That was part of what was so great about working undercover. The cars, the clothing allowance, the freedom of developing your own cases . . . But there was also the pressure to get results, to take more chances, to make the big arrests . . . You got caught up in the lifestyle, but still had to keep your lifeline attached, lest you get swept up in the maelstrom.

Is that what happened to me? he wondered. Is that why I'm here now, at the top of the department's shit list, divorced, separated from my kids, hating everybody, and driving a beat-up old Chevy that I should've traded in years ago?

He hadn't been back since the shooting. Everything had been handled via the phone while he proceeded with his recovery. Johnny DeWayne had been given a meritorious promotion to investigations for his role in the incident. Leal envied him momentarily, then reflected that

Johnny deserved it. Just like Leal deserved getting kicked back downstairs to uniform. Hell, he'd blown the case, gotten shot, lost one of his partners, and smarted off to a judge in court. What did he expect? A ribbon for being an asshole? For blowing the case? Was that why it happened? Had he failed somehow to see it coming?

Leal decided to stop doubting himself and concentrated on the driving as he cut through traffic and headed toward the Eisenhower Expressway. Self-doubts were the quickest way to get yourself killed in this business. He knew that. And, what the hell, he thought. Maybe it is time for a change.

Leal made good time exiting the Eisenhower at First Avenue, but caught the lights at Harrison and then again at Maybrooke. He watched the heavy stream of cars turning into the court parking lot and remembered the old days before the stop-and-go light had been installed and an officer had to be stationed there to direct traffic for a solid eight hours. It had been the preeminent shit detail for those who'd stepped on the wrong toes. Pure hell. He sighed, knowing that at least he wouldn't have to worry about drawing something that bad for his transgression.

After the Com Ed plant, Leal turned and joined the line going into the court parking lot. He knew there wouldn't be any room in either the headquarters or academy lots, so he circled wide and found a space near the fringes that placed him relatively close to the three-building complex that housed the administration, the headquarters, and the academy. Strange how he kept returning here at different stages in his career, like a pilgrim to Mecca. His initial training when he'd first come on the job right out of the army, his sheriff police training after he'd served his two years in the jail, and the various specialty courses over the years: self-defense training, investigations school, MEG school . . . Now, he knew whatever was ahead was waiting for him just beyond the four massive white pillars that made the front entrance look almost like some ersatz antebellum mansion instead of what the solid black lettering across the front said it was: COOK COUNTY SHERIFF'S POLICE.

He cut over to the side of the academy wing and pulled open the door, stepping into the coolness of the air-conditioning. To his right he saw some uniformed cadets sitting in a classroom, listening attentively. Been there, done that, Leal thought. But still, he was suddenly affected by a certain nostalgia. The pressure of cramming all that knowledge into just twelve weeks, the sweat of keeping up with the daily runs, the workouts in the defensive tactics class . . .

He heard the clanging of weights as he went by the gym and couldn't resist poking his head in for a look. On the far side he saw a lone figure seated at the Universal machine doing lat pull downs. He walked over and watched the lean muscular arms bulge and strain with each repetition. Collar-length blond hair hung over the back of a dingy gray sweatshirt with the sleeves cut off. The long hair made Leal wonder if the guy was a new MEG agent. Maybe his replacement. But when he was about four yards away the person stood up, and Leal suddenly realized that the "guy" was actually a heavily muscled woman. Her powerful curved legs sprung from a pair of red, French-cut gym shorts and seemed to ripple with each movement. She looked over at him and smiled.

"Hi," she said. "You want to do a quick set or something?"

Leal shook his head. "Nah, you made me tired just watching you."

She smiled again and went to the shelf holding the rows of chrome-plated dumbbells. Her features were well formed, although somewhat sharp-looking, so that her face was one of those that could be described as almost pretty. He noticed that her eyebrows were a shade darker than her blond hair, which was plastered to the side of her head now. Seating herself on a bench, she began to do concentration curls with a twenty-five-pound dumbbell, causing a network of veins to spread up her arm and coalesce into a larger vessel that snaked over her biceps. Nice strong teeth flared from her tan face as her lips rolled back from an obviously burning exertion.

Leal watched her do a few more curls, bracing her right elbow against her thigh. She switched hands, and he caught the tangy scent of her sweat when she shook her head, sending some droplets flying. The striations of her arms seemed to gleam under the sheen of perspiration. She completed the set. He was fascinated by her strength, yet somewhat repulsed by her massive muscularity.

She looks like the kind of babe that could knock *you* up, he thought as he turned and walked out of the gym. Probably sweats 98 percent testosterone.

As he headed down the hallway he remembered a joke he'd heard someone tell about a female bodybuilder: She's working out so she can develop into the man she always wanted to marry. He wondered what they were feeding these gals nowadays that they ended up looking like that. Put her out on the street, he thought as he passed the range, she'd kick a man's butt, that's for sure.

The winding staircase leading to the upstairs offices was just down the hall, and he glanced at his watch. Ten thirty-five. Not too bad a time for his post–grand jury appointment with Captain Sean O'Herlieghy, who would brief him on his reassignment.

It's time to get *my* butt kicked now, Leal thought as he started up the stairs.

CHAPTER FOUR

A Campaign Issue

The middle-aged secretary in the outer office glanced at Leal as he approached. Behind her he saw the pebbled translucence of the glass door of the captain's office. It looked ominous.

"May I help you?" the secretary asked.

"Sergeant Frank Leal. I have an appointment with Captain O'Herlieghy this morning."

She picked up the phone and pressed one of the intercom buttons. After a moment of hushed conversation, she replaced the phone in its cradle and told him to go right in.

"The captain's expecting you," she said.

I'll bet he is, Leal thought. But at least it would be his old mentor giving him the bad news. Maybe he'd let him down easy.

As Leal reached for the doorknob he saw a shadow behind the opaque glass and suddenly the door swung open. Sean O'Herlieghy stood there, smiling broadly.

"Frank," he said, extending his hand. "Get your butt in here."

Leal shook hands and was surprised at the captain's grip. It seemed overly flexed, as if he were trying to impress Leal or maybe break his hand. O'Herlieghy motioned him over to a green chair in front of a big gunmetal gray desk. Leal sat, feeling his mouth begin to dry up. The captain's desk was relatively uncluttered, except for a two-foot-high pistol-shooting trophy that sat off in the left corner. The gold cop figurine on top had his handgun extended, pointing right at whoever was sitting in the padded green chair. Leal's mouth suddenly felt a bit drier. But the sooner he got the bad news, probably the better.

"So how you been, Frank?" O'Herlieghy asked, settling into the chair behind his desk. "You all healed up?" He was a big man in his late fifties with sparse red hair combed over from one side. This gave his face a rather longish appearance, and didn't adequately hide the numerous places where his scalp shone through from under the long combover. His face looked weathered and massive, with an almost bulbous nose and pendulous jowls. A latticework of red veins climbed the tip of his nose and appeared again on his lower right cheek. O'Herlieghy leaned forward and placed his elbows on the desk.

"I'm okay, Captain. Getting better every day." He must be setting me up, so he can let me down easy, Leal thought.

"Good, good. That's what I hoped you'd say." O'Herlieghy reached in his desk drawer and removed two cigars, extending them toward Leal.

"No, thanks, I quit," Leal said. But he was tempted to take one just to have something to do with his hands.

O'Herlieghy nodded, stuck one of the cigars in his mouth, and put the other back in the drawer. He took out a lighter and held the flame to the cigar's rolled tip, puffing copiously to get it started.

"Times are a-changin', Frank." He drew on the cigar and exhaled a cloud of smoke with a smile. "Ahhhh, they don't allow you to smoke in the damn building anymore, except in designated areas. Ain't that a bite in the ass?"

Leal nodded, thinking that the pungent smell made him feel better than it should have.

"My point being," O'Herlieghy said, taking another draw, "is that when the times change, you gotta change with them, or you get left behind. It's a question of being smart. And acting smart, too."

Leal watched him closely. He sure was taking his time getting to the point.

"So that's why I called you in a little earlier than the rest," O'Herlieghy said. "You and me being from the old neighborhood, and me knowing your dad and all."

Leal wondered where this was going.

"I don't know if you heard or not," O'Herlieghy said, tapping the end of the cigar into an ashtray, "but I split up with Dora."

"No, I didn't. I'm sorry to hear that."

O'Herlieghy waved dismissively, then brought the cigar back to his mouth. "It was for the best. Besides, I met somebody new, and she's made me feel ten years younger. Her name's Bambi."

Bambi, thought Leal. That sounds like the name of the Playmate of the Month.

O'Herlieghy stood, turning so his profile faced Leal. "I lost fifteen pounds, too."

"You look good, Captain," he said. But he thought, What the hell is going on here? I came expecting to get my ass chewed out and bounced back to uniform, and he's acting like it's I-need-a-hug day on *Oprah*.

"Ahh, shit, Frank, can that 'Captain' shit, will ya? We got too much history for that."

Leal grinned and nodded, his hand instinctively patting his pocket for the pack of cigarettes that was no longer there. He leaned back in the chair and clamped his hands together.

"Like I said, we got history," O'Herlieghy continued, sitting down again. He took another drag on the cigar. His breath was cloudy when he spoke, staring directly at Leal.

"But I gotta tell you, telling off that fucking judge was stupid. But I guess you already know that, huh?"

Leal looked at the floor and nodded.

"Not that I ain't come close to doing it myself at times," O'Herlieghy said with a chuckle. "But do I have to tell you how many markers I had to call in to smooth it over?"

"No, sir."

O'Herlieghy winced slightly, then leaned back in his chair and took another long draw.

"So, you know that the sheriff's up for reelection next month, right?" he asked. "Well, with Shay gaining in the suburbs and parts of the city, it's gonna be a close one. Real close."

Leal nodded.

"Shay's making a big issue of the Walker case," O'Herlieghy said. "You're familiar with it, right?"

Leal recalled reading about it: Miriam Walker, female judge, wife of a prominent businessman, and a high-ranking board member of the nonprofit Coalition of Women Against Domestic Violence had disappeared the previous spring. Her body had been subsequently found in a pond in unincorporated Palos Township.

"Shay's been making it into a campaign issue," O'Herlieghy said. "Saying that if he's elected he'll get to the bottom of it." He leaned back and blew out a large smoke ring. "So Sheriff O'Hara's given the green light to the formation of a special task force to work the case."

Oh, my God, Leal thought, his fingers gripping the arms of the chair. "You mean I'm not going back into uniform?"

"Uniform? Nah. You're going to the Walker task force. At least until the election." He grinned broadly. "Didn't I tell you I'd take care of you when I came to see you in the hospital?"

Leal had been so doped up on pain medication that he

barely remembered anything of that period. But this was almost too good to be true.

"Sean," he said, his voice cracking, "I really owe you—"

"Ah, forget it," O'Herlieghy said, tapping some residual ash into the tray. His expression got serious. "But keep one thing in mind. We can't afford to stand around holding our cocks on this one. We're putting a couple of inexperienced people in the unit with you and Tom Ryan—he's the other sergeant—but the outcome of the election just might be riding on this."

Leal nodded, then asked the question. "What do you mean 'inexperienced'? Wouldn't it be better to put some real no-nonsense dicks on it with us?"

O'Herlieghy licked his lips before he spoke. "Well, part of the idea is for the sheriff to look . . . progressive and all. You know, giving new people a chance to show what they can do."

The phone rang before he could explain any more. He answered it and suddenly his whole face seemed to melt into a smile. "Hiya, babe. Just a minute." His big hand covered the mouthpiece, and he said to Leal, "Go out and get a fucking haircut and report back here down in the sheriff's pressroom at thirteen hundred sharp for a press conference."

He went back to cooing into the phone.

Leal stood up quickly and left, closing the door gently behind him. He winked at the secretary behind the desk and smiled as she blushed. As he walked down the hall toward the stairway, he felt like jumping up and clicking his heels like Gene Kelly in one of those old musicals.

CHAPTER FIVE
Catch-22

Leal pulled back into the court parking lot at twelve fifty, his hair freshly cut, and his mustache trimmed neatly. "Make it look politically correct," Leal had told the barber. The guy had smirked a bit and gone to work. The result was a bit shorter than Leal would have liked, but he figured the almost-military style would make him look like Mr. Conservative. His old drug contacts probably wouldn't even recognize him.

Several news vans were parked by the front doors, their antennae raised in anticipation of the feed-in to the afternoon news broadcasts. Leal strode by the technicians preparing their camcorders and took the steps with a jaunty bounce. He went immediately to the public information room on the first floor and saw Sean O'Herlieghy standing by the door, packing tobacco into a pipe.

"When did you take up pipe smoking?" Leal asked.

O'Herlieghy flashed a grin. "Frank, glad you're on time. The hair looks sharp." He held up the pipe. "This is Bambi's idea. Says it makes me look distinguished. Not extinguished. Besides, she likes the smell."

Without even having met the captain's new love, Leal had the feeling that his old mentor and friend was heading for heartbreak. No fool like an old fool, he thought. But he knew better than to try to interfere or offer unwanted advice, especially about such a delicate subject. He was grateful to Sean, though, for setting up this great opportunity after the fall from grace.

O'Herlieghy patted him on the back and they stepped into the sheriff's anteroom. But as they entered the room the hairs on the back of Leal's neck went up. In front of him were four people: a woman, a black guy, a white guy, and Paul Brice. Brice and Leal went back a long way.

"Frank, you know Lieutenant Brice, don't you?" O'Herlieghy asked. "He's running the task force."

Leal knew him, all right. From when he'd first started his stint at the county jail. Brice had been a sergeant back then. "King Shit" of all the jail guards. Someone everybody— guards and prisoners alike—stepped aside from. With a barrel-like chest and oak-tree arms, Brice liked to show off his prowess by challenging some of the bigger prisoners, with their jail-house bodies, to bench-pressing contests. He always won, one time doing 425 pounds with accomplished ease. But when Leal had fingered one of Brice's buddies to internal affairs for smuggling drugs into the jail, and the guard had lost his job because of it, Leal went to the top of Brice's shit list.

Leal's tours of duty became hellish as Brice made snide comments about stool pigeons, and how they were the lowest of the low. Finally, they'd been told to settle it by a senior commander. The commander, an ex-marine, suggested that they put on the boxing gloves and climb into the ring for a little "physical training exercise." Just before they squared off, Brice had leaned in to touch gloves, but instead knocked Leal's hands down sharply and said in a low voice, "I'm gonna beat the dog shit out of you."

Leal, a lean one-eighty, looked almost frail next to the heavily muscled Brice. But Leal, who had boxed golden gloves and been on an army boxing team, used his quickness to avoid the bigger man's punishing blows. Sticking and moving, Leal's jab repeatedly stung his opponent and set up overhand rights.

"Brice is getting hit with so many rights, he's begging for a left," one of the onlookers said.

Despite the large, sixteen-ounce gloves that minimized the blows, it soon became apparent that if anyone was getting the "dog shit" beat out of them, it sure wasn't Leal. Brice continued to absorb the punishment, following the wispy Leal around the ring on sodden legs that looked ready to crumble. The fight finally ended when the supervisor, tired of seeing the big sergeant used for a punching bag, stepped in and declared the fight a draw. Leal had a slight bump on his cheek from a head butt, but Brice's face was as swollen as a catcher's mitt. Word quickly spread, and the fight did little to end the animosity. Both men gave the other a wide berth, and soon they were each respectively transferred to the sheriff's police section and out of the jail. It was a big department, and their paths hadn't crossed in the intervening years. Until now.

With Brice running the show, this wasn't just the catch Leal had worried about; it was catch-22.

Brice still looked formidable. His shoulders had always been huge and his chest looked as solid as a wine keg. But his hair had thinned and turned steel gray. Large wrinkles fanned out from his eyes and bracketed his mouth. He held out a large right hand toward Leal, who accepted it.

"Lieutenant," Leal said, nodding in acknowledgment.

As Brice grabbed Leal's hand, it was all he could do not to wince. Brice had snared Leal's fingers in a grip of iron, pumping the hand slowly and squeezing until Leal felt like going up on his toes. It was an old trick of Brice's that Leal had forgotten about. Brice always called it "The Sissy Shake."

"Good to be working with you again," Brice said. He turned slightly, still holding Leal's hand, and pointed to the others in the room. "Let me introduce you to Tom

Ryan, Joe Smith, and Olivia Hart. This is Frank Leal, everybody." He punctuated each introduction with another bone-crushing squeeze.

Leal managed to extricate his hand from Brice's and waved an acknowledgment. Ryan he knew slightly, having met him before, but the other two were strangers. Or were they? Suddenly he recognized the woman. She was the bodybuilder he'd seen pumping iron in the gym, only now she didn't look quite so muscle-bound in a white blouse and navy blue skirt. She held a matching navy jacket folded over her arm.

Tom Ryan stepped over to him and flashed a quick grin as they shook hands. He was in his late thirties with a slender build and wire-rim glasses. His brown hair was flecked with a little gray, and his mustache was bushy. The black guy, Joe Smith, looked a decade younger than either Ryan or Leal, and appeared to be in good shape. He was tall, with a dark complexion and a razor-edge part cut into his very short hair. Leal noted that Smith's grip was friendly and strong.

Good, thought Leal. Maybe he can help get me into better shape if we get paired together.

Hart moved forward to shake also, but Brice interceded.

"You can get acquainted later," he said. "Right now we've got to get in the pressroom for the sheriff." He turned and led them down the hall, and then stopped abruptly. "Let me make this perfectly clear. At the conference nobody say nothing. Let Sheriff O'Hara handle the news media. He just wants us to be in the background as he introduces the new investigative team heading up the Walker case. Understand?" He seemed to glare at Leal in particular for a moment.

They walked down to the official pressroom. Reporters were just setting up in front of the podium with the dark green curtain draped behind it. Some cameramen perked up at their entrance, but deflated as Brice just shook his head.

"Ryan and Smith, sit over there," Brice said. "Leal and Hart, on the other side of the podium."

Leal and Hart glanced at each other. He noticed her eyes widen slightly and a quick smile flicked at the corners of her mouth.

She looks pretty nervous, Leal thought. I hope she knows her stuff.

The muffled conversations ended abruptly as Sheriff O'Hara strode in from an adjacent doorway with an undersheriff trailing behind him. As the harsh lights washed over O'Hara's square features and dark, slicked-back hair, he flashed a practiced smile at the reporters and stepped up on the podium, taking his place behind the lectern, which had been specially modified to offset O'Hara's rather short stature. The American flag and the Cook County flag stood at either side of the speaker's position. A dozen flashes popped silently, and the camcorders were shouldered as the cameramen began their simultaneous taping. O'Hara continued smiling as the undersheriff announced that a special task force had been assembled to take over the investigation of the Miriam Walker homicide, and a limited number of questions would be answered after a short statement by the sheriff.

Leal watched as O'Hara fumbled with his notes, then looked over at them and nodded. Donald O'Hara had always portrayed himself as a no-nonsense cop. "I'm just Get-the-Job-Done O'Hara," he was fond of saying at press conferences. And this might once have been true, Leal thought, but like most politicians who succeed themselves in elective office term after term, the street savvy and investigative acumen that had once made O'Hara a good cop had long since been glitzed over by high-priced PR firms selected to ensure the sheriff's continued election. But several recent high-profile setbacks in the sheriff's department had made some cracks appear in the highly protected image. And O'Hara's slick, media-conscious opponent, Michael Shay, had capitalized on these cracks to mount a skillful campaign depicting O'Hara as a faltering, out-of-touch official. *Michael Shay, a new leader for the new millennium,* the voice-over on his TV ads said, emphasizing Shay's rugged, blond handsomeness as his image was superimposed on the screen. This in contrast to O'Hara's middle-aged baldness and jowly appearance had the incumbent lagging behind in the polls.

So he gets on the five, six, and ten o'clock news being videotaped introducing his new, politically correct investigative team, thought Leal. A black guy, a woman, and two white guys. Then he thought for a moment. No, wait a minute, I must be the Hispanic entry. Yeah, he's got all the bases covered, he thought, wondering if Sean really had to pull those strings that he mentioned. And how long would they be here? That was the question.

O'Hara cleared his throat.

"Ladies and gentlemen," he said. "Thank you for your attendance here this afternoon. I take great pride in introducing to you the newest special investigative team in the department." He went on for a few minutes detailing how a search of the "best and brightest" young stars had been assembled to follow up every possible lead on "the heinous crime" with hopes of "bringing the perpetrators to justice soon."

Perpetrators, Leal thought. If he loses the election he can get a job reading stilted dialogue for David Letterman.

"Sheriff O'Hara," one reporter asked, standing. The technician focused the minicam on the speaker's podium. "Are we to take that to mean you feel the Walker case is solvable?"

"Any case is potentially solvable if you do enough legwork," O'Hara said. "It's just a question of tracing down every lead, leaving no stone unturned."

"Have there been any new developments?" another reporter said. "Some new leads you could share with us?"

"Let me just say," O'Hara said, smiling as he looked toward the camera, "that I have the utmost confidence in this group of officers here." He held his big palm toward Leal and Hart. "They will do their best to investigate what we believe are substantial new developments."

That sounded promising, Leal thought. Maybe this wouldn't be such a bad gig after all, if the boss wasn't just blowing smoke.

After a few more questions, the undersheriff stood and terminated the conference, saying that the sheriff had pressing issues to take care of. O'Hara took his cue and turned to shake hands with all of them before striding off the platform. A few of the old-time reporters crowded toward the doorway, trying to pump the undersheriff for more information as he left. Brice nodded for the task force to follow him out.

"My office," he said.

Brice's office was down the hall. The big room was separated by a drywall divider, with an assortment of plaques, awards, certificates, and photos decorating the wall behind the desk. A shelf of dust-covered law books was framed perpendicularly on the adjacent wall. Brice directed them to sit in the chairs opposite him. Leal noticed that the desk's surface was relatively clear, except for the phone, a tray of papers, a well-packed manila folder, and an ornately framed photograph that faced the other way. Picking up the thick manila folder, Brice sat on the corner of the desk.

"First of all, the ground rules," he said. "You'll all report to Ryan. He's in charge of the unit."

Leal noticed Ryan's eyebrows rise slightly, then he gave a slow, sideways glance in Leal's direction.

"And Ryan," Brice continued, "you'll report directly to me, and I'll expect daily updates. Smith's gonna be your partner, and Leal, you work with Hart. I don't need to tell you how important it is that we kick ass on this thing." He paused and stared at them, then thrust a manila folder, thick with papers, at Hart. "Here's the file. Would you mind making four copies for everybody? I got some more stuff to go over with the guys here."

Leal watched Hart's lips contract slightly, but she stood and left the room without saying anything. Brice watched her go, then turned back to the rest of them.

"I've had a temporary office set up for you in room one-ten. You can go check out whatever you need as far as radios, beepers, telephones, and cars, but," he stuck his thick forefinger out at Ryan, "let's see some goddamn results."

Ryan nodded and smiled crookedly.

"How long we got?" he asked.

"Let me put it this way," Brice said. "You'd better hope that you break something before the election. A new administration comes in here and who knows where we'll all be."

Ryan coughed and pulled out a pack of cigarettes.

"May I, boss?"

"Sure," Brice said, "in your own fucking office, not here."

Ryan grinned again, and stuck the unlighted cigarette behind his right ear.

"Well, I guess we might as well move to our new facilities then," he said, standing.

In the hallway they paused at the copying room to tell Hart where to meet them. She smiled and nodded, watching the machine automatically collate the pages. Ryan unlocked the door and gave the other key to Leal. The room had two desks, a typewriter on each, and a bulletin board on one wall. "Shit, no phones," Ryan said. "And only two keys. We'll have to get some organization here."

"Want me to run down to supply and get us some phones, Sarge?" Smith asked.

"Good idea, Joe," Ryan said. "And get us some beepers,

radios, and a couple of cell phones, too." He looked at Leal. "We gonna need anything else?"

Leal shrugged. "I'm sure we'll think of something when we need it."

Ryan laughed and closed the door, taking the cigarette from behind his ear and quickly holding the flame of his lighter to the end. He inhaled sharply, then let out a smoky breath along with a collective "Ahhhhh." He looked over at Leal and smiled, the cigarette still dangling from his mouth. "Look, I just want to get this up front so there's no problem between me and you. I didn't ask to be in charge of this thing, and I know you got seniority." He drew deeply on the cigarette again.

"Forget it. I'm just glad to be aboard."

Ryan exhaled a heavy cloud of smoke and grinned. "Great. How about we go for a drink? Just you and me. Today's about cashed anyway."

"Sounds good."

Hart came in with the file and four copies. She gave one to Ryan and another to Leal. Ryan flipped through the pages as though he was browsing a magazine.

"Jesus Christ, this is a lot of shit to sift through," he said.

Hart stood about three feet away, conspicuously silent. Leal took time to assess her again. She had her jacket on now and looked very angular. Beneath it, he knew, were the powerful muscles he'd seen earlier. He noticed she seemed sort of tentative, especially around Ryan and him. Her saw her blink several times and realized Ryan's cigarette was bothering her.

Let's see if she asserts herself, he thought.

A dark shadow banged against the opaque glass of the door.

"That's got to be Smith," Ryan said. "Open it, will you?"

She moved to the door and opened it just as Smith stumbled forward, carrying a load of regular and cell phones as well as four portable radios. Hart grabbed two of the portables in midair as they popped from Smith's grasp.

"Thanks," Smith said, moving to the desk and setting everything down clumsily. He pointed to his belt where four beepers were clipped. "This be enough, Sarge?"

"As long as they work," Ryan said. "I'll take one of the radios you didn't drop."

In a few minutes they had the phones hooked up, the beepers and portables distributed, and the seating arrangement determined. Ryan leaned back and lit another cigarette.

"Have to get an ashtray, too," he said, looking around. "We could use a LEADS terminal, but, Hart, with your background you'll be in charge of running anything we need, okay?"

Hart nodded. Leal noticed her lips compress into a thin line.

She's edgy, he thought. The cigarette? Or is it something more?

"Okay," Ryan said, glancing at his watch. "It's almost three. Let's all knock off for today. You two," he pointed at Smith and Hart, "finish getting yourselves squared away. Get your radios, shoulder holsters, whatever you have to get. Then we'll all go over the file tonight, and meet here tomorrow at zero nine hundred for a strategy session. Got it?"

Smith said he did, then immediately went to one of the phones and began dialing. "My wife's about ready to drop," he said. "Just want to check, see if there's anything she needs."

Ryan turned to Leal and smiled. "See you at Heaven's Gate?"

"Okay," Leal said, "fifteen minutes or so? I want to talk to my partner for a few."

"Sure. It'll save me from buying the first round." Ryan slipped on his sports jacket. It was a brown weave that looked almost a size too big for him. He took one final drag on his cigarette and then dropped it on the floor, crushing it under his shoe. "Have to get some filing cabinets in here, too. We'll have to lock up our reports so nothing walks. Joe, see to it before you leave, okay?"

Smith waved an assent.

Hart stood, holding her file copy in both hands.

Leal tried to smile in a disarming fashion as he took out one of his business cards and scribbled some numbers on the back.

"These are my numbers," he said, handing her the card. "Top one's my beeper, second's my cell phone, and the last one's my house."

Hart glanced at it, then grabbed her purse and sorted through it.

"I don't have any of my new cards yet," she said. "But let me give you my home number." She took out a gray-and-black business card with a pair of barbells on the front. As she leaned over the desk Leal noted that her handwriting was clear and neat, replete with all the typical feminine flourishes and loops. She wrote *Olivia Hart* along with a phone number.

Leal flipped the card over after she handed it to him. *The Body Center* was printed above the barbell design, with the address. Along the lower edge: *Rory H. Chalma, Proprietor*.

"That's the place where I work out," Hart said quickly. "If I'm not at home, you can usually catch me there."

I'll bet, Leal thought, pocketing the card.

"This looks like an Alsip exchange," he said.

"Right," she said.

"I live in Blue Island," he said. "Maybe we can carpool sometime since we'll be working together."

"Yeah, sure. And come by the gym to work out if you want," she said. "I know Rory, ah, the owner, real good."

A boyfriend? Leal wondered. She was beginning to

seem more feminine to him now, not that her sexuality really mattered as long as she knew what she was doing.

"I thought you worked out here?" he asked. "You looked like you were pretty much at home in that gym when I saw you earlier."

"I do, well, at least I used to," she said. "I'm . . . I was the aerobics instructor here, in charge of physical training."

Leal raised his eyebrows.

Smith hung up the phone and stood.

"Guess I need to run by supply and see about them filing cabinets," he said, smiling as he brushed past them.

"Wait," Hart said. "I'll go with you." She turned to Leal, smiling up at him as she held the file to her chest like a schoolgirl. "Well, I guess I'll see you tomorrow."

"Right," Leal said. "Tomorrow."

He watched the two of them walking briskly down the hall toward supply as he locked the office, the muscles of Hart's well-developed butt snaking powerfully under the brown fabric of her skirt.

Here I am stuck on a high-profile task force to investigate an unsolved homicide that just may decide the election, he thought. And I got Brice in charge and an ex-aerobics instructor for my partner.

Suddenly he wasn't feeling all that lucky. Maybe that drink in Heaven would be just what the doctor ordered.

CHAPTER SIX
Heaven's Gate

Ryan was already on his second drink when Leal arrived. The bar, Heaven's Gate, was practically empty, except for the usual group of hardcore regulars who seemed to begin their drinking as soon as the place opened. Most were retired from the railroad or steel industries, but a good portion of them, Leal figured, were ex-coppers, too. Not a pretty thought, he considered as the smoky, boozy air enveloped him. A cigarette haze hung over the stool where Ryan was sitting. He raised two fingers at Leal.

The bar itself was made of dark mahogany with a heavy polyurethane coating layered over the top. Suspended between the wood below and the top of the plastic was an asymmetrical arrangement of several thousand pennies. The result was not unlike one of those glass paperweights with suspended trinkets, bugs, or designs inside. Other than the "pennies from heaven" bar top, the rest of the tavern was pretty typical: a mirrored backdrop on the wall opposite the bar; rows of bottles, like old soldiers, lining the adjacent edge in solitary silence; some old-style pinball machines dinged away in a corner, accompanied by some video poker players; subdued conversations punctuated by an occasional hacking laugh, and the ubiquitous clouds of wispy smoke.

Sliding onto the red vinyl stool next to Ryan, Leal ordered a beer. Ryan drained the bourbon and water in front of him and signaled the bartender, a heavyset guy named Al, to hit him again. Al's hair looked a little too thick to be natural. And the shade didn't quite match his bushy eyebrows and the dark mustache that curved down on either side of his mouth like a winding snake. His teeth flashed brightly as he set the two glasses on the bar, then poured Leal's beer into the stein. Leal tossed some bills on the bar.

"That all you're having?" Ryan asked, squinting at him. "A beer?"

"Yeah, I got a long drive."

"Yeah, me, too. But my girlfriend's driving. She's gonna meet me here." He grinned and took a careful sip.

"She work around here?" Leal asked, picking up his stein. The beer tasted cold and good. He felt the carbonation sweep down to his stomach as he licked the foam off his mustache.

"Actually, she works at HQ. Personnel." He started to take another sip, but then set his drink down and took out his cigarettes instead. "That's how I knew about the seniority thing. I checked out everybody's files once I found out I was going to this task force."

"That's handy," Leal said, looking at Ryan over the edge of the stein.

"So, like I said, I hope there's no hard feelings about Brice putting me in charge and all."

"No problem," Leal said. "I came here today figuring I was getting bounced back to patrol."

Ryan stuck a cigarette between his lips and smiled. "Yeah, I heard about you telling off old Dark Gable," he said. He held the flame of his lighter to the cigarette, contorting his mouth as he did so. Then he exhaled a copious breath of smoke. "You got balls, I'll say that, man."

No secret's safe from his girlfriend's prying eyes, I guess, Leal thought.

"You've obviously read all about my dirty laundry," Leal said. "Now tell me about the rest of our crew."

"Okay. Smith put his time in at the jail. Took the sheriff police test about a year and a half ago and went on the street. He's made some good busts—dope, a couple of guns, but nothing really spectacular. Been on the street about fifteen months, tops." Ryan paused to belch slightly. He took another drag on his cigarette. "By all accounts he seems to be a good kid, but like most shines, he's slow upstairs." He tapped his temple with an index finger. "Probably need some help with the paperwork, but he should work out okay."

Like most shines, Leal reflected ironically, thinking how Johnny DeWayne's professionalism and quick thinking had made the life-and-death difference that night by the factory.

"And Hart?"

Ryan chuckled deeply, picking up his drink for another sip before talking. "She's twenty-eight, divorced, no kids, worked in the jail and in communications."

"Yeah, and how much street time she got?"

Ryan held up his left hand and made an O with his index finger and thumb.

"Huh?" asked Leal.

Ryan nodded. "Yep. Zilch."

"Then how the hell does she rate a position in a task force like this?"

Ryan shrugged and finished off the rest of his drink. He held up two fingers toward Al again, then turned to Leal. "You want another one?"

Leal nodded and drained his stein.

Ryan took a long drag on his cigarette and blew the smoke up toward the ceiling.

"I was asking myself that same question," he said. "I figure that it's one of two possibilities." His voice rose, emphasizing the middle syllables of the last word. The slurring was becoming more noticeable in his speech. "Either Miss Hart is one hell of a fuck for some sugar daddy in a high place, which, from the looks of her, ain't likely—I got her figured for a dyke myself."

Leal grunted noncommittally.

"Or," Ryan continued, holding up his finger in an exaggerated gesture, "they're setting us up."

"What do you mean?"

Al brought their new drinks, scooped up the bills that Leal had left on the bar, and slapped the change down.

Ryan took another sip and licked his lips.

Jesus, this guy's gotta be a stone alkie as well as a racist, Leal thought. *I wonder how he feels about somebody who's half-Mexican?*

"You know anything about this fucking case?" Ryan asked, taking one more drag before stubbing out his cigarette.

"Not much. Lady judge disappeared about six months ago. Discovered her body in a pond recently, stuffed in some kind of trunk. Never found her car anywhere. Shay made the incident into a campaign issue, saying it pointed to O'Hara's incompetence."

"You got it," Ryan said. "This fucking case is colder than Chicago in January. No way we'll solve it. Ain't gonna happen." He hunched forward, so close that Leal could smell the booze on the other man's conspiratorial whisper. "But that's just it. They expect us to fall on our faces on this one. We're getting set up to get hung out to dry, Leal. You, me, and the two inexperienced tokens they've thrown us in with. That's why you got the broad and I got the dog."

Leal leaned back slightly. "Maybe we'll get lucky."

"Shit. And maybe we'll figure out who killed Jimmy Hoffa, too." Ryan took a more substantial slug of his new drink, and began fumbling in his pocket for his smokes again. "But we gotta try, right?" He stuck another cigarette between his lips. "Yeah, sometimes you just gotta take a shot. Go for the gold, you know?"

"Yeah, I hear you."

Leal glanced at his watch. It was almost four. It's been a day of surprises, he thought. Might as well go for the gold myself.

"Look, Ryan—"

"Call me Tom, Francis."

"Okay, Tom," Leal said, standing up. "And it's Francisco, or Frank. I got to make a call. Be back in a minute."

Ryan nodded his head toward the drinks on the bar. "Okay. I'll hold your place for you."

Leal grabbed some of the change off the bar and headed toward the pay phones by the washrooms. A bleary-eyed guy stumbled out of the men's room as Leal brushed by him in the narrow hallway. He searched his notebook list of phone numbers, deposited the coins, and dialed. After several transfers she finally came on the line.

"ASA Devain."

"Ms. Devain, it's Sergeant Frank Leal. I was at the grand jury with you this morning."

After a pause, she said, "Right. What can I do for you, Sergeant?"

"Well, I know this may seem kind of abrupt, but I remembered that you said you were getting transferred . . ." He felt the awkward silence as he searched for the right words. "And I didn't know how to get a hold of you after today." More silence. "So I was just wondering if you'd like to maybe go out for a drink or dinner or something."

After another pause, her voice came back to him. "Well, I don't know. I'm kind of beat tonight . . ."

"Oh, okay. Where did you say you were getting transferred?"

"Felony Review. And I don't have my new voice mail number yet," she said. "So where did you end up? Back in uniform?"

"No, actually I kind of lucked out. I got assigned to a special task force. We'll be working the Walker case. You familiar with it?"

"Yeah, sure. I knew her slightly." She paused again, then said, "Why don't I give you my home number. Maybe we can make it another time." Leal scribbled the number down in his notebook as she repeated it for him. "But like I said, I'll be on call a lot, and I'm not sure what my hours are going to be."

"Okay."

"So give me a call sometime and maybe we can set something up. And congratulations on your new assignment."

"Thanks," he said. "If you're up tonight check out the news. We had a televised press conference today. Maybe you'll see us."

"Great. I'll have to try to remember to look for it. I've got to go, so maybe I'll talk to you again sometime." Her voice sounded less than enthusiastic.

That went real well, Leal thought, chastising himself for dropping the ball as he hung up the phone. He went into the washroom, urinated, and returned to the bar.

"What's the matter? You look like somebody just killed your dog," Ryan said.

"Yeah, I kind of struck out with a babe I met this morning at the Criminal Courts building."

"Oh? Anybody I'd know?"

This asshole seems to know everybody, Leal thought.

"A state's attorney. She prepped me for the grand jury."

"Not Sharon Divine?" Ryan asked, his upper lip curling into a salacious grin.

"I think it's Devain."

"Yeah, but I say Divine. She is a good-looking woman. But, listen, Frankie, you'd better be careful messing around with a chick like that. You don't know how much mileage she's got on her. Might have AIDS or something. If she had as many pricks sticking out of her as she's had stuck in her, she'd probably look like a porcupine."

Leal was finding himself growing very tired of Ryan and his stupid comments. Figuring that he'd gotten just about everything he needed from this meeting, he tossed a few bucks on the bar for a tip.

"I got to get going," he said.

"Aww, come on, Frankie. Stick around, at least till the rush hour is over. I'll buy the next round if you want."

Leal shook his head and stood up.

"No thanks," he said. "And the name's Frank."

Leal left the bar feeling a bit more light-headed than two beers called for; then he realized that he hadn't eaten all day. He pulled into the first fast food place he came to, a Burger King, and got a Whopper, fries, and a large coffee. Ryan had been right about the rush hour, so Leal ate slowly and watched the cars passing before him under the darkening canopy of the late summer sky.

I wonder if she was just brushing me off? he mused, thinking about his telephone conversation. But, hey, she did give me her home number. And she'd taken off her jacket this morning. What was that other than an invitation for me to check her out?

Then he realized that the beer must be fueling his logic as the memory of the stuffiness of the small State's Attorney's office came floating back to him. Hell, he'd felt uncomfortable in his sports coat this morning, too. But still, he wasn't ready to accept defeat in this matter just yet.

I'll call her tomorrow sometime, he thought.

The coffee had grown cold under the neglect of his ruminations. He went for a free refill, and thought about his new assignment with assholes Ryan and Brice leading the charge. Certainly Sean must have had something to do with me getting selected, Leal thought. But Brice must have agreed to it somehow. So was Ryan's setup theory right? Was the plan to toss two inexperienced cops, one apparently functional alcoholic, and one hot-tempered asshole who told off a judge, into the fray in case O'Hara needed some quick scapegoats? Maybe that was why Brice had disregarded the seniority factor and put Ryan in charge . . . *I had my reservations about that guy Leal,* he could almost hear Brice's raspy voice saying.

But there was a flip side: first of all, he hadn't been switched back to uniform. And second, if they did a thorough job and maybe got some good leads, they could come out looking professional even if O'Hara didn't win. And last, if they somehow got lucky, and managed to solve this one, they'd be able to write their own tickets, no matter who won the goddamn election.

CHAPTER SEVEN
A Call in the Night

The phone rang just as Martin Walker had finished snorting a line. The rush made him feel so much more capable and on top of things, especially when he had mundane tasks to do, like cutting and bagging the rest of the stuff he'd gotten from Nuke. He had to step on it heavily, to make up for the exceedingly larger cuts he was taking for his personal use each time. But no matter. The morons at the firm probably wouldn't know the difference if he slipped them granulated sugar. Just so he had enough for his special "guests" when he needed it. The loud ringing continued, breaking his trend of thought.

Dammit, who could be calling him? he wondered as he stared at the tray with the mannitol, coke, spatula, and envelopes in front of him. Gently, he pushed the tray back and got up. The main supply of his stash would be safe enough in his secret hiding place, he thought, then laughed as if the phone had eyes. Things were so much simpler when you were just a little bit smarter than everybody else. And right now he felt a lot smarter.

"Hello," he said, picking up the phone as he fumbled with his caller ID box. He saw the number was blocked. "Hello," Walker repeated.

"Marty, old buddy, how are you?"

It was Connors. Walker's brow furrowed slightly. He hated to be called Marty.

"Richard? What do you want?"

There was a pause on the line, then Connors' voice came back.

"You watch the news lately?"

"What?"

"Television," Connors said. "The fucking news. Did you watch it today?"

Walker sighed heavily into the receiver, demonstrating his irritation. "I generally wait till ten," he said. "Why? Look, is this really necessary, because I'm right in the middle of something."

"Are you alone?"

"Richard, I'm getting tired of this game."

"Just answer my fucking question," Connors repeated.

"Yes, I'm by myself. Now what is it?"

"All right, listen up. You're probably going to see the new task force they created to look into Miriam's death on the news tonight."

Martin Walker felt a momentary chill, as though someone had just touched an ice cube to his balls. But he knew the cocaine was making him react more than he should.

"So, is that something I should be concerned about?" he asked.

"Just relax," Connors' voice said. "I've got everything under control, just like always. We've got nothing to worry about as long as nobody panics. You'll probably be getting some visitors eventually, though."

Connors' tone did little to reassure Martin, who suddenly felt the high turning sour.

"Who? Nuke and his stooges?"

"No," Connors said, the irritation obvious in his tone. "The police. The new investigators. If they come to see you, just stick to the story. Nothing has changed, only a few faces, that's all."

"So you're saying that I shouldn't have to worry about some dumb cops?" Martin asked, his voice raising a few octaves at the end of the sentence.

"Just stick to the story," Connors repeated.

"The beauty of that is it's practically true," Martin said, trying unsuccessfully to sound more confident than he was feeling. It was the coke. That damn Connors had called at precisely the wrong time to take the edge off. Now he'd be going through the wringer instead of riding high.

"You're not coming apart on me now, are you?" Martin heard Connors ask.

"I'm fine," he said quickly. "I'm fine."

"Don't try to change anything."

"I know. I won't."

After another pause, Connors asked, "So how's everything else?"

Walker knew that this was a veiled code used to inquire about his investments.

"You're set to have a very profitable quarter," Martin said. "I'm ready for some more deposits."

"Okay, great." Connors said. "And, Marty, don't start sweating over this new task force thing, okay? My source tells me that we've got nothing to worry about. It's all smoke and mirrors."

"All right, Richard. Good night." He hung up the phone and began exploring his ambivalence about Connors, and how their symbiotic relationship had developed.

Strangely enough, they'd met in high school. Not that they were friends back then, or anything. No, far from it. Martin had been the bespectacled, nerdy, smart kid, in charge of all the scholastic things, and Connors the school troublemaker. The only passion they shared at the time was the chess club. And Martin had been astounded at Connors' proclivity for the game. He seemed to always be thinking one or two moves ahead. But Connors dropped out of the club late junior year shortly after turning sixteen and getting his driver's license. He bragged to a select few that he was helping his brother run drugs up from Florida on the weekends in a beat-up old van. Then, news spread the next fall that during the summer the pair had been stopped and arrested somewhere downstate. Connors' older brother got stuck with the brunt of the charges due to Connors still being a juvenile. He was absent for most of the term, but somehow managed to graduate, the line *Most Likely to Deal* printed under his yearbook photo.

The next time Martin happened to see him was at their ten-year reunion, where Connors, looking flashy and tan, pulled up in a silver Corvette with a girl who looked like a movie star on his arm. He explained his dark complexion as the result of some "Florida investments," and handed out tips to the waiters and bartenders that left little doubt in Martin's mind what that meant.

At their fifteen-year reunion, Connors literally bumped into Martin at the bar after making another equally splashy entrance. A short-tempered glance immediately softened when Connors looked at Martin's nametag.

"Marty, old buddy," he'd said. "Still playing chess?"

Martin replied that he hadn't much time for that now, as a CEO for a large savings and loan. Connors' eyebrows raised.

"Really?" he said. "We'll have to get together for a drink sometime." And they'd exchanged cards. That was the beginning of it. Martin began assisting him in "flying under the radar" to launder the very large sums that Connors made from his "business dealings" ever since. In return, he supplied Martin with a retainer fee, as well as the other perks when he found out more about him. The man had contacts everywhere, and for Martin, whose burgeoning aberrant appetites had begun to reassert themselves as his relationship with Miriam began to fail, these contacts were heaven-sent. These perks most recently had included a cut rate on an unlimited supply of cocaine, ecstasy, or virtually any other drug Walker had a yen for trying out as well as fodder for his "other sexual tastes."

But most of all, Martin owed Connors for so deftly solving the "Miriam problem." His wife had walked in on him during one of his special sessions with young Raul. The bitch. Why hadn't she stayed out that night like she'd said? He knew she'd been fucking someone on the side. But after the cat was out of the bag, Martin had little choice but to go to Connors for help. Exposure in some messy divorce case would have meant a disaster for both of them. Especially if Miriam had hired someone to check into his financial dealings a little too closely.

Connors had told him that Nuke would handle it. "Just go to your meeting for your fraternity reunion dinner, and it'll get done. Then all you have to do is report her missing in the morning."

It had all worked according to plan. The alibi, the disappearance, the body's discovery, it was like some bad dream remembered in a fog. And the best part of it was that he was in the clear. There was no way they could connect him to anything. Or so he hoped, as he began to gather up the rest of his stuff and resealed the baggie. He placed it all in the hollow section of the bronze statue of a satyr playing the flute. Satisfied it was packed solidly inside the base, he twisted the upper part of the figure back in place, inspecting it as always to assure himself that no one would be able to surmise what treasures it held. It's the perfect hiding place for an intellectual giant like myself, he thought. So why should I be concerned about a visit from some stupid cops? Especially with Richard having someone on the inside.

Martin looked at his reflection in the mirror above the statue and tried to smile confidently. But it looked weak and he knew it. Glancing downward, he caught a glimpse of the satyr. The lecherous goat-man stood in silent vigilance, his cold, metallic eyes seeming to twinkle with mischief as Martin looked on.

CHAPTER EIGHT
The Morass

Leal set the empty Styrofoam cup down on the counter and slowly crushed it in his fist. He'd tried to go over the file the previous night after he'd gotten home, but the beers and the way the unexpected events had played themselves out sapped all his powers of concentration. Despite repeated attempts to make sense of things, he found himself dozing as he sat at his desk. So he'd gone to bed, deciding to get up early and take another shot at it. Now, after several cups of strong Dunkin' Donuts coffee, he'd gone through it and found himself agreeing with Ryan. The trail was cold. The case wasn't just complicated and confusing, it was a morass.

Leal knew that the peak time for solving any homicide was in the first twenty-four to forty-eight hours after the crime. In some cases it might be extended to a week or so, but after that the solvability factors all dropped significantly: evidence perished, witnesses disappeared, recollections grew hazy. He reviewed the facts from the original case reports, trying to set the sequence straight in his mind.

Miriam Walker had left her board of directors meeting at the Women Against Domestic Violence coalition at six thirty. She'd gone to a restaurant in south suburban

Justice, and paid with her American Express card. From there, she'd effectively disappeared until her badly decomposed body was found in a pond adjacent to some Forest Preserve woods. The summer drought had caused a recession in the waterline, and two young boys looking for frogs had discovered a large trunk in the water. They attempted to pull it out, but the weight and terrible smell stopped them. The father of one of the boys had stuffed body bags during the Gulf War. When he went back with them to the pond, he knew the smell.

An entire alphabet soup of police agencies was called, and the case was initially assigned to the Forest Preserve police. Their detectives dutifully processed the scene, photographing and retrieving the trunk. The preliminary autopsy by the medical examiner revealed that it was the body of a Caucasian female between the ages of thirty and fifty. The corpse's dental records and fingerprints were cross-checked with the reported missing persons in that category, and the dental records provided the matchup. Miriam Walker had been found.

The Forest Preserve police, barely able to conceal their glee, immediately turned over the case to the sheriff's department, since it was the primary agency investigating the original disappearance. The Walker case quickly turned into what was known in the vernacular of homicide investigations as "a heater." The preliminary investigators had gone through all the standard motions: speaking with the husband (a prominent corporate attorney and CEO for a savings and loan), and questioning the rest of the victim's family, friends, business associates, and colleagues. No one could shed much light on any possible reasons for her death. Although a few friends mentioned that her marriage had been less than blissful of late, they also mentioned she had seemed quite happy recently and was totally devoted to her work both as a judge and an advocate against domestic violence. Martin Walker vehemently denied that he and his wife had been anything but totally happy, and embraced the role of the grieving widower, and promised to donate a hefty portion of her life insurance payment to the Coalition of Women Against Domestic Violence.

Leal flipped the file closed and looked up to see the young waitress standing over him with the glass coffee pot.

"Guess you need another cup, huh, mister?" she said.

He looked down at the crushed white fragments protruding from his fist and shook his head. Standing, Leal left her a tip and went out to his car. It was eight thirty, but he was just a few blocks away. Ryan had said nine and that still gave him plenty of time. When he got to their temporary office in room 110, he saw Ryan sitting at one of the desks, carefully sipping a large cup of steaming black coffee. He looked up and flashed a weak grin.

"You look raring to go," Ryan said.

"Yeah, that makes one of us."

Ryan shook his head slowly, as if it hurt to move.

"Oh, fuck me," he said. "The girlfriend ended up working late, and I kept drinking till she got to Heaven and joined me." His fingers massaged his temples. "We ended up closing the place down."

Obviously a match made in heaven, Leal thought.

"Then today the bitch calls in sick," Ryan said. "Shit, that's what I should've done." He took another small sip of the coffee.

The door opened and Hart came in wearing a tan pants suit with a white blouse. Leal nodded to her and smiled.

"Good morning," she said.

"Maybe for you it is," Ryan said. "You seen Smith?"

"No, Sergeant Ryan," she said.

"Oh, Christ, Hart," Ryan said. "Don't start with that 'Sergeant Ryan' shit this early in the morning." His vocal cords stretched for tenor as he mimicked her voice.

Leal watched Hart's face redden.

"Hey," he said, "lay off my partner." She glanced at him, her cheeks still showing circular red patches on each cheek. "Don't mind him. He's just extremely hungover."

Hart looked away without saying anything and Leal wondered if he'd done the wrong thing sticking up for her. Maybe she has to learn to hold her own around here, he thought.

Ryan had procured an electric coffeemaker that was still half-full. Leal grabbed the pot and a paper cup, refilling Ryan's before pouring his own. Just as he did this, the door flew open and Joe Smith hurried in, nodding and smiling. He looked sharp in a lightweight dark suit and pale blue shirt. His unknotted tie was draped around his lapels.

"Sorry I'm late," he said. "My wife's pregnant and I thought I was going to have to take her to the hospital this morning."

"False alarm?" Leal asked.

Smith nodded again.

"Fabulous," said Ryan. "Now why don't we all sit down and decide how to proceed with this cluster fuck." He drank some more coffee and closed his eyes.

They each sat at their respective desks, turning the chairs so they faced each other.

"Well, hopefully everybody's had the chance to review the file. Any ideas?" Ryan looked at Leal first.

Leal shook his head, holding his hand out for the others. At this point he was content to be a counterpuncher, seeing what the rest of them had to offer.

Smith leaned forward and smacked his file into the palm of his hand. "It's a cold trail, Sarge. The way I see it, she could've been a random victim. Somebody after her purse, her ride, or maybe even her. Maybe she got jacked, and it went too far, so they killed her and dumped the body."

Ryan stopped massaging his temples and looked up.

"All right, I'll buy that so far, but if it was just a simple car thief, why wouldn't he have just followed her and ripped the ride when she went in the restaurant? Or if it was a carjacking, why not just dump her on the road if the killer did ice her on the spot. Why take the chance of riding around with a dead body on the seat next to you?"

"Well, she was dumped in the pond," Hart offered.

"Yeah, in a fucking trunk," Ryan said. "How many carjackers carry one of those around?"

Hart sat back.

"So you're ruling out robbery then?" Leal asked.

Ryan scratched his cheek, then reached in his pocket, withdrawing a pack of cigarettes. He stuck one in his mouth and lit it, exhaling a stream of smoke.

"As big as this case is, we can't afford to rule out anything," Ryan said. "It could have been that she was targeted for a crime—robbery, rape, whatever, but we need to explore motives and figure out how they mesh with the facts we got."

"What about the husband?" Leal asked. "I remember something about them having a bad marriage."

Ryan wrote that down on his pad.

"It's definitely something we should check out," he said. "But he also supposedly donated half the insurance money, didn't he?"

Leal nodded. "Who was originally assigned to the case?"

"Roberts and Murphy," Ryan said. "Roberts is out with a heart attack and Murphy's been transferred to the State's Attorney's investigation section."

"We should talk to them," Leal said. "See what ground they already covered. Figure out what we might want to look at again."

"Yeah, I'll do that," Ryan said, bringing the cigarette up to his lips again. "You got any more ideas on this, Frank?"

Leal noticed that Hart was leaning way back, as if the cigarette smoke were killing her. He thought momentarily about telling Ryan to put it out, but then remembered he shouldn't be fighting any battles for her. He set his coffee cup down.

"It's been my experience that we'd have a lot more evidence if she was a random victim. Those types of crimes are usually based on opportunity, and a lot of unexpected things always go wrong. They throw the offender off his game. Cause him to make mistakes, drop the ball." Leal held up his hand and made a chopping action. "But this one's almost too neat. The car disappearing, the body being placed in a trunk, the trunk being dumped in a pond . . . It shows planning, not quick scrambling."

"You're right," Ryan said. "It's too nice a package." He blew twin plumes of smoke from his nostrils. "I was thinking along those lines myself."

Leal noticed both Hart and Smith looking at him. He continued. "And most of these planned things are engineered by somebody who knew the victim. Somebody had a reason, either monetary or emotional or both to kill her." Leal paused. "You always hurt the one you love."

Ryan drew deeply on his cigarette and blew the cloud of smoke up toward the ceiling.

"So you think it was the husband?"

"Alibi," Smith interjected. He smiled sheepishly when everybody looked at him. "Sorry, Sarge. But what I mean is, don't the file say he was at some kind of dinner or something?"

"A meeting for his fraternity reunion," Leal said. "But what I'm getting at is, what did he stand to gain from his wife's death?"

"He gave away half the insurance settlement to her abused women group, didn't he?" Ryan said.

"Supposedly," said Leal. "Anybody verify that? And the reason might not have been financial, either. We can't afford to rule anything out at this point."

"In other words he could have had ulterior motives and hired someone to do it," Hart said.

"Whoa, Iron Maiden," Ryan said. "Before we go jumping to conclusions, let's huddle. One thing's for sure, if we're gonna be taking on some executive with a law degree, we'd better be sure we've got all our bases covered. I'd better run it by Brice, too."

"And shouldn't we rule out the random victim theory first?" Hart asked. "I mean, if we can definitely eliminate it . . ."

"Then it'll point to a suspect familiar with the victim," Ryan said. His voice had an almost petulant edge to it. He took one more drag on his cigarette, then dropped it in his paper coffee cup and swirled it around. "Got to remember to get an ashtray for in here tomorrow. Everybody bring your own coffee cup, too." He tossed the cup into the trash can. "Okay, here's what we'll do. Joe, you run downtown and check out all the victim's associates, other judges, clerks, deputies, secretaries . . . anybody who remembers anything about her, especially how she was acting right before she disappeared. Write it all down, get names and phone numbers in case we have to follow up. Frank, you and Hart can check with the ME and see if he has anything to add as far as the autopsy. Then we'll start backtracking on the victim. Let's compile a list of people we should talk to. See what else she had going." He glanced at his watch. "We might as well get started and compare notes tomorrow at nine."

Ryan had obviously done his homework, Leal thought. He had it pretty well planned out for a guy who claimed to be as hungover as he looked. But he also had the luxury of reviewing the file before any of them.

"Getting close to lunchtime," Ryan said, grinning as he glanced at his watch. "An early lunch. Give me a buzz if you come up with any brainstorms. Otherwise, I'll see you all tomorrow. This is our first day, so let's all hit the ground running, as they used to say in the army." He stood and plucked his jacket off the back of his chair.

Leal concealed his displeasure with the rather lackadaisical approach. It was a step in the right direction, but a small step. If he were running things he would have really hit the ground running, not be going for an extended lunch break right off the bat. But then again, he wasn't.

Better not rock the boat at this point, he thought. Besides, if I get something good, I can always follow up on it myself. Or with my partner, he thought as he looked at Hart.

"You want to wait to eat?" he asked, "until after we get back from the medical examiner?"

"Oh, whatever you want," she said. "I'm just going to have salad anyway."

"Ever been to the morgue?"

She shook her head.

This could be a good character test, he thought. See how tough she is. See if she loses her cookies once she smells that smell.

She was his partner, so he knew he had to find out sooner or later. Better that it was sooner, just in case. She was a rookie, and totally unproven in his eyes. That would have to change if this partnership was going to work. Of course, she might have reservations about me, too, he thought. But still . . .

"Let's eat first," he said. "I know a place on the way."

CHAPTER NINE
Welcome to the Morgue

After checking out a dark blue Ford from the motor pool, Leal drove to a nearby fast-food chicken joint. Leal caught a glance of the teenaged girl behind the counter eyeing him and Hart as they sat at one of the Formica-topped tables in the small restaurant. Maybe she's wondering if we're lovers, he thought, smiling to himself. He dipped a few of his fries into the smear of catsup and watched Hart eating her salad. She'd folded her jacket over the chair next to her, but sat with her right side to the wall so no one could see her weapon. Her muscular arms extended from her sleeves, rippling as she ate her salad.

Jesus, why would a woman want to have muscles like that? he wondered. Maybe she is a lesbian, like Ryan said. In reality it shouldn't really make any difference, but he knew it would. If it were true, he'd have to be extra careful not to say something, anything that might be misconstrued as being antigay, or taken the wrong way.

Hart placed a bit of lettuce into her mouth with a daintiness that belied her powerful build.

She's feminine in a lot of ways, though, Leal thought. She looked up at him and seemed to notice his stare. He felt himself blush.

"Is something wrong?" she asked.

"No, why?"

"I was just wondering why were you looking at me like that just now?" she said, smiling. "Do I have something stuck between my teeth?"

"No, I was just wondering if you'd want to carpool tomorrow. That way I could drive the unmarked back and then we could start using the county's gas instead of our own."

"Sounds like a plan," she said. "Want me to pick you up?"

"Yeah, if you don't mind," he said, thinking that he didn't want her to see how pathetic his rust-bucket car looked from the inside. She took another bite of salad, then looked at him again, her plastic fork poised between them.

"Is that all?" she asked. "You look like you wanted to say something else."

"I was just admiring your rings," he said, pointing at twin topaz rings that she wore on each hand.

"Thanks, the necklace belonged to my grandmother," she said, holding up a matching blue stone set in ornate silver. "I wear the rings when I'm out in public so people won't notice my palms so much." She turned her hand over and displayed a thick crust of yellowish ridges. "Calluses from the weights. I've been wearing gloves more lately trying to get rid of them."

"Why did you get so heavy into weight lifting?" Leal asked. He tried to soften the bluntness his voice had betrayed by asking a quick follow-up question. "I mean, you trying to get ready for the police Olympics, or something?"

"Actually, I'm a bodybuilder, not a weight lifter. I still have to pump a lot of weights, but the aim is to develop and shape the muscles rather than lift more poundage."

"I see," Leal said, biting into his chicken sandwich, and wishing that he'd kept his mouth shut.

"My ex and I used to compete in couples' competitions,"

she said. "He was really into it, too. Unfortunately, he was also into 'roids real heavy."

"Those as bad as I've heard?"

Hart raised her eyebrows and nodded. "Worse, actually," she said. "Bodybuilding's all about looking good, not being healthy. The dieting, the training, it can all get to be too much sometimes. Add chemicals that destroy your liver into the mix and you can end up with some serious problems."

Leal found himself wondering if she was injecting anything to achieve her build. But that seemed a stretch for someone so health conscious.

"Is that how you met? In the couples' competitions?"

"No, actually we met at Western Illinois University," she said. "Both law enforcement majors. I was into track and field in those days. A little gymnastics until I got too big." She smiled. "We got married right after graduation. I got on County, and he became a personal trainer. He kept flunking the urine tests until he went off the juice. Then he finally got called by Chicago." She ate more of her salad, then said, "That's when I found out that cops make lousy husbands."

Leal smirked.

Hart looked at him quickly.

"Oh, I'm sorry. I didn't mean . . ."

He waved his hand dismissively. "Don't worry, it's true. I was so busy playing supercop, spending all my time at stakeouts and bars that I let my marriage go down the tubes."

"That's too bad," Hart said. "Kids?"

"Yeah. Two girls."

"Wow, how old?"

"Six and eight. They live with their mother. She remarried and moved to California. A suburb of LA. Thousand Oaks. Beautiful place, but far, far away."

"Oh, I'm sorry."

He blew out another slow breath and realized he was telling her much more than he had intended. But what the hell, we're partners, he thought. "I get them for two weeks around Christmas, and for a month in the summers. That's when I usually take my vacations."

"It must be hard not to see them more."

"Yeah, it is," he said, thinking that at least they didn't have to sit through the panic of seeing him in the emergency room with his chest half-open. "But they've got a stable family life, and they're both doing good in school. Great schools out there." His voice trailed off. "How about you? Kids?"

She shook her head. "I guess it's probably better that we didn't have any."

The ubiquitous odor of the dead and decaying bodies hung in the air so pervasively as Leal and Hart walked through the main refrigerated depository, that Leal was once again reminded of his initial trip to the morgue. It had been many years ago, but the memories never seemed to quite go away. His partner had taken him for a meal first, too. A late breakfast. Then he'd laughed as Leal subsequently covered the sidewalk with remnants of his scrambled eggs.

Leal glanced at Hart to see her reaction at the room full of black body bags, stacked on carts and shelves around the room. She seemed to be concentrating on just staring straight ahead, but he could see that her bare arms were already getting goose pimples from the cool temperature. Her nipples were starting to stand out, too.

I should have told her to keep her jacket on, thought Leal.

"Keep breathing through your nose," he said. "You'll get used to it quicker."

"You're supposed to get used to this?" she said.

Leroy, the attendant who was leading them to

Dr. Sprinklien, turned and grinned, showing his gold capped front tooth.

"We got a bunch of bodies from a fire," he said. "Them extra crispies don't smell real bad as a rule."

Leal chuckled. Morgue humor. He forgot how much he missed it.

The refrigerated room opened into a hallway, and another set of doors. Leroy pushed through them and they were all suddenly in a large autopsy room with several steel tables butting up against sinks and small desk areas. Numerous dead bodies lay naked on top of steel carts, lined up in haphazard order. Dr. Sprinklien looked up from over one of them, the body of a huge black man. The body's midsection had been sliced open, exposing layers of yellowish, waxy fat between the skin and organs. The doctor's half-glasses sat upon his rather longish nose. A blue cap covered his hair and a surgical mask hung around his throat. He looked to be in his late sixties or early seventies, and his face seemed slack and droopy.

"Ah, guests," he said as he finished snapping on a new pair of latex gloves. "To what do I owe this distinct pleasure, Officers?"

Leal introduced himself and Hart and said they were working on the Miriam Walker case. He noticed that Sprinklien took an unusually long time eyeing Hart. Maybe the doc's got the hots for her, he thought.

"We wanted to know if you had a few minutes to go over your file, Doctor?" Leal asked.

"Ah, most certainly," Sprinklien said. His speech had a distinctly foreign accent, although Leal couldn't quite place it. "Just give me a few minutes to complete some notes on this fellow." His gloved hand patted the distended stomach, causing it to jiggle lugubriously. Leal noticed that the dead man's flaccid penis was uncircumcised and looked like a dead anteater. He glanced over at Hart.

So far she hadn't said anything, but she hadn't thrown up, either. Maybe she was tougher than he thought.

Leroy pushed though the double doors, carrying a small baby by the feet. He swung the dead child up and dropped it on an adjacent steel table.

"Got your next one, Doc," he said.

"Thank you, Leroy," Sprinklien said. He was bending over the steel counter, writing on a plastic clipboard and talking alternately into a small pocket-sized tape recorder. After a few minutes he turned to them. Leal noticed that Hart hadn't taken her eyes off the baby's corpse.

"A child abuse case," Sprinklien said, nodding at the small body. "Those are always difficult. Now, which of my cases did you say you were interested in?"

"The Miriam Walker case," Leal said. "Lady judge, found in the water stuffed in a trunk in early July."

"You have the file, I take it?"

"Yes, sir," Leal said, handing it to him.

Sprinklien adjusted the glasses on his nose and opened the manila folder. As he read he motioned to Leroy to set up the baby for an autopsy. Leroy, who was also in green scrubs, adjusted a mask over his face and moved the cart with the child over toward one of the sinks. Hart seemed to recoil visibly.

"Oh, yes, I do remember this one," Sprinklien said. "She was quite a mess. We estimated that she'd been in the water a few months."

"She disappeared in April," Leal said. "You listed the cause of death as a broken neck?"

"Yes," Sprinklien said, his voice trailing along absently. "Compression fracture of the third cervical vertebra . . . collapsed trachea . . . no water in the lungs . . . post-mortem fractures to both legs . . . apparently to fit her into the specific container, what did you say it was? A trunk?"

"Right."

Sprinklien grunted. He was a short man, and moved

with a sidle, like some old-time comedian. "No sign of any other bruises, impossible to tell if she'd been sexually molested, and no semen was found." He pursed his lips and gave the file back to Leal. "Now, unless you have some specific questions, we are a little behind today, and I do have plans for dinner tonight."

Dinner? Leal thought. Great appetizers around here. He shot a quick look at Hart, who was still silent.

"Is there anything specific you could tell me about the way Miriam Walker died, Doctor?" Leal said. "We're trying to play catch-up on this one and we're under a lot of pressure."

Sprinklien went over to the body of the baby. Leroy had already split the torso open down the front, and was using a saw to open the skull. The doctor murmured an approval and stepped back over to the black man's corpse. Then his face wrinkled and he stepped over to another body, that of an older white female.

"This one's not as heavy to move," he said, wrapping his gloved fingers around the skull and lifting the head upward. "A compression fracture of the C-three, that's right here." His fingers touched an area just below the hairline. "I would venture to say that the damage most probably occurred as a result of the head being forced forward at the same time as the front of the neck was being compressed. That would account for the trauma to the trachea."

"Sort of like a sleeper hold in wrestling?" Leal asked.

Sprinklien waddled over to the table with the baby on it. Leroy had the top of the skull off now and had started a gentle flow of water over the steel surface to wash away residual fluids and tissues.

"Hulk Hogan once demonstrated a sleeper hold on a talk-show host," Sprinklien said. "This was in the old glory days of professional wrestling, before Goldberg, the Rock, and McMahon. I would say that type of hold may very well have been used to break the victim's neck."

"I didn't know you were a WWE fan, Doc," Leroy said.

"Oh, yes," Sprinklien said. "Never miss it, if I can help it. Great athletes, especially the women." He grabbed the mask and began to pull it up over his face, but stopped. "Officer, I would very much like to continue our conversation, but I doubt that I could add anything more than what is already in the file. Unless you have specifics you wish me to speculate on?"

"Just one, Doctor," Leal said. "How difficult is it to break someone's neck like that?"

Sprinklien canted his head slightly and frowned. The tip of his tongue rolled over his lips, and he said, "I suspect it would take a fairly powerful individual. A masculine assailant, most likely." He paused and smiled at Hart. "Unless, of course it was a female with remarkable physique, like your partner's here. Young lady, have you ever thought of donating your body to science?"

Leal cracked a smile, and glanced at Hart in time to see her blush. She compressed her lips, but said nothing.

Sprinklien laughed as he pulled his mask up all the way. Leroy stepped away from the baby on the cart, the front of his scrubs wet with water and blood.

"Don't mind us, ma'am," he said. "We got our own way of dealing with things here."

Hart looked away.

Welcome to the morgue, Leal thought as he thanked the doctor and began heading for the door.

The putrid smell seemed to linger on them even after they got outside into the sunshine. Leal unlocked his door, reached in and hit the unlocking button, and slipped off his sports jacket. Hart leaned over and spit, then got in the car.

Well, at least she held it together, he thought.

"You okay?" he asked. "I know this place is the pits. Sort of the ultimate in dehumanization."

Hart exhaled slowly before she answered him.

"I hope I never get that callous," she said, buckling her seat belt. "Slinging a baby around like so much meat. It was awful. Especially after all it suffered through in life. Why didn't the doctor tell him to stop?"

"I guess they don't see them as humans anymore. No respect for the dead." He tried a lame smile, but Hart just kept staring straight ahead. "A lot of it has to do with defense mechanisms. Keeping your sanity through black humor. But, believe me, if you start feeling sorry for all the victims you come across, all the tragic things you see on this job, you end up going nuts."

Hart gave him a sideways glance, which Leal detected as petulant. He realized that he must have sounded patronizing, although he hadn't meant to. But he had been somewhat troubled at being assigned with her, wondering if she was tough enough . . . She's so quiet, she doesn't even talk the talk, he thought. How the hell am I supposed to know if she can walk the walk? She hadn't paid her dues on the street, hadn't earned her right to be there. Still, she was his partner, and she had "passed" his little test of surviving the trip to the morgue without getting sick.

He pulled out into traffic and headed for the expressway. Maybe it's time to start giving her the benefit of the doubt, he thought.

The stench of the dead still stung his nostrils, hanging in the car and on them, having silently seeped into their clothes and hair. The light changed and they rode the rest of the way in silence.

CHAPTER TEN
Murphy's Law

Ryan sent Smith to check at the civic center downtown, where Miriam Walker had presided over civil litigations. "Make sure you call first," Ryan had told him, "to make sure they'll see you. You do know how to get down there, don't you?" He'd been somewhat surprised at Smith's expression, like the guy was pissed off or something. Christ, Ryan thought. Another prima donna. Next thing he'll be calling Jessie Jackson on me. Ryan also wanted to check out that organization that Judge Walker had belonged to, Women Against Domestic Violence, but he figured that it might be better to send Hart on that one considering that most of the bitches in an organization like that probably hated anything with two legs and a penis.

After waiting until Smith was gone, Ryan lit another cigarette and dialed the number for the State's Attorney investigations section for the fifth time that morning. It rang several times before someone answered.

"Yeah, this is Sergeant Ryan in Administration," he said, figuring the rank and the word *administration* would get the other person's attention. "I'm trying to get ahold of Investigator Murphy. He around?"

"Sure," the voice said. Ryan heard the man call, "Hey, Murph, phone."

"Yeah, Murphy," a voice at the other end said.

"Hey, Murph, Tom Ryan here."

"Ryan, my boy, how the hell are ya?"

"I'm up to my ears in shit. How about you?"

Murphy laughed heartily, then said, "I figured I'd be hearing from you sooner or later. Heard you caught the Walker case."

"Right. You available for a drink over an early lunch?"

"Always available for that kind of activity, as long as you're buying." Murphy said. "But the advice'll be free. Be here waiting on you."

Ryan stood and slipped on his sports jacket, taking a long drag on the cigarette before stubbing it out. He knew this was one assignment he had to handle alone, because old Murph wouldn't open up to just anyone, and if Smith had been along, forget it. He walked across the parking lot to the court building and flashed his badge at the deputies guarding the metal detectors and the entrance. He went up to the State's Attorney's office and nodded to the middle-aged clerk behind the counter.

"Murphy in?" he asked.

"Yes, sir," the clerk said, motioning with her thumb toward the back offices. Ryan went through the door and went down the hallway. He could hear the distinctive rasp of Murphy's voice even before he got to the doorway. The big man looked up quickly, then winked as Ryan entered. Two younger white guys sat hunched in front of Murphy's huge form, which was half saddling a large metal desk. He was heavyset with brownish-red hair slicked straight back from an expansive forehead. Wire-rimmed glasses with a slight tint rested on a nose that had obviously been broken more than once. He had a flaring mustache, and a sharp chin that seemed to jut out from a doughy dollop of flesh above his collar.

"Hiya, Ryan," Murphy said. His voice was husky and brassy-sounding. "Anybody else in the hall?"

Ryan shook his head.

Murphy swallowed and turned to the two seated men.

"So like I was saying, this pissant state's attorney wants me to do a fucking lineup, even though the victim's already seen him when we picked him up. So I says all right, and goes to pick this broad up. We go downstairs in the lockup, but it's Saturday and we have to wait for all the bond hearings to end. They're getting ready to load all the dogs on the bus to take 'em to Twenty-sixth Street, and I gotta hold everything up for this damn lineup." He paused to lick his lips. "But none of the other assholes will stand in the lineup for me. They're all afraid they'll get picked out and blamed for something." He lapsed into a poor imitation of a black accent. "Not me's, Officer. They's might pick me."

The other two men listening laughed appreciably.

"Time's running short, and I still got a ton of work to do before I can get to happy hour, so I had to use one of what I call Murphy's Laws. I improvised." He smiled broadly. "I got a couple of the deputies to stand in the lineup for me." Murphy paused for what seemed like a comedian going for dramatic effect. Ryan had heard the story before, so he knew what was coming. He'd worked with Murphy when they'd been in Vice.

"Two white deputies, two black deputies, all in T-shirts and black uniform pants, and one nigger defendant in funky-ass blue jeans. The witness didn't have no trouble picking the son of a bitch right out."

The two younger guys began laughing, and Murphy was, too, but he held up his hands. "And that ain't the best part of it. Get this. At the prelim, this little faggot of a public defender asks me if I conducted a lineup, so I says, 'Yes, sir, right in this very building, sir.' The asshole don't say nothing, either, leastwise not with me standing there glaring at him the whole time. He ended up copping to a plea and is now doing six years at Stateville. I thought about calling

Guinness to list the first racially balanced lineup in Cook County history, but figured I'd better let it ride. After all, I'm just here to serve and protect."

He stood up and brushed his hands together, as if expelling a coating of dust, then extended an open palm at Ryan.

"How you been doing, Tommy, my boy? And, more importantly, what can I do you out of?"

"I need some of your advice and expertise," Ryan said.

"Murphy's Law: If you can't fuck it or eat it, piss on it."

His two straight men laughed again, as if on cue.

Ryan realized he had to get Murphy away from his audience or he'd be in for a long afternoon.

"You eat yet?" he asked.

"No, I haven't," Murphy said, walking around to the chair. He grabbed a garish glen plaid sport coat that could have been powered by a battery from the rack and slipped it on, pausing to wink at the other guys. "In fact, I just might be tied up on an important investigation for the rest of the afternoon, boys."

At Heaven's Gate, Ryan waited until Murphy had downed his shot and was working on the beer chaser before asking about the Walker case. The reflection of the big man's face soured visibly in the mirror behind the bar.

"Anything you can tell me?" Ryan asked. "I'd like to avoid covering any dead ends."

Murphy snorted as he shook his massive head and set the mug of beer down on the bar.

"That whole case is a dead end," he said.

"You and Roberts like the husband for it at all?"

"We checked him out," Murphy said, after taking a long, slow drink from the mug. "His alibi checked out. He was at some kind of meeting bullshit, or something."

Ryan lit a cigarette and signaled the bartender for a refill. His own shot glass was still half-full.

Murphy smiled. "Trouble was, we had to run everything by the brass before we could make a move. Like they was afraid we'd step in some shit or something. Who you got in charge of you guys?"

"Paul Brice."

"I always got along with him good, until that case, that is." The bartender set another mug and shot in front of Murphy. The big man smiled and sipped the new beer. "Ahhh, nothing like the foam when you first get it from the tap." After licking his mustache, he continued. "He was directing us, too. Me and Roberts wanted to check out different angles, but all Brice wanted to do was keep checking on chop shops and carjackers."

"Because of the car disappearing?"

Murphy picked up the shot glass, held it to the lights, then nodded. He swallowed half of the amber liquid, exhaled heavily, then took a second more copious sip. "That's one thing I never knew about Brice. He's like a fucking bulldog once he gets something set in his mind." Murphy set the glass down and held up his open palms on either side of his temples. "Like he was wearing blinders. Only could see one angle. We was running down leads on every fucking Caddie recovered in four states. Never found the damn thing. Like it disappeared off the face of the earth, or something." He picked up the shot and finished the rest of the whiskey.

"How about the insurance angle?" Ryan asked. He sipped his own drink gingerly. He still had to report back to the office for a final check before he left. "The lady judge have anything other than the standard policy?"

Murphy shook his head, sloshing some beer around in his mouth.

"Just the usual hundred grand," he said. "And her old man donated half of it to that domestic violence thinga-majig that she belonged to." He squinted at Ryan through the smoke. "Of course, what's a measly hundred g's to some rich, fucking CEO? He probably farts more money than that."

Ryan smirked, then leaned closer.

"So tell me, Murph, how did you see it?"

Murphy took a long swallow of beer, holding the mug up so that the last bit of the foam drained into his mouth. After setting it down on the polished surface he forced a loud belch, then grinned at Ryan.

"Shit, I been on the job long enough to see it the way your boss tells you to see it," he said.

"Meaning?"

"Meaning, if Brice seen it as a carjacking gone bad, then that was that." One of the older regulars was at the jukebox and selected "One For My Baby (And One More For the Road)." Sinatra's voice filled the bar area. Murphy smirked and pointed to the empties on the bar. "They're playing my song," he said, rubbing his index finger and thumb together.

Ryan rolled his eyes, then motioned for the bartender to set Murphy up again.

"Christ, Murphy, I got an ex-wife and two kids to support."

"Here's to the wonderful institution of marriage," Murphy said, lifting the new shot glass in an exaggerated toast. He drained it in one protracted swallow.

Ryan looked at him carefully.

"Jesus, and I thought I could drink."

Murphy laughed and picked up the beer. "Every copper thinks he can until he comes up against the master. It's one of Murphy's Laws."

"Why'd Brice play it so cautious?" Ryan asked.

"Ah, you gotta remember that we were dealing with a bunch of judges and lawyers to begin with," Murphy said. He gripped the mug, but didn't drink. "I think Brice was afraid somebody'd step on his dick. He wanted to feel out every move, and it just worked against us, that's all."

Ryan considered this.

"So did you check out the husband real close or not?"

"Yeah," Murphy said, holding up his hand and wiggling it slightly. "Me and Roberts liked that angle, but like I said, the guy had an airtight alibi for the night of the disappearance. We tried to do some backtracking, but you gotta remember that it first came in as a missing person case. Plus we never even got to check the original crime scene. By the time we got handed it, the damn thing was colder than a dead mackerel." His voice sounded defensive. "So all things considered maybe Brice's approach wasn't so wrong after all. He's methodical, I give him that." He drank from the mug and leaned his arms on the bar. "As it turned out, Roberts had a heart attack, and they switched me outta dicks because we couldn't get nowhere. And then they ended up shelving the damn case anyway until all this stink got stirred up by that Shay asshole. Vote for me and I'll solve the fucking Walker case," he said with a mimicking lilt to his voice. Murphy turned and leaned forward, so close that Ryan could smell the other man's boozy breath.

"Now let me give you some real advice," Murphy said. "Southside Irish to Southside Irish. Don't make no waves. Just ride it out till we see how this election comes out."

Ryan's brow furrowed.

Murphy snorted. "Just remember you're dealing with fucking judges and lawyers here, my boy. So if the brass don't want to smell any stink, don't go stirring things up in the shitter."

"Lemme guess," Ryan said, reaching for a cigarette. "That's gotta be another one of Murphy's Law's, right?"

CHAPTER ELEVEN
The Box

Joe Smith had gotten downtown a little past eleven, and since then had searched up and down the massive Daley Center for anybody who'd known or worked under Judge Walker. Deputies, clerks, secretaries, even a few of her fellow judges had consented to talk to him, but none of them had provided anything that Smith felt could even remotely be considered a lead. Not that I'd know what a lead was, he readily admitted to himself. At the end of over four hours of interviews, he knew nothing more than what he had already gleaned from the case file: that Miriam Walker had been, in life, a rather attractive, intelligent, pleasant, and strong-willed woman. But each person punctuated his or her statement with the same question: Did they have any new ideas about who killed her?

Frustrated, Smith went to the cafeteria for a cup of coffee. He thought of calling home to check on Helena, but decided against it. He had to make some kind of sense of his notebook. He had things scribbled everywhere. Plus she would have beeped him if anything had happened. And she could always call her mother if she needed someone to stay with her at the hospital until he arrived. Smith looked up at the ceiling and blew out a long breath through pursed lips.

Why did all this have to be happening at once? he wondered.

"Excuse me," a voice said from behind him.

Smith looked up and saw a short white-haired deputy in a starched white shirt standing over him. The man appeared to be in his early sixties, and had a courtroom captain patch on his left sleeve.

"You the officer who's been asking about Judge Walker?" the deputy asked.

"Yes, sir," he said, still in the habit of automatic politeness from his patrol work.

"I'm Scotty," the older man said, extending his hand. "I was in charge of her courtroom before. I've since been promoted." Scotty pulled a chair out and sat across from Smith.

"Right. I was meaning to talk to you. People said you was the man to see," Smith lied. But what the hell, he figured. A little flattery never hurt. "Can you remember any particular cases that might have caused someone to hold a grudge against her?"

Scotty shook his head. "That's what I couldn't figure out. Most of the stuff she presided over was small potatoes. All civil hearings, small claims court . . . Nothing really to cause any waves."

Smith scribbled down more information as he asked the same standard questions that Ryan had told him to ask: How well did you know her? Had she been having trouble with anyone? Did she seem upset or distressed before her disappearance? To Smith's surprise, Scotty said that the judge had never seemed happier.

"Like she'd come into fresh clover," he said.

"How was she getting along at home? She ever talk about that?"

"Like I said, she never seemed happier."

Smith sighed. This was turning out to be more of the same. A wasted trip. He swished the last bit of his coffee around in the cup before he drank it.

Scotty was watching him, as if waiting.

"I was wondering how come they switched investigators?" he asked finally.

"New blood, I suppose," Smith said.

"I gotta tell you, I didn't think much of those other fellas," Scotty said, scratching his ear. "They came by, asked a few questions, made a big show about acting real interested, then they never even come by for the box after I called them."

"The box?"

"Yeah. I called them and said I'd found the box of stuff that we'd collected from her chambers. I was holding it for her husband, but he never came by for it, either. And that damn Murphy told me on the phone that he was definitely coming back, but he never did."

"You still got it?"

"Yeah, down in evidence storage," Scotty said. "Finish your coffee and we'll go find Big Fred to dig it up for you."

Locating Big Fred proved almost as difficult as finding a parking space on a downtown street. Finally, after Scotty had called him on the maintenance frequency for the third time, Big Fred answered.

"What's your twenty?" Scotty demanded, his knuckles whitening around the radio. "I've been calling you for fifteen minutes."

"Sorry, Captain," the voice said. "I was in the washroom."

"Well, get down to evidence storage on the double," Scotty said. He led Smith over to some elevators and they rode down to the basement. Big Fred, an immense man clad in a navy-blue uniform, slowly shuffled forward and grinned, his light-brown hair sticking out from under his cap.

Scotty glanced at his watch, his other arm cocked on his hip.

"Sorry I took so long, Captain," Big Fred said. "I got

diarrhea real bad." He rubbed his palm over his expansive stomach. "Might have to call off tomorrow if it don't get no better."

"Never mind your bowel problems," Scotty said. "We need that box of Judge Walker's personal effects that was logged in here."

"Oh yeah?" Big Fred turned to Smith. "You working that case now?"

Smith nodded.

"Yeah, them other guys never came back for that stuff, did they?" Big Fred pulled a cluttered ring of keys out of his pants pocket and opened a solid metal door set against a wall of thick steel mesh. Beyond the mesh were row after row of shelving with boxes piled high on each level. They stepped into a small anteroom on the other side of the door and Big Fred went to a desk that was covered with papers, magazines, coffee cups, pop cans, and numerous other items. He deftly plucked a black bound ledger book from the heap and paged through it, running his thick fingers down each column.

"I distinctly remember telling you to hold it for the investigators," Scotty said.

"Yeah, Captain," Big Fred said. "I know I got it in here somewheres." He paused. "Here it is."

"What did I tell you?" Scotty said in a triumphant tone. Then to Big Fred, "Go pull it for Detective Smith here. He'll be taking it with him. And make sure he signs the log for it." As Big Fred ambled off, the smaller man turned to Smith and extended his hand. "I sure hope this helps in some way. I'd like to see whoever killed her caught."

Smith shook Scotty's hand and thanked him profusely for his help.

When Scotty had gone, Big Fred came back carrying a cardboard box about three feet long, sealed with duct tape and written on with black Magic Marker. He set the box heavily on his desk and patted his pockets.

Smith began to hand his pen to Big Fred, but the other man shook his head, extracting a packet of cigars with the plastic tips. He held out the package to Smith, who declined.

Big Fred shrugged, peeled off the cellophane wrapper, and began fishing around in his pockets once again. Smith wished he'd brought a lighter, but spied a book of matches among the sea of papers on the desktop. He pointed to them and Big Fred smiled, the cigar dangling from the middle of his lips.

"Thanks, I been looking all over for them," he said, striking one and holding the flame to the end of the cigar. After a few seconds of copious puffing, he shook out the match and exhaled a plume of gray smoke. "So you think this'll help catch who done her?"

"Don't know right now," Smith said.

"Yeah, I figured it might be important. Them other guys seemed real interested on the phone, then they never came back. The captain was calling and bugging them, I guess." Big Fred tapped the page. "Just sign right here and it's all yours."

Smith scribbled his name, collected the evidence sheet, and hoisted the box onto his shoulder. It was heavier than it looked.

"Want me to get you a cart or something?" Big Fred asked.

"No thanks, I can handle it," Smith said. But by the time he'd waited for the elevator he'd switched shoulders two times and had the beginning of a crick in his back. He could also feel himself perspiring through the underarms of his shirt.

I sure hope this damn thing amounts to something after all this, he thought.

CHAPTER TWELVE
Random Victim

They spent the next day tracing down and assembling all the loose ends that Murphy and Roberts had glossed over: the insurance angle, Miriam Walker's lack of a will, the bank records preceding her death, the make and model of the trunk she'd been found in, interviews with all the friends and associates that had been listed, her final appearance at the Women Against Domestic Violence meeting . . . But as they sat in the office with the fading midafternoon sunlight streaming through the sole window, a sense of lassitude settled over them. Nothing had been appreciably accomplished by any of their efforts. Ryan had thumbtacked a set of the crime-scene photos on the bulletin board. He tapped a pen against his teeth.

"Well," Ryan said, "the boss wants to see us for an update. Anybody got any brainstorms before we go face the music?"

"It seems strange that she was a lawyer and had no will," Hart said.

"Actually, she was a judge," Ryan said. "Next comment."

Leal saw Hart blush. "Or somebody took it," he said, standing and walking over to the photos. "Maybe we should take another look at the original scene."

"Be my guest, Sherlock," Ryan said.

Leal studied the photos for several seconds more.

"I've been thinking about this," he said. "Look at the distance from the road to the location of the trunk in the water. It's got to be what, at least fifteen feet or so?" He saw the other three looking intently at the photos, too. "A trunk that size with a woman's body in it would have to weigh, what? Close to a buck and a half? That indicates a two-man job."

"Yeah, nobody could've thrown the fucking thing that far," Ryan said. "Not even Hart."

Hart looked at him and smirked. "With you inside, I might be tempted to try," she shot back.

Leal raised his eyebrows appreciably. Good, he thought. She's starting to stand up for herself. He remembered the pleasure that he got from watching a new recruit or partner gain in confidence and experience. In this case, he had both. The team seemed like it was coming together a little, too. They were all starting to work together for the same goals, with the same purpose. But it still gnawed at him that Ryan moved with all the speed of a tree sloth. He seemed to lack the fire in his belly to get everybody moving. Maybe it's time for me to exert some command authority, he thought.

"So, Joe," Leal said. "Anything from the rest of the judges yesterday?"

Smith pressed his lips into a frown and shook his head.

"Nobody seems to know much, or if they do, they ain't saying," he said, flipping open his notebook. "They all said she was smart, competent, and quiet. Stuck to herself . . . Seemed happy right before she disappeared . . . Nothing else significant."

"I noticed something in that box you brought back," Hart said.

"Yeah, me, too," Smith said. "It gave me one hell of a sore back."

He laughed to break the tension, but nobody else did.

Leal found himself admiring the way Hart's pants stretched tautly over her hips and butt as she bent over the box and sorted through it. He blinked twice and rubbed his temples, reminding himself that it was never a good idea to think those kinds of thoughts about your female partner. It could lead to problems. As he brought his hand down he saw Ryan grinning and licking his lips. He stared at Hart's back, then glanced at Leal and winked.

Leal was frowning just as Hart stood and turned around. She obviously caught his disapproving look and blushed again.

"What you got, Olivia?" Leal asked. Dammit, he thought. She's gonna think I meant that for her.

"This book," she said, setting a dark blue hardbound book on the desk.

"*Ap-hro-deet Rising*," Ryan said. "What the hell's this have to do with anything?"

"It's pronounced Aphrodite," Hart said. "Read the inside. The title page is signed by the author."

Ryan sighed heavily and paged through the book with sharp, quick movements. The inscription was handwritten in blue ink, just below the artfully scripted letters of the title: *To Aphrodite, Yours Always, Simon.*

"Okaaaay," Ryan said slowly. "I usually slept through English lit class. Want to bring me up to speed?"

"Simon Ellias is the author. That sounds pretty personal, doesn't it?" Hart said. "And Aphrodite is the Greek goddess of love."

"Yeah, I've heard all about Greek love," Ryan said. "But this ain't even personalized to her."

"Which could mean he didn't want to make it too obvious since she was married," Hart said.

"I don't know," Ryan said. "It seems like you're stretching it."

"Well, there had to be some reason why she kept this

book in her chambers, doesn't there?" she said. "And look in the acknowledgment section. He thanks the Lunge Hill Corporation for their 'gracious assistance.' According to the bank records Miriam Walker was a principal stock-holder in that company, wasn't she?"

"Yeah," Leal said. "Her father was some bigwig with them. Left her a lot of stock in it."

Ryan squinted and took out his cigarette pack.

"I think Olivia's got a good point," Leal said. "Let's go talk to this author guy."

"Okay, go get 'em, tiger," Ryan said, lighting a cigarette and drawing deeply on it. He paged to the back inside flap of the book and stared at the picture of Simon Ellias, then shook his head theatrically. "Nothing to look at, is he? But who knows, maybe they were doing the nasty. Says here he lives in Willow Springs, which is close enough to check on, I guess."

"That could go toward motive if the husband's in-volved," Leal said.

"Yeah," Ryan said, blowing some smoke through his nostrils, "but we don't even want to think about going there unless we got more than just a book of love poems by some asshole who may or may not have been jocking her."

"Come on, Tom," Leal said. "It's something we got to check out."

Ryan's cheeks hollowed as he drew on the cigarette more copiously this time. When he spoke his words came out amid a cloud of smoke. "Let's run it by the boss first. Like I said, he wants to talk to all of us today for a progress report."

Brice's sports jacket had been hung over the back of his chair, and the sleeves of his white shirt had been rolled up over his muscular forearms.

When they came into the office he stood up and moved around the desk with an anxious step, first slapping Ryan on the back and then extending his hand toward Leal. Taken somewhat aback, Leal reciprocated and got snared in Brice's patented "sissy shake," his big hand powerfully grinding the tips of Leal's trapped fingers together. Brice gripped Smith's palm in similar fashion, but Hart was seemingly spared.

Maybe he's afraid her grip will be stronger than his, Leal thought to himself, shaking his fingers.

Brice walked back behind his desk and opened a metal box next to the framed photograph of his wife and kids with dated-looking clothes and hairstyles. He removed a thick cigar from the box and bit off the end, leaning back and spitting into the waste can.

"Hope nobody minds," Brice said as he flicked the lighter and held it to the end of the cigar. "Thank God this no smoking thing doesn't apply to private offices."

Leal noticed the cords in Hart's neck tighten visibly. Suck it up, kid, he silently urged her.

Brice blew out a cloud of smoke and coughed several times.

"So how's the investigation going?" he asked.

Ryan took out his own cigarettes and held up the pack. "Boss, may I?"

Brice sat back and nodded, the cigar jutted at a sharp angle from the corner of his mouth.

"We've been going over the background of the victim," Ryan said, withdrawing his own cigarette after taking a quick puff. "Getting to know her, so to speak."

"What's that mean, Ryan?" Brice said. "She's dead. How the hell can you get to know her?"

"We were exploring possible motives," Leal said.

"Motives?" Brice said.

"Right," said Leal. He sensed the growing hostility in Brice's tone and sought to lighten it. At this stage of the game animosity would be counterproductive. He grinned. "After all, she didn't die of the flu."

But Brice didn't laugh or even smile. He removed the cigar from his mouth and said, "I'm well aware of that."

"So basically," Ryan cut in, "we were trying to establish her habits, who her friends were, her enemies . . . So we could try and develop a better understanding of what might have happened."

Brice wrinkled his nose, as if he were smelling a foul odor.

"Wait a minute," he said. "Didn't you people read the case file on this? Murphy and Roberts went over all that already. They pretty much established that Miriam Walker was a random victim." He looked at each of them and drew deeply on the cigar, causing the ash to redden. Leal glanced over at Hart. Between the lieutenant's pungent cigar, and Ryan's smoldering cigarette, she looked about ready to puke.

"I gotta say, I expected more from this group," Brice said. "But it seems that instead of hitting the ground running, you're just going over old ground."

"With all due respect, Lieu—" Leal started to say.

But Brice cut him off.

"Can it, Leal. I'm a lot more familiar with this case than any of you. I worked it before, you know."

Yeah, Leal thought. And you did real good, too, didn't you?

"So," Brice said, blowing out some more smoke, then coughing again. "I want you guys to concentrate on checking down every lead in two main areas. Random victim carjackings and chop shops. We find the car, if it still exists, then we got a good lead on who killed her."

Leal started to speak, but stopped as Ryan said, "You know, boss, I been thinking along those lines, too." Leal snorted and Brice stared at him sharply.

"You got a problem with that, Sergeant?" Brice said.

"Well, I gotta tell you, Lieu, I think it's gonna be like looking for a needle in a haystack. How many months has it been and the car still hasn't shown up? And I don't feel comfortable zeroing in on any one theory until we've ruled the others out."

Brice rolled his tongue over his teeth before he spoke. "Well, I'm really not interested very much in your 'comfort,' Leal. First of all," he held up the index finger of his non-cigar hand. "I been working this case a helluva lot longer than you, which means I've had plenty of time to sort out all the different theories and directions. And two," he held up another finger, "I am in charge of this investigation."

"I realize that, but—" Leal tried to say.

"No buts," Brice said, cutting him off again and waving his palm back and forth. Then he pointed to Ryan, "Check out the chop shops and random victims file. Trace down every lead. Look for similar MOs. Shit, maybe we even arrested some punk who knows something. Get 'em to flip. That's the way this thing's gonna be solved. Good old-fashioned police work." His eyes shot toward Leal momentarily. "And, Ryan, if you're not capable of leading and directing this group, I'll find someone else who is. Understood?"

"Sure thing, boss," Ryan said. His cigarette smoldered untouched between his fingers.

"Okay," Brice said, taking a careful draw on his cigar. "Give me a written report summarizing everything you've done so far. And I want it typed and on my desk by the end of business today. I'll expect one every three days. If things don't improve, I can increase that to every day."

Ryan stood and nodded. "Gotcha, boss." He turned and motioned toward the door, taking one more drag on his cigarette before exiting the office. He blew out the smoke, causing Hart to wave it away as they emerged in the secretary's office area. Ryan grinned and handed the butt to the secretary. "Take care of this for me, will ya, babe?" Then, he turned to Leal as they were out of earshot. "Jesus, Frank, could you have done any more to piss him off?"

"He's an asshole," Leal said. "Always has been, and always will be."

"Yeah, but he's also the head asshole," Ryan said. "Now we got to go curl up and kiss his ass."

"Maybe you do," Leal said.

Ryan gave Leal an imploring look. "Frank, he's got the authority to replace any of us if he wants."

"Bullshit, he's not going to replace anybody. He'd look like too much of an idiot after that big press conference. He was just blowing smoke out his ass."

Ryan sighed. "Well, if he was, I don't want to be standing behind him." He grinned, as if pleased with his own wit. "But right now we got bigger problems. Getting this summary to him. Hart, can you type?"

"Sure," she said. "As long as it's in a nonsmoking area."

CHAPTER THIRTEEN

Machines and Machinations

"Hi, I'm not in at the moment, but if you leave a message after the beep, I'll get back to you."

Leal exhaled loudly through his nostrils and waited for the series of electronic manipulations to give the desired signal. He hated talking to these damn machines, but after finally getting up the nerve to talk to her he didn't want to just hang up. Besides, if he did, and she had caller ID, she might trace the number, thinking it was a pervert or something.

"Ah, Sharon, this is Frank Leal," he said haltingly. "I wanted to give you a call to see if you were busy. I'll make it another time."

He left his departmental voice mail number and flipped the cellular closed, wondering if he should have left his home number, or at least his beeper. Nah, I got a long time to be disappointed, he thought. No sense waiting for a call that probably won't ever come.

It was quarter after three, and he was practically alone in the cafeteria section, which was why he'd chosen it. Some deputies and a few maintenance people sat at the far end in the smoking section. Leal stepped over to the vending machines and dropped some change into one of them.

A diet Pepsi for him, and a natural juice for Hart. As he gripped the can and the bottle and headed back to the office, he saw her standing by the wall, stretching.

"How's the typing coming?" he asked, setting the juice down on the desk.

"Just finished, Sarge," she said, completing her stretch and now flexing her fingers. Ryan and Smith had hung around for a little while, then silently departed, leaving the two of them to complete the investigation summary thus far. Hart hadn't seemed to mind that the typing duties fell to her, and she worked at incredible speed. Like a human typing machine, Leal thought. And since they'd ridden to work together that day, he was obligated to stay until the report was done. Not that he would have considered leaving with the others. She was, after all, his partner, for better or for worse.

"Here's your juice," he said, tapping the cap. "Let's go make some copies and get it to Brice so we can split."

Hart moved forward and twisted open the juice and drank some.

"He's gone for the day," she said. "I just called up there to tell him it was done. He left shortly after the meeting."

"That son of a bitch," Leal said. He regretted saying it a moment later, not wanting to criticize a higher-ranking officer in front of her. "We're going nowhere fast on this one."

"You think we're on the wrong track, huh?" she said, taking another sip of juice.

Why can't women ever drink things down in one or two gulps? He wondered. He took in a deep breath, then looked at her. He could say that he thought Brice and Ryan epitomized the term, "political hacks." Coppers who got their rank and appointments because of who they were and who they knew, not what they did. But still, he didn't really know her that well, and she was something of a mystery herself. "Let's just say that I don't have a lot of regard for the approach of our esteemed lieutenant."

"I get the feeling that there's history between you two. Am I right?"

Leal smirked. "We went a few rounds once," he said. "Literally. Back when we both worked at the jail. I don't think Brice has ever forgotten it."

Hart's eyebrows rose. "Wow, who won?"

Leal laughed. "It was a draw, I guess." He didn't want the word circulating again that he'd kicked Brice's ass. Not while he was working under him in this new assignment. "Come on, let's make those copies and get out of here."

They walked together toward the copying machine, which was on the way to Brice's office. The building was beginning to empty out, as the overstaffed day shift was slowly being replaced by those working afternoons.

"So, Olivia, what you got planned for tonight?"

She looked at him briefly, as if deciding what to say.

"Nothing much," she said slowly. "I've got to hit the gym. Tonight's my back and legs routine. Why?"

"I was just going to offer to buy you something to eat. Where do you work out?"

"The Body Center in Alsip. I gave you that card, remember?"

"Oh yeah," Leal said, remembering it now. "How long does it normally take?"

"Maybe an hour and a half," she said slowly.

He glanced at his watch.

"So if we leave right now, and traffic isn't too bad, you could be through with your workout by?"

"Maybe six thirty or seven, if I wasn't rushing it. Why all the questions? You thinking of joining me?"

"Actually, I was wondering if you were up to a little overtime?"

"Overtime?"

"Yeah, I think it's time to meet Mr. Walker face-to-face."

"But isn't that kind of going against what the lieutenant told us today?"

They stopped at the room with the copier. The door was open, but the place was empty.

"Yeah," Leal said. "But we're never gonna get anywhere with this case following Brice and Ryan's slow, careful, step-by-step directions. It's time for some initiative."

"But going over to his house at night? Wouldn't it be better to just interview him at his office tomorrow?"

Leal shook his head. "I'd rather see him in his natural habitat. Catch him off guard a little. He'll have too many defensive barriers set up at his office." He paused and considered what he was suggesting to her. He would be going to interview Martin Walker regardless, and she was his partner. But he knew that they could be risking Brice's wrath if he ever found out. But how the hell would that happen, anyway? Unless Walker complained, and if he did, that would tell them something, too. "So you up for it, partner? Or would you rather sit this one out?"

She seemed to consider his question for a couple of beats, looking down at the copies popping out of the machine. When she looked up, she smiled.

"Okay, I'm in," she said. "I'll do a light workout. You going to join me at the gym, or what?"

"I might," Leal said. "They got any punching bags there? A place to skip rope?"

"Sure."

Leal nodded approvingly, thinking how nice it might just be to do some boxing work again, imagining Brice's face on the front of the bag.

Leal pounded out a rhythm on the speed bag to warm up. He had been less than significantly impressed with the gym, although the proprietor had seemed nice enough. Hart had introduced Leal proudly as her new "partner." Rory Chalma had eyed him sharply as she'd said that, before extending an overdeveloped arm across the wooden counter and saying almost too gaily, "Mi casa es su casa."

Leal didn't know if the man was trying to impress him or what, but his pronunciation was totally anglo. Chalma looked to be about thirty-five, with a sparse crop of curly blond hair and a massive neck that appeared wider than his head. He had generously refused Leal's offer to pay for the workout.

"Any partner of Ollie's gets the first one on the house," he'd said. "We'll talk later if you want to sign up."

There was something different about the guy, but Leal didn't know what. Maybe he was a boyfriend of Hart's or something. Her name certainly was prominently displayed in the front window with a huge sign:

OLIVIA HART, MID-WESTERN FEMALE BODYBUILDING CHAMP TRAINS HERE

And numerous framed pictures of Hart doing various muscle poses in a small black bikini adorned the walls.

Leal noticed Chalma eyeing them as they walked toward the locker rooms. A few of the obviously hard-core lifters whistled and yelled, "Hey, Ollie" from their respective workout stations.

"You seem to be quite the celebrity here," Leal said.

"Just lucked out and won one of the top amateur contests, that's all," Hart said. "Small potatoes, really, but it qualifies me to compete in the Olympia this November."

Leal didn't know what the Olympia was, but didn't want to say so. An angular-looking woman in street clothes stepped out of the door marked *Women* and nodded to Hart.

"Hi, Ollie. I didn't know you were coming early tonight or I would have waited." Her voice was almost as low as Leal's.

"I didn't know, either," Hart said. "Oh, Marsha, this is Sergeant Frank Leal, my partner."

"Hi, Frank," the other woman said. "New member?"

"I don't know, maybe," Leal said.

"Hope so," Marsha said, giving him an obvious once-over. "See you two around sometime."

As she left, Leal thought that everyone in here seemed to be a weirdo. He turned to Hart.

"Ollie? Is that what people call you?"

She smiled and bit her lip slightly. "Yeah, it comes from growing up in a house with two brothers. My sister is the oldest, and I was always sort of a tomboy. Olivia never seemed to fit, so everybody started calling me Ollie."

"Okay, Ollie. See you on the floor," Leal said.

And he did sneak a few surreptitious glances at her between bag sessions. It was hard not to. She looked striking in a black nylon workout outfit that left her muscular shoulders and legs bare. Chalma was spotting her as she squatted down with an Olympic-sized barbell on her back. The bar was fitted with double forty-five-pound plates on each end, and Hart's thighs bulged in exquisite bas-relief with each repetition, showing more muscular definition than an anatomy book. But each movement, Leal noted, was accomplished with an underlying feminine grace. Fluid and lissome, like a female gymnast, yet, at the same time, undeniably powerful.

If she could develop the same confidence and self-assurance she shows around here, Leal thought, she could be a dynamite copper. He glanced at his watch and decided to eke out another round on the heavy bag. Maybe this place ain't such a dump after all, he thought. I could do worse for a regular workout place. And I could do a lot worse for a partner, too.

They arrived at Walker's house at seven thirty-five after a winding trip through the exclusive section of unincorporated Palos Park known as the Wooded Dells. Set just off the main highway, the area had obviously been tailored to maintain a bucolic appeal with lots of huge trees, curving roads, and picturesquely placed ponds. It was also devoid of street signs and lights, but the homes were all well lit by variously stationed floodlights to show off the perfectly sculpted hedges and well-manicured lawns. Every house seemed to have at least a three-car garage.

Leal drove slowly past the house, giving it a once-over.

"Isn't that it?" Hart asked.

"Yeah," he said. "But I just wanted to get a feel for things first. See what else is around, how close the neighbors are."

The houses were set far enough apart so as not to be within easy earshot of one another. There were no alleys, and each home had long, receding driveways that dropped back toward dark unknowns. A thick six-foot hedge separated Walker's residence from his neighbor to the right, and on the left a large undeveloped patch of woods extended about a hundred yards beyond the house, all the way to the adjacent roadway.

"Maybe somebody'll call the cops about a cruising ten thirty-seven," Hart joked.

"That'd tell us something, too," Leal said. "But I doubt it. If they would have been worried about security, they would have spent some money on street lights."

"And signs," she added.

Leal thought he detected something in her voice. A nervousness, perhaps? Maybe she was getting cold feet joining him on this violation of the Brice plan. After making a U-turn and following the road back to Walker's, Leal turned into the driveway. The headlights shone on a declining slope that descended to a lower level.

Probably the attached garage down there, he thought. As he shut off the car and grabbed the handle, he heard Hart say his name quickly. He glanced over at her.

"I'm . . . not sure what to do here," she said haltingly.

Leal let go of the door handle. "What do you mean?"

"I don't know if you've heard anything about me." Her voice full of pauses and breaths. "But I haven't really got a lot of experience doing this sort of thing."

He sighed quietly and grinned.

"Ollie, it's just like anything else. You've got to jump in and start paddling. You learn by doing. Just follow my lead. Let me ask the questions. See what you observe. You'll do fine."

Hart's lips pressed into a thin line.

"Okay," she said, exhaling. "I'll do my best."

"That's the spirit. Let's do it to it." Leal tried to smile reassuringly. It's the only way she'll learn anything, he thought. I just hope what she learns isn't how to get yourself in trouble with your boss.

CHAPTER FOURTEEN

First Impressions

The house was a two-level brick with a descending rear portion. The two large windows in the front both had heavy drapes securely closed, although lights appeared to be on inside. Leal found the doorbell next to the aluminum screen door. The interior door was solid-looking mahogany. He leaned on the button once, waited about five seconds, then hit it a couple more times. They heard chimes sounding wildly on the inside.

"That ought to get his attention," Leal said.

"To say the least," Hart said. He could tell she was still nervous.

Moments later the sound of movement came from the other side of the door. The ornate light above them flared to life, and a speaker below the doorbell asked, "Who is it?"

"Police," Leal said, holding up his badge case to the peephole. "We'd like to speak to you, Mr. Walker."

"What about?" the speaker asked.

Leal shot a quick glance at Hart, then said, "Your wife's death, sir. We've recently been assigned to the case."

There was a long pause.

"I see," the voice finally said. "I'll be with you in a moment."

The "moment" stretched to a good three or four minutes. Leal rang the bell again in impatience.

The door flew open and a balding, overweight man with wire-rimmed glasses stood glaring at them through the screen door. The petulance was obvious in his voice as he said, "You didn't have to ring the bell again. I was on my way."

Leal smiled. "Sorry, I thought you forgot about us."

Martin Walker sniffed and asked to see their identification again. He took a particularly long look at each, matching their faces to the photos. Leal placed him at around fifty, but knew from the case file that he was actually thirty-seven. This dude ain't into clean living, he thought. Walker's hair was light brown, and mostly gone in front, except for a peninsula-like section combed back from the center of his forehead. He had on a light blue bathrobe, striped pants, and house slippers. Leal realized that Walker was wearing pajamas. His skin had a loose, doughy look to it and his fingers toyed with the ends of the robe's sash. He sniffed again and asked, "I was in the bath. Now, what can I do for you?"

"We'd like to ask you a few questions about your wife, sir." Leal said. Hart stood by, watching Walker with intensity, her whole body stiff and tense.

"For God's sake," Walker said, "I've already told you people everything so many times." He drew in a sharp breath. "But I suppose if it helps . . . Come on."

They followed him down a hallway that opened into a large living room. Picture windows were set into each wall, one obviously meant to show a view of the front and the other the back, had the heavy drapes not been closed. A massive television in a wooden case with a VCR/DVD player underneath stood across from a curving white sofa. Several other matching chairs were strategically placed, along with a tall grandfather clock and other ornamental furnishings to give the place a decorative distinctness. At the room's entrance was an ornately carved and highly polished circular table upon which stood a bronze statue of a satyr. A floor-to-ceiling bookcase filled with brown leather-bound volumes lined other wall. Numerous video cassettes and DVDs were stacked haphazardly on a small metal table next to the television.

Walker went to the coffee table in front of the couch, picked up a remote control, and shut off some cable movie. He turned and rubbed his index finger quickly under his nose.

"I wish you would have called first, Officer . . ." He let his voice trail off, suggesting that he'd forgotten their names.

"Leal, Sergeant Francisco Leal. And this is my partner, Detective Hart."

She nodded and smiled politely.

Walker shifted his gaze to her momentarily, then glanced back at Leal, who strode past him and went to look at an oil painting of some running horses that was hanging over the couch. Leal stood there, waiting for Walker to follow him.

"Now, just what is it you wanted?" Walker asked, walking toward Leal. His voice sounded tight.

Leal didn't answer, but instead crossed his arms and stared at the painting. Slowly he turned his head and said, "That's a mighty nice painting."

"I'm glad you have an appreciation for art, Sergeant. But you surely didn't come here for that, did you?"

Leal shook his head slightly, grunted, and sat down on the sofa. He took out a small notebook and a pen from his sports jacket.

"Mr. Walker, we've been recently assigned to a task force investigating your wife's death," he said. "We're sort of reviewing things at this point."

Walker licked his lips. After a few moments he said, "That doesn't speak very well of the communications system in your police department." He picked up a pack of cigarettes, shook one out, and lit it. "Can we get on with this?"

"Sure," Leal said, speaking more slowly than usual. "What can you tell us about the day your wife disappeared?"

"Not much," Walker said. He perched on the arm of the sofa, his head swiveling occasionally toward Hart, who was standing silently on the left. "I worked till about four thirty, then I went to an alumni meeting of my old fraternity. We're planning a fifteen year reunion."

"Where was this meeting?"

Walker drew deeply on the cigarette before answering. He blew out some smoke. Leal watched Hart recoil visibly and smirked. She'd have to get used to dealing with smokers in this business.

"It was at a gentlemen's club on Wabash," Walker said. "My secretary could probably get you the address, as well as names of people who can verify that I was there." He took another quick puff on the cigarette. "You know, this would have been a lot simpler if you'd scheduled an appointment and come to my office."

"We were in the neighborhood," Leal said, smiling. "So what time did this meeting break up?"

"Actually, we had dinner there also." He brought the cigarette to his lips and sucked on it almost greedily this time. "I don't know. Maybe seven thirty or eight. I caught one of the late trains home and had to wait. I do remember that."

"And you arrived home at?"

"Around nine thirty or so."

"Was Mrs. Walker home at this time?"

"No, she also had a meeting that night," he said. He took a final drag and stubbed the cigarette out in an ashtray. "Her domestic violence committee. I didn't think anything of her not being home," he reached for the pack of cigarettes again, "but when it got close to midnight I began to make some calls. Orville Baker, another lawyer we know, said she hadn't even come to the meeting."

"Is that when you first called the police?" Hart asked.

The suddenness of her voice seemed to startle Walker. He paused with the cigarette unlit in his mouth.

"The first time, yes," Walker said, bringing up the lighter, which he flicked several times to no avail. Walker tossed the lighter down on the coffee table and leaned forward to pull open a drawer. He rummaged through it as he spoke, finally pulling out a white book of matches with glossy red letters. "They declined to do anything, saying she wasn't actually missing, and could just be"—he struck one of the matches on the safety slate and lit the cigarette—"making a late night of it with some friends, or something equally ridiculous." Walker shook out the match, dropped it into the ashtray, and placed the matchbook beside it. "I can't help feeling that if they'd done something right then and there, this whole thing might have turned out differently."

"You wife ever stay out late before?" Leal asked.

"Sometimes."

Leal rolled his pen between his fingers. "Would you have an address book of your wife's friends we could look at?"

Walker blinked several times before answering.

"Not really," he said, tapping the cigarette over the ashtray. "I do have a book of my associates, but I'm afraid it wouldn't do you any good. Miriam never used it. She had her own book, but I'm afraid I don't know where she might have kept it."

"Perhaps we could go through some of her things?" Hart asked.

Walker seemed startled again as he turned toward her. This guy's uneasy around women, Leal thought.

"Unfortunately, that's not possible, either," Walker said. He took a quick puff, exhaled, and squinted through the smoke. "I had our former housekeeper dispose of them. You see, I was so devastated by the entire incident, I just didn't want anything around to remind me."

Leal nodded, then asked, "So do you have any theories about what happened, Mr. Walker?"

Walker exhaled twin plumes of smoke through his nostrils.

"Isn't that supposed to be *your* job, Sergeant?"

"We'll need some names of some mutual friends of you and your wife."

Walker brought his hand up and pushed up his glasses to massage the bridge of his nose.

"Miriam and I had few friends in common," he said slowly. "That we saw socially, anyway."

"Maybe some of her friends, then?"

"I might be able to come up with some," he said. He blew up a thoughtful-looking cloud of smoke into the now hazy room. "But not off the top of my head."

"Okay," Leal said, standing. "Would you have a picture of her we could borrow? I'd like to get it reproduced. We'll make sure it gets returned."

Walker stood and compressed his lips. "I'll have to try and locate one."

"Anything will do," Leal said. "Maybe a wedding picture even."

Walker stared at him. "As I said, I'll have to look. Now is there anything else?"

Leal bit at his lip and squinted. "How about the housekeeper's name and number?"

"I can give you the agency's number. I had to let her go." Walker set the cigarette down in the ashtray and went over to a table with a telephone and picked up a black leather folder. Leal stepped over to the couch, stooped briefly to reset Walker's smoldering cigarette, then straightened up. Walker read off the number and Leal scribbled it down.

"Now," Walker said, flipping the book closed rather abruptly, "I really do have an early day tomorrow."

"Okay, sir," Leal said. "We'll be in touch later for that list of your wife's friends then." He started toward the door, then stopped. "Do you know the routes she usually took when she was going to those meetings?"

Walker frowned and shook his head.

"Those meetings were regular?" Leal asked.

"The third Tuesday of the month," Walker said. He wiped at his mouth.

"Did your wife wear any regular jewelry?" Leal asked. "You know there was none recovered with the body."

"I assume the people who killed her took it," Walker said in clipped tones.

"Okay. If you think of anything else in the meantime, sir," Leal said, handing him a card. Walker put the card into the pocket of his robe as Leal extended his hand. "Thanks for your time."

Walker and Leal shook hands, and Leal stared at Hart, cocking his head slightly. She returned his glance, then also held out her hand toward Walker. He shook hers with less enthusiasm. At the door Leal paused again, placing his hand on Walker's shoulder.

"Mr. Walker, I just want you to know that me and my partner are gonna stop at nothing to find the son of a bitch who did this to your wife, sir," Leal said. "You got our words on it."

Walker seemed to stiffen at the unexpected touch. He nodded, nervously this time, and smiled.

As they got to the car, Leal opened the door and watched Hart slide into the passenger seat and take a deep breath.

"Ugh, all that smoke," she said.

"Well, Ollie, what do you think?"

She compressed her lips, then licked them with the tip of her tongue.

"I don't know, Sarge. His reactions didn't seem right. Something was off. He sure didn't act like a husband should." She shook her hand exaggeratedly. "Sweaty palms, too."

"Yeah, the sure sign of a nervous liar," Leal said, twisting the keys in the ignition.

They sat down the road, blacked out, watching the Walker house just to see if maybe he'd leave or if someone else would drop by. He'd been nervous, all right. They'd both sensed that. And the perpetual sniffle suggested to Leal that Walker was putting something up his nose on a regular basis. Excited, they both talked about the inconsistencies of Walker's statements, his quick disposal of all his dead wife's clothes and belongings, and his professed ignorance of her friends.

"Not even a picture of her anywhere," Hart said.

She was really warming to the task, Leal noticed, and it made him feel good.

"And when you brought up that part about the jewelry," Hart said eagerly. "He said, 'the people who killed her.' Like he knew it was more than one person."

"Good point," said Leal. "You sure you haven't done this before?"

He grinned and could see that she held back from giving him a playful slap. Leal struck a match and let it flicker momentarily in the darkness before blowing it out and watching the smoke curl upward from it. "Need a light?"

"What are you talking about?"

He handed her the white book of matches with the red lettering. The design spelled out *The Kit Kat Club*. An address and phone number were printed in smaller letters. Hart looked at them, then looked up smiling.

"Why, Sarge, I was wondering why you adjusted his cigarette when you were getting up."

"Ever hear of that place?"

Hart strained to read the address, then shook her head.

"It's up around River North," Leal said. "Maybe we can go up there and show some pictures around."

Hart rotated her head slowly with her eyes closed, seeming to stifle a yawn.

"Tired?" Leal asked.

"A little, I guess."

Leal shifted into gear.

"We might as well call it a night, then. This isn't going to tell us anything else." He looked at her in the darkness. "You did all right in there tonight." In the moonlight he could see her smile ever so slightly.

He rolled well past Walker's house before turning on the lights. As they wound their way back toward the main highway a vehicle with its brights on came from the other direction. Leal flashed his brights, but the other car's didn't dim at all. A white Jaguar whizzed past them.

Nothing but rich assholes around here, Leal thought.

CHAPTER FIFTEEN

Messages

"You what?" Ryan asked, leaning back in his chair and letting his cigarette dangle loosely from his lips.

"We went out and interviewed Walker last night."

"At his fucking house?"

Leal nodded.

Ryan moved forward, resting his elbows on his knees. "Great move, Franko. Just fucking great."

Hart was standing off to the side, watching the contest between the two men.

"Christ, Ryan," Leal said. "If we don't start taking some proper investigative steps on this—"

Ryan cut him off: "We'll get Brice's boot shoved up our asses."

"Hey, fuck that," Leal said, massaging the back of his neck. He had almost said, "Fuck Brice."

Ryan smiled crookedly, as if he knew what Leal was thinking, and said, mimicking a black accent, "Brice be da boss." Smith hadn't shown up yet.

"Then maybe we got to start thinking about going over his head," said Leal. "There's less than two months till the election. If O'Hara's so set on us clearing this damn thing, he's got to give us the leeway to check everything."

"Nobody from upstairs has been in lately," Ryan said.

"All out campaigning at those county luncheons, putting the arm on everybody's wallets." He stubbed his cigarette out after taking a last drag. "Anyway, we got to go through the motions on Brice's suppositions. Me and Smith are going to check with DCI today. They were supposed to be running a big chop-shop sting. If the brother ever gets here, that is."

Leal said nothing.

"Look, Frank," Ryan said, leaning forward again. "Like I said, we gotta at least go through the motions, right? And in covering that stuff we're at least able to rule it out."

Leal was still silent.

"Let's try this," Ryan offered. "I'll run this chop-shop angle to pacify the boss. You and Hart take the rest of today and tomorrow off. Then Sunday you guys can run down some of the personal angles on the housekeeper and maybe that author dude if you want. And I'll bring up our suspicions about checking out the husband to Brice when the time's right."

Leal looked at Hart, then back to Ryan.

"That would give us weekend coverage, I guess," he said. *And keep us out of Brice's hair for today, too,* he thought. "Sounds okay to me. Ollie?"

"Sure, Sarge," she said. "I have to get in a heavy workout tonight anyway."

Ryan clapped his hands together. "Good, now that we've got that settled," he moved over to a stack of papers on his desk and rummaged through it. He selected a pink message slip and shoved it toward Leal. "Here, this is for you."

It was a telephone number under which was written *S.A. Devain. Please call.*

"I assume that's Sharon *Divine?*" Ryan asked salaciously.

Leal noticed that it was her home, not her work number.

"Who's that?" Hart asked.

"A state's attorney I know," Leal said quickly. He stood and started to head for the door. "I'd better make this call."

"Hey, wait, Franko," Ryan said. "Just use one of these phones, why don't ya?"

"I want to get some coffee," Leal said. He pushed out the door as Ryan smirked triumphantly.

Leal took out his cell phone as he walked, but noticed the low battery signal as soon as he turned it on. He snapped it shut and debated going back to the office to get a new one. To hell with that, he thought. I'll just use the pay phone in the cafeteria. Proceeding down the hall, Leal took a dollar bill out of his pocket and put it in the coin changer. A set of pay phones was on the opposite wall. She answered on the third ring.

"Hi, Sharon. It's Frank Leal. Returning your call."

"How are you?" she asked. Her voice had a coolness that seemed more distinct over the phone. "I got your message on my machine, but I didn't get in until late last night."

"I see," Leal said, wondering what that meant. "How's Felony Review?"

"It's not too bad. Keeps me hopping. We work twelve-hour shifts, on call seven to seven. Four days, four nights, then four days off."

"Doesn't sound too bad."

"It's not, really, once you get used to it. I had my off days, so I went up to Michigan with my sister. They've got a summer place up there."

That sounded innocuous enough, Leal thought. At least it doesn't sound like she went someplace with a boyfriend.

"Well, ah," he began, finding himself fumbling over the words, like a teenager. "I was wondering if you'd be interested in going out to dinner?"

"Hmm," she said slowly. "When?"

Oh, great, he thought. Another brush-off.

"Whenever's best for you," he said. "Depending on your

schedule and plans, of course." He was beginning to feel stupid.

"Well, I'm scheduled to go back on call tomorrow morning."

"Oh, I see," he said, feeling crushed.

"But I haven't got anything planned for tonight."

There was an abrupt dropping sound and at first Leal thought he'd been disconnected. Then a computerized voice said, "Ten cents more, please." He fished in his pocket for more coins and quickly fed a dime into the slot.

"You still there?" he asked.

"Where are you? I thought you hung up on me."

"The battery was dead in my cell phone," he said. She laughed and gave him her address, agreeing to expect him at seven.

Leal walked back to the office, sipping from a cup of coffee and smiling. Maybe things are finally starting to go my way, he thought. Then he remembered his car. There was no way he wanted to show up in his beat-up old Chevy with holes in the seat covers. Maybe he could borrow a car, but from whom? He wouldn't even consider asking Ryan . . . Hart maybe? But she drove a Toyota, with a stick shift at that. It had been a while since he'd driven one of those. Plus the car seemed so small.

Dammit, he thought. I got too used to driving those sharp confiscated numbers when I was in MEG. Should've taken care of business and bought a new car when I got transferred.

There was only one other alternative, and it wasn't pretty. Use the unmarked and hope Sharon wouldn't notice.

Leal managed to sidestep all of Ryan's idiotic questions as Hart gathered up her stuff and they left. When they got to the unmarked, Leal immediately went to the driver's side and got in. Hart opened her door and slid inside.

"I was wondering if you'd mind me using the squad this weekend?" she asked as he headed for the expressway.

"Why's that?"

"I was thinking of going in tomorrow to run a few things on the computer," she said.

Oh great, he thought. But what the hell, I'm the sergeant here.

"Actually, I'm going to need it," he said.

Out of the corner of his eye he saw Hart nod and quickly look away. She said very little else as he got on the entrance ramp and began the ride home.

Hart slammed the door of her apartment, angry at herself for the way she was feeling. Her reflection in the full-length mirror opposite the door stared back at her and she canted her head slightly, looking at her face from various angles before drifting lower. She tossed her jacket toward the sofa, watching the muscles of her arm and shoulder bulge and jump at the action. Her body, even unpumped, looked so big. So . . . massive. Taking a deep breath, she immediately went to a double biceps pose, turning to scrutinize the well-defined, tautly bundled tissue that seemed ready to burst through her skin.

Olivia Hart, Mid-Western Female Bodybuilding Champion, she thought. Yeah, that's me. And my partner won't even trust me alone with the squad car.

Going to her bedroom she quickly assembled her "heavy workout" clothes: a pair of black nylon shorts, a baggy sweatshirt with the sleeves cut off, and her usual socks and gym shoes. She stuffed a towel and clean underwear into her bag and zipped it closed. As she straightened, she brushed back her hair and again studied her reflection in the mirror above the dresser. The sunlight streamed through the windows, seemingly softening her image and making her hair seem lighter. It had been obvious from Leal's conversation with Ryan that the state's attorney they'd talked about was more than a professional contact. And Leal had seemed in such a good mood leaving that place, too.

He must be seeing her, Hart thought, and wondered if Leal found her attractive. She certainly felt the sizzle when she was with him, but as partners she knew that could complicate things.

Yeah, she thought. Those kinds of complications I don't need. Not after what she'd been through with Jim Markham. He'd been teaching at the academy, and she began reporting to him when the aerobics instructor position opened up. They'd seen each other every day, and he'd taken a genuine interest in her activities. He asked her out to lunch, and then dinner. The wedding band on his finger was an imposing obstacle, but she'd conveniently ignored it, telling herself that she was, after all, just going out to dinner with a colleague.

Then, of course, came the sex. She was still on the rebound from her divorce, she told herself, and his wife didn't understand him. Whatever the reasons, they provided all the necessary rationalizations as the affair stretched from weeks to months. And despite the occasional guilt, Hart found herself feeling strangely happy for the first time in a long time. There was somebody for her to share her dreams with, albeit limited. They held each other in bed after making love and she'd tell him of her dream to get into investigations one day. And he kept listening and encouraging her, saying he knew she'd make it one day.

It had ended abruptly. She came in one Monday and found that he'd transferred back to a street assignment. Not so much as an explanation as to why, and he wouldn't answer her pages or calls. Hart wondered if his wife had found out, or if the duplicity of their relationship had gotten to him. Finally, after more than a week she found a pink message slip left in her box. It was unsigned, but she recognized his scrawl:

Ollie, Sorry the way things worked out. I put in a good word about you for that assignment you wanted. You should hear something soon. Take care.

J.

J, she remembered thinking. He didn't even have the balls to sign his name. Not even a, "If you need anything call me . . ." As she crumpled the pink message slip and felt the rush of the tears down her face, she became immediately cognizant of the secretaries watching her.

And then, the next week Captain O'Herlieghy had called her in and interviewed her about this position. She knew then that some strings had been pulled, but so what? She'd earned it, in a twisted sort of way, hadn't she?

No, I've had enough of cops, she thought. *Frank's sweet, and he's nice-looking, but since we're working together as partners it's better if it doesn't develop into anything more.* She picked up her gym bag and car keys. *Besides,* she added mentally, *he's obviously got someone else on his mind anyway.*

She continued her ruminations on the drive to the gym, and when she pulled open the door and saw Rory Chalma's surprised expression, she felt a surge of resentment. Unjustified resentment, she knew, but she didn't feel like answering what she knew would be twenty questions. She just wanted to do her workout.

"What are you doing in so early?" Rory asked. "I didn't expect to see you till tonight."

Walk on by, Hart thought. But she couldn't.

"I got the day off. Tomorrow, too. Thought I'd go heavy and then work on my routine."

"Do the routine first. Otherwise you'll be too tired." Chalma's head bobbled as he looked past her. "Where's your new boyfriend?"

Hart crinkled her face. "What are you talking about?"

"What's his name? Frank? You two made quite a couple."

He put a slight lilt in his voice. "Everybody was talking about it in here."

"Don't they have anything better to talk about?" Hart said, a little more sharply than she intended. "I mean, he's just my partner."

"Whatever," Chalma said, smiling slyly.

"Rory, get a life."

"Whoa," Chalma said, raising his hands to his chest and fluttering his fingers. "Aren't we testy today?"

Hart headed for the locker room and slammed her gym bag onto the bench. Get it together, girlfriend, she thought. Focus.

She undressed slowly, thinking about what Chalma had said. *Everybody was talking about it* . . . Didn't they have lives of their own to worry about, instead of speculating about mine?

Hart removed the tiny pink posing bikini she wore for the contests and looked at it. Maybe she should go with black instead. She held the bottom against her hips and stared in the mirror. She'd have to wax again soon, she thought. But that could wait until right before the contest. Today was just a dress rehearsal anyway.

When she stepped out of the locker room a couple of the guys working out sounded off with wolf whistles. Hart tried to ignore them, juggling the CD player and towel. She felt slightly cold and regretted not wearing a robe or something.

Chalma jogged back to her and yelled for one of the others to watch the front desk for him. They walked past the weight room area to the aerobics section. Two smaller rooms with tanning beds were off to the side.

"You'll want to get some tanning in, too," Chalma said.

"Okay," Hart said. She hated the thought of lying there naked in the ultraviolet glow. "But I'm thinking about using some instant tanning lotion instead."

Chalma looked at her.

"Oh?" he said.

"I read where too much of that artificial tanning isn't good for you."

"Whatever," he said. They stopped in front of the floor-to-ceiling mirrors that covered the back wall. "What CDs do you have?"

Hart studied her mirrored image. The overhead lighting made her muscles look heavier, more defined. She turned.

"Earth to Ollie," Chalma said, mimicking a person on a telephone. "The songs?"

"I don't know," she said. "I think I've been working with 'If You're Not In It For Love.'"

Chalma wrinkled his nose.

"Shania's out," he said. "Too much like an old Revlon commercial. Let's use something from Madonna. 'Impressive Instant.'"

"You're just saying that because she made that movie with Rupert Everett a couple of years ago," Hart said. "It bombed, remember?"

Chalma fluttered his eyebrows. "But Rupert looked sooooo good."

Hart frowned.

"Trust my instincts, babe," he said. "Rory knows best."

"Yeah, right."

"It'll give you an edge. The judges will remember you better."

They were standing side by side now and Hart caught a glimpse of their flattened reflections again. She towered over Chalma by what looked like half a foot, with his squat, muscular frame and thickly muscled arms giving him a barrel-like appearance. Hart flexed her broad shoulders and deltoids. The muscles jumped to attention under her skin.

"How do I look?" she asked.

"Great. Fabulous."

"You really think so?" She turned and stood, arms akimbo, and flexed her lats. Her V-shape accentuated distinctively.

"Look for yourself," Chalma said, his eyes suddenly narrowing. "I've never seen you better."

"I mean . . ." Hart said, turning sideways and drawing her hand over the chiseled symmetry of her legs. "Do I look feminine?"

"What is this all about?" Chalma said, frowning now. His tongue swept over his upper lip. "Are you having man trouble or something?"

"No, I just—"

"It's that guy Frank, isn't it?" Chalma asked, cutting her off. "He's messing up your head, isn't he?"

"No, he's not." Hart dropped her pose and looked down at him. "Really, he's just a friend, that's all."

Chalma pursed his lips.

"Look, this thing's ninety percent preparation. You can't afford to get de-psyched. Otherwise, you'll be finished before you even start."

Hart nodded. "I know."

"I'm worried about you since you started this new job. I can see it's putting a strain on you."

"There's no strain," she said. "And I'm getting all my workouts in."

He shook his head dubiously.

"It's more than that," he said. "It's mentally preparing, too. You know how important this is."

Hart had to suddenly fight back the urge to cry. Important? she thought. Important to you, maybe. But what about me? What's really best for me? But there was no way she was going to break now in front of Rory. No way in hell.

"Just lay off, okay? This new position is very important to me career-wise."

"We can't afford to have you get your head messed up by some guy."

"Will you stop? I told you, Frank's just my partner. A friend. And he's very supportive."

"I'll bet he is."

Hart started to say something, but instead just stared down at him.

"Are we going to get started, or what?" she asked.

Chalma drew his lips into a thin line and nodded.

Hart reached down and selected a CD out of her bag and handed it to him.

"Shania," she said. "'If You're Not In It For Love (I'm Outta Here).'"

CHAPTER SIXTEEN
Doing Juice

Richard Connors swung the white Jaguar into the parking place directly in front of the ornately painted sign that advertised: THE IRON MAN GYM: OPEN 24 HOURS. The front of the building, which was set at the end of a curving strip mall, was composed of large windows set into brick pillars. From the parking lot Connors could see numerous people inside working out. He got out of his car and began walking toward the glass doors, passing a young girl with a blond ponytail and tight-fitting blue jeans. She eyed the car, and then Connors. He smiled as he passed her, regretting that he was too pressed for time to strike up a conversation and get her number. He liked a girl who knew class when she saw it, and he knew he looked good in his gray short-sleeve shirt and tailored black pants.

Several blocks away to the west the massive white brick walls of the Joliet Correctional Center loomed in the background. Connors was cognizant of them, too, and felt the tinge of regret about the girl fade as he concentrated on setting up the task at hand. He reached out for the angular metallic door handle, resting his fingers lightly on it until he saw Tex behind the front counter hit the buzzer. Stenciled across the front of the door in solid black letters outlined in gold was: MEMBERS ONLY.

"Hiya, boss," Tex said, giving a respectful wave. The high counter hid his lower body from view. A portable television sat a few feet away, playing a cable sports channel. "Come to check things out?"

"Nah, I'm looking for Nuke."

Tex cocked his head toward the back and said, "Locker room."

Connors nodded and began to weave his way across the floor where several sets of heavily muscled men strained and screamed as they struggled with metallic plates on iron bars. Floor-to-ceiling mirrors made the inside look twice as big as it really was, reflecting back the rows of dumbbells, weight machines, and stationary bicycles. The rubber-tiled floor was littered with discarded plates and two short Hispanic men in maintenance outfits scurried around, replacing the weights in the appropriate racks.

Connors pushed through the swinging wooden doors that marked the men's locker room and glanced around. The rows of lockers and benches were empty, but at the far end, where the toilet and shower facilities were, Connors saw two sets of masculine-looking feet inside the same cubicle. Both sets of feet were pointed in the same direction toward the porcelain bowl. Connors blew a snort out his nose.

Nuke's bearded face appeared around the corner of the open stall and gave a leering wink of acknowledgment before disappearing again into the confines of the cubicle. The front pair of feet shifted slightly, and Connors heard someone grunt sharply. Nuke backed out of the stall, dropping a hypodermic syringe and a blood-spotted sheet of toilet paper into a paper bag. He was followed by another man, a muscular but short young blond guy, about nineteen or twenty, who was fiddling with the drawstring of his sweat pants. He stopped suddenly when he saw Connors and looked at Nuke.

"It's okay," Nuke said, adjusting a wad of tobacco inside

his lower lip. "He owns this place." The sleeves of Nuke's black Harley Davidson sweatshirt had been chopped off to accommodate his massive shoulders and arms. A brocade of veins stood out, forming a trellis of bas-relief on his swollen forearms, and a crude, homemade tattoo spelled out *NUKE* on the well-developed left deltoid. On his right shoulder a professionally done mushroom cloud exploded upward, under which was lettered *DON'T FUCK WITH ME.*

The young blond guy shook his leg a couple of times and grimaced.

"Well, shit, go workout, you dumb fuck," Nuke said, slapping the kid's head. "You'll feel the difference doing squats."

The young guy grinned, nodded to Connors, and left. They watched him hobble out.

"What the hell was that all about?" he asked.

"Just trying out some new juice," Nuke said. He unlocked his locker, reached in his pocket, and pulled out two fifties. "What's up?"

Connors frowned. "What if I'd been an undercover cop or something?"

"Relax, boss. I'm careful about things." He removed a roll of bills from his boot and slipped the fifties around it. "Ain't no way I'm going back inside for nothing. Besides, I got cops who work out here that are on the juice, too."

"That's good to know," Connors said, letting the sarcasm drift into his voice. "Look, I'm not fronting the bills here to see it go up in smoke from somebody being careless."

Nuke smirked. "Like I said, it ain't no big deal. Besides, I'm making a pretty good buck from it, too. Almost as much as I make working for you."

Connors nostrils flared. "Meaning what?"

Nuke smiled again, less derisively this time. "Okay, if it makes you feel better I'll watch my ass. You been pretty square with me, fronting for that fancy lawyer the last time, and all. I got no complaints."

Connors realized that this conciliation was probably as far as he was going to get with this big, dumb prick. And he wasn't ready to sever all ties yet. He still needed Nuke to make those little trips to Mexico to pick up those special shipments. What did it matter if he brought back some steroids along the way? It was an arrangement of mutual benefit. And Nuke was another layer of insulation between Connors and the more sordid aspects of the business.

"For a minute I thought you were butt-fucking him," Connors said, trying to inject some humor into the conversation.

But it seemed lost on Nuke. He shook his head and said, "Nah, with that AIDS shit, I never even done that on the inside. I'd just get my bitch and make him give me a blow job."

"Look," Connors said. "I need you to do something pretty quick."

"Oh yeah?" Nuke said. His big fingers fumbled through his clothes hanging in the locker, and he withdrew a dark brown vial and a hypodermic syringe. "This is the good stuff. Sustanon 250," he said, inverting the vial, and sticking the needle through the gray rubber top of the bottle. After filling the reservoir of the syringe, he set the vial back inside the locker and slammed the door shut, pressing the padlock closed. Nuke cocked his head, indicating the toilet area. Connors followed Nuke to the cubicle and watched as the big man entered the stall and carefully set the syringe on the paper dispenser.

"So what you need, boss?" he said, and dropped his pants, exposing his big, hairy ass. The muscles of his legs bulged like bundles of steel cables under the skin. "You gotta excuse me, but I'm way overdue for this."

"Better bodies through chemistry," Connors said, more than a little pissed off at Nuke's inattention. But, he reminded himself, he needed him. For the present, anyway. Especially for the task at hand. "Go ahead and take care of business," Connors said. "I'll wait."

Nuke nodded and picked up the syringe, tapping it to consolidate the tiny air bubbles, then depressing the plunger until a viscous drop of yellow liquid appeared at the end of the needle. He worked the needle into a thorny patch of skin on the top of his buttocks and injected the two cubic centimeters of the steroid.

"Like I mentioned, I've got a problem," Connors said.

"Haaaah," Nuke slowly grunted as he finished depressing the plunger. "No problem's too great. What is it?"

"There's someone," Connors said, "I want you to eliminate."

CHAPTER SEVENTEEN
Chinatown

Leal went through his mental checklist as he prepared to embark on what he hoped would be a very pleasant evening. He checked his watch: six twenty-five. No sense rushing, he thought. It's only in Evergreen Park. Twenty minutes tops. And he didn't want to arrive early, although that was preferable to arriving late. Grinning, he slipped on his sports jacket and grabbed his keys, taking a final look around to make sure his earlier cleaning sprint had been successful.

Gone were the unseemly stacks of dirty clothes, old newspapers, and scattered dishes. In the off chance that he'd invite Sharon over, he wanted to be sure the place was at least presentable. Plus it was overdue for a cleaning anyway. The straightening, dusting, and vacuuming had been almost as exhausting as the workout the night before with Hart. Leal thought about her and the progression of the case.

Hart was starting to shape up. He felt he could do worse for a partner. At least she listened and always gave it her best shot. With a little more confidence, she could turn out real good. Maybe. Leal remembered her sudden nervousness right before they'd gone in to interview

Walker. *I haven't really got a lot of experience doing this sort of thing*, she'd said. But she had picked up on the inconsistencies in Walker's actions and statements. That was an intuitive ability. You either had it or you didn't. It couldn't be taught. Refined and developed, yes. Taught, no. Someone like Brice just didn't have it. Never had, never would.

Brice, he thought. The epitome of the Peter Principle. Yeah, he's a Peter all right. Random victims, carjackings, chop-shop rings . . . The bastard couldn't find his ass with both hands. And Ryan going right along with Brice's half-assed theories. The consummate yes-man.

Shit, thought Leal, checking his watch again. I'm supposed to be relaxing on my night off, I got a date with an angel, and here I am thinking about the stupid case.

It was time to get going.

As he walked out to the unmarked squad, he grabbed the box of condoms that he'd picked up, just in case, at the drug store. Being prepared was essential, even though his expectations only fell into the realm of a pleasant dinner and stimulating conversation.

But, if we really hit it off, who knows, he thought, whistling as he appraised the job the guys had done at the car wash. At least it smelled nice with the aromatic air freshener. Like strawberries or something. He removed two of the condoms from the box and slipped them in his inside jacket pocket. Unobtrusive, yet easily obtainable if needed. The box was another matter.

Should've left it at home, he thought. But now it was already six thirty-five. Where did the extra time go? He opened the glove box and stuck the box under the maps and gas-log papers, then closed it.

I hope she doesn't mind the county car, he thought, twisting the key. He felt a slight twinge in his side. This was his first real date since the shooting, too. If things did get that far, he wondered how she'd react to the railroad track scar on his chest.

One step at a time, he thought. One step at a time.

Sharon's apartment was one of those two-story brownstones that had proliferated on the south side and its contiguous suburbs. The name next to the upper buzzer read S.A. *Devain*. Sharon Ann? he wondered. Her distorted voice came out of the speaker and the door buzzed. Leal went inside the little foyer and glanced up the stairway to his left. A door popped open at the top and he heard her call, "Come on up."

After trotting up the stairs he pushed open the door and she stood there smiling at him in a light blue silk blouse and navy skirt. The blouse was open at the neck and he could see the delicate serpentine loops of a gold chain against her neck. Her hair looked freshly curled and her makeup perfectly accented her eyes and high cheekbones.

"I'm almost ready," she said. "Make yourself at home."

She closed the door behind him and disappeared into another room. Leal saw the apartment was furnished with a big, comfortable-looking couch opposite a television and VCR. A coffee table with a lace doily in the middle was in front of the couch. An original oil painting, a landscape depicting effulgent trees and bodies of water, hung on the wall. Looking closer he saw the name S. Devain printed along the bottom. The next room looked more lived-in, with a computer sitting on a long table and a paperbound volume of the criminal statutes next to it. Probably her office, he thought.

Sharon came into the room, slipping on a dark jacket and grabbing her purse from the couch. She flipped on the light switch and said, "Okay, I'm ready."

Leal smiled, appraising her, thinking she looked like a million dollars.

"Where would you like to go?" he asked. "Anyplace special?"

"You decide. But I have to be back by eleven, or so."

Why was she giving him the time constraint up front? Was she trying to tell him something? He compressed his lips. Remember, he thought, a pleasant dinner is all I'm hoping for. But he had to ask.

"Why?" he asked, trying to sound light. "Afraid my car will turn into a pumpkin or something?"

Sharon laughed. It sounded almost musical.

"Oh, I guess I should have told you, I got sort of roped into starting my next shift a little early. You see, my partner on Felony Review was supposed to be on call tonight, but his sister's getting married tomorrow and he asked if I could take anything after midnight."

Leal felt his confidence returning.

"I can understand that," he said. "I'm on call a lot, too."

Sharon smiled as they walked outside.

"Is that why you brought your squad car?"

Oh, shit, Leal thought, trying to think of an appropriate comeback. Suddenly his preplanned response that he might get called at any time to handle a life-threatening emergency seemed pretty lame. But, his mind raced, I can't very well tell her my personal car is a piece of shit, can I? Deciding to hell with pretension, he said, "Actually, my personal car's worse than this one. It's due for the auto graveyard, but I've been too busy to look for a new one." He watched her reaction as he opened the door and she slid inside. "Plus, I don't have to worry about parking tickets."

Sharon smiled.

They decided on dinner at Chinatown, and Leal headed down Ninety-fifth Street to the expressway. Sharon dug into her purse for a cigarette and Leal immediately reached to press in the lighter. Except the lighter had been removed so that the emergency light could be plugged in. Dammit, he thought, glancing over at her.

Sharon must have noticed his dilemma and smiled, flicking her own lighter and holding it to the cigarette.

"I hope you don't mind, but I need this," she said, cracking the window. She blew a cloud of smoke to the side. "You don't smoke, right?"

"I quit."

"Wow, I wish I could. I've tried to so many times. How'd you do it? The patch?"

"I got shot in the chest," he said. "But I wouldn't recommend it."

"Yeah, I remember hearing about that. When they told me about you telling off Judge Gable."

He grimaced. "That was really more of a misunderstanding."

"Oh, I'll bet," she said, looking over at him with a wide grin. "I thought it was great that you did. It was about time somebody told the son of a bitch what an asshole he is."

Leal glanced over at her and smiled back. This girl doesn't mince words, he thought.

They ate at the big Mandarin Restaurant on Twenty-second Street, the conversation floating along so pleasantly that Leal was reluctant to even surreptitiously glance at his watch. For an after-dinner drink they each ordered wine.

"But only one glass," Sharon said, smiling. "I have to keep my wits about me."

He liked her smile. He liked everything about her.

"So tell me," she said. "When you testified before the grand jury you gave your name as Francisco. Is that Hispanic?"

"Actually, it comes from my dad's side of the family. My mom's Irish, my dad's Mexican. Guess you could call me sort of new generation Black Irish."

Her eyes swept over him. "So, do you speak Spanish?"

"Yeah. That's why I did so well in MEG. Everybody

thought I was your typical Latino drug dealer." He grinned. "The bastard probably wouldn't have shot me if he'd thought I was a cop."

"Fran-cis-co," she said, drawing out the pronunciation. "I like that. So it's Frank for short."

"Actually, my mother calls me Cisco. And that was a primary motivation for me taking up boxing in school."

She laughed again.

"What about you?" he asked. "I saw those paintings in your apartment. Did you paint them?"

Sharon sipped the wine slowly, looking at him over the rim.

"I wish," she said. "My sister Sara did. She got all the artistic talent in the family. I, on the other hand, inherited all the brashness. Hence, my profession."

The waiter came over to their table with a small platter containing the check and two fortune cookies. Leal slipped some money in the folder and told him to keep the change. The waiter bowed deferentially and left. Sharon was already breaking open her cookie.

"What does yours say?" she asked.

He snapped in two and pulled out the slip of paper. "Great things are in store for you," he read. "Yours?"

She smiled slowly, her tongue darting over her teeth for only a second.

"It says I'm going to meet a tall, dark, handsome man," she said. She twisted the paper and put it in her pocket. "But I already have. Maybe we both can share yours."

Outside the night was cooling off, but it was still comfortable enough for them to walk down Wentworth through a few of the blocks that comprised Chinatown, looking at all the shops, the bright neon signs displaying foreign lettering, the designs on the windows, and the throngs of Asians crowding the sidewalks and speaking in foreign tongues. They walked back to the car holding hands, stopping in front of the big ceremonial gate to admire the ornate Chinese characters. Sharon lit a cigarette and asked him what time it was.

"Almost ten," he said. Dammit, where had the time gone?

"I guess we'd better head back then," she said.

He nodded. Just dinner and some pleasant conversation, that's all, he reminded himself.

The ride home went uneventfully, with the traffic seeming lighter than usual. When they pulled up in front of her building, she turned toward him.

"I had a nice time, Frank," she said.

"Yeah, me, too. Maybe we can do it again sometime."

She nodded, staring up at him, her fine features illuminated by the overhead streetlights, and kissed him softly on the lips. "Do you want to come up for a while?"

Do I? Leal thought.

"Yeah," he said. "I'd like that very much."

She looked at him for a moment, then smiled wickedly.

"Just remember, Francisco, that I'm subject to get beeped after midnight."

The beep came while they were still making love. Abrupt and intrusive, its piercing sharpness shocked both of them. Sharon, who was on top, inhaled quickly with a sudden sharpness, kissed him, and then was off padding around in the darkness.

"Shit," she said. "Where did I put that fucking thing?"

Leal rolled on his side, watching her naked ass, opalescent in the moonlight, as she moved around the bedroom sorting through the helter-skelter array of clothes they'd left lying in their wake. Finally she stooped over and grabbed something from the floor. The insistent chirping stopped.

She came back and sat on the edge of the bed, her back to him, and turned on the night-light. The phone was on the table next to the lamp.

"We've only got so many minutes to answer these damn

pages," she said, dialing the number. He reached up and softly caressed her shoulder. To his surprise she turned and faced him, kissing his fingers lightly, then leaned forward to kiss him on the lips.

"Yes, this is ASA Sharon Devain. What have you got?" she said into the phone.

Leal leaned back, trying to follow the periphery of the conversation, but losing much of it due to her monosyllabic responses. "Okay, I'll call them in a few minutes." She hung up after scribbling down a number and turned back to him.

"Looks like I'll have to go," she said, her long legs snuggling down next to his. "They've got an armed robbery/rape, and I'll have to go interview the offender before he lawyers up."

Leal didn't know what to say, sensing that the mood of the moment had faded.

"So do you want me to go with you?" he asked.

She shook her head. "And how would that look?"

He laughed slightly. "Not too good, I guess."

She kissed him again, harder, and said, "I told you I was subject to getting beeped in the night, so we'll just have to continue this another time, okay?"

For the first time, Leal sensed that the roles had been strangely reversed for him. Getting kicked out of bed while she went off to fight crime in the middle of the night. Was this what it felt like to be the girl? Looks like both of us got beeped tonight, he thought.

CHAPTER EIGHTEEN
No Need To Ask

Leal pulled up in front of Hart's apartment building late Sunday morning and debated whether to honk the horn or just trust that his partner, ever observant, would be watching for him. Screw that, he thought, and tapped the horn twice. Everybody who isn't up by now should be. He stretched and settled back in the seat, reflecting on what had turned out to be a pretty damn good couple of days for him.

He'd spent most of Saturday looking at new cars, and finally found a used red Pontiac Firebird in fairly decent shape with a reasonable price tag. Plus, when the dealer found out Leal was a cop, he offered to slip in a few extras, like a CD player and a free recharge on the air-conditioning. Leal had also managed to tag up with Sharon at her place again, after she'd recovered from her night session interviewing felons and witnesses, and they'd ended up in bed again. They'd started early enough this time to preclude any beeping interruptions and he'd ended up spending the night.

I'd better be careful, he thought, and he glanced out the window. Or this could develop into a habit. But maybe that wouldn't be so bad, either.

Hart was still conspicuously absent, and Leal tapped the horn again. What the hell was keeping her? He looked up at her picture window and saw her wave, using an "I'll be right there" gesture. Leal nodded and settled back again, thinking that next week he'd pick up his new wheels and drive to Sharon's in style. No more using this beast, he thought. It had felt good to relax with Sharon for a couple of days. Ryan had been right to suggest the time off. It was great not having to think about the goddamn Walker case, or that fucker Brice and his horseshit theories, or that ass-kisser Ryan with his nose so far up Brice's butt that he was probably having trouble breathing.

He saw Hart jogging across the lawn, carrying a blue windbreaker and a spiral notebook. She had on a beige sleeveless blouse and black slacks, the big Model 19 bouncing in the holster on her hip. Leal hit the door lock and she jumped in looking, he noticed, raring to go.

"Hi," she said, looking him over. "Am I dressed okay?"

"Sure," he said. "How were your days off?"

"Oh, pretty good. I got a real heavy workout in Friday and did some posing routines. Yesterday I took a light one and did some work on the case."

"Huh? What was that?"

"I ran a check on Simon Ellias, the poet," she said, turning to look at him. "Guess what?"

He shrugged.

"He doesn't exist," she said.

Leal squinted at her. "Run that by me again."

"I ran a Soundex on him and came up with zilch in Willow Springs," she said, opening her notebook. Leal could see pages of notes in her neat cursive. "Remember that's where the book said he lived?"

Leal nodded.

"So I went to the library and traced him down." She paused and smiled. "Well, actually, this real helpful librarian did, but I found out his real name. Are you ready for this?"

Leal nodded again.

"Randall S. Pecker. No lie. That's it." Her grin looked a mile wide. "Simon might be his middle name. I guess we can surmise why he used Ellias, right?"

"I guess," Leal said, smiling.

"And," she said, paging through her notebook, "I also called that agency where Walker's former housekeeper worked and persuaded them to give me her address. They wouldn't do it over the phone so I went there and flashed my badge."

Leal felt proud of her. She'd done some good legwork on this and he told her so.

"Thanks," she said. "But I gotta tell you, Sarge, I could've used this baby instead of burning up a half a tank of my own gas driving back and forth."

She said it good-naturedly, but Leal realized she'd felt slighted that he'd taken the squad. He suddenly remembered that she'd asked him if she could use it Friday when they were driving back. She must have been planning this all along, he thought.

"Yeah, well, sorry about that," he said. What the hell, he thought, might as well level with her. "Actually, I had a date and my personal car is a wreck. I had to use the squad."

"Oh," Hart said, her eyebrows rising. "I see."

"But I bought a new one, yesterday."

"Great," Hart said, prying open the glove compartment. "Anyway, I think I can find Ellias' address on this." As she pulled out the folded maps the opened box of prophylactics fell out onto her lap, spilling a few folded foil packettes. Leal silently cursed himself for having forgotten about them being in there.

Hart carefully placed the box back in the glove compartment and said, "So I guess there's no need to ask how your date went, huh?"

Leal was silent on the drive to Willow Springs. Hart's verve and initiative had left him feeling guilty, but what the hell, he told himself, I deserve a day off once in a while, don't I? It helped me come back renewed. But his argument flattened before the scrutiny of his own conscience. The fact of the matter was, his partner, the rookie, had acted while he just laid back. Or got laid, whichever way you looked at it. The wordplay brought a smile to his lips.

"What are you smiling at?" Hart asked.

"Oh, just thinking what a great detective you're turning into."

Hart smiled back, then pointed. "There's our street."

Randall S. Pecker, aka Simon Ellias, lived in the bottom half of a brown two-flat near the Des Plaines River. The house was wood frame over a solid-looking brick and mortar foundation. Hart pointed to the doorbell and Leal nodded. The faint noise of a stereo could be heard inside. She pressed hard on the bell, and suddenly they heard the heavy barking of what had to be a sizeable dog.

"Who is it?" a man's voice said from the other side of the door.

"Police," Leal said, holding up his badge case in front of the peephole. The interior door opened and a bearded man of medium height stood behind the screen door. His shaggy hair hung unkempt almost to his shoulders, and he was wearing a plaid flannel shirt with the sleeves rolled up. Leal placed him at about forty. The dog, a rottweiler, continued barking until the man called its name.

"May I see your identifications again?"

Leal and Hart held up their badges and the man's eyes narrowed slightly as he read them.

"What can I do for you?" he asked.

"We need to talk you about Miriam Walker," Leal said. "Can we come in?"

Pecker looked stunned, then recovered, opening the door. The dog, ever vigilant, growled slightly. "Shadow," he said. The growling stopped.

The inside of the house was filled with stacks of wood, half-finished paintings, crude statues, and rolls of paper. Off to the side a computer was on a desk playing a CD of classical music. Leal saw Hart staring at some of the paintings, abstractions of the human form, that were leaning against one of the chairs. A small television set sat on a coffee table in the center of the room.

"Pardon the mess," Pecker said. "I'm right in the middle of a few projects."

"Simon Ellias projects?" Leal asked.

Pecker smiled. "I see you've done your homework, Officer."

"What do you have all this wood for?" Leal said.

"I'm a cabinetmaker. I work in my shop out back."

Hart pulled the poetry book from her purse.

"Did you write this?"

Pecker wiped his hands on his shirt and accepted the book, immediately opening it to the title page and reading the inscription. His mouth hung slightly open as he looked up and asked, "Where did you get this?"

"From Miriam Walker's private effects," Leal said. "Why don't you tell us about your relationship with her?"

Pecker licked his lips and went over to shut off the CD. "Let's go in the kitchen."

They sat at his table, a heavy wooden piece with ornately carved legs. Pecker offered them coffee, which they both declined.

"I was wondering why no one ever came to talk to me," he said, finally. "I thought about going to the police myself, but then again, illicit lovers really don't have a right to inquire, do they?"

"You were having an affair with her?" Leal asked.

Pecker nodded. "It was much more than that. The word 'affair' sounds so meretricious."

Leal frowned. "So how did you meet? And how long had you been seeing her?"

Pecker sighed. "Do I really have to go into that now?"

"Now or later," Leal said. "Your choice."

"Simon," Hart said, putting a hand on his shoulder. "I know you must have cared for her very much. We need your help if we're going to find the people who killed her."

When he looked up his eyes were glistening. He quickly recounted the beginning of their relationship, as he put it, from their initial meeting when he did some cabinetwork at an abused women's shelter that Miriam had sponsored. How Miriam's interest in the arts lead to a drink, and the drink to a subsequent dinner.

"She was very unhappy at home," he said. "And we shared so much in common."

"She ever talk about her husband?" Leal asked.

"Only occasionally. About what an insensitive bastard he was. Her marriage was practically arranged by her father, you know."

Yeah, I'll bet, Leal thought. But he said, "So was she going to divorce her husband?"

"That was problematic," Pecker said. "You see, Miriam came from a very wealthy family, and had just received control of her inheritance from a trust. She was worried that under the community property laws, she'd lose half of what she felt was essentially her money."

Leal nodded. "So what was the plan? Keep meeting in secret?"

"Actually, things seemed to change the last few weeks before she disappeared," Pecker said. "She told me that our problems would soon be solved, that we could be together. She was ebullient, but she was also enigmatic."

"Try that again in plain English," Leal said.

Hart smirked at him.

"Well, she seemed happy, confident that the divorce wouldn't be as much of an obstacle as she'd thought," Pecker said. "But at the same time she seemed very nervous. She wanted both of us to get HIV tests."

"She say why?"

Pecker shook his head. "Only that if we were going to stay in a monogamous relationship, we should both be tested. We both came back negative, of course. She then told me that we shouldn't see each other until after the formal separation papers were filed."

Leal asked, "Was it because of something her husband did?"

Pecker shrugged. "I surmised as much, but I didn't ask." He brought his hand up to wipe at his eyes. "When I didn't hear from her, I assumed that everything was all right. Then I saw that she was missing on the news. I knew something had gone wrong, but kept hoping that she was merely hiding somewhere for her own purposes. When they found her, I didn't know what to do. The police kept saying that it was apparently a random street crime."

"So you just sat on your hands?" Leal said.

"What else could I do?" Pecker raised his head and Leal saw there were tears streaming down his face. Hart reached out and patted the man on the shoulder. "What else could I do?" he asked again.

They spoke to Pecker for about twenty minutes more, assembling the dates and locations of their trysts, trying to get a picture of Miriam Walker's habits and routines during her last few months.

"Okay," said Leal, once they were back in the car. "She was planning on dumping her old man, and was initially concerned about losing her money . . ." He waited for Hart to pick up his trend of thought.

"But then she suddenly gets something on her husband that makes the divorce less of a problem," Hart said.

Leal nodded. "So we gotta assume that she picked up on Martin Walker's secret life. Only what could it be? Drugs? Hookers? Why the concern about HIV?"

"Maybe he's AC/DC?" Hart said.

Leal grunted, remembering Ryan's comments questioning Hart's sexuality. "That's what we gotta find out," he said, twisting the keys in the ignition. "Let's go talk to the housekeeper. Maybe she can give us more on the enigmatic Mr. Walker."

Hart looked at him and smiled. "Nice word. For a cop."

It was near noon by the time they pulled in front of the dull gray apartment building near the Cal-Sag Channel. Two children, a boy in a blue shirt and pants, and a little girl in a dirty white dress were playing in the yard. They both stopped as Leal and Hart approached.

"Does Mrs. Martinez live here?" Hart asked.

The girl nodded, showing them a gap-toothed smile, and pointed to the second floor. After walking up the sagging wooden steps, Hart rang the buzzer and presently a heavyset woman in her forties opened the interior door. Her dark eyes flashed suspiciously at the badges.

"Mrs. Martinez," Hart said. "We're the police. We'd like to speak to you."

The woman tried a weak smile. "My English no too good."

"*Señora, no importa,*" Leal said. "*Hablo español.*"

The woman seemed more at ease as Leal continued to chat with her so rapidly that Hart was left stranded trying to follow the conversation through overheard cognates. She understood *Señora Walker* and *el señor,* but everything else was lost.

Mrs. Martinez bent her left elbow and patted the point of it with her right hand, saying something else. Hart looked to Leal, who grinned.

"She says Miriam was always very nice, but Mr. Walker was a stingy bastard."

"*Muy tacaño*," Mrs. Martinez said, again patting her elbow.

"Did I hear you ask her something about a divorce?" Hart said.

"Right. They were sleeping in separate bedrooms," Leal said. He said something else in Spanish. Hart heard the word *drogas*. She knew what that meant.

"*Creo que si*," Mrs. Martinez said. "*Pero no lo vi.*"

She says she never saw him using drugs, but suspected it," Leal said.

"*Después de la señora despareció, el me dio calabazas.*"

"*¿Cuando?*" asked Leal. "*¿Immediamente?*"

"*Sí.*"

"She says that he fired her right after Miriam disappeared," Leal said.

"Almost like he knew his wife wasn't just missing," Hart said. "More like she was gone for good."

"Sure enough."

"You know, Sarge, this is sounding more and more like we figured, and not like," Hart dropped her voice in an attempt to mimic Brice's raspy voice, "a random victim killing."

Leal grinned. Back in the car she asked him what their next move should be.

"We've got to pressure Walker," he said. "We can't pull him in just yet, but maybe we should follow him. See what his quirks really are. Then if we find something, we can use that as a lever in an interrogation."

"Interrogation?" Hart said. "This guy's a lawyer as well as a CEO, isn't he? What makes you think he'll talk?"

"Yeah, well his experience is as a pissant corporate

lawyer, not a criminal one," Leal said. "Maybe he does have some street smarts. It'd be nice to catch him buying some dope or something."

"It sure would."

"But one thing's certain. To clear this one we're probably going to need a confession, or something pretty damn close to it." He sighed and pulled away from the curb. "You check our messages today?"

"No," Hart said, sorting through her purse for her cellular phone. She punched in the numbers and the codes to release the voice mail. After listening she pressed another key and turned to him. "Guess what?"

He glanced at her.

"Miriam Walker's father called," she said. "He wants to talk to us."

CHAPTER NINETEEN
Everybody Hates Mondays

Leal kept remembering the image of the old man as he and Hart drove in to work the following Monday. With the wisps of white hair, the oxygen tubes hooked under his nose, Miriam's father had looked virtually played out. He was at the end of it, Leal figured, and was searching for some hope that his daughter's killer would be found. He blamed himself for his daughter's death.

"I was the one who encouraged her to marry Martin," the old man had said. "It seemed a good move for her, career-wise and financially, but," he paused to gather a few breaths, "I never thought about her long-term adjustment or happiness."

Their interview with him had yielded little. Only that Miriam hadn't been close with her father in the past several years. The old man's pleading look had prompted Leal to make a premature promise as they left. "We'll get the people responsible for your daughter's death, sir. You have my word on it."

Now he found himself wishing he hadn't said that. Just what I need, he thought. More pressure to solve a cold case. He turned to Hart as they walked up the steps toward the office.

"You type up all our summaries of the interviews?" he asked.

She nodded. "Sure did, Sarge."

Leal grabbed the door and pulled it open, debating whether or not he should tell her to call him Frank. But that will come, he thought, if this partnership works out. Inside they were met by a group of trainees getting a tour of the facility on their first day at the academy. Looking at all the eager young faces brought back more memories for Leal.

"God, I hate Mondays," he said. "You can't even move around this damn place."

"Everybody hates Mondays," Hart said, dodging the group by going along the wall. She tugged at his sleeve. "But it's sort of like Wednesday for us, remember?"

Inside the office Ryan was standing at his desk with one foot on the seat of his chair. His right elbow rested on his thigh as he read a copy of the *Sun-Times*. He smiled at them, pointing to Hart's in-box where an eleven-by-fourteen manila envelope denoting interdepartmental mail lay. "You got some goodies, babe."

She opened it and flashed several large photos of Martin and Miriam Walker at Leal.

"I ordered some duplicates made of our file photo of Miriam last week," she said. "Thought it might be useful to get Martin's driver's license digital, too."

Leal nodded approvingly.

"You look ready to go," Leal said, turning to Ryan.

"Not hardly. That fucking Smith's late again." Ryan rolled his eyes toward the ceiling. "But get a load of this." He tapped the newspaper. "This dog-ass in New York went into the ER with a real problem. Seems he shot up his dick with cocaine to improve his performance with the ladies." Ryan flashed a rakish grin under his bushy mustache. "And it worked. Sort of. He had a hard-on for three fucking days, but found that he couldn't take a piss. It's called . . ." he looked down at the paper, "Priapism. Can you imagine that? A hard-on for three days?"

"Not like little Ryan, who rises and falls on demand, huh?" Leal said. He wondered how Hart was reacting to this.

Ryan smirked. "Well, they catheterized him and it deflated. The only problem was his johnson turned gangrene and fell off."

"I love a story with a happy ending," Hart said.

"It says here," Ryan continued, patting the paper again, "that injecting cocaine into the penis to enhance sexual performance is a commonly held, but false, belief. In the ghetto, no doubt."

Christ, thought Leal, the asshole's more interested in that fucking story than he is in solving the damn case.

Suddenly the door opened and Smith came in smiling.

"Sorry about being late, Sarge," he said. "Another false alarm with the baby."

Ryan rolled his eyes again. "Well, now that we're all present and accounted for, let's compare notes. The boss wants a progress report in half an hour. Hart, can you make us a pot, please."

Leal bristled at the impropriety of the request, but remembered that he couldn't fight her battles for her. And at least he did say please, he thought.

Over coffee they discussed their separate efforts on the investigation. Ryan and Smith had touched bases with the Illinois State Police Criminal Investigations Division and SSATIN, the auto-theft section.

"You should've seen the layout they had there," Ryan said. "They set up their own sting operation for buying stolen cars. Videotaped every transaction."

"So you get anything on that angle?" Leal asked.

Ryan shook his head. "One thing that is funny. They said that parts for Caddies ain't been much in demand this year."

"Which makes the chances that someone murdered her for a chop shop ring kind of small," Smith said. He'd sat passively while Ryan had been relating their activities.

"We looked over all the files of carjackers and auto thieves who've been active in the South Suburbs in the last year or so," Ryan said, taking out his cigarettes and shaking one out of the pack. "Nothing really matches up. I guess we can spend today digging through some more files."

"That's a dead end, Tom," Leal said, realizing that the anger in his voice was more than he intended. He took a deep breath and explained about the interviews he and Hart had done. "We got to start focusing on the husband."

"So, you saying we should tag him?" Ryan asked, leaning forward, the smoke from his cigarette trailing up toward the ceiling. Hart moved back away from it.

"It'd be a start," said Leal. "We got to get some leverage on the guy."

"All right, then," Ryan said. "Let's go run it by the boss. Give me your summary reports."

Leal and Ryan spent ten minutes waiting outside Brice's office while he finished a telephone call. Then he opened the door and admitted them. Leal noticed that Brice looked pale and haggard, and wondered if he was getting some pressure from upstairs. Good, Leal thought. Maybe it'll shake his ass up so we can move on this thing. But Brice seemed unfazed by their reports. He meticulously bit off the end of a cigar as he listened to the synopsis.

"Go run down those MOs, Ryan," he said, twirling the cigar in the flame of his lighter. "Any robbery teams that've been preying on lone females."

"What about the husband?" Leal said.

"What about him?" Brice answered, blowing out a mouthful of smoke.

"I think we should set up a surveillance on him."

"For what?" Brice said. "You ain't got dick. So she was fucking around, supposedly. That don't mean nothing."

"It could show a motive," Leal shot back. "He's our best suspect. Let's ask him to take a polygraph."

"Those ain't worth shit," Brice said.

"Not in court," Leal said. "But it's a good investigative tool. If we pressure this fucker, he'll crack. I just know it." As soon as he said it, he regretted it. Brice's reaction was plain.

"Look," he said, his face reddening, "until we've eliminated all other possibilities, we'll do this by the book."

What book is that, Lieutenant? Leal thought. But he clamped his mouth shut. Brice seemed to sense the defiance anyway.

"Tell me if you got a problem with that, Leal," he said. The veins in his thick neck were standing out against a flush of red.

Leal glanced to Ryan, who was leaning back in his chair massaging his temples.

"Well, do you, Sergeant?" Brice said. His lips curled downward as the cigar snapped in two between his fingers. Glaring, he stubbed it out in an ashtray, the trail of gray smoke winding upward toward the ceiling.

Leal shook his head, but then thought, what the fuck. If we're going to solve this thing . . . "I just feel it's something we should be looking into, Lieu." He met Brice's stare with one of his own.

"And I feel that you're disregarding the team approach to this investigation," Brice said, pointing with his index finger. Ryan started to speak, but Brice just turned to him and said, "Shut up." He berated Leal for a few more minutes, then sat back, exhaling a long, slow breath through flaring nostrils. "All right, this is what we'll do. I'll review your report summaries. Ryan, you go over that offender's file like I told you. Leal, you and your partner can go check with the state's attorney. See if we got enough to get a tap on the husband's phone."

Leal knew that they didn't have nearly enough to meet the stringent applications of the law, but he nodded.

"And," Brice continued, "be back here tonight at nineteen hundred. Sharp. And dress nice. The sheriff wants to go over our case so far and the press might be here."

Marvelous, thought Leal. This is nothing but busywork.

"In the meantime," Brice said, "I'm gonna look up Investigator Murphy. See what he thinks of your theories. What they did along those lines. No sense covering the same ground twice."

Murphy, Leal thought. That fat fuck had his shot and he blew it. But he said nothing.

"Make sure the whole team makes it tonight," Brice said. "No exceptions."

"We got it, boss," Ryan said, standing.

In the hallway Leal and Ryan exchanged looks.

"Man, I thought he was gonna lose it there for a minute," Ryan said.

"Nah," said Leal, "you gotta *have* it in order to lose it."

"Well, he's under a lot of pressure," Ryan said slowly. He fumbled for his pack of cigarettes.

"Shit, man, we all are."

"Yeah," Ryan said, squinting. "But I happen to know that he's having some personal problems."

Leal looked at him. Ryan shrugged.

"Brice sort of opened up to me the other day," he said. "I guess his kid Max is causing him all kinds of grief. Has some kind of a learning disability or something. Messed up big time in school, now he's dropped out totally."

Leal frowned. Sometimes it was better not to say anything. He wished he'd remembered that earlier.

"Of course," Ryan grinned, popping the unlit cigarette between his lips, "going through life with a name like Maxwell Brice can't be a picnic, no matter how you cut it."

Neither can having an asshole for an old man, Leal thought.

Back at the office, Hart and Smith reacted predictably to the change in plans.

"Damn," Smith said. "That's gonna throw a big wrench in my Lamaze class tonight."

"And I was hoping to get a workout in," Hart said.

"Hey, kids," Ryan said, grinning and fishing out a cigarette. "I'm just the fucking messenger." He stuck the cigarette between his lips. "Tell you guys what. Let's all do what we gotta do and knock off after lunch. That way we can all be back here tonight refreshed. Sound like a plan?"

"Not a good one," Leal said. "If we keep spinning our wheels, we'll never get this thing solved."

Ryan flicked his lighter and drew on the cigarette.

"Don't I know it," he said. "So maybe we can bring that out to the sheriff tonight. It's his ass on the line in the election, not ours."

Leal could imagine who the "we" would be, if they got the chance to talk at all. Probably that asshole Brice will be the only one saying anything, he thought He noticed Hart recoiling from the smoke and asked, "You ready?"

As they started down the hallway, Leal heard someone call to them. He turned and saw Joe Smith jogging toward them.

"Sarge," Smith said, "I just wanted to tell you I talked to Miriam Walker's doctor Friday."

Leal raised his eyebrows.

"He said he wouldn't release anything without a subpoena," Smith continued. "Figured you should know, since you're going to talk to the state's attorney." He glanced over his shoulder. "I did it on my own time. Thought it was an angle we should check out."

"Good thinking, Joe. Thanks," Leal said. He was sensing

something about this man. A simmering anger just under the surface.

"So what else you want me to do?" Smith asked.

"Well," Leal said. "Brice wants—"

"Not Brice, Sarge," Smith said. "Or Ryan, either. You're the one I respect."

Leal smiled slightly.

"Look, Sarge, I know the story on Brice, and Ryan, too. And I talked to Johnny DeWayne about you. I know you're straight."

"Thanks, Joe," Leal said. He thought for a minute and took out his notebook. "Tell you what. Call this person and mention that you're working with me on an investigation." He wrote down the information and handed it to Smith. "She works for National Credit. I used to use her sometimes when I was in MEG. Ask if she'll run a credit check on Martin Walker for us. On the sly, so we don't get in trouble with the privacy act."

Smith grinned and nodded.

"And see what you can find out about this Lunge Hill Corporation," Leal said. "Maybe check the Hall of Records if you have time."

"Will do, Sarge. And I'll have plenty of time. Ryan will probably be delighted to get rid of me. You know how he feels about my kind of people."

They watched him walk away, and Hart said, "You also know what they say about disregarding the coach's instructions in the huddle, right?"

"When the coach is an idiot, sometimes you have to call an audible if you want to win the game," he said, pulling out the car keys. "Come on."

"Aren't we going to walk? It's only across the lot."

Leal smiled. "Brice didn't say which state's attorney he wanted me to ask. I got somebody special in mind."

CHAPTER TWENTY

Imperfect Matches

Leal watched Hart picking away at her salad as he ate a burger and fries. Their trip all the way out to the Fifth District had gone pretty much as he expected, with the added benefit of his getting to see Sharon, since he'd remembered that she said she had a meeting there this morning. He was struck by the differences between her and Hart as he'd introduced them, Sharon looking drop-dead gorgeous with the jacket of her gray suit draped over her arm. Hart had looked angular and very sleek, like a thoroughbred racing horse, or rather, a professional athlete. But, hell, he thought, that's what she is. For the first time he wondered what it would be like to go to bed with Hart, eyeing the sweep of her sleeveless shoulders. He'd already dismissed Ryan's theory that she was gay. But she might as well have been. She was his partner, and thinking carnal thoughts about somebody you worked with every day was not a good thing. He noticed her watching him.

"What?" he asked.

"Just wondering what you were thinking," she said.

"Trying to figure out our next move," he said, smiling. "You sure are drinking a lot of water today."

"I got up early and ran." She speared some more lettuce and began to raise it to her mouth. "So is that the person you've been seeing? Sharon?"

Leal nodded, remembering that Sharon had kept it pretty much professional as they all met in the hallway. She'd introduced him to her supervisor, Jack Fretters, and he'd introduced them to Hart. Sharon sat in for a few minutes as they began to explain the basics of their case and ask about the wiretap.

"Don't you guys work up by the Fourth District?" Fretters had asked. "Why did you come all the way down here?"

"We were in the neighborhood," Leal said.

Sharon smiled slightly and stood to go, giving Leal a surreptitious wink and mouthing, "Call me," so only he could see. A promise of good things to come, he hoped.

"Yeah, that's her," Leal said.

"She's very pretty," Hart said. "Too bad her boss shot down our hopes for a tap."

"I figured he would," Leal said. "We just don't have enough right now. That's why we need to start pressuring our buddy Martin a little."

"You know, I thought of something," Hart said, pushing aside her plastic plate and wiping her fingers on a napkin. She reached for her purse and took out the big envelope with the pictures of Miriam Walker inside. "I looked in the case file while you and Ryan were up with the LT. Martin gave the original investigators a picture, and there's no note that it was ever returned to him." She handed him the photos. Leal wiped his own fingers before accepting them. "Notice anything?"

Leal scanned the photos. The original had a matte finish and was on heavy card stock. The copies were glossy, thinner, and obviously cheaper.

"These are the duplicates," he said, indicating the copies. "Which means that after all this time, he didn't even inquire about getting the original back," she said. "Don't you think that's just a little bit strange?"

Leal nodded approvingly, then grabbed his chin. "You still set on working out this afternoon?"

"Yeah, I need to, especially since we have the meeting tonight. Why?"

"How about a little ride downtown first? Then I'll join you for the workout."

She canted her head and looked at him.

"What have you got in mind?"

"In India, when they used to go tiger hunting, they'd send a bunch of natives in to beat the bushes," he said. "It's usually to stir the tigers out of hiding so the hunters could shoot them."

"I've always kind of liked tigers," she said. "There's not a lot of them left, you know."

Leal smiled. "Yeah, I like real tigers, too. But this guy's made of paper. If we start to push, he'll crumple."

Martin Walker's secretary was an attractive, dark-haired woman who looked to be in her midthirties. She eyed the badges that Leal and Hart hung in front of her, then dutifully picked up the phone and spoke very softly into the receiver. Leal pocketed his badge and removed the cigar that he'd bought in the tobacco shop in the lobby. Hart had looked at him quizzically until he explained his plan in the elevator.

"Mr. Walker will see you now," the secretary said.

They followed her to a sturdy-looking, darkly stained wooden door. The office itself was sumptuous, with thick carpeting, a large polished oak desk, and several black leather chairs. One wall contained a built-in bookcase and wet bar. Martin Walker stood up and slipped his jacket over his narrow shoulders, nodding curtly.

"I'm very busy, Officers," he said. "I hope this is important."

Leal moved forward and held out his hand. Walker shook it with reluctance.

"We wanted to return your wife's picture," Leal said, opening the envelope and removing one of the cheap copies. "We appreciate you loaning it to us."

Walker set the picture on his neatly arranged desk. "That's perfectly all right." He looked down at it, then back to Leal. "Do you have any new information?"

"We're exploring some new leads," Leal said, sticking the envelope under his arm and peeling open the cigar.

"New leads?" Walker asked.

"Yeah," Leal said, taking out a book of matches. "You mind if I smoke?"

"Well, this is not a designated smoking area," Walker said. "But go ahead. What type of new information do you have?"

Leal shook his head. "I'd better not do this. I've been trying to quit anyway." He dropped the book of matches onto Walker's desk and went around behind the desk. "Is that a trash can?"

"Yes." Walker's gaze dropped to the desk, and he seemed to be visually startled. "What, err, what were you saying?"

Leal dropped the unlit cigar into the can, and looked at Walker.

"Ah, it's nothing we can go over at the moment," he said. "But rest assured, when the time is right, you'll be the first to know." He smiled again.

"Sarge," Hart said, "we'd better get over to see the state's attorney like the lieutenant wanted."

"Yeah, right," Leal said. He held out his hand again. "Like I told you before, Mr. Walker, we'll get whoever did this to your wife. You can count on it."

"I would like to be kept informed of the progress of the investigation," Walker said, extending his hand to shake Leal's. But Leal snared just the ends of Walker's fingers and pumped his hand.

"Well, now that you mention it," Leal said, "there is something else you can do."

"What's that?"

Leal kept squeezing Walker's fingers while he spoke. "The list of your wife's friends you were supposed to make for us. Have you finished them yet?"

"No, I've been rather busy."

Leal released Walker's hand and clucked sympathetically.

"Yeah, I know how that is," he said. "But you know what else? Could you also include a list of the people who were with you the night your wife disappeared?"

"Yes," Walker said slowly. "I guess I could do that." He inhaled quickly. "If you think it's pertinent."

Leal smiled. "Everything's pertinent until we figure out what isn't. Right, Hart?"

"It factors in the reconstructive process," she said. "We try to learn as much about the victim as possible, to better understand her actions."

Walker swallowed, then nodded. "I'll get to it."

"Thanks, we appreciate it," Leal said. "Maybe we'll drop by later in the week."

"Why don't I give you a call instead?" Walker said. "I have a very busy schedule."

"Sure. You still got my card?"

Walker nodded.

"We can always drop by your house," Hart said. "We work a lot of nights."

"I'll call you as soon as I finish," Walker said.

In the elevator going down Hart smiled at Leal.

"He didn't even look at the picture," she said. "Don't you think you'd notice it was a copy if you really cared about someone?"

"He's nervous. And nervous people make mistakes."

"Well, if he needs a cigarette," she said, "at least you gave him back his matches."

Richard Connors was just setting up his traditionally carved white-and-black chessmen for a game against his computer adversary when his private line rang. It helped him, when he had a lot on his mind, to keep the game going on the actual board as well as the screen. Frowning, he picked up the phone and listened to a frantic Martin Walker describe what Connors knew must be an embellished version of the visit by the two cops.

"Marty, Marty, Marty, you're making more out of it than it really was."

"Easy for you to say. They weren't in your fucking office breathing down your neck. They know, I tell you. They know."

"Calm down, for Christ's sake." Connors set the white queen on her square. "I got things covered."

"Yeah, right. That's what you said the last time." Walker's voice sounded close to cracking.

"They don't have anything," Connors said. "Believe me, I know."

"Oh no? Well, what about the matches?"

"It don't mean shit. I told you, I've got things covered."

"Your supposed inside man?" Walker said. "Well, you'd better do something fast, Richard, because I don't plan on going down alone."

Connors picked up the white king and set him beside his queen. "Like I said, calm down. And call me tonight at seven thirty, as planned, okay?" He could hear the other man's rapid breathing on the line.

"All right."

"Good," said Connors, setting a black knight in place. "I'll be expecting your call, so don't forget. I should have some very good news for you."

After a few more reassurances, Connors hung up. The chess pieces were still in their places from his half-played game. He studied the uneven symmetry of the board. Marty had been useful to him, in his own way, but he was too stiff and unimaginative. Plus he panicked. Couldn't deal with the pressure. Sort of like a bishop, powerful, but only able to move along one set of colors. This guy Leal was a knight, capable of outmaneuvering Marty, as long as the cop stayed one move ahead. The two rooks were the insurance. With the business dealings pretty well set in place, Connors felt it was time for a bold move. He imagined pieces scattered all over the board, himself a king, directing others to cut down pawn and knight. And bishop as well. A sacrifice move. Marty had outlived his usefulness, having completed the setups of all the dummy corporations, the foreign accounts, the realty trusts in the names of more dummy companies. The complex layering that would insulate him, just as the rows of pawns and other pieces safeguarded their king.

A king must remain above the fray, Connors thought, as he made a castling move with his king's rook. Nuke was this rook, his insurance. The sacrifice move would be necessary to eliminate the swirling turbulence below him. Perhaps at a later date Nuke would have to be sacrificed, too, but, after all, there were two rooks.

CHAPTER TWENTY-ONE

Perception Becomes Reality

At seven P.M. sharp they met outside Brice's office. Leal was a bit miffed that Ryan had paged both him and Hart reminding them to "dress nice." As if we'd dress sloppy? he thought. He mulled over the events of the day in his mind, wondering if they'd catch any flack over rattling Martin Walker's cage a little bit. But what the hell, he thought, sometimes you just gotta take the bull by the tail if you can't reach the horns.

Suddenly Brice's door opened and he ushered them in, asking, "Where's Smith?"

Leal shrugged. "Guess he'll be along shortly."

Inside Ryan was seated next to a big guy Leal knew was Murphy. Murph hadn't changed much since Leal had last seen him, except the expanse of his gut seemed a bit more magnified. His cheeks had the red flush of someone who'd already had a couple at dinner.

Ryan looked at them and flashed a thumbs-up. Turning, he introduced Murphy.

"Glad to meet you," Murphy said, rising to shake hands with Hart. "I know who I want for *my* partner." He looked at the rest of them and laughed. "Wanna go out for a drink later?"

"I don't drink," Hart said, extricating her hand from his.

"That's okay," Murphy said, "I probably drink enough for both of us." He laughed again and shook hands with Leal.

Leal wondered what the three of them had been discussing behind closed doors. The "nineteen hundred, sharp" order obviously hadn't applied to all of the team, but Leal figured he wouldn't really have wanted to come in any earlier to listen to any more of Brice's half-assed theories. Or his personal problems. Leal caught a glimpse of the framed photo on the desk of Brice, his wife, and their two sons.

This one must be the one having the problems, Leal thought, looking at the fat, rotund face that stared back from the photo like a leering buddha, the strange-looking eyes enlarged behind the lenses of thick glasses. He remembered the kid's name was Max or something.

Brice returned to his position behind the desk and looked at Ryan.

"You tell Smith to be here at nineteen hundred?"

"He's usually running on colored people's time," Ryan said.

Murphy laughed out loud and grinned. Leal shot a harsh look at the man, then said, "Give the guy a break, why don't ya? His wife's almost due and he's all excited about it."

"We ain't here to get excited about nothing but catching a killer," Brice said. He looked at his watch again, and said to Ryan, "Go call him."

Ryan started to get up when the door opened after a shallow knock and Smith came in.

"Sorry, Lieu," he said. "Heavy traffic."

"Nice of you to join us," Brice said as he motioned Smith to the empty chair beside Hart. "Joe Smith, this is Bill Murphy. He was assigned the case before you guys."

Smith and Murphy shook hands.

"All right," Brice said. "I had a chance to go over all the report summaries thus far, and I got to say that you've done a pretty decent job of getting this investigation off the ground again. I also want to say that I agree with Leal that we should be looking at the husband more closely."

Leal raised his eyebrows. At last he's seen the light, he thought, and knew he should keep his mouth shut. But he couldn't help himself.

"Why the change of heart, Lieu?" Leal asked.

Brice stared at him before answering.

"No change really," Brice said. "Just going through basic investigative procedure. You *always* should look at the spouse in cases like this, but this time he happens to be a rather prominent citizen, not to mention an attorney, too. So we had to eliminate the random victim possibility first, understand, Sergeant?"

The way he said "Sergeant" made it clear what he meant. Leal just nodded, figuring it was best to back off. He saw Hart widening her eyes in warning as she looked at him.

"His alibi was rock solid," Murphy said, after clearing his throat. "Don't mean that he couldn't have hired somebody, though."

"I want to start looking into that alibi," Brice said. "Start focusing on this fucker." He pointed at Hart. "What did the state's attorney say?"

"Not enough for a wiretap."

"Figures," Brice said. "So we're gonna start zeroing in on Martin Walker. His relationship with his wife, associates, any history of domestic violence, all that shit. Let's see if Financial Crimes can give us anything, too." He turned and looked at Leal. "Miriam's old man called me. Said you talked to him."

Leal nodded.

"The old guy was pretty impressed with you two. Feels you're gonna get to the bottom of this." Brice glanced at his watch again. "All right, it's time to go downstairs and meet with the sheriff. Everybody take a five-minute break and hit the john. Make sure your hair is combed and your ties are on straight." He stood up.

What the hell, thought Leal. Is he losing it, or what?

Martin Walker listened to the loud dialogue of some television program on the other end of the line and lit another cigarette. He hated waiting, and this was trying his patience even more. Finally he heard some fumbling and Richard's voice came back on the line.

"Sorry, Marty, I had to make another call."

"Well, why did you make such a big deal about me calling you at seven thirty then?" Walker asked, the anger and stress spilling into his voice. "I don't appreciate being on hold for two minutes, either."

"You weren't on hold," Connors said. "And I told you, I had to page someone."

"Whatever. Now what's the plan to get rid of these fucking cops?" Walker's voice was close to cracking. He blew out a lungful of smoke. "You said you could handle things. Well, it sure doesn't seem that you're doing a very good job."

"Take it easy, Marty. I told you, I got it covered."

"How?"

Suddenly Walker heard the sound of an electrical motor, followed by a slight vibration. Then he realized it was his garage door opener.

"You okay, Marty?" Connors asked.

"Yes, I just heard something." He got up and moved to the upstairs windows overlooking his sloping rear yard and driveway. "My garage door is going up. There's some kind of van down there."

"Yeah, I know," Connors said. "It's Nuke. I told him to drop by."

"What? I don't want him *here*. What if my neighbors see?"

"Will you relax. I told him to pull around to the back, just like the last time," Connors said.

Walker felt a shiver go up his spine. The last time had been when they'd killed Miriam.

"Well?" Connors asked. "Look out the window again. The van's out of sight, right?"

"Yes, but that's not the point. What is that big idiot doing here?" He took another drag on the cigarette. "And how did he get my garage door open?"

"He has the frequency, remember? From the garage door opener in Miriam's car."

Walker could hear the heavy sounds of footsteps on the stairs coming up to the second level. It sounded like more than one person.

"Richard, is this your idea of how to handle things? Sending some big clown over here?"

"Relax, Marty. Just go give the phone to Nuke. I gotta talk to him."

Walker sighed heavily and walked to the dining room and stood by the door to the circular staircase. He pulled it open and saw Nuke standing there grinning in a dark-colored shirt and his dirty Levi's jacket with the sleeves cut off. The shirt was sleeveless, too, showing the obscene tattoo on the overdeveloped shoulder. Walker could see the two young stooges behind him, the heavyset one with the exotropic left eye, and the skinny blond one with the collar-length hair.

Oh, God, thought Walker. I hope none of the neighbors saw them come in. Luckily, he remembered, the garage was set under the bedrooms, and the cement reinforcement wall would block the sight of the van from his neighbor's house.

He handed the phone to Nuke and said, "Here, it's Richard."

Nuke accepted it and spoke into the receiver, moving up into the dining room from the stairwell. The other two followed. Walker noticed that their hands looked funny. Slick and almost shiny, and he realized they were all wearing latex gloves. The wall-eyed one, Moose, moved forward and closed the drapes. Nuke set the phone down and looked at Walker.

"You alone?" he asked.

"Yes," Walker said. "Did anyone see you come in?"

Nuke smiled and shook his head. The soft rubber squeaked as he squeezed his hands together.

"What does Richard want?" Walker asked, wishing he had retrieved the snub-nosed .38 he kept in his desk drawer. He tried to make his voice sound forceful. "I said, what does he want?"

"Shut up, bitch," Nuke said. He moved forward and gave Walker a hard shove. "Bring the shit over here," he said over his shoulder.

Walker did a little stutter step to regain his footing, then turned and tried to run into the living room. But Nuke grabbed him, snaring his shirt. A second latex-covered hand closed over the top of Walker's face.

Walker tried to scream, but couldn't. A huge arm had circled his throat, cutting off his air. He reached up, scratching furiously at the arm. He heard Nuke grunt, almost like an animalistic hiss. Or roar. Walker felt himself being lifted off his feet as the powerful grip around his neck tightened and his air was cut off. He stuck the burning end of the lit cigarette to Nuke's forearm as he struggled for a few more moments, kicking and scratching until the myriad of black dots that swarmed before him leapt up and engulfed his consciousness.

Undersheriff Lucas was standing just down the hall from the conference room, watching their approach. Lucas was a waspish man with brown glasses and a neatly trimmed haircut. His slender right hand held the bowl of an unlit pipe, and his other hand rested in the outside pocket of his suit, the thumb outside. Leal thought the guy looked like he was trying out for an ad in *Gentlemen's Quarterly.*

"Who's this man?" Lucas asked, pointing the pipe stem at Murphy.

"That's Bill Murphy," Brice said. "He used to work on the Walker case and was here for a meeting."

Leal watched Lucas give Murphy a quick once-over. The big man's face seemed to stretch into a nervous smile and it looked as though he was trying to hold in his massive stomach.

"I think we'll just go with these four," Lucas said, waving his hand. "Thank you, Murphy."

Murphy sputtered some reply and turned to go, his huge gut billowing outward again. Leal silently chuckled. Lucas opened the door to the conference room and ushered them in. Several sets of large wooden chairs had been placed around an oval table. Sheriff O'Hara sat at the head, while a thin guy with a ponytail leaned over him. The thin guy held a towel and an eyebrow pencil. A white bib covered the sheriff's shirt, and the jacket of his blue suit was draped over a nearby chair. Leal could see the large circles of sweat under each of the man's arms.

"Please, Sheriff, hold still," the thin guy said. His voice was a couple of octaves above tenor. "I'm trying to eliminate some shadows. And remember to keep your chin tucked when we shoot."

The sheriff grunted as the thin guy leaned back, studied him, and picked up a powder puff and makeup brush. In the corner two men were setting up some video equipment. One held a camcorder on his shoulder. The other had a camera mounted on a tripod base. A television monitor sat on the table. A third man in a dark brown suit came forward to talk to Lucas. "Are you almost finished, Henry?"

"He's about as good as I can get him, Mr. Tillis," the thin guy said.

"Okay," Tillis said, looking at Leal. "Let's do the Latino guy next. Can you make him more swarthy?"

Latino guy? thought Leal. What the hell is this?

Henry moved over toward Leal, his makeup brush and powder puff poised for action.

"Touch me with that and I'll shove it up your ass sideways," Leal said, his voice pitched low and tight.

"Goodness," Henry said, recoiling.

"Dammit, Ted," Tillis said. "How the hell am I supposed to get this right if your people won't cooperate?"

"Take it easy, Glenn," Lucas said. "Now listen to me, all of you. We're going to tape this meeting tonight, and I expect each of you to cooperate in the fullest. Is that clear?"

A murmur of lukewarm assent went through the group. Henry moved forward, more cautiously this time, and handed Leal a green bib similar to the one the sheriff had been wearing. Leal blew a slow breath out his nostrils and tied it around his neck.

"Sit down and close your eyes, please," Henry said.

"Do it!" Nuke shouted as he used his superior weight to force Martin Walker's body to the floor. "Do it now!"

Moose came forward, his left eye staring off at some odd angle as he fumbled with the purple Crown Royal bag he was holding, spilling the contents on the rug.

"Which arm?" he asked.

"Who the fuck cares," Nuke said. He face was a contorted mask of rage. Walker's body flailed effetely, his legs making spasmodic kicks.

Nuke flopped the limp man over onto his back. Moose rolled up Walker's left shirtsleeve and tied a rubber band around his bicep. He then uncapped the syringe and tapped it twice, looking at the fluid reservoir.

"Just fucking do it," Nuke said. "I don't give a shit about air bubbles."

Moose nodded and began scanning Walker's bare arm.

"Shit, man, this fucker's veins ain't coming up."

Nuke grunted and released his grip from around Walker's neck and watched the flabby shoulders slump lifelessly to the floor. The phone, next to them on the floor, was repeating in a computerized tone, "If you'd like to make a call, please hang up and try again."

Nuke squeezed Walker's cheeks together and touched a thumb to the hooded, blank-looking eyes. No reaction.

"Shee-it," Nuke said. "Gimme that phone."

After Henry had finished prepping each of them, the "meeting" began with O'Hara back at the head of the table, Leal and Hart on one side, and Smith, Ryan, and Brice on the other. Leal had taken particular pleasure in watching Brice get the fluffy treatment. It almost made the whole thing worth it. But, Christ, he thought, what a waste of time.

"Which way should I look?" O'Hara asked.

"Never mind that," Tillis called out. "Just look forceful. Like a leader. We're not taping any dialogue. We're going to use a voice-over for this spot."

"So we can talk about the Cubs?" Leal asked, smiling.

"Knock off the shit," Brice said.

"Aww, I thought it was pretty funny," O'Hara said, smiling. "I'm a Sox man myself."

"Cut it, Dorry," Tillis called out. The cameraman stopped filming and assumed a relaxed position, the camcorder canted on his shoulder. The brightness of the lights was unbelievable, and Leal felt a trickle of sweat run down from his armpits. Henry darted between each of them, dabbing at their faces with some gauzelike material.

"Can't afford a shiny nose," he said to Hart, who smiled.

Asshole, thought Leal.

"Don," Tillis said. "Come over and take a look at this, please."

O'Hara rose ponderously, his face drooping, and went over to the television monitor.

"See how you keep picking up that stack of papers and doing this?" Tillis bounced his own papers on the table a few times. "It makes you look nervous, and hence, what? Insecure."

"Well, dammit, I gotta do something with my hands, don't I?"

Tillis patted the sheriff's shoulder. "I know, Don, but remember, we're talking image here. People are going to see this for maybe thirty seconds, and we want you coming off looking totally in control. Let's try it again, and this time, hold a pen. Write something when I tell you, then use it as a pointer, like you're a teacher calling on some students."

O'Hara nodded.

"And let's get a couple shots of you doing this," Tillis said, steepling his hands. "Let's practice that a few times, okay? Remember, perception becomes reality."

The sheriff nodded again and Leal saw the sweat stains were starting to seep through the underarms of O'Hara's suit. For the first time that evening Leal felt sorry for the old man. Jumping through hoops at a dog and pony show, he thought, and wondered if he'd do the same if he wanted something that bad. But after all, perception becomes reality.

CHAPTER TWENTY-TWO

Night Moves

Everything had changed now, due to Nuke's steroid-accelerated mood swing. Snake hated him when he was heavily into the cycle. And now with Moose doing the shit, too, it was like tiptoeing around in a volcano. He watched as Nuke talked with the boss on the cell phone. Snake could see that even the big man was nervous now. Shit, we're on damage control, he thought as he eyed the sumptuous furnishings in the house. For Snake, who was an inveterate burglar, it was closely akin to being in heaven.

"Okay, boss," Nuke said. He spat a loop of tobacco juice on the rug. "Yeah, that ain't gonna be no problem. We'll get right on it."

Snake listened intently as Nuke repeated the instructions back to the boss over the phone, stopping when he was apparently directed to go back over important details. "Get his files, Rolodex, and pack a bag. Take him outta there, and go park his car up at O'Hare." Nuke stopped. "But ain't they gonna find it up there?" He paused and listened. Snake could hear the faint humming of Connors' voice coming over the line. "Oh, okay, I see. The wallet . . . uh, okay . . . Yeah, I got it, boss."

Nuke hung up and snapped his fingers at them.

"Go take the file cabinet in the office downstairs and load it into the van," he said. Snake saw Nuke shift the plug of tobacco to the front of his lower lip as he knelt by the corpse and removed Walker's wallet.

Snake and Moose moved quickly to the other room. The filing cabinet was heavy and although Moose seemed to handle his end with ease, it slipped from Snake's grip and crashed to the floor.

Nuke slapped him on the back of the head.

"Get outta the way." He grabbed the end of the cabinet himself. "Go get something to roll him in," he said to Snake. And then to Moose, "Careful not to hit the walls going down. Take it nice and slow."

Slow . . . That was like a magic word to Snake. He moved into the bedroom and grabbed a folded blanket off the bed. A huge dresser loomed to his right, with a jewelry box, several rings, some cash, and a credit card on top. Snake glanced around and licked his lips.

Won't hurt anything, he thought. Who's to know?

He rolled down the bedspread and slipped a case off a pillow. A burglar's best friend. Pocketing the cash and rings, he dropped the credit card and jewelry box into the pillow case. A cordless telephone next to the bed caught his eye so he unsnapped the jack and put that in, too. He was going through the rest of the drawers when he heard footsteps coming up the stairs.

Scampering as silently as he could to Walker's body, he skidded to his knees and stashed the pillowcase under a chair. He was busily spreading the blanket out on the floor when Nuke and Moose came back.

"Hey, Nuke," Snake asked, smiling, "can I take his watch and beeper?"

Nuke strode over and jerked him upright, bundling his shirt in one hand and slapping him across the face with the other.

"Quit fucking off," he said.

Snake recoiled as the redness crept up his cheek.

"Sorry," he muttered.

Nuke released him. "Find the keys to his ride, and his Rolodex," he said. Then to Moose, "Take his legs and let's roll him in that blanket."

Snake felt the stinging in his face as he watched them flip Walker's limp form over. A slight trickle of blood rolled from the dead man's mouth.

"Take the feet," Nuke directed. "And keep him level. I don't want nothing spilling out of him."

They went through the stairway door again with the inert form in the rolled blanket, Nuke shouting directions as they descended. Snake knew his time was limited, so he wasted none of it. His fingers were already twisting the wires from the rear of the DVD/VCR, and he deftly stuck them behind the cabinet as he slipped the machine into the pillowcase. Moving to the desk he found the keys on top as well as the Rolodex. But something else caught his eye in the partially open center drawer: a snubnose, nickel-plated revolver. Snake picked it up and held it at arm's length, sighting down the barrel at the bronze statue of some fairy-looking guy playing a flute.

Then he lowered the gun and kept looking at the statue as something clicked. He'd seen one of those before, in *Get High* magazine, the publication for sophisticated heads. It was some kind of fancy way of hiding your stash. A false bottom. He picked up the statue and grinned broadly as he hefted it, testing the weight.

Yeah, something was in there, all right.

He stuck that in the pillowcase, too, noticing how bulky it now looked, and went back to wipe the telltale dust pattern off the table where the statue had been.

Nuke and Moose came in moments later.

"You find 'em?" Nuke asked.

Snake held up the keys in one hand and the pistol in the other.

"Look what else I found."

"Put it back where you found it, fuckhead," Nuke said. "We don't take nothing except what I told ya."

Snake nodded and returned to the desk, eyeing the bulky pillowcase next to a chair, and hoping like hell that Nuke didn't see that.

Nuke grabbed the keys and pointed to the Rolodex.

"Put that in the van. I'm gonna pack a couple of suitcases for this fucker."

Moose followed him out the room and Snake sensed his opportunity. He lagged behind, snaring the pillowcase and then moving down the stairs with desperate urgency. He pulled open the rear door of the van and set the Rolodex next to the blanket. Looking over his shoulder, he quickly pulled at the inside panel in the left rear section. Normally, it was used to transport weapons or drugs, but since the White Wolves had ceased to be a viable motorcycle gang in recent months, the artillery was in short supply. The pillowcase fit snugly inside, and Snake replaced the panel and smiled as he patted the blanketed body beside him.

"Keep an eye on them things for me, would ya?" he whispered.

The skyline of the factories was barely visible through the fog, and the dark figures moved with a stealth that filled Leal with dread. Everything made sense, even though it didn't. Johnny DeWayne was there. And Bob Hilton. But so was Brice, who just kept harping that Leal wasn't a team player. Then Sheriff O'Hara stepped forward, the enormous circles of sweat soaking through the armpits of his suit, and said, "Thank you very much for your contribution tonight."

Is he talking to me? Leal wondered.

Then Marcus LeRigg smiled, showing the gleaming gold-capped tooth, a look of conspiracy in his eyes. Leal knew something was wrong. Dreadfully wrong. He set the briefcase with the buy money on the trunk of his car. Brice yelled again about being a team player.

"Ready to do the do?" LeRigg asked, still smiling.

Suddenly Leal knew it had all gone sour and he reached for his gun. Beside him, Bob Hilton screamed, clutching his chest and twisting down into a heap. Two "gangstas" stood blazing away. Leal raised his gun, but it wouldn't fire. The trigger wouldn't go back. He squeezed harder. Nothing. Brice yelled. LeRigg laughed. The guns in front of him flashed again, and he felt the rounds whizzing by his head. Then the pain in his chest. Like someone hit him with a hammer. No, a poker. A red-hot poker. Everything was red.

He was screaming as he snapped awake, breathing hard, Sharon shaking his arm. The room was dark.

"What's wrong?" she asked. "You were tossing so much you woke me up."

He swallowed hard and rubbed a hand over his face. It was wet with sweat. It hadn't been this bad since right after the shooting.

"Sorry," he said, swinging his legs from under the sheet. "Bad dream."

"It must have been," she said, following him as he headed for the bathroom. "Are you all right?"

He nodded, pausing to flip on the light and check himself in the mirror. It hurt his eyes. "It was an anxiety dream."

"Oh, I get those, too," Sharon said, leaning against the door frame and crossing her arms in front of her breasts. "Like when I'm in school sometime and I'm late for a final and can't find the room."

"Yeah," he said, rinsing his face and mouth. "In mine, I'm dead."

He lifted the toilet seat and she moved out of the doorway as he urinated, and stepped back in as he padded out.

"My turn," she said, lowering the seat again.

When she came back, he was sitting on the edge of the bed.

"You got a cigarette?" he asked.

"I thought you quit," she said, kneeling beside him and massaging the back of his neck. "You don't really want to start again, do you?" Her fingers traced over his neck, and she leaned down to kiss him. "Are you sure you're okay?"

"Yeah, it's just . . . that damn dream . . . When it comes, it usually means something bad is about to happen. My body's way of telling me there's something I missed."

Her hands squeezed his neck, then crept lower and she leaned forward and kissed him on the lips.

"Let me see if we can change that," she said, "because you don't miss anything."

CHAPTER TWENTY-THREE
Venn Diagrams

The chirping of the beeper woke them both.

"Yours or mine?" Sharon asked, raising her head and arm from Leal's chest to allow him to get out of bed.

"Mine," he said as he pressed the acknowledge button and looked at the screen. "Shit, it's HQ. Mind if I call?"

"Sure, go ahead," she said. "I'll just lie here and admire your nice butt."

He smiled. "If I said that, you'd call me a sexist, right?"

"No, I'd call you observant," she said, sitting up and reaching for her cigarettes. "This going to bother you?"

He shook his head as he dialed, seeing 9:25 A.M. on the digital clock next to the bed. After explaining to the communications personnel that he'd been beeped, he was subsequently put through to Joe Smith.

"Hey, Sarge, didn't mean to bother you, but I showed up here today and I'm by myself. Did I miss something, or what?"

"Yeah, sorry, Joe," Leal said. "Ryan told me last night that he had some family emergency and might take a personal day."

"You think he could've at least told me. I'm supposed to be his partner."

Even over the phone Leal could sense Smith's resentment.

"Joe, we were all pretty burnt out after filming that commercial last night. He only mentioned it to me as we were walking out."

Sharon got on her knees beside him and mouthed *commercial.*

He grinned and she messed with his hair. Leal shook his head and gave her what he hoped passed for a stern look.

"Yeah, right," Smith said.

"Well, Hart and I are going to hit some of Walker's favorite haunts up around River North tonight. You're welcome to come along."

"Thanks, Sarge, but we've got a Lamaze class. I appreciate you keeping me in the loop, though. And I mean that."

"How'd you do on that other stuff we talked about?"

"Your friend at the credit bureau wasn't there, but I did make it to the Hall of Records to check on that Lunge Hill Corporation."

"Great. What'd you find?"

"Not a helluva lot," Smith said. Leal could hear him flipping through papers on the other end. "It's owned by some company in the Virgin Islands. That's as far as I got on it. I can keep digging, though."

"Sounds good. Touch bases with the guys in Financial Crimes for some help. And run that credit check, too. Like I said, if Margie's working, she'll do it on the sly for you if you mention my name."

"Gotcha, Sarge. Will do."

"And Joe, after you finish those things, take the rest of the afternoon off. We'll meet tomorrow morning and discuss what we've got, with or without your partner."

"Okay," Smith said. "And thanks for the faith in me. I'm learning a lot."

After Leal hung up, Sharon pointed an accusatory finger at him, and said, "Did I just hear a police sergeant tell one of his men to circumvent the law?"

Despite the playfulness in her tone, Leal could tell there was some seriousness mixed in. "I love it when you use big words. Circumvent? What does that mean?"

"You know very well what it means," she said. "Sounds like you're being too lazy or too sloppy to get a warrant."

"Not lazy or sloppy, just smart."

"Since when is circumventing the legal system smart?"

"Since it was set up so that lawyers can play their games and get people off on technicalities."

She shook her head. He could tell he'd struck a nerve.

"Hey, it's not that way," she said. "Those are all our rights, yours, mine, everybody's. A person doesn't just lose them because they've been accused of a crime."

"Sorry, I forgot I was sleeping with a lawyer," he said, regretting it almost immediately.

"What's that supposed to mean?"

Leal let out a slow breath. "Let's just drop it, okay?"

"No, it's not okay," she said, stubbing out her cigarette. "Every time I try to have a meaningful discussion with you, where I might be able to get to know you better, you retreat behind your wall."

He looked at her for a moment, then smoothed some errant hairs away from her face. "Can't we just agree to disagree?" he said. "Maybe say that you deal with legal abstractions, while I work in the real world. The two have to meet down the line somewhere, but sometimes they just run parallel. Idealized reality versus practical reality."

She traced the scar on the side of his chest with her fingers.

"Practical reality," she said softly. "I guess we are like Venn diagrams, aren't we?"

"Huh? What's that?"

Those diagrams that they use in schools," she said, drawing circles on his chest. "You know, where one circle overlaps another, and they share this common, shaded area."

Yeah, he thought as he pulled her close, and I know which areas I'd like to have overlapping right now, too.

"So now you want to cancel the payment for the flight on your credit card and pay cash, Mr. Walker?" the girl behind the United counter asked. She smiled politely. "I'm sorry, but we don't accept cash. Regulations."

"Fine," Richard Connors said, bumping up the dark glasses on his nose in his best imitation of one of Martin's nervous gestures. "Can you hurry, please? I still have to get through the security checkpoint, don't I?" He felt a slight tremor, but the false ID that he had showed his picture with Martin Walker's information. It should be a cakewalk. They looked enough alike that it shouldn't be a problem when the police showed her Martin's picture. All he had to do was imitate an innocuous-looking asshole for a few more minutes.

"It'll just take a moment more, sir."

He looked at his watch. "What time will we arrive in San Juan?"

"About three o'clock, Chicago time," the girl said. She pressed some keys on her computer terminal. "Bear with me, please."

Connors heaved what he hoped would pass for an impatient sigh. He turned and studied the surging crowds behind him and wondered if she would remember anything about his face when they questioned her.

"You'll lose the hour going, but gain it coming back," the girl said, obviously trying to be convivial.

"Yes, I know that," Connors said, letting a little lilt of petulance creep into his tone. Walker did not relate well to women. Give her enough to remember that I'm an asshole, but not enough to recall any details, he thought. It was like walking a tightrope. Or sacrificing a pawn to take a knight.

"And you won't need your hat and overcoat there, either," she said, handing him the ticket and boarding pass. "It's a lot warmer than here."

Connors nodded curtly, the same way he imagined Martin Walker would have done, and murmured something in reply. "Which way is it to the gate?"

She pointed, her smile almost flagging, and said, "Gate three, thank you for flying United."

He left, uttering a purposefully exaggerated hiss.

They found the Kit Kat Club sandwiched between an adult bookstore and another club called Games & Faces. The streets were moderately crowded and there were absolutely no parking places. Finally, Leal pulled into an alley and stuck the red light on the dashboard. Hart looked at him.

"It's not like anybody's not going to know it's an unmarked anyway, right?" he said.

She nodded.

Crazily dressed young punks walked by them, some with the Goth look, all in black, and others with multiple piercings and spiked hair. A few yuppies strolled by dressed in high-fashion clothes, interspersed with young lovers and groups of college-age kids.

"Some of them don't look old enough to drink," Hart said.

"But old enough to get laid," Leal said. He pointed across the street to a group of hookers in tight, abbreviated dresses spilling abundant cleavage.

Most of the buildings in this section were two-story brick, with the lights of the skyscrapers looming to the south. The bookstore next to the Kit Kat had a protruding neon sign depicting a woman's exaggerated figure. The words *Adult Books* covered the area where her nipples should have been. *Movies* was centered across her hips.

"Nice neighborhood," Hart said. She was a little miffed that Leal had insisted she dress up a bit so they wouldn't look conspicuous if the chance somehow arose to start a surveillance on Walker in his unnatural habitat. That's fine for him, she thought. He can wear his gun in a pancake under his sports jacket, but now I've got to keep mine in my purse. But the warmth of the day had lasted into the evening, and Hart had left her jacket in the car, feeling comfortable in her sleeveless white blouse and dark slacks. But Leal couldn't take off his jacket without people noticing. She adjusted the strap of her purse on her shoulder and smiled. Maybe there is some justice after all.

"Let's check out the Kit Kat first," Leal said. "Maybe somebody will know him."

They pushed though the glass doors and into the foyer. The blaring music engulfed them even before they entered the bar area. It was set up as a restaurant on the ground level. Beyond that, a sunken area served as dance floor. Several nearly nude girls strolled along a raised platform, next to a sign that advertised Tuesday night as Wiggle Night. Flashing laser lights reflected off mirrored walls, and in the center a young black man with a needlelike mustache sorted out CDs in a glass booth. The bar was rectangular, with padded stools and the customary mirrored back wall. Two bartenders filled orders, slapping beer steins down on the lacquered surface and filling glasses for several waitresses. One of the bartenders was a big white guy with a shaved head and handlebar mustache. The other, a thin blond in her late twenties, looked like death warmed over.

Leal and Hart moved to the lower portion of the club toward a large guy in a dark turtleneck with a weightlifter's build. *Security* was labeled across the breast pocket. He stepped in front of them.

"Three-dollar cover charge for Wiggle Night," he said.

Leal held up his badge. Hart began to reach in her purse, but the security guard backed away. They descended the steps, trying to survey the crowd. Baldy came over to them first, as they managed to squeeze into an empty space that was almost too small for them. Hart felt herself pressed against Leal's side. She could feel his weapon pressing into her ribs, and she moved her purse around to the front.

"What'll it be?" the bartender asked.

"Information," Leal said, flashing his badge again. He took out the copy of Martin Walker's driver's license photo. "Ever seen this guy in here?"

The bartender leaned over and Hart thought that his head looked as shiny as a cue ball.

"Hard to say," baldy said. "What did he do?"

Leal ignored his question. "How about your partner?"

Baldy shrugged and moved away, going over to whisper to the blond girl who was mixing a B and B. She held up her fingers and smiled. One of the waitresses glanced across at them, then looked away. After setting the glass on a tray, the blond girl walked over. Her teeth were going to need some dental work soon, Hart noticed.

"Hi. Whatcha need?" Her name tag said Crystal.

Leal tapped the picture on the bar and asked the same question.

She studied the picture and handed it back.

"You know, I mighta seen him in here, but not recently," she said.

"When was the last time?" Leal asked.

She shrugged. "We get so many people."

"What was he like?" Hart asked. "Did he hang with anybody?"

Crystal shrugged again and wiped her nose.

"I remember he was a lousy tipper," she said. "What's he done, anyway?"

"We just want to talk to him," Leal said, putting the picture back in his pocket.

"Yeah, right," Crystal said. "With two cops asking for him?" She tossed her head defiantly and walked back to the center of the bar.

They tried to survey the crowd again from this vantage point, but the noise and dim lighting made it next to impossible. Hart turned and placed her mouth next to Leal's right ear.

"Maybe showing Walker the matchbook wasn't such a good idea," she said, hoping he could understand her over the beat-driven cacophony. The disc jockey had put on a remix version of "I'm So Excited."

Leal nodded and started to say something. Instead, he jerked his head toward the door. As they walked away he leaned close and said, "I wish I would've known Brice was gonna see it our way, or I might not have done it." They started up the stairs. "Anyway, let's check some of the other clubs and come back. They may know more than they're telling."

Games & Faces seemed geared toward a younger crowd. A couple of punk rockers eyed them suspiciously as they walked in, and Leal snorted. The club was designed with a domination motif, the small dance floor a gesticulating mass of postadolescent bodies in black, punctuated with gleaming metal studs. Gigantic video screens played music videos in frenzied cuts.

"Come on," Leal said, after the bartender laughed and shook his head after seeing Walker's picture. "We're about as inconspicuous as two nuns at a Madonna concert."

"Yeah, I doubt he would have gotten in here without a lip stud," Hart said.

After checking three more clubs with similar results, Hart was ready to quit. She just knew her hair would smell totally like cigarette smoke, and the thought of washing it again before she went to sleep didn't gel with her plans of an early morning run. So she wasn't happy when Leal said he wanted to go back to the Kit Kat.

"There was something about that female bartender," he said. "The way she looked at us."

"Okay," she said, not wanting him to know how she really felt. It was time to suck it up, she thought. Learn from the best.

"If that doesn't work, maybe we can tag up with a couple of vice boys from CPD and lean on the street people a little," he said.

A group of women stood in front of the adult bookstore adjacent to the Kit Kat. Hart eyed them warily. Several of them wore opulent miniskirts and tight halter tops leaving little to the imagination. One of the women, a dark-skinned girl with large breasts and skinny legs, called out as they passed.

"Looking for a little action, Officers?"

The other girls laughed hysterically.

"No problem making us, huh?" Hart said.

Leal waved back at the hookers and smiled.

"The wagon's on the way, ladies," he said, pulling Hart toward them. "Say, you girls mind helping us out a bit?" He took the picture of Martin Walker out and showed it to them. "Seen this dude around here lately?"

"Shit," the hooker said. "This boy's so ugly he have to pay for it."

"Pay me double," another one said, looking over her shoulder.

A Lincoln town car pulled up and slowed as the passenger-side window lowered into the door. "Hey, good-looking," the driver called.

The girls waved him away and stared at Leal and Hart.

The picture got quickly passed around and returned.

"Let's go take us a smoke break, girlfriend," one of the white hookers said, sounding like she was doing her best to emulate a black accent.

"I do know this dude," the first hooker said, turning to go. "Look like one of Bobbi's boys."

"Hey," Leal said, holding up a bill. "Who's that?"

The girl did a quick about-face and snatched the bill. "Bobbi work that club there now," she said, pointing to the Kit Kat.

"She in the life?" asked Leal.

The hooker nodded. "Bobbi into a whole 'nother kind of kink. But lately, she pretty much dealing in chemical transactions, if you get my drift."

Leal nodded. "Can you point her out to us?"

The hooker's face scrunched up.

"Don't want to be narcing on nobody," she said. "I got a reputation to uphold." She smiled.

Leal smiled back. He held up another bill.

"Maybe we can do it on the sly?" he said.

She grabbed the bill and tucked it into her Wonderbra.

"You know, I guess I could use a trip to the ladies' room," she said.

As they went inside, the security guy stopped the hooker at the door.

"Get your motherfuckin' hands off me, bitch," she said.

He looked about ready to slap her and throw her out the door when Leal said, "She's with us."

The security guard raised his hands in an I-give-up gesture, and took a step back.

"Thank you," the hooker said in a smug voice, and went down the steps. She paused in the darkness, her voice barely audible between the squeals from the crowd and the pervasive beat. "Let me go in and look around. If I see her, I'll lean over and talk to her and put my hand on her like this." She touched Hart on the shoulder, then said, "Damn, girl, you strong. Come by and see me, honey, and I'll show you some good times." Hart recoiled slightly at the thought and suddenness of being touched, and the hooker laughed. The song ended and the disc jockey said something special, really special, was coming up.

The hooker circled the floor, taking the long route to the ladies' room. They watched her progress as she went inside, and after coming out, she stopped, pausing to take out a cigarette. Through the haze Hart saw the hooker stop at the bar and lean between two patrons, her hand resting on the shoulder of a slender white chick with dark shoulder-length hair feathered back to just above her collar. Her excessive eye makeup gave an almost grotesque exaggeration to her slim face.

"The broad in the black leather," Leal said, moving down the stairs. "Let's go down and check her out."

Hart followed, trying to watch as the hooker grabbed a book of matches off the counter, lit her cigarette, and then looked up. She melted into the crowd as Leal and Hart drew closer. The blond bartender seemed to see them coming, as she was refilling a customer's drink. She leaned forward and said something, and Hart saw the brunette's extreme outlined eyes seek them out. They pushed past a couple of stumbling drunks who were all hands and apologies.

"I think Blondie tipped her off to us," Leal said, shoving past the drunks.

Hart saw Bobbi pick up her shoulder-strap purse and slip off the stool, her sequined stockings sweeping together as she headed for the back of the room.

"She's booking," Leal said.

They watched as Bobbi pushed open the washroom door.

"What do you want to do?" Hart asked.

"I wonder if there's a window in the ladies' room."

She shrugged. "Want me to check?"

"Yeah," he said. "Ask her to step outside and we'll question her about Walker. It'd be nice to set something up so we could catch him with a hooker or some drugs."

Hart smiled, thinking that maybe they had a chance to catch that break they needed. She pushed past a few people to the ladies' room.

"I'll guard the door," she heard Leal say. "Be careful in there."

I can handle it, she thought.

Leal stopped just outside the door as Hart went in.

Surprisingly, the room was fairly spacious as club washrooms went, and empty, too. Hart looked at the rear wall and saw a partially open window and thought, Oh, shit. But the window was pretty high off the floor, and Hart just couldn't see Bobbi risking her tight leather dress to scurry up the wall and belly out of a window. She decided to check the stalls.

Hart paused at the sinks to take out her badge. Then she bent at the waist and looked under the three stalls, but saw no feet. She checked the doorknob of a small closet on the opposite wall and found it locked.

Things aren't always what they seem, she thought and pushed open the first stall door.

Empty.

Giving the middle door a shove, she saw that one was empty, too.

The third one's the charm, she thought, and pushed the door. It was locked. Peering between the space between the frame and the door, Hart saw black leather, sequined stockings, and black patent-leather pumps resting on the horseshoe toilet seat.

"Come on out, Bobbi," Hart said. "We need to talk."

"What the fuck do you want, bitch?" came the husky whisper.

Hart was in no mood for a smart-ass comment from a smart-ass whore.

"Police," she said, grabbing the stall door and giving it a shove. The door flew backward, swishing past Bobbi's hunched up knees. Hart held up her badge. "Let's step outside for a minute."

Bobbi stepped lightly off the toilet with a dancer's grace, and strolled to the sinks. She leaned over and looked in the mirror, one hand digging in her big black purse. Hart was having trouble stuffing the badge case back in her purse, wishing she had pants with pockets big enough, when the little alarm inside her head started to go off.

I'd better not let her go digging in there, she thought. "Hey, keep your hands where I can see them."

Bobbi smirked and removed a lipstick tube, holding it up. Hart relaxed slightly.

"So what do you want?" Bobbi asked, slipping the gold top off the tube.

A remix version of "I Want to Dance With Somebody" began blaring over the sound system. Hart moved her head at the sudden noise, and when she looked back in front she saw Bobbi whirling toward her. Hart raised her arm to block what she thought was just a punch, not seeing the hooking blade protruding from the top of the lipstick tube. The blade sliced down the underside of Hart's left arm. She felt a cutting sensation, then the pain and gushing of blood. Bobbi tore Hart's purse away with a sudden quick jerking motion. Hart backed away, but Bobbi followed, grabbing at her with long, black fingernails. Hart tried to snatch away the blade, but only got a slice across her hand. Bobbi slashed outward, obviously aiming for the throat, but hitting Hart's left shoulder and back, ripping and tearing her blouse as she tried to run for the door.

Summoning all her strength, Hart grabbed Bobbi's right hand, the one with the blade, held it in both of hers, and yelled, "Frank, help!"

Leal, who had positioned himself outside the ladies' room door to prevent anyone else from going in, heard what he thought was a scream mixed in with the lyrics of the Whitney Houston song that was blasting from the speakers. He pushed open the door and the sight of the bloody struggle sent a shock up his spine.

Inside in seconds Leal seized the raven-colored hair only to have it come off in his hand, exposing a shortly cropped head covered by a murky hairnet. Tossing the wig down, he slammed into them, the force sending everyone crashing against the stall assembly. Leal grabbed Bobbi's right wrist, his fingers meeting around the slimness of the bones, and together with Hart, managed to twist the bladed lipstick tube loose. It fell to the floor, rolling over Leal's arm. His gaze followed it for only seconds until an elbow smashed into his temple. Long black talons raked over his face. Leal backed away slightly, but it was enough to loosen his grasp and Bobbi wormed free of them. He saw Hart slip to the floor, a bloody mess, and half a second later a sequined leg snapped up to catch him in the crotch. Leal stumbled forward, his balls on fire, and braced, half a second later, for the inevitable gut-wrenching nausea that usually accompanies a deftly delivered groin blow. The black fingernails flashed for his eyes, but suddenly fell short, and Leal saw Hart's bloody arms looped around Bobbi's legs, sending her plopping down on the hard tile floor.

Waving off the nausea, Leal gritted his teeth and drove his right fist into Bobbi's jaw as she was getting up. The blow staggered her, and her wobbly two-step bought her within range again. Leal put his legs behind a body blow, catching the leather dress at the midpoint. Bobbi sunk to her knees, and Leal pivoted, slamming the close-cropped head into the nearest porcelain sink. Then, using his superior weight, he forced Bobbi to the floor and reached for his cuffs, snapping them over the slender wrists as he twisted them behind her back.

"Get my purse," Hart said. She looked groggy, out of it.

Leal shook off his own dazed fuzziness and picked up the

lipstick blade. As he straightened up he saw the short leather skirt riding up over Bobbi's hips as she writhed on the floor, twisting on her side. Through the sequined panty hose Leal could see some sort of black padded sheath, and spilling from the side of it was the unmistakable bulge of a dick and balls.

"Fucking freak," he said, giving Bobbi a kick in the gut.

He moved to Hart, kneeling beside her as he fished his cell phone out of his inside pocket. The front of her blouse was in shreds, and he could see her breasts and the lacy edges of her bra. She was bleeding so much he couldn't tell how bad the wounds were. But they were bad enough, he knew, as he put an arm around her and dialed *999 on his cell.

What the hell's the address here? he wondered as he waited for the emergency operator to connect.

"Is it bad?" Hart asked.

Shock. He had to keep her from going into shock. "Easy, Ollie. It'll be all right. You're gonna be okay."

She murmured something.

The door pushed open just as the operator came on the line. The hulking security guard stuck his face inside, his mouth gaping.

"What the hell's going on?"

"We need an ambulance," Leal said. "Tell them we have an officer down."

CHAPTER TWENTY-FOUR

Lost In the System

The paramedic holding the IV bag was staring down at the front of Hart's torn blouse. Leal reached over and pulled the white sheet up over her breasts and the guy looked away. The other paramedic pierced a vein on her right forearm and wiped away the trickle of blood as he taped the needle in place.

"No problem finding a vein on her," he said.

"Where you taking her?" Leal asked.

"Augustana's the closest."

"That place good?" Leal asked.

The paramedic nodded.

"She your wife or girlfriend, sir?" the first guy asked as he fastened the glucose bag to the metal clip and adjusted the flow meter.

"She's my partner," Leal said. He held up his badge and realized he still had Hart's purse slung over his shoulder. He lowered the purse to his hand.

"So you gonna ride over with us?"

Leal turned to the uniformed Chicago copper who was standing by the open rear doors.

"Can you guys keep the asshole for me while I see to my partner?"

The cop nodded. Behind him Leal could see Bobbi being shoved none too gently into the back of a squad car.

"We'll take him over to eighteen," the cop said. "I assume you'll want to go felony, right?"

"Fuck, yeah," Leal said. He looked over at Hart again.

"Okay, Sarge, we'll put him in the lockup and the dicks will do a follow-up to the violent crime report."

"Did I mention that we originally wanted to talk to her . . ." Leal stopped and shook his head. He was tired, and feeling it. ". . . him, in connection with a homicide case we're working?"

"No shit? He a suspect?"

Leal shook his head. "Maybe one of his johns is. So can you keep him on ice for me till tomorrow?"

"Not a problem," the copper said. "We'll run his prints, get a rap sheet, have everything for you by the morning when you come back."

Leal nodded a thanks. "Ah, no phone calls?"

"Lost in the system," the copper said, grinning.

"You'll have to ride up front if you want to go with us," the paramedic said.

Leal moved closer to Hart and said, "Ollie, I'm going to take the unmarked over to the ER. I'll be right behind you, okay?"

"Okay, Sarge," she said. "I'll be fine."

He smiled and got out of the ambulance. The siren wailed and the heavy vehicle moved off with an array of flashing lights.

Leal badged his way past the security guards in the emergency room and went into the space where they had Hart. He squeezed her hand slightly and sat down next to her.

"How you doing, kid?"

"I've had better days," she said, holding up her bandaged

arm. The blood was already beginning to seep through the gauze. "Does it look very bad?"

"Not too bad," Leal said. "You'll be all right. I locked your purse in the trunk, by the way."

"Thanks," she said. "You didn't get hurt, did you?"

"No, I'm okay."

"God, she was so strong. I couldn't believe it. It all happened so fast."

"Well, don't feel bad," Leal said. "She wasn't a 'she' at all. She was a 'he.'"

He saw her forehead wrinkle.

"Woman on the top, man on the bottom."

"Oh, my God," said Hart.

He saw a tear roll down her cheek. "It's okay, Ollie. Everything's going to be fine." He patted her head with his left hand and reached for the seam in the curtain with his right. Leal had been in emergency rooms enough times to know they always give you a number and have you wait, no matter where you were. But that's not going to happen in this case, he thought.

"Nurse, I want a doctor over here now," he said, holding up his badge. "We've got an injured police officer."

The nurse looked at him, nodded, and walked away from the cubicle area where she'd been standing. Several other people in the cubicle glared at him, but Leal just stared them down.

Presently a young-looking guy with glasses and reddish hair walked up. The stitching above his left pocket said Dr. Forrester.

He stepped inside the curtain and grabbed the chart.

"Good evening," he said, slipping on some rubber gloves and unwinding the gauze on Hart's arm a bit. "How are you feeling, miss?"

"It's Officer," Leal said.

The doctor looked at Leal. "And you are?"

"Her partner."

A nurse came through the curtain carrying a tray of instruments, a hypodermic syringe, and more rubber gloves.

"Would you mind waiting outside, sir?" she said.

Leal looked at Hart, who nodded and smiled. She squeezed his hand as he left.

"So how's Hart?" Ryan asked on the other end.

Leal, who was standing amid a group of hospital employees taking a smoke break outside the emergency room doors, sighed into the cell phone.

"They had some plastic surgeon who was on call come in to stitch her up," he said. Leal looked down at his jacket and shirt, both of which were covered with dark crimson stains. *God, she lost a lot of blood*, he thought. "They don't think the scarring will be too bad. They're gonna keep her the rest of the night and I'll take her home tomorrow."

"Aha," Ryan said. "I knew it. You're gonna get her to switch back to men, right?"

"Will you knock it off?" Leal said. "You're gonna talk to Brice, right?"

"Of course. Say, Frank," Ryan's voice sounded conspiratorial. "How does this all connect to the Walker case?"

"Bobbi, the pervert, was wanted on a warrant," Leal said. "That's probably why he fought so hard. I won't know much until I can lean on him a little tomorrow, but he was supposed to be one of Walker's associates."

"Okay," Ryan said. "I'll contact the brass in the morning and give 'em a heads-up. Then I'll come by and help you with the interview."

"I'd appreciate that," Leal said. "Me and Bobbi don't exactly have a good rapport."

Bobbi slouched forward, elbows on his knees, smoking a cigarette. He still had on his leather blouse and miniskirt, but was without his wig, and the crew cut, coupled with the mascara, gave him a faintly reptilian cast. The bruise under his left eye was beginning to turn purple. He flicked the ash into the empty paper cup in front of him on the sparse wooden table. No other furniture was in the interview room except for the chairs in which the three of the four sat. Leal paced back and forth by the door.

"So we talking deal, Bobbi?" Steve Megally asked. He was one of the honchos from the State's Attorney's office who had come down personally to handle the interview after Sheriff O'Hara had called. "No goddamn pervert slices up one of *my* officers, much less a female officer, and gets away with it," he'd raved. That's why they'd sent a seasoned pro like Megally, to discuss all the aspects of the case before the interview began.

"Deal?" Leal said. "You got to be kidding." His voice was filled with rising intensity.

"Frank, take it easy," Ryan said, standing up as Leal began moving toward Bobbi from across the room.

Leal halted but continued his tirade.

"That fucking little bastard tried to kill my partner and me, and you're talking a fucking deal? No way."

"Look, Frank," Ryan said. "I know you're upset, but—"

"Upset? I'll show you fucking upset," Leal said, and he lurched forward again as Megally jumped up and helped Ryan hold Leal back. "C'mere, you little piece of shit."

"Keep him away from me," Bobbi said. "I've got rights, you know."

"I'll give you some rights," Leal yelled. His face looked flushed as the other two men struggled to restrain him.

"Easy, big guy," Ryan yelled.

"Get him out of here, Ryan," Megally said. "That's an order."

Leal seemed to deflate a bit, and Ryan walked him to the door.

Leal opened it, poised to leave, but pointed back at Bobbi and said, "I'll find you later, you little fuck."

Bobbi stared at Leal for a moment, and then looked downward. Ryan pushed Leal all the way out and closed the door behind him. He turned to Bobbi, taking out his cigarettes.

"To put it mildly," he said, shaking the pack and holding it toward Megally, who shook his head, and Bobbi, who grabbed one and lit it from the one still smoldering in the ashtray, "you have pissed a lot of people off, to a high degree of pisstasity."

He watched as Bobbi began to hot-box the cigarette.

"Look at it logically, Bobbi," he continued. "Attempted murder of a cop, and a female cop no less. No judge in his right mind is gonna let you off with anything less than the maximum." He paused and took a drag on his own square. "This is, after all, an election year."

"My office would concur," Megally said.

"So we're talking major time here, Bobbi," Ryan said. "Hard time. No good time. In Stateville. For a white boy with big titties and a pretty face, that could be an eternity." He watched Bobbi staring at the tabletop, the smoke trailing out of his dainty nostrils. "You'll be getting butt-fucked by every nigger and Puerto Rican in the joint. You'll be kept property, just something to be passed around."

"So what kind of deal we talking?" Bobbi asked.

Ryan raised his eyebrows and looked at Megally.

"You give us the straight scoop on this Walker guy," Megally said, "and we'll drop the attempt murder and go with one count of agg batt."

"Which translates to what?" Bobbi asked.

"A substantial reduction," Megally said. He looked to Ryan.

"Don't try to fucking jack me off," Bobbi said.

"I wouldn't dream of it," Ryan said. He nodded fractionally to Megally.

"All right, here's our final offer," he said. "As good as it gets. You can plead to felony probation on the agg batt."

Bobbi stared at him. "I can walk with felony paper?"

Megally frowned and nodded. "But what you'll have to trade has got to be the real goods."

"It is," Bobbi said, and bit his upper lip. "Okay, I'll do it. But I want it in writing."

"How about we call in a stenographer?" Megally asked, smiling up at Ryan.

Approximately two and a half hours later, Leal woke up to see Ryan and Megally standing by the coffee machine, laughing and slapping each other on their backs. Leal stood up and stretched, feeling the stiffness of having fallen asleep sitting in a straight-backed chair. He walked over to them.

"So how'd it go?" he asked.

"Great," Ryan said, rubbing his palms together and grinning broadly. "The he-she-it gave us Martin Walker on a silver platter. The fucker's a kink. Likes to have sex with boys, and lately has been preferring them younger and younger."

"That's what Bobbi's been supplying," Megally said. "Mostly runaways."

"And in return," Ryan said, "Old Marty's been giving Bobbi his blow supply."

He dropped some coins in the coffee machine and held his hand out to Leal. "Go ahead, Frank. We couldn't have done it without you."

Leal smirked and pressed the button marked black.

"Thanks," he said.

"No, he's right," Megally said. "If I ever need a bad guy again, I know who to call. You even had me shaking."

Leal removed the cup from under the spout and brought it to his lips.

"Intimidation is my business," he said, before taking a cautious sip.

"And the beauty of it is," Megally said, "we'll keep him remanded until he pleads, at which time we'll also violate his probation for the pandering charge and send him bye-bye to Joliet for two to four." He grinned and pressed the buttons for cream and sugar.

Leal knew that two to four for Bobbi meant he'd probably be out in a year and a half, but a year and a half in Stateville, for someone with his silicon-acquired attributes, would be time in pure hell. If he survived at all.

"Well," Megally said, "I'm going to finish up my file." He shook hands with Ryan and Leal. "Nice working with you two."

After Megally had left, Ryan slapped Leal on the back with a familiarity that made Leal tighten.

"We did it, buddy," Ryan said. "I never in my wildest dreams, thought we would, but we are this close," he held up his thumb and forefinger and narrowed the gap to about a centimeter, "to clearing the Miriam Walker murder case."

"Let's hope so," Leal said.

But he knew he still had to break the news of Bobbi's deal to Hart.

Leal was heading to the hospital elevators when he spotted Rory Chalma, head down, walking slowly toward him. After debating for a split second whether or not to say something, Chalma looked up and stopped.

"Oh, Frank," he said. "Isn't this terrible?"

"How's she doing?"

Chalma swallowed hard and Leal wondered if the man was holding back tears.

"She's a trooper," he said. "I got the feeling that she was just putting on a happy face, though. She said you were coming to take her home."

Leal wondered if that was what had Chalma so upset. Maybe he and Ollie did have something more besides the trainer/protégée relationship.

"Yeah," Leal said. He was about to say that he'd brought

her some new undies and clothes, since hers had been taken as evidence, but thought better of it. No sense pissing this big guy off, if they are seeing each other, he thought, even though Leal had asked the nurse to get Hart's sizes the night before. Him going through her stuff seemed too much like another violation.

"And the doctor was saying no sun," Chalma was saying. "I don't know what we're going to do with the contest coming up. I mean, looking bronzed is half of looking buffed."

Leal nodded as though he'd been following Chalma's line of conversation.

"They say anything about the scarring?" Leal asked.

"Oh, thank God you saw to it that she got proper treatment last night," Chalma said, laying a hand on Leal's forearm. "She said the doctor that stitched her up was a plastic surgeon specialist."

Leal nodded again.

"He said her fair skin usually doesn't scar too badly," Chalma said. He brought his hand to his face, and suddenly looked like he was on the verge of breaking down completely. "I don't know what I'd do if I lost Ollie."

Leal felt almost like patting the man on the shoulder or something, but Chalma mumbled something about having to leave and hurried off. Leal decided to make a quick detour to the hospital gift shop for a minimal bouquet. If Hart was depressed, maybe flowers would cheer her up.

He knocked lightly on the door frame before stepping into her room. She was in the bed closest to the door with the back angled up so she could watch the small TV. Her blond hair was spread over the pillow, and she had a large gauze bandage around her left arm from the wrist to the elbow. A greenish-blue hospital gown and the bedsheets covered the rest of her, but the taut lines of her superb figure were easily discernible.

That Rory's a lucky guy, thought Leal.

Hart looked over and smiled as he came in.

"How you doing, kid?" Leal asked, holding the bouquet behind his back and the bag with the underwear and clothes out in front. "I brought you some clean clothes."

"Oh, thanks, Sarge, but Rory already brought me some things. He just left. I called him after I realized they took my underwear."

"Yeah, I bumped into him downstairs," Leal said, thinking, Rory knows her sizes, huh? "Anyway, I had the nurse check your sizes last night and write them down. I didn't look."

"Like you'd really want to, huh? I'll bet that stuff was terrible. They said I bled like a stuffed pig."

"You," Leal said, bringing the flowers out from behind his back, "could never be a pig."

"Oh, thank you, they're so pretty," she said, grabbing the flowers and smelling the fragrance. She winced slightly as she tried to move her left arm. "Still a little sore. Can you put them in the water pitcher? They told me I could take that."

"Sure," Leal said. "You ready to leave?"

"Am I ever. I just have to wait for the doctor to release me. Shouldn't be too much longer."

"How come Rory didn't wait?" Leal asked, sticking the bouquet into the plastic pitcher. "He got pretty emotional downstairs."

"He did?"

"Yeah, I sensed he really cares about you."

"We've been friends for a long time."

"I think it's more than that," Leal said. "I wouldn't be surprised if this doesn't cause him to pop the question."

"What? Rory?" she said, smiling. "I don't think so."

"Trust me," Leal said. "I've got a feeling about these things. It's a knack."

"Your knack's a bit off in this case."

"I don't think so," Leal teased. "I'm seldom wrong about reading people."

"You are in this case," she said. Then, lowering her voice to a whisper, "He's gay. And he has a partner."

"Him? With those arms? I was worried he'd break me in half downstairs if he found out I was bringing you underwear."

"I'm not sure he would have approved," she said. "But for purely professional reasons. He thinks you and I are having an affair, and that it's messing up my training. It was all I could do to convince him you weren't interested in getting into my pants."

Leal felt his mouth drop open and he couldn't think of anything to say. The thoughts of what it might be like "getting into her pants" flashed through his mind, and so did a picture of Rory. He tried to blank out both images. Fortunately the doctor saved him from having to speak, and he went down the hall to the nurse's station for a cup of coffee. When he came back, the doctor was just leaving.

"Are you a relative?" the doctor asked, pausing.

"Her partner."

The other man nodded. "Well, she's getting dressed now. See to it that she rests for a day or two. I don't want those stitches to get popped loose."

Leal said he would, and knocked on the door again. Hart pulled open the curtain and told him she was going to need one of the female nurses to help her get dressed.

"Okay, I'll get one," Leal said. He paused. "So what did the doc say?"

"That I'll have to stay out of the sun for at least a year, and hold off on my workouts until the cuts heal," she said. "But since I'm in such great shape, it shouldn't take too long."

"That's good, right?"

He saw her bite her lower lip.

"What?" he asked.

"I'm worried about the scars," she said. A couple of tears rolled down her face and she quickly wiped them away. "Can I have a hug?"

"Hey, sure," he said, moving forward because it seemed like the natural thing to do, but it felt like he was holding a greyhound. She was all solid muscle on top of muscle, and suddenly his hands were moving over the bare skin of her back. He immediately stopped to move away, but didn't. She made no move, either. "You're pretty fair-skinned, and everybody knows that fair-skinned people don't scar much." He patted her back lightly and she seemed to relax a bit. As they parted he suddenly dreaded having to tell her about Bobbi's deal on the way home. How's she gonna react to that? "Don't worry, you'll still be gorgeous."

"Oh, Sarge, you're such a shmoozer."

"I think it's about time you started calling me Frank," he said. We'll see about the other on the ride home.

CHAPTER TWENTY-FIVE

The Games People Play

The sunlight streamed in through the windows of Brice's office as he leaned back in his chair and ran a hand over his oily hair.

"Okay, we went over everything with the state's attorney this morning," he said. "Here's our game plan."

Leal, Ryan, and Smith leaned forward attentively.

"Nobody's seen Martin Walker for two days. He ain't been at work, and he's not answering his phone at home. I got a surveillance team on both places, the house and the River North apartment he was renting. In addition, his picture's on the Chicago Daily Bulletin under a pick-up order, and we got a type-three message in LEADS."

Ryan took out his pack of cigarettes and held them up.

"You mind, boss?"

Brice waved his hand nonchalantly, and patted his own pocket for a cigar. He bit off the end and spat it into the wastebasket. Leaning forward, he held the end of the cigar into the flame of Ryan's lighter and puffed a few times before continuing.

"This morning we get those warrants all squared away," he said. "After we get 'em set, we hit the apartment first, then his house, then the office. We're going step by step on this one building our case. You see anything suspicious in either location, anything relating to the Miriam Walker homicide, we're gonna have evidence technicians with us to process." He blew out a cloud of smoke.

Leal pushed back in his chair and away from Ryan as well, thinking, It's a good thing Ollie isn't here.

"In the meantime," Brice continued, "if Walker gets picked up, we'll let him sweat it out."

"What if he lawyers up?" Leal asked.

"What if he does?" Brice said, grinning. "We'll just tell him we'll put him in a bullpen with a bunch of guys named Bubba. Then we can spring the real kinky shit on him during the interview. He'll crack." He pointed the two fingers holding the cigar at Leal. "How's Hart doing?"

"She's all right," Leal said. His thoughts drifted back to the quiet car ride when he told her how the deal with Bobbi had played out. The silent tears splashing down her face, her not wanting him to see, and him not wanting to let her know he saw them. Her stoic attitude to go along with the deal for "the sake of the investigation." Man, she had grit, he thought. "She just needs some rest."

Brice nodded. "Yeah, tell her to take a couple of days off. Undersheriff Lucas is already talking about presenting her with some kind of award. Maybe even the Medal of Valor." He paused to draw on the cigar again.

"The Medal of Valor?" Ryan said. "Christ, all she did was get herself cut up."

"Hey," Leal said, "you weren't there."

"Take it easy, you two." Brice clasped his hands behind his head and leaned back, the embers of the cigar glowing. "Maybe the award isn't totally called for in this case, but it is an election year."

"And this'll score with the female voters," Ryan said. He smirked.

Leal was boiling, but decided to keep his mouth shut. As

far as he was concerned, Hart deserved the medal. He remembered how, cut and bleeding, she'd still managed to snare Bobbi's foot and trip him after the pervert had delivered the ball-busting kick. Probably saved me from getting my throat slashed, he thought.

"So, anyway, that's our game plan," Brice said. "Any questions?"

"What about getting a subpoena for a credit check and his phone records?" Leal asked. He gave a quick surreptitious wink to Smith. "Maybe see if he's been using his credit cards, too. If he's on the lam, he's got to be leaving a trail."

"Good idea," Brice said. He brought the cigar away from his mouth and exhaled a large cloud of smoke. "Yeah, that's a real good idea about the credit cards. Find out all his recent transactions." He tapped some ash into the tray, and leaned forward, placing his hands on his desk. "I know this has been a difficult case, a cold case, but you've all done a good job. I'm proud of you. So now we can afford to coast a little today, take our time doing the subpoenas and getting the warrants prepared."

Huh? Leal thought. Now was the time to kick it in gear. To really push it.

Brice grinned. "We also got to come up with a plausible explanation of why it's taken so long to crack this one. In case the press demands it."

Just tell them you were in charge of the investigation, Leal thought. He smiled.

Brice glared at him, as if reading Leal's thoughts.

"Something funny, Leal?"

"Nope, just considering plausible explanations, Lieu," Leal said. At this stage of the game, he didn't want to risk locking horns with the lieutenant and get kicked off. Not when they were this close to clearing a major case.

"I'm pulling Murphy out of investigations to replace Hart," Brice said. "He'll be available to give you a hand."

"Hey, wait a minute," Leal said. "I think Hart deserves to be in on this."

Brice shook his head. "She's out on sick leave, remember? Everything can't come to a stop while we wait for her to get better. Plus Murph worked the case before, and he's familiar with it. I think he's a good choice."

Yeah, he worked it before and fucked it up, Leal thought. He knew there was no way he was going to let Hart get excluded from this one. Not after all she'd been through.

"Anyway, that's my decision, and it's not open to debate." Brice continued staring at Leal for a few more seconds, then got up and went to the window. "Great looking day, ain't it? Pretty soon it'll be hunting season." He raised an imaginary shotgun toward the sky and made a sound mimicking a gunshot. Leal rolled his eyes and saw Ryan's face contorting to stifle a laugh. Quickly averting his eyes from Ryan, so as not to break out laughing, Leal focused on the family picture on Brice's desk. The blond woman and Brice flanked by two boys who looked like scaled-down versions of their father: bull-faced, thick-necked, and stocky. The picture was obviously several years old, judging from the clothes and Brice's face, and Leal wondered which kid it was causing the problems now. The younger of the two had on a pair of thick glasses that made his eyes seem unusually large. Too bad they didn't have the kid take them off for the picture, he thought.

"Okay," Brice said, turning. "Get to work putting the finishing touches on everything. I want a thorough search at each place, especially for drugs, in view of what that pervert told us. What's the story with him, anyway?"

"They're handling the bond hearing this morning," Ryan said. "The state's attorney's gonna ask for a high bond so we can keep the asshole on ice at the jail without a chance for an I-Bond in case we need him. We can send Hart down to the grand jury and get an indictment before the prelim." He laughed. "The sorry fucker's already gloating over the plea bargain agreement we handed him. Wait till he finds out they're violating his probation. He'll be keeping them standing in line in the jail."

"Just wait till he gets to Stateville," Leal said.

"Yeah," Ryan said. "He'll really get it in the end there."

Brice laughed, too. Leal took a deep breath.

"One other thing's bothering me, Lieu," he said. "Martin Walker seemed to have a solid alibi for the night of the murder. That means he didn't act alone."

"We don't really know that," Brice said. "Plus, that's the purpose of sweating him once we get him into an interrogation setting. He'll crack. Maybe we'll ask him to take a polygraph test."

Yeah, right, Leal thought. But he had to admit that he was optimistic about breaking Walker in an interview. And he wanted to get the chance.

"We got him by the balls," Brice said, holding up his big hand and flexing it. "Soon as we get him, we start squeezing. He'll flip and spill his guts."

"Think we'll be able to find him?" Smith asked.

"He'll turn up sooner or later," Brice said. "Just a matter of time. Anyway, the prick ran, and that shows his guilt. We had a high-profile case, and we got it solved for all practical purposes, at a crucial time. That's what really counts."

"Maybe we'll all get on Most Wanted," Ryan said.

"There's another thing," Leal said. "Where was Walker getting his dope from? That person might be involved."

Brice shook his head. "You're not working MEG anymore, Leal. Forget about the small stuff. This is the big leagues now. A whole different ball game."

Leal stifled his response, figuring again, it was better to keep his mouth shut than to risk getting tossed off over some bullshit argument.

"Okay," Brice said. "You guys know what you have to do. Let's get to it."

"So how do your buddies feel about you sneaking off to have lunch with me while they do all the work?" Sharon asked, sipping her iced tea.

"It's about time they did some of the work." Leal grinned. "Actually, Ryan encouraged me to come here. He's having someone type everything up, and I told him Smith already did the credit check, so he could walk him through it."

"Really? What did he say to that? Ryan hates blacks, right?"

Leal nodded. "He said, 'You know, maybe I was wrong about him.'" Leal shook his head. "I said, 'Maybe you were wrong about a lot of things.'"

Sharon smiled.

"Well, I'm just glad you're going through the proper procedures this time," she said. "Just in case I end up in private practice and have to defend Walker."

"You wouldn't do that, would you?" He was being playful.

Sharon sort of half smiled, then set her drink down. The waitress came by and asked if everything was all right.

"Yeah," Leal said, but he was suddenly sensing that everything wasn't. I don't like the way she's looking at me, he thought. When they were alone again, he asked, "What's up?"

Sharon reached over and touched his hand, her eyes staring at the tabletop. "Something came up. A real good opportunity for me. In private practice. Big prestigious law firm, lots of money. But . . ." She sighed. "It's in New York."

"New York?"

"Yeah. I have an interview there tomorrow." She looked at him. "Feinstein and Royale."

"Huh?"

"That's the name of the firm. Feinstein and Royale."

"Oh." It was all he could think of to say.

"My ex-supervisor, Steve Megally, he's a friend of Mr. Feinstein's son. He set up the interview for me."

"Sounds pretty important," Leal said. On the inside he was doing his best to hold that churning feeling in his stomach in check.

She rubbed her fingers over his hand. "So I just wanted to tell you. I'm not sure what's going to happen, and . . ." The sentence trailed off.

He tried to smile.

"I mean, it's double what I'm making here, and the opportunity is so good," she said. "On the other hand, I do like being a prosecutor, and I might even have a chance at a judgeship, somewhere down the road. And things have been nice with us, too." Her fingertips traced over his hand again. "You're not saying anything. Talk to me. Tell me what you think."

"It sounds," he said slowly, "like a great opportunity." Leal was still feeling the pinch way down in his gut. Why is it as soon as I meet somebody really special, he thought, they end up getting taken away from me? "As far as us, I like you a lot, but I don't want to stand in your way. We haven't got any strings on each other. But I would miss you if you left."

She squeezed his hand.

"What time are you leaving?" he asked.

"This afternoon. I want to get there early so I'm fresh for the interview in the morning. New York's an hour ahead of us."

He looked at his watch.

"You need a ride to the airport?"

"No," she said. "My sister's taking me. But maybe I'll call you for a ride when I get back. I'll be there tonight and Friday. Coming back Saturday night."

Leal made an attempt at a smile.

"Well, I guess I should say good luck, then." And goodbye, too, he thought.

CHAPTER TWENTY-SIX

No False Moves

The apartment proved to be a mixed bag. It was on the top floor of one of those stylish brick buildings that proliferated on the North Side. Leal, Ryan, and Smith showed up with a legion of county cops, evidence technicians, and a K-9 officer. Martin Walker was not there, the landlord said. The guy had been renting it for the past year, only his name wasn't Walker, it was Brian Tubbs.

"He left me alone and paid his rent on time," the old man said, looking at the picture. "What do I care what name he used? He wasn't there much, anyway."

"How about this person?" Leal asked, showing him a mug shot of the battered Bobbi with his wig.

"Yeah, she's been here, too," the landlord said. "Looks like she has some lumps there."

"Man, you don't know the half of it," Ryan said, grinning from ear to ear. "Now, all we ask is that you open the door for us. Otherwise, we'll do it ourselves." He pointed to Smith, who was holding a big sledgehammer.

"Okay," the old man said, "but that dog's not going to pee on anything, is he?" He looked down at the large German shepherd sitting on the landing, panting.

"The dog's completely housebroken, sir," the K-9 officer said.

"Believe me, compared with your tenant, he's a real sweetheart," Leal said.

The old man grunted and pulled his passkey from the loop on his belt. It unlocked the bottom door lock, but not the top dead bolt. "That's funny," he said.

"How long since you've done an inspection?" Leal asked.

The old man scratched his chin, and shrugged.

Smith frowned and gently moved the old man away from the door. He swung the hammer with a pivoting motion that made a sharp cracking sound when it hit just below the lock, and the door swung inward.

All the rooms were checked and photographed. The dog alerted on several places, but no substantive amounts of drugs were found. They did find a scale and a quantity of Pony-Pak rolling papers along with some crack-baking supplies.

"Bobbi told us he'd been expanding their product a bit," Ryan said, directing the ET to photograph and tag the stuff.

What they found next bothered them more so, although it, too, had been described by Bobbi. Several kiddie-porn movies and a VCR, along with a Polaroid camera, were in a cabinet in the bedroom, along with a stack of stoned-looking young boys masturbating and performing fellatio. From the background in the photos, it was apparent that the pictures had been taken in the bedroom. Some of the photos had obviously been taken by one of the participants, a flabby middle-aged white male.

"That son of a bitch," Leal said.

"More fuel for the fire," Ryan said, handing the stack to an ET with an evidence bag. He snapped at his latex gloves after he dropped the photos. "Makes me still feel like washing my hands, you know?"

"Really," Leal said. "If I find him, he's going down hard."

"The way it looks, we'll probably be figuring out who we want to play us on *Most Wanted*," Ryan said.

"I want Eddie Murphy to play me," Smith said. "Him or Laurence Fishburne. How 'bout you, Sarge?"

Leal shrugged.

"I've been told I resemble Tom Selleck," Ryan said. "But he hasn't been doing much lately. Maybe somebody more popular."

"Gain a few pounds and we'll see if Drew Carey is busy," Leal said. Smith laughed, and Ryan smirked. It was the first time Leal could remember that the three of them had shared a light moment together.

"Okay," Ryan said, imitating John Wayne. "Looks like this little fracas is about over." He went back to his regular voice as he took out his cell phone. "The state's attorney wanted us to check with him before we hit the house to review anything new that we might want on the warrant." He began dialing.

"What about the office?" Leal asked.

"We can do that next," Ryan said. "All we're looking for there are copies of his records. We got some dudes from Financial Crimes to do most of that one. They know what to look for." He put his hand over the receiver. "The boss wants to come along when we hit the house."

"Look," Leal said, "why don't you guys finish up here. I gotta go outside and make a call."

"Got a hot date?" Ryan asked. "With Sharon Divine?"

The comment stung, but Leal just replied, "No, I told Hart I'd call and give her a heads-up after we were done."

Leal was just on the verge of disconnecting when Hart finally answered. He figured her caller ID had identified him, because she answered with a, "Hi, Frank, how did it go?"

"We just got finished sorting through the apartment. About what we expected."

"Did he have a lot of kiddie porn?" she asked hesitantly.

"Yeah, including some homemade shit. Polaroids."

"What a creep. I hope I can be there when we nail him good."

Leal hoped that, too, and debated telling her about Brice's decision to bring Murphy into the picture.

"What took you so long to answer the phone?" he asked instead.

"I just got out of the bathtub," she said. "The doctor said I could do some light exercise, so I went for a walk. Then I have this special ointment that's supposed to minimize any scarring. What a trip trying to put that on my back."

"Need any help?" Leal said.

"Oh, yeah, right," she said, her tone light.

It's good to hear her laugh, at least, Leal thought.

"So what's your next move?" she asked.

"We've got the warrants all set. Financial Crimes is going to the office with us and we'll grab all the records we can. Then we'll hit his house."

"Wish I could be there for that."

"Yeah, me, too," he said. "But I do have some other good news."

"What?"

"You've been nominated for an award for pinching Bobbi and helping break open the case. Undersheriff Lucas will be contacting you. And," he purposely waited, "it just might be the Medal of Valor."

He waited for her to say something. "Ollie?"

"You're kidding, right?"

"No, why?"

Leal looked up to see Ryan, Smith, and a host of others coming out of the apartment, Ryan grinning at him and pantomiming kissing into a mock telephone.

"Look, Ollie, I have to go. But don't worry, I'll call you later and give you a heads-up, okay?"

Ryan slapped Leal on the back and said, "Time to go, Frankie, unless you want to keep making time with your girlfriend."

"I got to go," Leal said.

"I heard him," Hart said. "Good luck, and be careful, Frank."

"You, too, kid," he said, hoping she'd get through this all right. But then he reflected a moment more and figured she would. She has cojones. He smiled at the thought. In a figurative sense, she's got 'em.

Ryan called on the tac frequency for Leal to meet him at the small ice cream shop that was about half a mile from Walker's house. Orders were that they were supposed to use that as a staging area, and when Leal pulled up he saw a line of perhaps a dozen squads parked along the road, with all the coppers standing there eating ice cream cones. He spied Ryan and Smith sitting in some wire chairs under a large umbrella on the back patio.

Ryan grinned at him and licked at an immense cone of tutti fruiti.

"Have a double-decker, on me, Frankie," he said as Leal walked across the street.

"What kind of bullshit is this?" Leal asked. He nodded a hello to Smith.

"Orders," Ryan said, dabbing at his mustache. "The boss called. Doesn't want us to go in yet."

"Why's that?"

Ryan grinned again. "Because he wants to be in on the entry team."

"Great. And when the fuck will that be?"

"Relax, Frankie." He rolled his tongue around the side of the cone. "We got a surveillance team on the house."

"How do you know they aren't out having ice cream, too?" Leal said, sitting down in a huff.

Ryan snapped his fingers and a young girl dressed in a white shirt with an embroidered horse on it came over.

"Please get my friend here one of these," he said, holding up his cone. He made a show of reaching in his pocket for his wallet, removing a five, and winking. "And I'll need a receipt, too, please."

The girl hurried off and Leal said, "Don't you think she's a little bit too young for you?"

"Hey, old enough to bleed, old enough to breed, I always say."

Leal frowned, thinking of his own daughters and hoping that they never met someone like Ryan. He took out his notebook and a pen and placed it on the table.

"All right, as long as we're here fucking off," he said, "we might as well do some planning."

"What's to plan?" Ryan said. "We hit the house and break down his front door."

"Uh-uh," said Leal. "We'll do it MEG style." He drew a quick diagram of the house, and made notations where he wanted each officer to go in. Then he checked in with the surveillance team, asking if they saw any activity.

"Negative, Sarge," came the reply.

"All right," Leal said, turning to Smith. "Joe, you and I will go into together, all right? Our objective is to get to the bathroom as quickly as possible in case Walker is home."

Smith nodded, smiling. "So nothing gets flushed, right?"

"With a two-level house like that," Leal continued, "you can't rule out a bathroom on the lower level as well. If it is there, it'll probably be right below the one upstairs."

"And how do we know where that one is?" Ryan asked.

"Simple, you just look for the standpipe coming out of the roof."

Ryan raised his eyebrows. "I can see your time in narcotics really sharpened you up."

Leal glanced at his watch and frowned.

"Why the hell does Brice want to be on the entry team?"

Ryan shrugged. "Maybe he misses it, being saddled to a

desk all day. The LT is a hands-on type of guy, though. I know this for a fact."

"Oh yeah?" Leal said.

"I remember being with him on a barricaded suspect call once," Ryan said. "He was the sergeant and I was still a patrolman. This asshole barricaded himself in this trailer in Stickney. Every once in a while he'd peek out with a rifle. Hadn't fired it, but he'd threatened a couple of people." He licked some more of the ice cream cone.

"So we got this fucking trailer surrounded, see, and this candy-ass lieutenant, who didn't know his butt from a hole in the ground, is running the show, trying to talk this guy out with a bullhorn. The guy keeps giving him the finger, and the lieutenant is getting madder and madder. Meanwhile, they got the old thirty-seven millimeter gas gun all ready to go, but the lieutenant's afraid to make a decision."

"Sounds typical," Leal said, thinking of Brice.

"Anyway, Brice is off to my left behind a squad, and next to me is this rookie, been on the street only a couple of weeks." Ryan paused to grin. "This kid calls over and asks Brice what he should do, 'cause he has to take a shit real bad. Only he's saying he has to go 'number two.' Now by this time, it was getting a little bit dark, and I'm thinking that we're probably gonna be there all fucking night, when Brice tells the kid to just go squat in the bushes and take a crap." Ryan swirled the cone against his tongue. "'Just squat down there,' Brice tells him. So just when the rookie drops his pants, old Brice whips a rock over at the kid's squad and says, 'Look out, he's got a silencer.'"

Ryan paused to laugh, and Leal and Smith were chuckling, too.

"But the kid had his shotgun propped up next to him and grabs for it, and the thing discharges into the air. Well, the lieutenant thinks we're under fire and finally gives the command to use the gas. The kid wound up with pants full of shit, and the poor dumb asshole had to dive through a glass window 'cause he'd barricaded the doors to the place."

"I think I remember hearing about that," Leal said. "Wasn't there a fire, too?"

"Yeah," said Ryan. "The fucking trailer burned down. Man, those things go up like Christmas trees. But I did learn one thing. If you have to go, go now, or forever hold your pants."

"And your shotgun," Leal said.

The waitress reappeared with Leal's cone. She dropped the receipt and change in Ryan's hand and Leal was just about to take a bite when he heard one of the other officers say, "Hiya, boss."

"What the hell is this? A goddamned party?" Brice's gruff voice carried over to them. "Doesn't anybody do any real police work anymore?"

Ryan and Smith stood up quickly and dumped their cones in the trash. Ryan then grabbed the one from Leal and dumped that one also.

Brice walked up to them and glared.

"This a fucking Sunday social?" he said.

"We were waiting on you, boss," Ryan said. "Figured the men could use a little break."

"Listen," Brice said. "When I run an operation, it's done by the book. No false moves."

Leal glanced obliquely at Ryan, who still had some vestiges of pink ice cream on his mustache.

"Everybody in position?" Brice asked.

"Roger that," Ryan said. "We were just going over the house diagram."

Brice stared at him a moment more, then raised his radio to his lips. "This is Lieutenant Brice. Get in position. We'll move on my command."

They went to their vehicles and slipped on the Kevlar vests with *POLICE* printed in white block letters across the front and back. Everyone was grimly silent as they drove up to the adjacent houses, which in this neighborhood were a good fifty yards away. Cutting across lawns on foot, they moved to the far side of the evergreen shrubs along Martin Walker's driveway, then strode quickly to the front door. Brice opened the screen door, and rang the doorbell. "Police," he yelled. "Search warrant." He motioned to Smith who was holding the sledgehammer. Smith set his feet and slammed the hammer into the solid oak door as though he was swinging for the fences. The door buckled and slammed inward.

"Police," yelled Leal as he went through the door. He and Smith made a quick but cautious trek to the upstairs bathroom and listened as, one by one, the rooms were cleared. At the end it was apparent that they'd hit still another empty house.

"Now what?" Smith asked as they stood in the confines of the bathroom.

Leal looked around, popping open the medicine cabinet. "We'll let the dog do his stuff, and the ETs. Maybe we'll find something, but I think this dude felt the heat and booked up days ago."

Smith nodded. "If only we'd moved quicker."

"No false moves," Leal said, placing a hand on the other man's shoulder. "Remember?"

Brice surprised everybody by finding four folded packets of cocaine in the top dresser drawer in the master bedroom and spotting a counterfeit soft drink can with a hinged top with more drugs in the kitchen. One of the ETs did a quick field test before bagging and tagging it. They watched as he broke the sequential glass cylinders and the resulting liquid turned a bright blue.

"Looks pretty pure," Leal said.

"Great," Brice said. "We got that fucker by the balls, now. All we gotta do is wait till he's picked up."

Leal went to the living room and wanted to look around, trying to remember how the room looked the night he and Hart were there. Something was different, but he couldn't place it. But in the dim lighting and with the drapes drawn, he couldn't see much.

"Hey, Sarge," one the ETs called from the center of the room. Look at this." He swung a black light in an arc over the rug and two spots glowed. "Know what this looks like?"

Leal grunted. He knew all right. It looked like blood.

CHAPTER TWENTY-SEVEN
Heart-to-Heart Conversations

Leal had tried to call Sharon again after he'd gotten home. It was after seven, and the weight of the exceptionally long day was starting to wear on him. He'd popped a beer, ate some chicken, and settled down in front of the TV. He looked at his clock. Nine thirty-five. That meant ten thirty-five in New York. No sense calling her this late, especially when she had to get up early. Maybe she'd shut off her phone. Maybe that's why there had been no answer on either of his previous calls.

He decided to drink another beer to celebrate the successful completion of the search warrants. Man, they were really close to cracking this one. The biggest case of his career.

Too bad I don't have anyone to share it with right now, he thought.

He leaned back as the ten o'clock news came on. No word about the Walker case, he noted, suddenly wondering when he was going to see the new commercial he was in. He closed his eyes just for a minute as the weatherman talked about some storms possibly moving this way. The next thing he knew when he opened them it was two in the morning and the television was playing some old movie. Getting up, he felt incredibly stiff and sore, especially his neck. After shuffling to the bathroom to urinate, he tossed his clothes off and went straight to bed.

The sound of the alarm at six thirty brought the dull pain in his head bubbling to the surface. It felt like someone had used his temples for an anvil. Even the steady stream of hot water from the shower did little to alleviate it. Black coffee and aspirin for breakfast helped a little, but on the drive in he regretted not eating something more substantial. When he walked in the office he found a bright-eyed Smith pinning up all the search warrant photos from each respective location on the bulletin board.

"Ryan called," Smith said. "He's running late."

At least somebody feels worse than I do, Leal thought. He sat at his desk.

"Man, Sarge, you look terrible. Want some coffee?" As Smith poured the coffee he gestured toward the board.

"Those were developed last night," he said. "They put a rush on them."

Leal looked at each one of the pictures, sipping his coffee and suddenly recalling the uneasy feeling he'd had the day before in Walker's living room. They'd found tapes and DVDs in the television cabinet, but no tape player on the shelf. Only twin wires hanging down behind it. It could have meant that Walker had taken it in for repairs. After all, he had another VHS player in the bedroom. But there was something else that still bothered him, something else missing, but he couldn't put his finger on it. He searched his memory for the sight of the room the night he and Hart had visited Walker.

He sipped the coffee that Smith had prepared and together they looked at the rest of the photos.

Leal tapped the photo of the bedroom.

"Here's something else that bugs me," he said. "No pillowcase."

Smith rubbed his forehead.

"Maybe he put it in the wash?"

Leal frowned. "That's something we should've checked. Too late now." He studied the photo some more. "But look at this, Joe. Nothing else is out of place. Even the tapes here are evenly stacked."

"Yeah, his drawers were lined up inside, too. No wonder he fired his housekeeper."

Leal grinned. The second cup of coffee was starting to do the trick.

"So what do you make of it?" Smith asked.

Leal shook his head. "Don't know yet."

The door opened and Ryan walked in holding his head. He virtually collapsed in his chair and said, "Oooh, fuck me."

Smith got up and poured a cup of coffee for Ryan, putting in extra cream and sugar. He handed it to him and said, "Here, Sarge."

"Thanks, Joe," Ryan said, still holding his head. "Brice wants to see us. He wants us to bring Murphy up to speed today."

"No fucking way," Leal said. "He's trying to close Hart out of this investigation, and I'm not standing for it."

"Right. She deserves to be in to the end," Smith said.

"All right, all right," Ryan said, rubbing his temples. "Let me talk to him. As soon as I have this coffee."

As Ryan, the master of compromise, sat in Brice's office he felt as if the pounding in his head would never stop, but he knew neither would Leal's bitching if Hart got dropped. Maybe he *was* jocking her. Regardless, on the way up the stairs, Ryan had decided on a tactic that he felt would work. First, he brought up that Smith's wife was ready to drop any day now, and Murphy would be needed to replace him more than Hart, who was expected back soon.

"Smith's been holding his vacation so he can stay home with her and the kid," Ryan said.

"You look like shit," Brice said. "What's the matter? Somebody piss in your beer last night?"

Ryan smirked. "Wouldn't surprise me. And don't forget there's also the publicity mileage that the sheriff will get when he presents our esteemed female detective with the Medal of Valor."

"Yeah, but the only problem is, she looks so much like a guy," Brice said, snickering. He took out a cigar and bit off the end. "I'll tell Murph to sit tight for another day or two. In the meantime, start checking around. Maybe Walker flew out of O'Hare or Midway. We got a subpoena for his credit card records, right?"

"Yeah, boss. And he's got a safety deposit box, too. We gotta go through his papers more and take the list of stuff recovered back to the judge."

"Okay, get to work on that, then." Brice took out his lighter and held the flame to the end of the cigar. "You still sitting here?"

Ryan slowly got to his feet.

At the United counter at O'Hare Airport, Leal and Ryan managed to pull the clerk off to the side, much to the chagrin of her coworkers, who struggled to address the constant flow of people in front of them.

"Now this is very important, miss," Ryan said. "Would you recognize this man if you saw him again?"

The airline clerk's eyes widened as she shook her head. "You know, we get so many people through here . . ."

Leal showed her the passenger list that the Chicago PD detective from the O'Hare detail had found on last Tuesday's departures for San Juan.

Ryan held the picture of Martin Walker.

"Ring any bells?" he asked.

Her eyes narrowed again as she scanned the photograph.

"I'm sorry," she said, drawing back her lower lip nervously, "but I really can't be sure."

"That's okay, honey," Ryan said, giving her shoulder a reassuring pat. "What did you say your first name was?"

"Elena."

"Okay, what's your home phone number?" Ryan asked, his pen poised above his notebook. "You know, this might be on *Most Wanted*. I know John Walsh real good. You done any modeling, or anything?"

As they walked away, Leal shook his head. "You know, Ryan, if you spent half as much time working as you do trying to get laid . . ."

"Yeah, I know, I'd be a captain by now," Ryan said, grinning. "But you can't blame me for trying. After all, I don't have Sharon Divine waiting to tuck me in at night, now, do I?"

Neither do I, thought Leal. "How'd you like a size twelve up your ass?"

"Not me. I'm a lover, not a fighter." Ryan smiled. "Come on, let's go fill the boss in. Who knows, maybe he'll send us to Puerto Rico."

"Yeah, right," Leal said.

"The clerk remembers the guy. He tried to cancel the ticket on his MasterCard and pay for it with cash," Ryan said. "But she wasn't sure about the picture, though."

Brice nodded. "Anything else?"

"No recent transactions beyond the ticket," Ryan said. "Looks like he's switched to cash to avoid a trail."

"There is something the lab boys came up with, Lieu," Smith said. "That section of carpet where they found the bloodstains was inconclusive. Definitely blood, but someone tried to wash it."

"Yeah, I figured it would just be trace amounts," Brice said. "No way to know how old it was, either, but it would've been nice to be able to match it up to Miriam Walker."

"They also found a small shred of chewing tobacco with the vacuuming," Smith said.

"Was Walker a dipper?" asked Ryan.

"I doubt it," Leal said. "He was too much of a city rat for a habit like that. Are they sure it didn't come from a cigarette?"

"I asked the same thing," Smith said. "They said they're positive it came from a wad."

"Maybe they'll be able to get some DNA traces," Leal said.

"You got the subpoenas for the credit card records and the warrant for the safe-deposit box, right?" Brice asked. He rubbed the bridge of his nose.

"Right, Lieu," Smith said, setting the stack of papers on Brice's desk. "You want to look them over?"

Brice nodded.

"What about his phone records?" Leal asked.

Brice considered this for a moment, then said, "Yeah, Monday's soon enough for them. You guys been working pretty hard on this, so just take the rest of the weekend off. Keep your cell phones and beepers on in case he gets picked up."

He seems to be falling back into his old, lazy habits, Leal thought. Now was the time to push. They were close.

After the meeting broke up Ryan went downstairs to check on his lady love, and Leal and Smith walked slowly back to their office.

"You find out anything on that credit check, Joe?"

Smith grinned and shook his head.

"I was beginning to wonder if you were going to ask me about that." He pulled a list of printed numbers from his inside pocket. "No missed payments, the usual credit card stuff, mortgage on the house, leased car for business expenses. Nothing to indicate he was hurting financially."

Leal sighed. "Well, we never figured greed was the motive, did we?"

"I also called the credit card companies and asked them to monitor his numbers for any new transactions."

"Good thinking," Leal said. "They gonna do it?"

Smith smiled. "Some told me they'd do what they could, but a couple pretty much said they couldn't do anything without a court order."

"Typical," Leal said. "We'll have to move and get an indictment against this guy sooner rather than later. Don't know why Brice is slowing up again. It's like he loses focus."

"Well, at least we got those type-three's out," Smith said.

"Yeah. Joe, you take care. You've done a lot of good work on this one. And good luck if this is the weekend for the baby."

Smith smiled again. "If it ain't, we gonna go in for a C-section. I'm tired of waiting. Something better happen soon."

There was still no answer, but he let the phone continue to ring. Finally, the hotel operator came back on and asked if he'd like to leave a voice-mail message. Leal muttered a few words about wondering how the interview went, and ended with, "Call me if you have a chance. I should be home."

Yeah, where else am I going to go at seven o'clock on Friday night? he wondered.

After he hung up, Leal's mind continued to play twenty questions. It was eight in New York, right? So where the hell was she? But was it any of his business? They weren't, after all, anything more than casual lovers at this point. No strings . . . Wasn't that what he'd told her? When the phone rang it jarred him out of his reverie, and his heart leapt, hoping it was her.

"Frank? It's Ollie," the voice at the other end said. "I hope I'm not bothering you."

"What? No, not at all. I was just deep in thought."

"That sounds interesting," she said. "About the case?"

"Ahh, yeah. Sort of. What's up?"

"Well, I thought you were going to call me and give me a heads-up?"

It suddenly dawned on him that he had promised that.

"Sorry," he said. "Actually, there isn't much to report. Brice seems to have taken a slowdown."

"Are you kidding me? I figured now would be the time to push."

"Yeah, me, too." His voice sounded listless, even to him.

"Are you going out or anything?"

"No, just sitting in the dark, contemplating a TV dinner."

"Well, why don't you come over?" she said. "I'm going stir crazy in here doing nothing and I've fixed way too much food as a result."

What if Sharon calls? he thought. But then again, why not? He couldn't shake the sinking feeling that his days, and nights, with Sharon had most probably come to an end. Especially after this New York deal.

"I'll be right over," he said. "Need me to bring anything?"

"Just yourself. And a hearty appetite, of course."

It was the first time he'd actually been up to Hart's apartment and he was struck both by its neatness and feminine simplicity. Her living room had a large couch with a floral slipcover, two chairs and a coffee table. Several vases with bouquets of flowers sat on each end of the table and on another smaller table by the window. Next to it was a framed eight-by-ten picture of Hart in a black posing bikini, wearing a large gold medal. Her muscles in the photograph gleamed like polished marble.

"Everybody from the gym sent me flowers," she said, smiling and directing him to the kitchen. "I hope Rocky leaves them alone." She indicated a large tiger-colored cat curled up in a corner of the sofa. The cat regarded Leal for a few moments then went back to sleep.

Leal sat at a circular wooden table with a lazy Susan in the middle. Hart set a dish and silverware in front of him, along with a glass.

"I hope you don't mind cranberry juice to drink," she said. "Otherwise, I can make you some coffee."

"No," Leal said, taking a sip. "This is fine."

The meal consisted of steamed rice, vegetables, and a whole wheat muffin. Leal kept waiting for the main course, then suddenly realized there wasn't one.

"Is there any butter for this muffin?" he asked.

She shook her head, chewing and holding up her hand. He'd noticed before that she chewed everything forever and a day, mixing it thoroughly with saliva, she'd told him.

"Sorry, I can't have any dairy products until after the contest," she said. "I don't keep them here so I won't be tempted." She smiled. "But what I wouldn't give for an ice-cream sundae right about now."

Leal raised his eyebrows, impressed with her dedication, but still wishing he had some butter.

Hart smiled and asked him if he was ready for dessert.

"Sure," he said. Not realizing that the sliced apple she was putting in front of him was it.

Looks like it's White Castle on the way home tonight, he thought as he bit into the slice.

After dinner they sat on the living room couch with two cups of herbal tea, and he told her about the new developments.

"So it looks like he left the country?" she asked. "Where does that leave us with the case?"

"I don't know. I originally thought that Brice was moving too slow on everything. But maybe now, with Walker being gone, it isn't such a bad idea to just take our time building a case against him. I'd like to see us get an indictment against him for the drugs and other stuff we recovered in the raids. Then maybe let it leak that we're close to a suspect and that we're seeking him." He smiled. "Hopefully, they'll time the announcement to coincide with you getting the Medal of Valor."

Hart looked down suddenly.

"What's wrong?" Leal asked.

It took several seconds for her to answer.

"Frank, I can't accept that medal."

"What? Why not?"

"Because," she said. "I don't deserve it."

"Sure you do."

"No, you're the one who does, not me."

"How do you figure that?" He couldn't understand her reticence. Didn't she know that most coppers would give their right nut for a chance to get the Medal of Valor?

But I can't very well say that to her, can I? he thought.

"All I did was get myself cut to pieces," she said. Her eyes were glistening now.

"Ollie," he said, reaching out for her hand.

"Oh, Frank, I can't accept something like that."

"You got it coming. You kept me from getting my throat slashed by that asshole."

"That's sweet of you to say that, but I think you saved me. I was so lax," she said. He could hear the crack in her voice. "I keep going over it and over it in my mind. I almost got us both killed."

"Bullshit, you weren't lax. The bastard thought we were coming after him on a warrant. That's why he fought the way he did. There was no way you could have known that. Sometimes you get blindsided, and there's nothing you can do to prevent it."

He heard no response.

"Just like when I got shot," he said. "And my partner went down. It was unpreventable. Besides, like I said, you saved my life. He'd kicked me in the groin and was just getting set to cut my throat when you tripped him."

"I don't remember it too clearly," she said. The first tears started to fall.

"Yeah, I know how that is, but in the long run, it's good. It just might keep your dreams clear at night."

"I hope so." She wiped at her face. He offered his handkerchief.

It seemed natural when she came forward, crying and circling his neck with her arms. He held her there on the couch, listening to her sobs, feeling her powerful shoulders and back quivering under his hands.

"I'm sorry," she said. "I feel like such a weakling."

"No, that's okay, kid," he said, patting her softly. "Sometimes you just gotta let it all come out."

The next day Leal was packing two weeks' worth of dirty laundry into the machine and contemplating how, if things had been different, he might have ended up in bed with Hart instead of just holding and comforting her. He'd felt the sizzle, all right. But she needed a friend more than a lover. And a good partner couldn't be both. Or could he?

The phone rang, intruding on his thoughts, and he picked it up on the third ring.

"Hi," Sharon said.

"Hi. Where you at? New York?"

"No, I just got back a little while ago. I figured I'd take the shuttle bus back to that place in Alsip if you can pick me up."

"You sure you don't want me to shoot up there?" he asked.

"No, the shuttle is fine," she said. "Why fight the traffic in this rain? Besides, I need some quiet time to think."

"Okay," Leal said. Uh-oh, that doesn't sound good.

An hour later Leal was walking into the Holiday Inn

bar, which was just off to the left of the main entrance. He scanned the sparse group of customers, and saw her almost immediately. Her legs were crossed and he could see her calf making a slow, rhythmic kicking motion as she smoked and talked with the bartender. He straightened up when he saw Leal approaching them.

Sharon turned and smiled. "Hiya, handsome. Want a drink?" She gave him a light kiss as he sat next to her.

"That depends. You want another one?"

She looked at the amber fluid in her glass, swirled it a couple of times, and then stubbed out her cigarette. "Nah, let's just go home."

Leal grabbed her suitcase from beside the stool, and Sharon gave a little wave to the bartender.

"You bring enough stuff?" Leal asked, hefting the suitcase. "This thing weighs a ton."

"You don't think I'd go to New York without doing some heavy-duty shopping, do you?"

As they went outside the rain had been replaced by a fine mist. Leal placed the suitcase in his trunk and slammed the lid.

"Feels more like September should," she said, getting in the car.

"Yeah, I always thought September should be called the cruelest month, instead of April," Leal said. He shifted into drive. "You want to go get something to eat, and you can tell me about your trip?"

But he was wondering if he really wanted to know.

"Sure," she said. "That place down the road is fine." She stretched her arms over her head and leaned her head back. "Oooh, it feels so good to be back."

That sounds kind of promising, he thought.

"The interview went real well," she said, looking over at him. "When I got there Thursday night Mr. Feinstein had left this message at the hotel to join them for his office party. God, was that neat. We were in this real tall building in the heart of Manhattan, with these huge glass windows overlooking all the lights of the city. New York is endless."

She went on to explain how well the interview went the next day. "Everyone was so nice. I felt totally comfortable. They told me the work I've done in the State's Attorney's office was a big plus."

Uh-oh. Sounds like all systems are go for a relocation, he thought.

"But afterward one of the junior partners, a guy named Tim Fenner, invited me to dinner and the Letterman Show." Her tone seemed to change a bit.

A little mist was collecting on the windshield, and Leal flicked on the wipers.

"How'd you like it?" was all he could muster.

"Oh, that part was great. David Letterman is so funny. He's just like he is on TV, only better." She took a deep breath. "Things started to get a little bit strained on the way back to the hotel."

"Strained?"

"Yeah, you know, friendly little pats on the arm in the taxi. Then he began touching my leg, insisted on seeing me all the way up to my room—'New York's a dangerous place, you know.' And then the asshole really started pawing me in the elevator. Finally, I had to tell him to cool it or I'd call hotel security."

Leal felt his knuckles turning white as he gripped the steering wheel.

"He got real insulted and said, 'What's the matter, honey? Don't you want the job?' Oooh, I hate it when some drunken idiot who's all hands calls me 'honey.'"

"So what did you do?"

She laughed. "I told him to go do to himself what he wanted to do to me," she said. "Only not exactly in those terms. You should have seen Mr. Lady-killer's face then. I swear, he should go practice those expressions in a mirror."

"Swift, decisive, direct," Leal said, smiling. "Good qualities for a lawyer. So does this mean you'll be staying for a while?"

"Well, I'm certainly going to tell Steve Megally about it," she said. "I was so shaken that I had them put me in a new room. I mean, I want to get to the top of my profession, but not by sleeping with the boss."

"Sounds like it was a pretty rough trip in a lot of ways," Leal said, still wondering what her final decision would be.

"Oh, there were some good things," she said. "Remind me to tell you about them sometime. But right now, all I want to do is grab something to eat, go home, and hop into a nice hot tub."

He nodded, making the turn into the restaurant. She reached over and squeezed his arm.

"And I want you to scrub my back, okay?" she said.

CHAPTER TWENTY-EIGHT
Name Games

It was early Sunday morning when Leal's beeper went off the first time. The intrusive alarm woke him immediately, and he struggled to extricate himself from Sharon and the sheet in which they'd become entangled. Then he had to stumble around the bedroom looking for his pants. The beeper, which was still attached to his belt, had transformed into a periodic chirp by the time he pressed the button and stared at the unfamiliar number.

"Oh, God, what time is it?" Sharon asked, pulling a pillow over her head.

"Quarter after six," Leal said, wondering who the fuck would be calling him at this hour on a Sunday morning. He punched in the numbers on his cell phone. Joe Smith answered on the first ring.

"Sarge? I'm sorry to bug you this early, man, but it finally happened."

Leal rubbed his eyes. "Slow down, Joe. What happened?"

"The baby, Sarge. Just about an hour ago. Took us damn near the whole night, but, man, was it worth it. I got me a son."

"Hey, that's great, Joe. You decided on a name yet?"

"Helena wants to call him Joe Junior, but I'm leaning toward Matthew Harold."

"They both sound good to me," Leal said. He eased himself back into bed next to Sharon, who was now lying on her side smoking a cigarette as the conversation came to a close.

"One of the guys on my team," he said, hanging up the phone. "His wife just had their baby."

She nodded slowly, her hand propping up her head, and the sheet barely covering the fullness of her breasts.

"Must be nice, having the time for kids," she said, blowing the smoke up and away from him.

He'd already told her about his daughters and his unhappy first marriage. The look she was giving him now worried him. Was she starting to think along those lines?

"You look deep in thought," he said.

"Just thinking."

"About having kids?"

"Yeah," she said, taking another drag on the cigarette and then reaching to stub it out. "But I'm not ready to get pregnant at this point in my life."

He heaved an exaggerated sigh of relief, hoping to make her smile, but instead she stared him straight in the eye.

"But that doesn't mean that I'm not up for a bit more practicing, though," she said with a sly smile.

At late breakfast Sharon mentioned that she was going to her parents' house for dinner and that he was welcome to come along if he wanted. Then, when she later asked when she was going to get to see his place, he really began to wonder how much Smith's phone call that morning had affected her.

Sounds like she's ready to set up house, he thought. And that was a good thing, wasn't it?

Changing the subject, he mentioned that the arrival of the baby would start Smith's two-week vacation.

"He's been planning it for a while now," Leal said. "But we're getting that asshole Murphy to replace him."

"Ugh," Sharon said. "I've had the misfortune of meeting him a few times. What a pig."

"Yeah, Brice wanted him to replace Hart when she got hurt, but I told them no way."

"Oh, that's right," Sharon said. "How's she doing?"

"Good," Leal said. "Or I guess I should say, as well as could be expected considering the trauma. She's worried about the scarring and how it'll affect her bodybuilding."

"She's lucky to have someone like you to support her," Sharon said, squeezing his arm.

After helping her clean up the dishes, Leal went back to his house, remembering the cleaning that he'd started and needed to finish. Stacks of dirty dishes waited for him in his kitchen sink. But he spent most of the ride thinking about Sharon and how much she meant to him. But liking her was one thing. Meeting her family was another, and not something he looked forward to at this stage in their relationship. Too much like meeting the girl's dad on a teenage date. The looks, the scrutiny, the false smiles . . . He could certainly think of a better way to spend a Sunday afternoon.

His reprieve came at two fifteen. His beeper went off again and this time it was headquarters. When he called in, the communication personnel told him that there'd been a response to his type-three on Martin Walker.

"They got him?" Leal asked.

"No, a Detective Brown in Joliet says they've got someone using one of his credit cards."

"Give me his number," Leal said, reaching for a pad and pencil.

After he hung up he quickly dialed.

"Detective Brown," the voice on the other end of the line said, its deeply resonant timbre suggesting a black man.

Leal explained who he was and about the type-threes.

"Yeah, I read them last week," Brown said. "Here's what we got. One of our local hypes was charging up a storm at the mall using a Visa card belonging to Martin Walker. The card wasn't coming back stolen, or anything, but the credit card company had some kind of security alert on it. They notified the store security, and they grabbed her and called us. She had a syringe on her, too. I remembered the name on the type-threes and thought I'd give you a call. Still interested?"

"Am I ever," Leal said. "My partner and I will be right out."

After calling Sharon and explaining that he wouldn't be able to meet her folks for dinner, he called Hart. She answered on the first ring.

"Hey, pretty lady, you up to doing some police work?"

"Sure. What you got?"

"I'll fill you in on the way," he said. "We gotta drive to Joliet. A break in the Walker case."

Hart was standing in the doorway of her apartment building when he pulled up. She was wearing dressy-looking blue jeans, a white blouse, and tan jacket. Leal had told her to dress casual and dress quickly. They took I-57 to I-80 and headed west. It was close to four when they got to Jefferson Street.

Detective Brown met them at the front desk and shook both their hands. He was a black man, as Leal surmised, but he was a lot bigger and younger. He had the physique of someone who spent a lot of time in the weight room.

"Connie Arpegio," he said as he led them to the lockup area. "One of our locals. You want anything out of her you can usually get it."

The lockup was cinder block walls covered with blue paint. They followed Brown through a corridor with several heavy metal doors, and finally came to a narrow table.

A twenty-something-looking girl sat on a bench talking on the phone, her dark brown hair drawn back from her face in a frizzy perm. The heavy mascara gave her eyes a stark look in comparison to her drawn cheeks.

"Come on, Mom, it's only a hundred fucking dollars," she yelled into the phone. "Whaddya mean, not this time? I'll pay you back with that check I got coming."

She continued her litany of profanity into the phone until the uniformed officer who'd been sitting across from her snapped his fingers and motioned for her to hang up.

She nodded but continued to plead. He made the gesture again, and she nodded once more.

"Come on, Mom, I gotta get off the phone. You coming, or what?" She paused, listened, and then yelled into the receiver, "Oh, Mother, you're such a fucking bitch." She slammed down the phone and stared up at Brown. He smiled amiably.

"Connie, these are Detectives Leal and Hart," he said.

The girl's feral eyes scanned both of them, lingering longer on Hart than Leal.

"They'd like to talk to you about the card," Brown said.

"If I want to talk to somebody, it better be about getting the fuck outta here," Connie said.

"So you want to cooperate then?" asked Leal.

"Fuck you, asshole," she said. Then added, "Can I have a cigarette?"

"Looks like she's coming down," Leal said, pointing to the bruises and scabs where her left forearm met the biceps.

Brown nodded.

"Where'd you get the card, babe?" Leal asked.

"What card? I don't know nothing about no card."

"Maybe we should let her sit all night and come back tomorrow," Leal said.

"We could do that," Brown said.

"What are you talking about?" Connie said. "You told me I could walk with a hundred."

Brown shrugged and smiled. "That was before I knew we were holding you for investigation."

"Investigation?"

"Right, babe," Leal said. "We got a couple of days before we even have to think about what we want to charge you with."

"You big pricks," she said. "Always fucking with people. That's what you like to do, ain't it?"

"We live for nothing else," Leal said.

Connie jumped up suddenly and before Leal could grab her, Hart moved forward and slammed the girl's back against the wall.

"You just be cool," Hart said.

"Don't put your hands on me, bitch," Connie said, spitting in Hart's face.

Hart's fingers seized Connie's jaw and racked her head back hard against the cinder blocks, making a plunking sound. Connie emitted what passed for a muffled scream and then sunk back down to the bench. Leal took out his handkerchief and handed it to Hart.

"This is getting to be a habit," she said, dabbing at her face.

"I'll have to buy you one of your own," Leal said.

"That little bit of bullshit just elevated your charges to a felony," Brown said. "This is Will County, bitch. Battery to a police officer is something our state's attorney takes a real dim view of." He turned to the uniformed officer. "Go place her in a cell. I'll call Felony Review."

Connie looked up at them, the heavy black lines descending from her eyes and the mucous bubbling from her nose making her face a grotesque mask.

"You just blew your fucking chances for an I-Bond, babe," Leal said.

With the mention of the last words, the sobbing abruptly ceased. Connie wiped at her face, and leaned back against the wall. Brown handed her a paper towel for her nose.

"Can I have a cigarette?" she asked. Brown nodded and the uniformed copper gave her one from his pack.

She sucked on the cigarette so hard, Leal noticed, that he thought she'd take half of it down in one long drag.

"Okay, what is it you wanna know?" she said with a cloudy breath.

"The White Wolves," Brown said, placing a heavy tan folder on the desk in front of Leal and Hart. Brown seated himself and began sorting through the papers, some of which had photographs attached.

"They used to hang out on Collins Street, not far from the correctional center. We didn't originally have them classified as a one-percent gang," he said. "That is, most of the members had some kinda jobs and just met on the weekends, instead of being full-time assholes like the Hell's Angels."

Leal nodded.

"They got some hard-core leadership from this guy, though." Brown handed them a paper with a photograph attached to it. The face staring back at them from the black-and-white mug shot was a bearded white male with a crazed Charles Manson–type look. "Raymond Griggs, aka Marauder. All these motorcycle assholes go for these crazy-ass nicknames. He tried to transform them into a real one-percent club. Got in over his head when he got into a turf war with one of the bigger, tougher established gangs. Griggs was shot to death. His lieutenant, a guy named Nick Stevens, aka Nick Smith," he flipped a second sheet onto the table. This one showed another white guy with a slender face and longish hair. "He went to Stateville for robbery back about ten years ago at age twenty. Pulled two years, came out looking for a surrogate family and took up with the Wolves.

"Well, him and Griggs hit it off pretty well." Brown stopped and poured a cup of coffee from the pot behind him. He held the cup toward Hart, who smiled and took it. Then Brown did the same for Leal. He poured his own cup last.

"There may have been some kind of homosexual bond between the two of them," he said, tapping the photos. "They both did hard time together. When Griggs got it trying to make the Wolves into a big power gang, Stevens went down for murder. He killed the guy who iced his buddy." Brown put another photo on the table. It was a picture of the same face as the slender, long-haired boy, but this one was more mature and much more massive-looking.

"This is one of our more recent pictures of him," Brown said. "Calls himself Nuke."

"Look at his traps," Hart said, indicating the sloping bulge on either side of the bull neck. "And his jawline. See that bloat? He's on juice."

Brown nodded and smiled. "Very perceptive. He built up a real jailhouse body, all right. Did four years on the murder rap—typical, right? Then got out. Nobody's been able to get anything on him since. A couple arrests for possession of a syringe, and PCS, but no convictions."

"A syringe?" Leal asked. "He a hype?"

Brown shook his head.

"He probably injects the steroids," Hart said. "Less strain on the liver than taking them orally." Leal noticed her blush as they both looked at her.

"Can we run his ISB number and get a rap sheet?" Leal asked. "I'd like to see where he's been arrested lately."

"Sure," Brown said. "He's had some top quality attorneys since he got out. The Wolves kind of went by the wayside after Griggs got killed and Nuke went to prison. Now our boy kinda just hangs out at a local gym, pushing steroids to the rest of the muscle heads. Real cautious, though. It's a members-only thing."

Leal nodded. "Who's the one Connie was telling us about?"

"Him," Brown said, dropping a third picture on the table. "Stanley Willard, one of Nuke's little asshole buddies. There's another young punk that hangs out, too, but we haven't got anything on him. Only seen him a couple of times. Got something wrong with one of his eyes." He pointed off to the side. "Wall-eyed. Calls himself Moose, or something. But Willard I know from way back. A little fucking burglar. Did a couple of stretches here and in Chicago, but never any hard time."

"How about the address that shows up on the printout?" Leal asked. "Think it's current?"

"That's his mother's house," Brown said. "It's over in the older section of the city. Connie said something about an apartment. That's probably where the stuff is."

Leal skimmed the printouts. "Any idea what kind of car he drives? There's a Ford van listed here that comes back to him."

"That sounds like Stanley," Brown said. "He was always a van man. His little ass looks pretty funny bouncing around on top of one of those big Harleys."

Leal smiled.

"You want me to have one of the marked units look for him and Nuke?" Brown asked. "Maybe pull 'em down on a traffic stop or something?"

Leal considered this, then shook his head.

"Thanks, but I don't want to take a chance on spooking them just yet," he said. "At least not until we get a fix on where this place actually is."

"Okay," Brown said. "We'll keep Connie on ice for you tonight. You'll be back in the morning for her, then?"

"Right," Leal said. "Thanks for all the help, brother." He extended his hand toward Brown, who shook it. "Oh, by the way, I forgot to ask you. What's Stanley's street name?"

Brown smiled broadly.

"It's Snake," he said.

CHAPTER TWENTY-NINE

Clockwork

God, he looks hungover, Leal thought the next morning as he briefed Ryan on the new developments and the interrogation of Connie. Ryan sat, his left hand supporting his head, occasionally sipping from his coffee cup and massaging his temples. Murphy, Ryan told them at the start of the meeting, had been handpicked by Brice to replace Smith, who was now on vacation.

Man, I'm gonna miss Joe, Leal thought as he shook hands with Murphy. But with a new baby he won't feel like working long hours of surveillance, either. The bags under Murphy's eyes rivaled Ryan's, and his color seemed to darken as Leal explained how the case had developed over the weekend.

"We're gonna pick her up this morning," Leal said. "Brown will arrange an I-Bond for the hypo charge. Then we'll sign a complaint on her for the credit card."

"But them cards ain't even been reported stolen yet, have they?" Murphy asked.

"It doesn't matter at this point," Leal said. "We'll sign for receiving the card of another. That'll keep her on ice tonight in the Will County jail."

"Will County?" Murphy said.

"Technically," Hart said, "she has to be brought before a judge in the county where she's arrested."

"Yeah, I know that," Murphy said, his head bobbling angrily. "Just seems that we ain't doing much as a team, that's all."

"All right," Leal said. "She's agreed to show us the apartment building where the stuff's at if we get her into a drug treatment program. We're going to take her for some methadone this morning. I know somebody at a clinic in Joliet. When we get the address, we sit on it until the warrant comes through."

"This is the boyfriend's place?" Ryan asked. "The guy who gave her the card?"

"Actually, he didn't give it to her," Hart said. "They partied hard for a couple of days with some heroin and coke that Stanley had. It seems his nose is falling apart fast, and he's just started mainlining. She was teaching him."

"Nice girl," Ryan said, taking out one of his cigarettes.

"Maybe we can get her cleaned up in time for the Miss America Pageant," Murphy said. He took out a cigar and motioned for Ryan's lighter.

"How about holding up on the smokes, guys?" Leal said. They both stared at him, but didn't light up. "Anyway, after a few days of sex, drugs, and rock and roll she lifted the card and decided to go shopping. She played it pretty smart, telling people she was Martin Walker's daughter, and just buying stuff she could fence real easy. Jewelry, sheets, CDs."

"So she could buy more shit," Ryan said. He stuck the unlit cigarette between his lips.

"Then she tried to get some cash refunds on some of the stuff she bought," Hart said. "That's when the store security checked with the credit card company and saw the alert."

"And the rest is history," Ryan said. "So where's this taking us?"

"She gives us the apartment where Snake stashed the

stuff," Leal said, "and they give her an I-Bond tomorrow and take her to the drug rehab place."

"Christ," Ryan said. "I hate working with hypes. What if she tips the fucker off we're coming?"

Leal shook his head. "After we get her the methadone and she shows us the house, Brown will keep her for us."

"She'll probably just sleep all day anyway," Hart said.

"Just so she doesn't make any calls to shithead," Ryan said. "What's he supposedly got?"

"The DVD/VCR definitely," Leal said. "They used it to watch porno flicks. We'll have to make the warrant non-specific, though."

"Too bad we missed the party," Ryan said. "So we get this guy Willard—Snake to his friends and lovers—and maybe we get the connection between him and Walker, huh? Maybe he's one of Walker's boys."

"Or his supplier," Leal said. "Anyway, once we get him we find out the connection. I think these wannabe motor-cycle gangsters are involved somehow."

"Sounds like you're kinda stretching it," Murphy said.

Leal just shot him an angry look. *If I can get through the rest of this investigation without punching this fat fucker's lights out, I'll be happy.*

"Okay," Ryan said, standing. "One step at a time, okay? You guys go out there and take care of business. Murphy, go in with a second car. I'll get with the state's attorney. As soon as you got the address, call me and I'll set up the warrant. You guys can sit on the apartment until it comes through."

Leal nodded and handed Ryan copies of Connie's statement and the report.

"I want to make sure Snake's in there when we hit it," he said.

Ryan nodded, looking over the paperwork. "You got a picture of this bitch?"

Leal handed him a Polaroid mug shot.

"Jesus Christ," Ryan said. "Talk about coyote ugly. That's where you wake up next to her in the morning and have to gnaw your arm off to get out of the bed."

Murphy guffawed with a heavy chuckle.

Those two fit together like a perverse Laurel and Hardy, Leal thought.

"I'd better touch bases with Brice on this, too," Ryan said. "He took a personal day today, so I'll beep him. At a reasonable hour, of course."

"Get started on the warrant first," Leal said. "I don't want to lose the momentum on this."

"Roger that, Franko," Ryan said, with a grin and a salute. "Just get me the address and I'll start the ball rolling."

It went like clockwork once they got back to Joliet. Connie was "enrolled" in the drug counseling program, thanks to Leal's connection, a middle-aged Hispanic woman named Maria. She and Leal talked in Spanish for a good five minutes before she turned to Connie and greeted her with a cordial firmness.

"How have you been, Connie?"

The girl mumbled something unintelligible, her gaze on the floor.

"So are you ready to reinstate yourself?"

"Yeah."

"All right, I'll set up your counseling sessions and support group," Maria said.

"I don't have to go through that shit again, do I?"

"You know the rules. Either you agree, or it's no deal." Leal watched as Maria met the girl's insolent-looking stare. "I'm already stretching things by letting you bypass our waiting list."

"Okay, okay, for Christ's sake," Connie said. "I'll do whatever the fuck you say. Now can I *please* just have my medicine?"

Maria exhaled, then took out a book and a set of keys. After making a few notations in the ledger, she left the room. When she returned she had a small plastic vial filled with a pink liquid.

"Cisco," she said. "*Lo quieres?*"

"*Sí,*" Leal said, taking the vial. Then to Connie, "I'll just hold on to this for now, babe."

They ignored her pleading protests as they escorted her back to the squad car. Murphy was sitting behind the wheel of his car, smoking.

"Can the cigar and get in with us," Leal said, directing him to the front passenger seat. Hart opened the back door for Connie, whose eyes stayed on the vial as Leal stuck it by the windshield.

"The quicker you show us the house," he said, "the sooner you get your stuff."

It was a brick three-flat situated in the middle of the block in one of the city's older, decaying sections. Connie told them Snake's apartment was the one on top. The building had a small entranceway recessed into the northeast side. The trim and gutters had been painted a dull green, with chips of paint peeling and flaking off, showing the gray patches underneath like a torn checkerboard. The house on the left was also a three-flat, with a long canopied gangway that ran to the rear yards. A chain-link fence separated the two. On the right side there were two more apartment buildings of identical design. Leal circled the block and cut down an alley that ran parallel to the street.

The rear of the buildings had three-tiered, enclosed wooden porches ascending from the ground to the roof. A large three-car garage, almost as wide as the apartment building itself, blocked the view of the rear yard. Three overhead garage doors and a metal gate faced the alley. Leal drove around to the front again, checking the area.

He stopped halfway down the block and told Murphy to get out and check it.

Murphy breathed laboriously as he got out of the car and shuffled toward the middle building.

"This is where I'm really gonna miss Joe," Leal said. "Now we got to deal with Jabba the Hutt with a badge."

He saw Hart smile in the rearview mirror.

"So what was that Maria called you back at the clinic?" she asked. "Cisco?"

Leal sighed. "Yeah, like the Cisco Kid, right?"

"Actually," she said, "I was thinking of that old Willie Nelson song."

He grinned. "Either way, you know who that makes you, right?"

"All right, I won't call you Cisco if you don't call me Pancho then. Okay?"

"It's a deal," he said. "For now." He saw Murphy leisurely ambling back toward them. "Good thing we're not in a hurry."

"Stanley Willard's name is next to buzzer three," Murphy said, settling back into the car.

"See?" Connie said. "Now can I have my medicine?"

Leal removed the vial from the dashboard, shook it several times, and handed it back to her. He watched as she drank it in one long gulp then settled back into the seat.

After dropping Connie off and thanking Detective Brown for his help, Leal called Ryan back to get any progress on the search warrant.

"I'm writing the complaint as we speak," Ryan said. "Keep your pants on, will ya, Frankie?"

Leal glanced at his watch: twelve thirty-five.

"Okay, we're going to set up on the house and wait," he said. "Call me back when you get the warrant."

"Is the stroke even there?" Ryan asked.

"I didn't want to ring the bell. He's supposed to drive a

blue Ford van, and that's in the garage. But he has a Harley, too, and that's not here."

"Okay," Ryan said. "I beeped Brice twice so far and he ain't called yet."

Leal wasn't worried about Brice. He told Ryan to keep working on the warrant and hung up. Afterward, he called Sharon and told her he'd be tied up till late.

"Oh, damn," she said. "It figures that you'd be on nights when I'm on days. I was kind of hoping you'd come over so I could fix you dinner."

"How about a rain check?" he asked.

"Sure," she said.

He detected some hesitancy in her tone.

"Everything okay?"

"Yeah," she said. "Well, I got a call from Mr. Feinstein in New York this morning."

"Oh?"

"Yeah, I mentioned to Steve what happened, and apparently it got back to the big boss." She was speaking rapidly. "So, anyway, he apologized to me and said that he was going to reprimand that guy Fenner for his—How did he put it? 'Unconscionable behavior.'"

Leal licked his lips. "Good. Did he talk to you about the job, too?"

"Yeah," she answered slowly. "He asked me to reconsider and offered to up the salary considerably."

Leal was silent for a moment.

"Sounds like he still wants you," he said. "What did you say?"

"Frank, I—" Her voice trailed off. "I told him I'd have to think about it. Maybe I shouldn't have mentioned this over the phone. It's just that I was really hoping that you could stop by tonight so we could talk."

It's all over but the crying, he thought.

"It depends how this thing goes down," Leal said. "I'll call you later."

"Okay, be careful."

Leal pressed the "end" button on his portable and slipped it back in his pocket, gritting his teeth and trying to force the conversation out of his mind. He knew he didn't need any extra baggage right now, but it still grated on him.

Yeah, all over but the crying.

Leal told Murphy to park near the mouth of the alley and watch the rear of the place, and directed Hart to pull down the street from the front. She deftly pulled in behind a parked car, and they both slouched in the seat. Since they were only a few hundred yards away from each other, Leal told Murphy to go to tac band on his portable.

They waited in silence, watching people come and go. The afternoon slipped away, boredom replacing their initial enthusiasm.

"Hey, Sarge," Murphy's voice said over the tactical frequency. "How much longer?"

"How the fuck should I know?" Leal said to Hart. He keyed the mike. "Unknown, Murph."

"Well, Sarge, could I be excused for a little bit?"

"Negative."

Leal squinted at the radio as it squawked again.

"Awww, Sarge, I gotta relieve myself," Murphy said.

Just be glad I reminded you not to have too much to drink when we stopped for lunch before, Leal thought. You'd probably have pissed your pants by now.

"Just stand by," Leal said.

"Sarge, come on. I gotta go bad. How about sending your partner back here to relieve me."

"No way," Hart said. "Just the sight of him makes me sick."

"Negative," Leal said into the radio.

Murphy muttered something indistinct that could have possibly been a curse word. Leal's lips tightened into a thin line and he gripped the door handle and wrenched it upward.

"That settles it," he said. "I'm going back there to have a *talk* with that fat fucker."

"Frank, take it easy," Hart said. "Remember, we still need him to cover the back."

Leal blew out a slow breath and massaged his temple. Nothing on this fucking case was going smoothly. Every time he managed to take a few steps forward, somebody threw a roadblock in his path. But this lead was too hot. With a little luck, they could break this one wide-open. He brought the radio to his lips and told Murphy that he was clear to take a quick break. "Get something to eat, too, but make it as fast as possible. You ten-four?"

"That's affirmative, Sarge. Thanks."

Leal told Hart he'd be back and got out of the squad. He walked down the block, working out the kinks that inevitably occurred from sitting in the cramped position for so long. It felt good to move a little. As he neared the alley he saw the unmarked whiz by. Leal turned and went past the spot where Murphy had been parked. It was littered with cigar butts and candy wrappers. A small gray tendril drifted upward from the most recently discarded butt. Leal smashed it under his sole and cursed Murphy for leaving such a distinguishable trail. From all accounts this idiot Snake wasn't a rocket scientist, but Murphy's detritus was enough to send out smoke signals. The smell from the nearby garbage cans was putrid. How the man could even have an appetite after sitting back here was amazing to Leal.

He leaned against the wall of a nearby garage so he could keep an eye on things. There was no movement that he could see in the apartment. No lights, either. But it was still pretty early. He glanced at his watch. Quarter after four. Christ, where the hell was Ryan? On his way, hopefully.

Leal took out his cell phone to call and check, but the LoBatt light was on. Shit, thought Leal. It figures. Nothing was going right. He put the phone back in his jacket pocket and blew out a slow breath.

He's got to be on his way, Leal thought. He'd let Ollie take a break next. She probably had to take a leak, too, and couldn't go standing in the alley like he could. The first rule of being a good sergeant was taking care of your people.

The slight chill in the air made him snap the buttons of his windbreaker. The hot, humid weather that had held on all summer long and for most of September had suddenly vanished, and an autumnlike coolness was descending. Like March, only in reverse. Getting colder now instead of warmer. Then the real cold would start. But this one would have to be wrapped up long before that. Their informal deadline, the November election, was only a few weeks away. By that time he'd most likely know how this thing with Sharon would turn out, too.

Murphy was gone for a good forty-five minutes. When he returned Leal was waiting to chew his ass out royally.

"Sorry, Sarge," Murphy said, wiping his thick mustache with a Burger King napkin. "But, Christ, I didn't think this was gonna take so long. I didn't eat much at lunch, remember?"

Leal nodded.

"Well, now that you're fed, get ready to stay in position until Ryan gets here with the warrant."

"Any idea how much longer it'll be?"

Leal shook his head. "As long as it takes." He eyed the heavyset patrolman. "You got your vest?"

"Yeah, it's in the trunk."

"Well get it on, then," Leal said. "I want you to be ready in case anything goes down. We might have to hit that door in a hurry. And give me your cell phone. Mine's dead."

"Okay, boss," Murphy said. His big mustache drooped over his upper lip. "Hmm, looks like mine's dead, too."

Hart reluctantly agreed to go grab something to eat, leaving Leal sitting on the curbside. She said she'd go pick up food for both of them and be back as soon as possible. He told her to call or page Ryan, too, and find out his ETA. She gave him a smile and a nod as she sped off. Leal leaned against the telephone pole and watched a group of Hispanic youths, boys and girls, walking down the street with a boom box. They spoke in a mixture of Spanish and English, and he could tell by their accents that they were Puerto Ricans. One guy glanced at him as they went by and Leal noted the twin teardrops tattooed on his left cheek.

Gangbanger asshole, Leal thought. But at least he didn't feel too out of place—What was it that idiot director had called him when they were filming that stupid campaign commercial? That swarthy-looking Latino type. He grinned and made a mental note to try and get a tape of it from the sheriff's campaign manager.

Hart was gone for fifteen minutes. The parking space that they'd had before got taken by a yuppie-looking guy who parked his Ford Mustang and made a show of hitting his alarm as he walked away. Luckily Hart pulled into another spot farther up the block that gave them an even better view. Leal strolled down and slipped in the passenger seat. She handed him a bag and a medium drink cup.

"What'd you get?" he asked.

"Chicken sandwiches and iced tea." She had the remnants of a half-eaten one on a piece of paper on her lap.

"You must be starving to eat this kind of crap."

"Too hungry not to get something," she said. "After all, I am a big girl. Just don't tell Rory I broke my diet."

"You get ahold of Ryan?" Leal asked, taking a bite of the sandwich.

She shook her head as she chewed.

"He didn't answer. I paged him to your cell phone."

"Shit, my battery's out."

"Oh no," she said. "Sorry."

"No sweat. I should've told you. But he must be on his way by now. Let's get our vests on and get ready."

The streetlights were glowing at eight and it seemed about as dark as it was going to get. Leal was repeating his umpteenth curse of that asshole Ryan when they heard the thunderous roar of a powerful motorcycle engine.

"Sounds like a Harley," Leal said, trying to slip down in the seat.

They saw a slim figure with straggly blond hair blowing away from his face shoot by them. The motorcyclist slowed directly in front of the apartment building, angled the Harley in a semicircle, and then managed to sandwich it between two parked cars. He looked around warily, then bounced up over the curb, across the parkway and side-walk, and toward the three-flat.

"That's got to be him," Leal said, bringing the radio to his lips as the cycle disappeared between the buildings. "Murphy?"

No response. They waited a few more minutes.

"Frank, looks like a light just came on in the third-floor apartment," Hart said.

"Murphy," Leal repeated into the radio. He glanced up at the third floor. A translucent glare of lights could be seen through the front picture window. "I'd better see what the son of a bitch is doing back there."

Leal got out and walked slowly around the end of the block. When he was sure that he was out of the line of sight of Snake's apartment, he ran back to where Murphy was parked.

The unmarked was there, idling. Murphy's head was leaning against the headrest in repose. His pendulous jowls quivered as he snapped awake when Leal slammed the flat of his hand against Murphy's shoulder.

"What the fuck?" he said.

"Yeah, what the fuck?" said Leal.

Murphy breathed rapidly through his mouth several times before stammering out a profuse apology, culminating with, "I didn't get much sleep last night, Sarge."

"I don't give a flying fuck how much sleep you didn't get," Leal said. "The asshole just got home. And answer me on the fucking radio next time I call you." He pointed his finger in Murphy's face. "Got it?"

Instead of walking back around the way he'd come, Leal went straight east down the alley so he could pass by the rear garage of Snake's place. He gave a quick sideways glance as he passed. No lights on in the rear of the apartment that he could see. Continuing, he circled the block. There were enough recesses and thick telephone poles in the alley to provide good cover if he had to go there on foot. He reviewed his mental notes of the area as he crossed over to the opposite side of the street, making his way back to Hart.

"That asshole was sleeping," he said slipping in.

"Sleeping? What the hell's wrong with that man?"

"I don't know, but I read him the riot act. I'll write his ass up later. Right now I just wish that damn Ryan would get here."

Another hour passed, with nothing much happening. The lights in the front of the house were still on. Leal tried to call Ryan on the regular radio several more times, but couldn't raise him. He didn't even know if he was in range of any repeating stations. The activity in the neighborhood had increased slightly as teenagers came home from dates and people drifted back from the bars. Then it dropped off. Several more groups of kids wandered by, some on Rollerblades, others in groups, but they seemed to scatter when a Joliet patrol car drove down the block.

Still no Ryan, and no warrant.

Murphy checked in, asking if he could go call to see what the holdup was.

"Negative," Leal said into the radio. "That fat-ass son of a bitch . . ."

"At least we know he's awake."

Leal sighed and looked at Hart, her profile intent on the building, her arms stretched forward, hands clenching the steering wheel. Suddenly she turned to look at him and raised her eyebrows.

"What?" she said.

He looked at her questioningly.

"You were staring at me," she said. "I was just wondering why."

"Oh, you're the best scenery around here."

She smiled. "You're just lucky I'm not big into sexual harassment filings, or you'd be in trouble for saying something like that."

"Yeah, that's me, all right. Always putting my foot in my mouth. You need to take another break?"

"No, I'm okay. Plus, I don't want to miss anything. This is my first search warrant. Besides, Ryan'll be here any minute now."

"How do you know that?"

"Woman's intuition."

"The vest bothering you?"

"I'm okay." She looked quickly back at the building. "Frank, I thought I saw movement at the window."

Leal scanned the apartment but saw nothing. He raised the radio to his lips and spoke into it. "Murphy, anything moving back there?" Leal called him again, but there was no reply. "Goddamn him. If he's sleeping again, I'll have his fucking badge."

"You want me to go check?" Hart asked.

"No, I'll go." Leal forced himself to pull up on the door handle slowly, instead of ripping it open like he wanted to do. He got out and trotted around to the alley, expecting to find Murphy dozing again. He was doubly shocked when he didn't see the car at all.

"Ollie," Leal said into the radio. "Murphy's gone. He must have changed locations or something. I'm going to set up back here."

"Okay, Frank."

The twin streetlights at either end of the alley provided enough ambient lighting to make him moderately visible to anyone looking down from the apartments. Continuing onward down the alley, Leal stopped by a telephone pole and pretended like he was urinating. While he was doing so, he glanced around, hoping to appear as the late returnee from the bars, pausing to water the weeds after drinking one too many beers.

More lights burning up on the third floor, especially toward the back. A shaggy-haired silhouette appeared in the window, and Leal flattened against the wall. When the shadow disappeared, Leal moved over to the adjacent garage, stopping behind another telephone pole. He strained his ears and heard some sort of muffled sounds. But what were they? He whispered into the radio.

"Ollie, something might be going down soon. Get ready."

Leal took out his weapon and listened again. Someone was huffing and puffing coming down the wooden stairs in back. Was it Snake? Christ, thought Leal. He may be just going out for shits and giggles to score some dope. He glanced at the shadowy figure again. Or he may have the fucking evidence with him. Without knowing the status of the damn warrant, I could be stepping on my dick big time.

Crouching in the alley Leal heard the scuffling sound of footsteps coming down the sidewalk toward him. The garage between him and whoever it was gave him cover, but it also made it impossible to see.

"Ollie," Leal whispered into the radio. "Move up in front and cover the motorcycle. He might be trying to book outta here."

Hart clicked a reply.

Leal heard the squealing of hinges on the side door of the garage. No lights came on inside. A car door opened. He listened intently, leaning sideways against the telephone pole to keep out of sight. A starter ground and an engine came to life. The overhead door of the garage swung upward.

It's now or never, Leal thought. If he does have evidence, then it'll be totally lost if he leaves now. Twisting on his Minimag flashlight, Leal ran forward. Goddamn that fucking Murphy. If he'd been there they could have blocked the asshole in.

Leal was suddenly illuminated by the twin headlights of a van. The vehicle began to pull out of the garage, the driver's door still cracked open. It was Willard, all right. He's getting out to shut the overhead door, Leal thought, running now, reaching for the driver's door, and wrenching it all the way open. "Ollie, get back here!" he yelled into his radio. Then to Willard, "Police, don't move."

The van lurched forward. The flashlight fell from Leal's hand as he made a frantic grab through the open window at the driver. His fingers managed to snare a handful of shirt, but the van began to accelerate. Leal had a sudden fear of being crushed against the telephone pole. He twisted and pulled the shirt, trying to pull Willard out of the car. Leal's side slammed hard against the door, closing it.

"Lemme go, motherfucker!" Snake grunted. He clawed at Leal's face and arm.

Leal felt his feet leave the ground and knew he was dead if the van got moving or bumped against something. He pulled the shirt again, feeling the slender body lift up from the seat. Snake's head banged against the door frame. It was enough to cause a lull in the acceleration. Gaining purchase with his feet momentarily, Leal shoved the Beretta at Snake's face, the butt of the weapon glancing off his head. The van slowed, impelled only by the automatic transmission. Leal pulled him almost completely out the window. The van rolled forward and Snake cried out, then gurgled, as Leal's fingers curled around the skinny neck. Suddenly the vehicle smacked into the adjacent telephone pole, coming to such an abrupt stop that Leal was thrown to the ground. He got up immediately, reaching forward and grabbing at Snake, who was frantically scrambling to get back in the driver's seat.

"Police, hold it, motherfucker!" Leal shouted again, managing this time to reach through and grab for the keys with his left hand. Their fingers fought for a moment, then Leal grasped the gearshift lever and pulled it back and up, shoving the van into park. His hand caught Snake's neck and he brought the Beretta up to the other man's left eye, letting the extended barrel loom in front of him.

"Give it up or die," Leal said.

Hart suddenly was on the passenger side, pointing her gun at Snake also.

"Police, don't move," she said.

Snake's eyes worked over toward her, and he tensed for a moment before going limp.

"Move again and I'll blow your fucking head off, asshole," Leal said.

Hart came around and they pulled Snake's arms up and tugged him through the window. He didn't resist and fell to the alley with a resounding plop. When his body hit, he made a few attempts to squirm away, but Leal brought his knee and the full weight of his body down on Snake's lower back. They twisted his arms behind him, and Hart ratcheted her cuffs over the thin wrists and he was secured.

"What's the matter, man?" he said. "I didn't do nothing. What you hassling me for?"

"I dropped my flashlight," Leal said, afraid to look in the van for fear of what he might not find.

Hart stood and swung her flashlight into the van's interior. A DVD/VCR player was perpendicular on the floor between the seat and the dash. She stepped in and shone the beam directly on the back.

Smiling, she turned and smiled at Leal, holding a thumb's-up.

"I'll buy you a new Minimag if we can't find yours," she said.

Leal felt a surge of relief wash over him.

Suddenly they both heard the roar of an engine and saw the headlights coming toward them. The car screeched to a halt, and Murphy lumbered toward them, his gun drawn.

"What's going down?" he asked.

"Everything," Leal said, still trying to get his breathing under control.

"This him?" Murphy asked, giving the handcuffed man a swift kick in the side. Snake gasped and curled over. "You piece of shit."

"Knock it off, Murphy," Leal said. "The man's cuffed."

Murphy glowered at Snake.

"Where the fuck were you?" Leal said. "I needed some help back here."

"I had to leave," Murphy said.

"What?"

"I had to take a shit, Sarge," the big man said. "Real bad. Couldn't wait. Besides, somebody beeped me and I thought it might be about the warrant. My cell was out, remember?"

"Why didn't you call me on the radio?" Leal asked.

"The fucking thing wasn't working," Murphy said. "I tried and nobody answered. I was afraid of going around to the front for fear of blowing the stakeout."

"Give me that," Leal said, reaching for Murphy's radio. He keyed the transmit button and heard the slight crackle of a radio wave on his own radio. "Seems to be working fine."

"Well it wasn't then, Sarge. Honest." Murphy's portly face was wet with sweat. "As soon as I seen what was going down back here I beat feet."

Leal was about to suspend him on the spot when Ryan's voice came over the radio.

"Anybody out there?"

Leal answered him.

"Ah, I've got the warrant," Ryan said. "I'm a few blocks away. I'll stop by Joliet PD and get some big guys with sledgehammers and axes."

Leal stared over at Murphy, realizing that he still needed another body for containment and searching. I'll deal with this fat fuck tomorrow, he thought.

"Just come directly to the scene," he said. "You won't need the axes. We're in the alley."

CHAPTER THIRTY
Wild Cards

After making arrangements to have Snake's van towed to Maywood, they took their time searching the apartment. The place was a pigsty, with stacks of pornographic and drug-oriented magazines, video tapes, and old pizza boxes scattered everywhere. They'd found what they'd expected initially: a cache of drugs, assorted syringes, and two handguns. In contrast to the coolness of the night, the inside was hot, and Leal found himself covered with sweat. Be lucky if I don't catch cold, he thought. But the search began to get interesting as he found a pillowcase with some rings inside. One of them, a class ring, had the initials MHW on the inside band. Martin H. Walker? Leal wondered. He'd also noticed that Snake had been wearing a very expensive-looking watch when they'd cuffed him. A Rolex.

"Looks like it was the maid's day off," Ryan said, chuckling. He looked at Leal. "Like I said, Frankie, sorry it took me so long, but everything that could go wrong, did." He began holding up fingers as he ticked off each point. "First, the damn complaint for the warrant was like nine fucking pages. Brice didn't make it into HQ till almost two, and then I had to play twenty questions with him. By that time it was getting late, and I still had to get the thing typed. Then there weren't any judges left in Four, so I had to run down to Twenty-sixth Street and find a night judge." He heaved a theatric sigh. "Naturally, the State's Attorney there wanted to go over every fucking detail before we presented it to the judge. Then we had to wait for hizzoner to finish his call."

"Okay, okay, I get the idea," said Leal, but his gaze was on something else. He walked to a small table in the living room and looked at an ornate bronze statue on the floor next to the TV. It was a satyr playing a flute.

"Ollie, does this look familiar?"

She went over and stood beside him. As she studied it, Leal noticed her blond hair was plastered to her head with sweat.

"You okay?" he asked.

She nodded. "Didn't we see a statue like that at Walker's?"

Leal grinned. "Let's bag this, too," he said to Ryan. Then to Hart, "Are you hot? Want me to help you out of that vest?"

She shook her head. "No, I've got it," she said as she carefully slipped out of the windbreaker and protective vest. Leal saw a crimson stain on the back of her blue T-shirt.

"Ollie," he said.

"I know," she said. "Must have torn something open."

"Dammit," Leal said. "You want me to call the paramedics?"

"I'll be okay," she said.

Leal nodded, thinking, Man, she's tough.

They watched Stanley "Snake" Willard through the panel of one-way glass as he sat in the interview room, his arms crossed, his legs thrust sullenly under the table.

"How do you want to handle this?" Ryan asked.

Leal stood beside him. They'd sent Murphy on a coffee run and Hart to the emergency room to get her wound checked.

"Let's go over what we know," Leal said. He held up the plastic bags containing the recovered ring and watch. "These most likely belong to Martin Walker. The same with the credit card, the DVD/VCR, and the drug statue. Question is, how did this asshole get them?"

"Maybe Walker gave them to him?" Ryan said.

"Yeah, but why?" Leal asked.

Ryan shrugged. "In exchange for taking him to the airport, maybe? Or maybe in exchange for some dope?"

Leal shook his head, frowning. "No, I can't see Walker giving him the credit card."

"Maybe he stole it?" Ryan said. "Or maybe he's one of Walker's fag boys." He'd lit up a cigarette.

"We got to be very careful how we approach this," Leal said. "He obviously knows more than we do. We gotta convince him he doesn't."

"Good cop/bad cop?" Ryan asked, grinning.

Before Leal could reply, Murphy came strolling in holding a cardboard tray of coffees.

"I got the brews," he said. "Here you go."

Murphy passed over the other cups and then took his own and collapsed heavily into a nearby chair.

"And, I talked to the boss," the big man said. "He told me to tell you to shut it down till he gets here."

"What?" Leal said. "Now's the best time. He's still shook up from the arrest. If we wait he might lawyer up."

Murphy shrugged. "That's what he said."

"Let's give him one more shot," Leal said.

He saw Murphy stare at him. Leal looked at Ryan.

"You ready?"

Ryan blew smoke out of both nostrils, then nodded. "Murph, do me a favor, will ya? Forget you told us what you told us."

As they went in the interview room Willard looked up.

"Hiya, Stanley," Ryan said. "Need a smoke?"

"Yeah," Willard said, sitting up.

Ryan took one out of his pack, passed it to Willard, and lit it.

"We gotta advise you of your rights," Ryan said, holding up the pre-printed Miranda warning. He read it verbatim, then passed it to Willard. "Just sign here, my man, to show we read it to you."

Willard placed the cigarette in the corner of his mouth and accepted the pen.

Initial cooperation, Leal thought. This is going better than I figured it would.

"So you ever hear of a guy named Martin Walker?" Leal asked.

"Who?"

Leal blew out a slow breath. "Don't fuck with us, Stanley. You had his stuff. You were using his credit card."

"Well, yeah. Maybe."

"No maybes about it," Ryan said. "You're in deep, my man. In fact, you're in shit up to your knees. Pretty soon it'll be over your head."

"This is your last chance to help yourself," Leal said. "Cooperate at this point and we'll mention it to the state's attorney."

"Maybe I should talk to a lawyer," Willard said. Leal detected a hesitancy in his voice.

"Maybe you should," Ryan said, smiling.

"And maybe we should tell Nuke that you flipped for us, Stanley," Leal said.

The reaction was visible.

"No, you guys can't do that," Willard said. "Please. He'd kill me if he knew."

"If he knew what?" Leal asked.

Willard swallowed hard and took a last drag on the cigarette.

"Can I have another square, sir?" he asked.

Ryan sighed, but took his pack out of his pocket. "You know," he said, leaning forward to light it for Willard. "It's getting pretty late, and I'm getting pretty tired of playing fucking games. You want to talk, or what?"

Willard nodded a "thanks," and drew deeply on the new cigarette.

"Okay," he said. "Tell me this. If I play ball with you guys, what's it gonna get me?"

"That depends on what you got to offer," Leal said. Willard looked at him, and Leal added, "Look, we got all the pieces. We just haven't put them all together yet. But we will."

Willard looked at the floor, obviously considering his options.

"I think you want to tell us," Ryan said. "Don't cha?"

"Like, could I get immunity, or something?" Willard asked.

"Immunity?" Leal said. "What do you think this is? TV?"

Ryan leaned forward, smiling like he was consoling his little brother after striking out at the ballpark. He placed his hand on Willard's shoulder.

"At this point we're all you got going for you, kid," he said.

Leal was remembering Detective Brown mentioning the fancy lawyers that Nuke and Willard had before. But he seemed scared of Nuke.

"I just gotta think about it, is all," Willard said.

Suddenly Leal began to worry that it could all come apart. Willard could refuse to talk, and lawyer up. Brice's order that they wait for him meant they'd lose all the momentum they'd gained. And he wasn't about to let that go down the drain.

"Well, think fast," he said, letting a hint of anger and menace creep into his voice. "Like my partner told you, it's late, and you're out of second chances."

"It's either shit, or get off the pot," Ryan said, leaning back in his chair.

"Okay, suppose I told you I took the DVD/VCR and other stuff from his house?"

"Cut the shit," Leal said. "We all know the DVD/VCR is just a small part of this."

"Don't insult our intelligence," Ryan said.

Willard buried his face in his hands for a moment, then drew his fingers back through his greasy hair. He sat up straighter and said, "All right, just tell me this. If I show you where the body is, can you guarantee you'll protect me from Nuke?"

They continued talking to him over a parade of soft drinks and cigarettes. In forty-five minutes they had the whole story outlined and down in a preliminary statement. The initial murder of Miriam Walker, the disposal of her body, the subsequent drug deals, and the eventual murder of Martin Walker. Once the dam broke, Willard was like a faucet they couldn't shut off. Not that they wanted to. The body, he told them, was buried in a forest preserve off Route 83. He'd slipped the Rolex off Walker's limp wrist while Nuke and Moose were digging the grave.

"What's Moose's real name?" Ryan asked.

Willard shrugged. "I don't know."

"Take a guess."

He shrugged again. "I just know him by Moose, is all."

"All you motorcycle guys have nicknames, huh?" Leal said.

Willard nodded.

"What about Nuke?" Leal asked. "Where'd you hook up with him?"

"Will County jail. He protected me from the niggers."

"And got you a lawyer," Leal said.

"Yeah, well, the boss did that. Nuke's connected," Willard said. "Me, him, and Moose go for pickups down in Mexico and Texas for his boss."

Ah, Leal thought. So there's a wild card in the deck.

"Who's his boss?"

Willard shrugged. "Don't know his name. Nuke just

calls him 'boss.' But, man, he's a cool guy, though. Owns a gym and a truck rental place and all kinds of stuff. The trucks is what we use to bring the shit up in."

"What's he look like?" Ryan asked, offering Willard another cigarette.

"White guy. Brown hair. Maybe about your age. Always dresses cool and has some awesome-looking bitch with him in his car."

"What kind of car?" Leal asked.

"Shit, man, he's got lots of 'em." He drew on the cigarette and blew out a cloud of smoke. "A Bimmer, a Mercedes, an XJ6."

"An XJ6?" Leal asked. "What color?"

Willard rolled his shoulders and sucked on the cigarette again. "White, I think."

A white Jaguar tripped something in Leal's mind. Of course, he thought. The first night we went to Walker's, one passed us.

"Can you think of anything else you want to tell us, Stanley?" Ryan asked.

Willard took a final drag on the cigarette and stubbed it out.

"Shit, man," he said. "To tell you guys the truth, if I wasn't afraid Nuke would kill me for taking the stuff outta the house that night, I probably wouldn't even be talking to you."

"One other thing I'd like to ask you," Leal said. "Why'd you try to split tonight? You see us out there?"

Willard shook his head. "Moose called me. Told me to ditch the stuff right away. Said Nuke was suspicious and coming over to check."

When they came out of the interview room Leal saw Brice standing by the window with a haggard look on his face.

"Howdy, Lieu," Ryan said. "Man, have we got a statement for you."

"Yeah, I been here for a while. I heard most of it," Brice said, pointing to the speaker above the window. "I got here when you were reading it back to him. He say anything else about the other guys involved in this?"

"Just two biker types named Nuke and Moose," Leal said. "I got the goods on Nuke from Joliet PD. All we got on the other guy is his street name."

Brice nodded, pinching the bridge of his nose. He glanced at his watch. "All right, it's almost two in the morning. Put this little fucker on ice till tomorrow and we'll figure out our next move." He turned to go, then paused and looked back. "Good job. Everybody. I'm proud of you guys."

Right, Leal thought. Random victim, my ass.

CHAPTER THIRTY-ONE
The Underground Man

The woods seemed to retreat at their encroachment, punctuated by the quick, scurrying movements of small animals and birds as the morning sunlight filtered down between the thick tangle of branches. Even the chirping of the ubiquitous insects was replaced by a sudden, uneasy tranquility as the group of humans, led by the big German shepherd and his handler, moved along the dirt trail. Leal, Hart, Ryan, and Murphy followed with a host of evidence technicians carrying an assortment of digging tools and boxes. Willard, clad in handcuffs and leg irons, had led them to a gravel road that intersected with Route 83 just west of the Swallow Cliffs toboggan slides. The road was secured with a rusty chain suspended between two posts. Nuke, Willard explained, had cut the padlock and replaced it with one of his own.

They'd gone down the road until it angled to the right, out of sight of the highway. Willard lost his bearings several times, before pointing to a patch of coniferous trees and saying, "I think it's that way."

Leal looked down the path and saw nothing but a sea of changing colors.

"Think your partner can help steer us the right way?" he asked the K-9 officer.

The big man, whose name was Weaver, was dressed in army-style BDUs and a baseball cap. He scanned the area, and said, "Let's give it a try. How old's this body supposed to be?"

"About a week," Leal said.

Weaver nodded and reached down, patting his dog and letting him sniff some of Walker's clothes. He whispered and cajoled the animal, then put him on a thirty-foot leash. The dog's head whipped around, then he went off through the underbrush, circling and smelling, looking one way, then another, his large black tail curling upward expectantly.

"What do you think?" Ryan asked.

"How do we know the pooch won't be looking for jack rabbits?" Murphy said. "Goddamn waste of time, if you ask me."

"Nobody's asking you," Leal said. He felt mad enough to bust Murphy's lip just for being such a pain in the ass yesterday on the warrant. Today he was in no mood for the man's complaining.

"He's pretty good at finding bodies," Weaver said. "Remember that mob graveyard up north? We worked that one."

"Any of this looking familiar?" Ryan asked Willard.

He looked around and blinked. "It looks a lot different at night."

About twenty feet ahead the dog barked and sniffed the ground.

"What you got, Dino?" Weaver said, moving forward.

Dino barked again, and dug at the ground. Weaver knelt beside him. "Give me a bag," he said.

"What is it?" Leal asked.

"Looks like raccoon shit to me," Murphy said.

Leal was about to tell him to shut the fuck up when Weaver made a stunning pronouncement.

"It looks like a wad of something. Chewing tobacco, I think."

"Yeah, Nuke chews," Willard said.

"Great," Leal said. "We found a trace of that at Walker's house, remember?"

"Bet he never loses a bone," Ryan said, staring down at the dog.

Dino emitted a low growl, lips curling back from twin rows of perfectly aligned teeth.

"Dogs don't like eye contact," Weaver said, getting to his feet. "Too adversarial."

"That's something we have in common," Hart said, smiling. "At least where you're concerned." She patted Ryan's shoulder as she walked by. They followed the dog farther into the woods. In a small clearing he began to sniff and scratch violently at the ground. He barked several times, and began digging again. Leal studied the area, and suddenly noticed it looked somehow more artificially arranged than the rest of the surroundings. Dino sent a shower of dirt from between his back legs as he dug furiously. Weaver pulled him back.

"If I had to guess," he said, "I'd say this is it."

The evidence technicians went over the area first, photographing and carefully sweeping. A button was found and bagged. Then they started with the shovels.

"How deep is he?" Ryan asked.

"Couple of feet, I guess," Willard said.

With each shovelful Leal's expectations rose. He had the feeling they were getting closer. His nose told him so, too. When they'd gone down about four feet one of the technicians grunted.

"I think we found something."

It was a strip of beige cloth.

"Look familiar?" Leal asked.

Willard nodded. "They wrapped him in a sheet to carry him out."

Renewed by the discovery, yet wary of going too fast, they had the techs set up a camcorder so that they could videotape the rest of the unearthing.

They found his feet first. Then the rest of him. Uncovered, the underground man didn't look much like Martin Walker anymore. He lay on his right side, his head twisted grotesquely backward, dirt stuck in his eye sockets and filling his gaping mouth. The bloated discoloration of the shirt and pants made it almost impossible to tell the actual colors, and the putrid odor wafting upward made it undesirable to try.

"Whooeee," Ryan said, reeling back from the hole. "If he woulda smelled that bad at the airport, they'd never let him on a plane to Puerto Rico."

"Right," said Hart. "Like that was really him at the airport."

Leal spotted an ET pulling something out of the dirt by Walker's feet.

"What you got?" he asked.

"Looks like a beeper," the ET said. He held it out carefully and gently brushed away the dirt with latex-covered fingers.

"Can you see any numbers on it?" Leal asked.

After carefully inspecting it some more, the ET said, "How about that? It's still working."

"They ought to use that for the commercial with the Energizer Bunny," Ryan said. "He could pop up outta the grave and somebody could smack him with a shovel."

"Read me the numbers on it," Leal said as he took out his notebook and pen. His elation was almost enough to make him forget the smell.

Brice looked more haggard than usual as he sat behind his desk, puffing on one of his cigars while they briefed him on finding the body.

"We got no doubt it's Martin Walker?" he asked.

"The ME's confirming it now," Leal said. "The number on the beeper's nonpublished, too. We need to get a subpoena for telephone security."

"Shit, I remember when all you had to do was call," Murphy said.

"Irregardless," Brice said, leaning forward on his desk. The ash of the cigar glowed brightly. "We can follow up on the small stuff later. Right now, we gotta keep moving forward." He tapped the end of the cigar into the ashtray. "I want you to put out a pickup order on that Nuke fucker. And when the state's attorney is through taking that little shit Willard's statement, run him over to the jail."

"We better put him in isolation," Leal said. "Just to be on the safe side."

"I already stapled the isolation request to his file," Ryan said.

Brice grunted and ran his tongue over his teeth.

"What about Nuke's associate?" Leal asked. "That guy Willard called Moose."

Brice frowned. "Yeah, I suppose we can include him, but we really don't know enough about him right now. No, just concentrate on picking up Nuke." He looked at his watch. "Okay, let's get ready to touch bases with Undersheriff Lucas. He's going to be talking with the press shortly, but all we're gonna say is that we're working on a new development in the Miriam Walker case. We got to be careful so we don't spook this other fucker before he's picked up." He stood up, extinguishing his cigar. "You've all done an outstanding job. Write that warrant up and I'll see you all tomorrow."

In the hallway Leal and Hart drifted behind Ryan and Murphy.

"Why so pensive, Cisco?" she asked.

Leal smirked.

"I thought we agreed you weren't going to call me that?"

"I kind of like it."

"I'll have to remember that." He glanced down the hallway to make sure Ryan and Murphy were far enough

-ahead to be out of earshot. "That damn phone number's bothering me. So is Willard's statement about that high roller bankrolling them."

"Like maybe he's the real brains behind everything?"

He nodded. "Let's get that subpoena for the number today, and also pull the MUDs for all the calls made by Walker in the last few weeks. We'd better run a check on that beeper, too. Okay, Pancho?"

She looked up at him and smiled.

White knight takes black rook, Richard Connors thought, making the move on the board of chess figures. Then black rook takes white knight. One move away from mate.

He realized now that he had perhaps underestimated this guy Leal. He'd considered him merely a knight, a minor annoyance, a burnt-out case. But he'd turned out to be a bit more than that. More persistent, more crafty. What was the word? Tenacious. Smarter, at any rate, than was originally anticipated.

He picked up the white knight, studying the ornate curves of the burnished ivory. With Leal gone, it would be for all practical purposes over. Or should he use the sacrifice move and jettison Nuke? The big man was showing signs of slipping. The way he'd bungled the second "Walker visit" was proof enough of that. Still, he did have an unswerving loyalty. But so did a dog, and a dog wouldn't turn state's evidence. Not that he thought Nuke would ever flip. No, that big fucker was hardcore. He'd go to prison for life rather than be labeled a squealer. But there were the other factors to consider.

He replaced the white knight on his square. It was time for a deft stroke. A bold move. He started to make a castling move with his black rook and then remembered that he'd already made one earlier in the game. But what the hell, he thought as he set the king safely into the corner square, and picked up the phone. I make my own rules.

Nuke was grinding out a set of concentration curls on the preacher's bench with Moose spotting him with a two-fingered assist. Nuke's arms bulged with a brocade of veins, looking as big as gallon milk jugs. Just as he was reaching the peak of his curl, the blaring rock music stopped for a moment, and the guy behind the counter called out, "Hey, Nuke, phone call."

Moose's exotropic eye swiveled in front of Nuke's face. He let the bar slam down into the cradle and stood up.

"Jesus fuck, man," he yelled. "Don't ever do that again. You blew my concentration."

"Sorry," Moose said, looking down.

Nuke didn't acknowledge the apology as he strode over to the counter, still scowling, then snatched the phone.

"Hello," he said, then snapped his fingers at the counterman, indicating that he should lower the volume on the stereo.

"Where the hell you been?" Richard Connors asked. "I beeped you twice."

"Yeah, I know," Nuke said. "I lost that fucking thing."

"Where?"

"How the hell should I know? If I knew where it was it wouldn't be lost, would it?"

He listened to silence on the other end and knew that he'd pissed Connors off.

"Is your contact still set at the jail?" Connors asked finally.

"Uh-huh, but I thought they were still holding the little shit at the Fourth District lockup?"

"Not anymore. He's been moved to Twenty-sixth Street this afternoon."

"They gonna have him in isolation?" Nuke asked.

"That's been taken care of."

Nuke grinned, even though he knew the other man couldn't see it. He grinned because he knew what was coming.

"I usually get my collect call from the jail at around six," Nuke said. "I'll just tell him it's a go, then. For the usual nominal fee."

"Just don't fuck it up like you did the other one," Connors said.

"Hey, listen, we didn't fuck up nothing," Nuke said. He was angry now at the very thought of *him* messing up.

"Yeah, right," Connors said. "Forget about it. Just listen. I need you and Moose to lay low after this is set up, all right? They got a pickup order out on you guys."

"Huh?" Nuke said. "When did this happen?"

"Today. And we've got another troublesome end to tie up, too."

"I'm listening," Nuke said.

"This one's a cop," Connors said.

"We're at your old stomping grounds," Leal said into his cell phone as he paced in the massive hallway. "The grand jury."

"Really?" Sharon said. "What are you doing there?"

"We're getting some subpoenas. Say, things have slowed down a little and I thought we might get dinner."

"Tonight?" Her voice sounded uncertain.

"Well, yeah."

He waited for her reply.

"Frank, I can't," she said slowly. "I have some other plans that I just can't cancel." She paused. "I'm sorry. Really. Steve Megally and I are having dinner. A business dinner." She was speaking rapidly now. "To discuss my future with the State's Attorney's office as opposed to Feinstein and Royale."

"Oh, I see."

After a long pause she said, "Look, why don't we plan on dinner together Friday night? I'll be off for the weekend."

"Okay."

"Look, Frank," she said, her voice taking on more of an edge now. "I have a lot of heavy decisions coming up in my life, and I need this time to consider all my options."

"Yeah, I understand," he said, trying to sound sincere. "Friday then, all right?"

After he disconnected Leal compressed his lips and fought the urge to throw the phone against the wall and watch it smash into a million pieces. I wonder if it really is just a business dinner, he thought, as the scene of her and Megally having dinner together lingered his mind's eye.

No strings, he thought, and exhaled a long breath through his nose. He saw Hart coming down the hall with one of the grand jury state's attorneys.

Yeah, lawyers and cops.

CHAPTER THIRTY-TWO
Damage Control

When Leal and Hart arrived at the office the next morning they saw a note taped to the outside of the door, instructing them to report to Brice's office ASAP. Ryan and Murphy were already inside, and the air was gray with smoke. Leal saw Hart grimace as she sat down. Brice had an expression of suppressed rage on his face, a solitary vein bulging on his left temple. Murphy's expression was equally dour, and Ryan looked ashen.

"Sit down," Brice said. He exhaled loudly and crushed out his cigar. "When we're this close to clearing a case," he held up his thumb and forefinger, keeping them a few millimeters apart, "I don't expect a fuckup like this."

Leal's brow furrowed. "What are you talking about, Lieu?"

Brice glared at Ryan.

"You tell him," he said.

Ryan swallowed hard, took a drag on his cigarette, and exhaled a cloudy breath.

"Ah, Stanley Willard," he said. "He was found in the jail this morning. Dead. They're interviewing some of the jailhouse snitches, but so far, nobody saw nothing."

Leal stared at him, dumbfounded.

"What the hell? I thought we had an isolation order on him?"

Ryan shrugged and shook his head. "Somehow he ended up in general population."

"Yeah, Sergeant Ryan," Brice said. "Isn't that what we discussed here in my office yesterday?"

Ryan jammed another cigarette between his lips and flicked his lighter. When he spoke his gaze was down toward the tabletop, his chin lowered.

"I coulda swore I attached it to the file, boss."

Brice cleared his throat.

"Well, our case, our important career-making case, is now in jeopardy," he said. "We've let one of the principal witnesses slip through our fingers. We still have his statement, but now it ain't worth shit without the testimony to back it up." He picked at some lint on the sleeve of his jacket. "So, without further delay, I want you guys to go get an arrest warrant for that guy Nuke. Then go out to Joliet and try to serve it right away. With this new development, we gotta consider him a flight risk. Maybe, if we can grab that bastard before he skips town, we can still salvage this thing."

"Dammit," Ryan said. "I still can't understand how this could happen."

"I can," Brice said. He was rotating another cigar in the flame of his lighter. "You've been a step behind on this from the beginning, Ryan. I never shoulda put you in charge." He blew out some smoke, licked his lips, and then spat into the waste can beside his desk. "Consider yourself on administrative leave. I want a written report of your actions. Report to me Monday morning at nine for disciplinary review."

Ryan's jaw dropped open and he almost lost his cigarette.

"Look, boss," he said, "I realize I might have stepped on my dick, but—"

"No buts," Brice said, cutting him off.

"But I'd really to stay on this one, Lieu."

Brice shook his head, twisting his lips into a frown. "Not only did you step on *your* dick, Ryan . . . You stepped on *mine*."

Ryan looked stunned. He lowered his head and rubbed the bridge of his nose.

Leal was stunned, too. Did this mean Brice was putting him in charge?

Murphy asked the question before Leal could.

"You'll all report directly to me," Brice said. "I'm taking personal command of this one. Murphy, you and Leal pull out all the stops and get that warrant pushed through. And then go serve it. You should be able to get a last known address from Joliet PD."

"What about the beeper and the phone numbers?" Leal asked. "We're in the process of checking them out."

Brice compressed his lips.

"Yeah," he said, "but the arrest of this Nuke guy should take top priority. All the rest of this stuff is secondary and can be followed up at a later date. Once this hits the grand jury, it'll be out in the open. I gotta work on damage control." Brice cleared his throat. "Hart, take the rest of today and go get yourself fixed up at the beauty parlor, or something. Tomorrow morning's the awards ceremony here, and the press is gonna be all over it. Get your uniform pressed. The sheriff wants some shots of you and him together when he's giving you the medal."

"Lieutenant, I'm supposed to get my stitches out tomorrow," she said.

"What time?"

"Nine o'clock."

"Uh-uh," Brice said, shaking his head. "Reschedule that for the afternoon. After the ceremony you can take an early weekend."

They filed out singly, Murphy, Ryan, Hart, and Leal. In the hallway Murphy slapped Ryan on the back and ambled down the hall. Leal and Hart stopped to talk to him.

"Tom, I'm sorry," Hart said. "I don't know what to say."

"Same here," Leal said. "You didn't deserve that."

Ryan seemed to regain a little of his composure. He shrugged and managed a weak smile.

"I could tell he had a hair up his ass when he called and told me to report in early," he said. "But I didn't expect this."

"He looked really wound up," Leal said.

"Tighter than a six-day clock running backward," Ryan said. "Damn, I was sure I put that isolation order in the file." He exhaled a long, slow breath. "Well, I'm gonna miss you guys. And Joe, too. Tell him I learned a lot working with him, will you?"

Leal nodded and they shook hands.

"Well," Ryan said. "I'd better go break the news to my girlfriend, then head over and start drowning my sorrows." His posture looked bent and defeated as he walked away.

At the office Murphy surprised Leal by apologizing for his conduct at the search warrant stakeout.

"I appreciate you not dropping a dime on me to Brice, Sarge," he said. "And I won't forget it, neither."

Leal nodded an acknowledgment, but said nothing. He'd actually been too busy to put pen to paper to write Murphy up.

"I can get that warrant walked through, no problem," Murphy said. "I got plenty of buddies in the State's Attorney's office."

"We'd better handle that right away," Leal said. "Go ahead and get things rolling at Felony Review, and I'll meet you over there in a couple of minutes. I've got to talk to my partner before she leaves for the beauty parlor."

A simpering grin spread across Murphy's face. He took the file and left.

Leal turned and saw Hart looking at him.

"Beauty parlor?" she said, raising her eyebrows.

"You know, you're the only girl I know who looks great without any makeovers," he said.

"Right. Now tell me what you really want."

"I need you to follow up on those phone calls and the beeper," he said. "The subpoenas came through. I picked them up earlier."

"Anything else?" she asked, smiling. "While I'm at the beauty parlor, that is."

"Yeah, give Joe a call. He was supposed to check out that Lunge Hill Corporation for me." He handed her the keys. "Here, you take the car. I'll have Murphy give me a ride home."

"Better you than me," she said, smiling. "If I had to spend that much time alone with him you'd have another homicide to investigate."

Leal and Murphy had no luck trying to locate Nuke to serve the warrant. The last known address proved to be a boarded-up old apartment building with dark smudges coloring the front wooden panels where someone had obviously tried to start a fire. Detective Brown shook his head and smiled.

"Why is it when you're not looking for some scumbag, you see him all over the place?" he said. "I put the word out on him with the patrol guys, though. If they see him, they'll grab him and call you."

"That would probably be the best way to handle it," Leal said. "If he hears about too many coppers poking around it might spook him."

"If he ain't spooked already," Murphy said.

"We won't know that until we catch him," Leal said. He turned to Detective Brown and thanked him for his help.

"I'll give some of my buddies on Will County a call about him, too," Brown said. "Sooner or later he'll turn up."

"Sounds good," Leal said. "I'd also like to grab that other asshole that hangs with him."

Brown nodded.

"Maybe if you get 'em both, you can play one off against the other," he said.

The drive back on the expressway slowed considerably as they caught the tail end of the rush hour. Leal leaned back in the seat and told Murphy not to even think about smoking the fat cigar he was unwrapping. A couple of rain drops splashed against the windshield.

"Aww, come on, Sarge. How 'bout if I open the window?"

"Uh-uh," Leal said. He didn't want to have any more conversation than necessary with a man he detested so much. His beeper went off as they were exiting at 127th Street near Leal's house.

Perfect timing, he thought as he pressed the acknowledge button and saw Hart's home number flash into view.

"Who's that?" Murphy asked. "HQ?"

"No," Leal said. "My dinner date."

"I hope you're hungry," Hart said, opening the door to her apartment. Rocky, the cat, looked up from his sleeping perch atop the edge of the sofa, and resumed his slumber. "I made your favorite. Steamed vegetables and rice."

"Sounds delicious," Leal said, mentally calculating how many sliders he was going to get at White Castle on the way home. "Your hair looks great. You did get to the beauty parlor, huh?"

"Just a quick trip. I have a friend who does hair," Hart said.

"I mean it. It looks really nice."

"It's okay for Thursday evening. Now come on. I'm starving." She led him into the dining room and motioned for him to sit.

After wolfing down the Spartan-sized meal, and washing it down with two glasses of unsweetened, low-calorie cranberry juice, Leal was still famished. He waited while she finished, and declined her offer of herbal tea.

"What happened in Joliet?" she asked. "Get any leads on Nuke?"

Leal shook his head. "Just that his last known address was bogus."

"How about Willard? Anything new there?"

"Nothing. Even the snitches are clamming up on this one."

"So aren't you going to ask *me* what I found out?" she said, placing her muscular forearms on the table and leaning forward. The cut on her left arm had forged itself into a crusty-looking scab, punctuated by the perpendicular row of stitches.

"I figured you were saving that for dessert," Leal said.

She smiled and tapped his arm playfully. After pouring more juice for both of them, she cleared the table, and took the dirty dishes into the kitchen. She came back in with her notebook and motioned for him to join her on the couch. They pulled the coffee table closer in front of them and Hart placed her notebook on top.

"I'm not sure how all this connects to the Walker case," she said. "But there's some pretty interesting developments."

"I'm all ears," Leal said.

Hart took a sheet of paper with columns of numbers printed on it. Some rows had been highlighted with a yellow magic marker.

"This is a listing of all of Martin Walker's phone calls for the past month," she said. "Home and office. This number shows up with more frequency than any other in both columns." She tapped the paper with her pencil eraser. "It's nonpublished, but the telephone security gave it to me after I faxed them a copy of the subpoena. It comes back to a Richard Connors in Orland Park."

"Doesn't sound familiar," Leal said.

"Well, it will. I ran a Soundex and some title searches

on Mr. Connors. Found that he owns four cars—a BMW, a Jaguar, a Mercedes, and a Corvette. Plus, he owns a boat, too."

Leal raised his eyebrows.

"I also checked his credit rating. Thanks to your friend at the credit bureau," Hart said, smiling. "I hope you take care of her from time to time. Just the mention of your name was enough to get her to help me."

"What can I say? My natural charm. It's a gift."

"Don't forget your modesty," she said. "Anyway, guess what? Our friend Mr. Connors has no credit rating. Absolutely none."

Leal hunched forward and stared at her. She tapped the pencil eraser against her strong-looking teeth.

"Which means he deals strictly in cash," she said. "I called a friend of mine in real estate, and had her do some checking. She got back to me and said that she talked to the realtor who handled the sale in Orland."

"And?"

"And," she said, "he paid cash for it. Can you believe it? That house had to go for several hundred, easy."

"Yeah, I can believe it, if what we heard about this guy is true. He's got to be the high roller that Willard the Snake told us about. Any arrest history?"

Hart shook her head. "No record, but I do have more. Oh, I called Joe Smith, by the way. Both baby and mother doing fine."

"Good," he said. "Now tell me what else you got."

"The Lunge Hill Corporation that Miriam Walker was on the board of directors?" Hart said.

Leal nodded.

"Guess who the major stockholder is?"

"Connors?"

She smiled. "You win. And I'd be willing to bet that this Lunge Hill thing, which is a conglomeration of several smaller businesses, had Martin Walker on the payroll somewhere as a consultant, or something."

"And used his savings and loan for money laundering," Leal said. "Having a respected lady judge as a board member, and allowing her to give away money to philanthropic causes would certainly be a good cover."

"So do we figure that Miriam knew about the operation then?"

"Maybe," Leal said. "But maybe not. At this point, we can only speculate on that. And on why she was killed. We know that Nuke and his cronies carried it out, and that Martin wanted it done. Maybe she threatened to spill the beans, so she became a threat to them. Anyway, the exact reasons are still murky right now. Can we tie this Connors guy to Nuke?"

"I was saving the best for last," Hart said. She paused, increasing his anxiety level.

"What?" he said. "Tell me."

"That beeper we found in the grave," she said.

He nodded.

"The phone number on it was Connors' home, nonpublished number. And guess whose beeper it was?"

"I figured it was Walker's."

"So did I, but I decided to check on it anyway. The beeper was leased from Chi-Metro Communications to Richard J. Connors."

Leal's brow wrinkled. "But how did it end up with Walker? And why would a guy have his own, privately listed number on it? Unless . . ."

"He loaned it out to somebody," Hart said, completing the thought. "Somebody like Nuke, maybe?"

Leal gave a low whistle.

"Ollie, you've done a helluva job. If I wasn't afraid of a sexual harassment suit, I'd kiss you."

"Well, don't let that stop you," she said, blushing slightly.

He leaned over and kissed her gently on the forehead.

"Thanks," she said. "So where do we go from here?"

Leal considered this for a moment.

"Right now, let's just document what we've got so far," he said. "And let's just keep it between you and me."

"We don't tell the LT?"

Leal shook his head. "Brice is too ham-handed and single-minded. He's got it in his head to get this Nuke guy before anything, which isn't really a bad way to go. Plus, this white-collar angle is a little too complex to throw at him until we've got all the answers." He thought for a moment. "I've got a couple of buddies in Financial Crimes. I'll touch bases with them and put them on to our Mr. Connors. Plus I want to check him out a little myself."

"Okay by me," Hart said.

"And one more thing," he said. "I'll take the responsibility for pursuing this angle. For now, anyway. If Brice finds out about it and gets pissed, I don't want him going after you."

"Hey, we're partners," she said.

"I know that. You're the best partner I've ever had," he said, reaching out and squeezing her hand. "But after what happened to Ryan today, I don't want it to appear that you've done anything that Brice could interpret as insubordination."

"Like not following his orders and going straight to the beauty shop?"

"Yeah, but when the time comes," he said. "I'll make sure you get the credit you deserve. And Joe, too."

She squeezed his hand back.

"Frank, I *want* to be in on the rest of it. Plus, I'd like a chance at this Nuke guy when we get him."

"Sure," Leal said, realizing that he and Ryan had monopolized every interview so far. "I'll make sure you get in on the arrest, too, if you want. I promise." He held up three fingers in a mock Boy Scout salute.

Hart smiled, then suddenly looked downward.

"Frank, I've got to tell you how much getting this assignment, and working with you, has meant to me." She paused, and he was reasonably certain that he saw her eyes starting to mist over. "It was the kind of case I've always dreamed about. And when I started, I had so many doubts. But having you as a partner . . . it's been . . ." She shook her head slightly and wiped at her cheek. "I can't seem to find the right words. It's just that I've learned so much. I've come so far . . ." Her arms encircled his neck.

He reached out to hug her.

"We both have, kid," he said. "We both have."

CHAPTER THIRTY-THREE
Comrades and Adversaries

The long row of white TV vans with emblazoned logos and extended antennae lined the circular curb in front of headquarters as Leal and Hart pulled into adjacent spaces near the outer edge of the parking lot. She'd called him earlier and told him she was driving down in her own car since she had the doctor's appointment. They'd coincidentally tagged up on the expressway and driven the rest of the way almost side by side. Hart stepped out of her car first and stood there waiting for him.

Man, Leal thought as he looked at her freshly pressed tan uniform and patent-leather shoes. She looks sharp. She'd let her blond hair fall gently over her shoulders in a profusion of curls instead of wearing it back, and had more clothes covered in plastic slung over her shoulder.

"You look great," he said. "You going to change into soft clothes afterward?"

"Yeah, I had to shift the doctor's appointment to this afternoon, so I'm taking off right afterward." They began walking toward the front of the building where groups of reporters were filming backdrops for their upcoming newscasts. "As soon as they get all the pictures they need, that is."

"Want me to snap a few extra of you?"

"No, but thanks anyway." He watched as her eyes surveyed the news vans. Her pace slowed. "Frank, I still don't feel totally right about this."

"Ollie, we already talked about that, remember? You got to do this one for the Gipper." He smiled. "Besides, I'm proud of you. And as far as I'm concerned, you deserve it."

"Thanks," she said, and reached out and squeezed his arm as they got to the front steps. "You won't forget about including me in the wrap-up, will you?"

"I won't forget. We're partners, Pancho."

"I thought you didn't want me to call you that?"

"Call me what?" he asked, pulling open the door for her.

"You know. Cisco."

"Well," he said, smiling broadly. "It is permissible under certain circumstances."

Laughing, they went to the office where Hart hung up her clothes, and they were dismayed to not find the coffeemaker turned on.

"Guess I'm actually starting to miss Ryan," Leal said.

"Well, you've still got Murph," she said.

Leal groaned and rolled his eyes.

They found Murphy in Brice's office, sucking on his own cup of machine coffee from the cafeteria. Undersheriff Lucas was there with a script of the ceremony. He huddled with Hart, explaining exactly how they wanted her to stand, how they wanted her to approach the sheriff, and, most importantly, what not to say. That included virtually anything about the ongoing investigation, how she got injured, and so forth.

"If they push you," Lucas said, "just say, 'I'm unable to comment on that at this time,' and I'll step in. Got it?"

"Yes, sir," she said.

"Good. Now after the sheriff presents you with the Medal of Valor, a short photo session will follow." Lucas looked at his watch. "You're more than welcome to join us at the postconference luncheon."

"Thanks, but I have to change clothes and go to my doctor's appointment," she said.

"Well, if you need any help changing," Murphy said, "I'm available."

He laughed, apparently thinking that would ingratiate him to the others, but all it did was bring a flush to Hart's cheeks.

"I think I can manage, thanks," she said.

Lucas emitted a short, forced laugh, but it, too, fell short, creating a feeling of distance rather than one of camaraderie.

"You've all done an excellent job on this," Lucas said. "Lieutenant Brice will brief you on the next phase of the investigation. You'll have to excuse me while I check on the sheriff."

He's got his nose so far up O'Hara's ass, it's a wonder he's still breathing, thought Leal.

"Okay, here's the game plan," Brice said. "The warrant for Nick Stevens, aka Nuke, is going to be placed in LEADS and NCIC by the end of the day. So if he's stopped or picked up, we'll be notified. I've reached out to several friends in various agencies, too. Joliet and Will County are both looking for him, and his picture's also been put on the Chicago Daily Bulletin. I'm confident we'll bag him this weekend."

Brice stopped to glance at his watch. He kneaded his forehead with big fingers, and smoothed back his hair. His face looked creased and haggard, the strain evident in the heavy bags under each eye.

"So everybody keep either your beeper or cell phone on at all times." He sighed. "In the event we don't grab him in the next forty-eight hours, the sheriff has scheduled a news conference for Monday evening. He's going to cover some of the aspects of the Walker investigation, including finding the body."

"That's going to make it worse for us," Leal said.

"How so?" Brice said.

"Well, we still have some loose ends to tie up," Leal said slowly. "I'd like to do a little more digging into Walker's affairs. Find out who the brains behind this really is. Nuke's not running the show himself, and if we tip our hand, we'll lose him."

"We won't know that till we bring Nuke in," Brice said. "And we can't sit on finding the body too long. The press will crucify us. Anyway, the topic's not open for discussion. If we get Nuke, we can grill him. If not, we let the truth about Walker being a sex pervert and hiring them motorcycle assholes to do his old lady come out at the conference."

"But just how did a guy like Walker connect with someone like Nuke?" Leal asked. "It doesn't make sense. There's a piece of the puzzle missing."

"Who gives a shit?" Brice said. His voice had risen to a high whine. "They probably were into drugs or something together. Anyway, that ain't what's important."

Leal gave a reluctant nod. He was missing Ryan's interdiction skills already. Brice was just too stubborn and single-minded.

"So, you've all worked really hard on this, and I'm proud of you," Brice said. "After the ceremony, you can all take the weekend off. But like I said, stay close to your beepers and phones, and consider yourselves on call. That means no drinking. Well, one or two beers is all right, but this thing could jump out at us at any time. If I need you, I'll beep you to my cell with a nine-one-one behind it. That means call me back immediately."

Leal leaned back and tried to tune out Brice as he spoke. The weekend off. What a crock. But he already had something planned for this afternoon, and tonight, hopefully, his dinner with Sharon wouldn't be interrupted.

The awards ceremony was set up in the gym to accommodate the overabundance of people. An academy class was graduating, and besides Hart's medal, several other awards were being given out. Leal made the mistake of sitting next to Murphy near the back, watching the heavyset cop surreptitiously pick at his nose. Finally, Murphy bowed his head and he started to snore. The son of a bitch is dozing, he thought. Rather than rouse his partner with an errant elbow, Leal carefully slipped out of his seat and left the row of chairs. He collared one of the photographers and told him to take an extra roll of Hart receiving the Medal. He'd have it developed and printed himself. This is something she'll want to look back on, he thought.

"And our recipient of the Cook County Medal of Valor," the announcer's voice said, echoing through the large auditorium, "is Officer Olivia Hart . . ."

Leal listened while a brief summary of the incident, obviously tailored to sound dynamically succinct while saying very little in the way of facts, was read. Hart stepped forward, stopped, and stood at attention. From the distance O'Hara looked short and paunchy as he moved next to her and held out the Medal in his left hand, while extending his right. As they shook hands and the flashes popped, Hart appeared infinitely more impressive, all blond curls, broad shoulders, and tapering waist. Like Wonder Woman receiving an award from one of the Seven Dwarfs.

That asshole Lucas ain't gonna like the rushes on this one, Leal thought. Maybe that's why he scheduled another photo shoot after the ceremony. Give them time to find a box for O'Hara to stand on for that one, and photograph him from the waist up. Just like early Elvis.

Leal chuckled at the thought, then, out of the corner of

his eye, he caught sight of Brice standing about fifty feet away staring at him.

Leal cruised by Richard Connors' home twice before he called the unlisted number on his cell phone. He'd done that same thing when he'd been in MEG—driven by to get a feel for the place. He pulled to the edge of the sweeping cul-de-sac and appreciated the lush, green lawn. The front door was recessed behind a brick archway, and the white XJ6 sat in the driveway like a gleaming trophy. Leal pressed the "send" button.

Connors answered on the second ring with a clipped hello. The voice became totally cordial and relaxed when Leal identified himself as a police officer.

"I'm conducting a death investigation. This number was among the decedent's possessions."

"Oh, yeah. Who died?" He sounded mildly curious.

"I'd rather speak in person about this, Mr. Connors," Leal said. "Would you mind if I stopped in? I'm in the neighborhood."

"Well, I was on my way out," Connors said, a trickle of doubt seemed to invade his tone for the first time. "But I certainly want to do everything to cooperate. And since you're in the neighborhood. You need my address?"

"No," Leal said.

He waited down the block for about five minutes just to see if Connors was going to rabbit on him. Then he made the slow turn and pulled up in front of the house. A forced space between two of the closed blinds in the picture window cracked shut.

Connors looked pretty much like Leal had imagined: midthirties, fit-looking, a wavy crop of brown hair, and with a fashionable tan.

"We spoke on the phone," Leal said, holding up his badge.

"Yeah, come on in," Connors said, stepping back and

extending his arm. "I hope you can at least tell me who it was that got murdered."

"How'd you know it was a murder?"

Connors looked almost startled, then relaxed into a smile.

"I didn't," he said. "I just assumed. That's a dangerous thing to do with a guy like you, isn't it?"

The house was dimly lit and the light pastel walls blended effortlessly into each other. The floor was lined with a thick, bluish carpeting, and the hallway was bordered by a row of ceiling-to-floor burnished wooden posts. Through the gaps Leal could see into a sunken dayroom where a large-screen television played some cable movie. A pair of well-formed female legs and a bare arm protruded from the corner area of a curving sofa. The legs shifted suddenly and a young girl in a purple bikini padded to the bottom of the stairs. Leal admired her curves for a moment and she smiled up at him.

"Candy, this is Sergeant Leal," Connors said. "We're going to be talking in the den for a bit."

"Oh, okay," the girl said. Her eyes swept over Leal for a moment, as if assessing him, and she returned to the sofa.

"Come on this way," Connors said. "Want something to drink?"

Leal shook his head.

"Oh, that's right, you're on duty, aren't you?" Connors smiled. He turned and spoke over his shoulder as they walked. "So tell me, what's it like being a cop?"

"Like anything else, I guess. It has its moments." Leal followed him down an adjacent hallway. "What type of work do you do, Mr. Connors?"

"I'm what you might call an entrepreneur. Made a killing with a dot-com company when they first started. Got out before they went belly-up." He opened a finely polished door, paused, and grinned. "I didn't mean the killing part literally, now."

The room was spacious, with a large teakwood desk at

the rear wall. A computer sprawled across the desk, along with a set of assembled chess pieces. Two comfortable-looking leather chairs sat on either side of the desk, and a gun cabinet with an array of rifles was off to the right. The walls were decorated with the stuffed heads of several animals: a ten-point buck, an elk, a brown bear. On the opposite wall were three big snarling cat heads: a male lion, his female counterpart, and the striped head of a tiger.

Leal studied the animals as he sat down.

"Trophies," Connors said. "I like to hunt."

"I thought tigers were an endangered species," Leal said. Connors smiled.

"Actually, those came from a game farm. One of those private zoos down in Texas. It was going out of business and my guide bought them. We tried to set them free on his preserve so we could hunt them, but it turned out to be a bust. They were so tame all they wanted to do was hide, even after we set the dogs loose."

Leal nodded, continuing to size the other man up. If he was nervous, he sure wasn't showing it.

"Not much of a challenge, really," Connors said. "But they make a helluva conversation piece. I'm hoping to bag a bison next year. It's one of the big ten, you know."

Leal shook his head. He'd learned a long time ago to listen more and talk less. It gave him a chance to observe the other person. Size them up.

"So tell, me," Connors said, "who is it that was killed? I'm dying to know." He laughed.

"Do know Martin Walker?"

Connors wrinkled his brow. "Martin, yeah, sure. We went to high school together. Used to be in the chess club." He stared at Leal for a moment. "It's him? Oh, wow, that's a trip. After what happened to his wife, and now him." He shook his head. "How did it happen?"

Leal ignored the question. "When was the last time you spoke to him?"

Connors licked his lips, shaking his head slightly.

"You know, I couldn't really tell you. We bumped into each other a few years ago at one of our high school reunions. Our fifteenth, I think." He smiled. "It was right after I'd started making some money with my company, and he offered to help me invest some of it. But we weren't particularly close."

"Why would he have your home number?"

"Well, like I said, he was my investor," Connors said. "But a lot of people have my number. Can you tell me what happened?"

Leal shook his head. "You knew his wife, too?"

"Actually, I found a place for her on the board of directors of one of my companies," Connors said. "It was strictly for show, though. I mean, she was a sharp lady, and it didn't hurt to have a female judge associated with me. She liked to give away money to artistic and avant-garde causes, like her little domestic violence thing. It was a good tax write-off for me."

"Was she a victim of domestic violence?"

Connors shrugged. "No idea about that. If she was, she never told me. Anyway, I hardly knew her. Or Marty, either, for that matter. It was more of a business relationship."

"What about Nick Stevens?"

"Who?"

"Nicholas Stevens," Leal said. "Big guy. Calls himself Nuke."

Connors raised his eyebrows. "Doesn't ring a bell, but maybe if I saw him . . ." He looked at his watch. "Is this gonna take much longer? I did promise my girlfriend we'd go down to the lakefront."

"You have a boat?"

"Yeah, I do," he said slowly. "You're asking an awful lot of questions about me, aren't you? I thought you wanted to know about Marty."

"Just curious," Leal said, standing. This bastard's too crafty. "I appreciate your time, Mr. Connors." Leal extended his hand.

They shook. Leal noticed Connors' grip was strong. Next time, he thought, we'll finish this on my turf.

Connors watched the unmarked back out of his driveway and pull away. So that was Leal, he thought. Bigger than I expected. And smarter, too. Can't afford to underestimate him anymore. Candy came up the stairs and pressed herself against his back, her arms encircling his waist.

"What did that cop want?" she asked.

He unclasped her hands from around him and turned.

"Never mind," he said. "Go get the hot tub warmed up for me. I gotta make a call."

He watched her ass as she bounced down the stairs, undoing her bikini top.

I wonder how much he knows? he thought as he picked up the phone and dialed. There's only one way to play this one now.

The voice at the other end of the line answered with a gruff "Hello."

"Nuke?"

"Yeah."

"It's me. Everything cool?"

"Sure, just waiting for instructions, just like you said."

"All right," Connors said. "Tell Moose to call his dad now. I want it done right away. Tonight. No later. Got it?"

Connors heard a low chuckle on the other end.

"Sure, boss," Nuke said. "We'll take care of things for you."

After he hung up Connors felt a slight tickle move up his spine. A tinge of regret that he wouldn't be able to pull the trigger himself? Or was it a trace of fear that Leal was striking so close to home? Either way, the guy was dangerous. It was time for a decisive move. But it would be almost like stalking one of those big cats that had lost their cunning. Black rook takes troublesome white knight. Black king out of check. Poor Leal, he thought. He's about to get blindsided by a freight train out of nowhere.

CHAPTER THIRTY-FOUR
Commitments and Cop-Outs

When Leal picked Sharon up at seven thirty he was stunned at how attractive she looked. She'd obviously gotten her hair done, and worked carefully on her makeup. Her white silk blouse was open just enough to let him appreciate the swell of her breasts, and he caught the delicate smell of her perfume as he closed the car door behind her. On the phone he'd told her that he had a reservation at a very fine restaurant, and he wanted to make the evening very special.

Who knows, this could be our last one together, he thought. The beginning of the end before she flies off to New York and out of my life.

At the restaurant they lingered over the menu, drinking white wine and appreciating the European motif. Baroque designs and long flowing curtains extended from the ceiling to the floor. They ordered and she began telling him about the cases she'd been involved in on her two night shifts: an armed robbery, an aggravated battery, several thefts, and an aggravated sexual abuse case.

"An eight-year-old girl who'd been repeatedly molested by her stepfather," she said looking at the table and shaking her head. "I mean, it's bad enough when something like that happens to an adult, but an eight-year-old?"

"It's always rough when kids are involved," he said. "A loss of innocence."

She gazed up at him, after taking another sip of her wine, and asked how his case was going.

"Did I mention that Brice is now in charge?" he said. "He relieved Ryan."

"Wow. As in fired?"

"Pretty much." Leal smiled slightly. "You know, I really didn't care for Ryan, but he took one on the chin for a mess-up that wasn't entirely his fault. Now that he's gone, I kind of miss him. At least he had some street sense."

"And your favorite lieutenant doesn't?"

"Brice is too one-dimensional." He drank some more from his glass. "Plus he brought that idiot Murphy back into it. Between the two of them, they've mishandled things from the beginning."

"Well, it sounds like you've almost got it tied up now," she said, smiling.

The waiter came back with their orders and they ate leisurely, enjoying the wine, the food, and the conversation. For dessert they ordered ice cream and more wine.

"Brice would kill me if he knew I was drinking tonight," Leal said. "We're officially on call in case they pick up Nuke."

"Well, I won't tell," she said. She looked at him over the rim of her glass. "So how come you haven't asked me?"

"Asked you what?"

"If I'm going to take the job in New York at Feinstein and Royale?"

He looked into her face for a moment.

"I guess I've been afraid to."

Her nostrils flared slightly as she took in a deep breath.

"It's been a tough decision," she said. "I was really shocked when he called me and apologized. And the money that he offered was a lot more than I'd ever make at the State's Attorney's office." She took out her cigarettes and shook one from the pack. "Do you mind?"

He shook his head. Here it comes, he thought.

She lit it and blew the cloud of smoke away from him.

"But, on the other hand, I've got a lot holding me here, too. My parents, my sister, my friends, you. It's not easy just to leave." She paused to inhale once more on the cigarette, and then stubbed it out. "I'm trying to quit," she said, and smiled. "Steve was pretty honest about my future here, too. I'll be getting assigned to do felony trials after about six months, and there's a lot of opportunities opening up in the office for women." Glancing downward, she reached for his hand. "And I'm not so sure I'd ever be happy doing defense work. Not after all the things I've seen as a prosecutor. That little girl last night . . ."

She brought his hand up to her lips, touching his fingers to her face. "And then there's us. We've got something nice here, Frank. I don't know how it is for you, and I'm not trying to press you for a commitment or anything, but, I guess what I'm trying to say is that I think you're a pretty special guy."

"I feel the same about you," he said. His voice sounded hoarse.

"So, I'm staying," she said, squeezing his hand.

Leal was stunned. A feeling of relief flooded through him, but so did a small bit of fear. She said she wasn't pushing him, but did she mean it? Was she really prodding him to make a reciprocal commitment? Visions danced through his mind of Sharon and him arguing while a trio of screaming kids cried in the background. But maybe he was just drudging up the unpleasant memories of his first marriage. He'd grown since then, hadn't he? And what the hell, he thought. Am I ever gonna be happy about anything? Maybe it was the wine. He pushed the glass aside, silently vowing, no more tonight.

"So you want to go to your place or mine?" she asked.

"Well," he said, mentally trying to review the degree of disarray of each of his rooms, "mine's a lot closer."

"I hope this doesn't frighten you into reconsidering about New York," he said, opening the front door. Luckily, he'd felt a burst of energy after he'd gotten home yesterday and pulled out the vacuum cleaner and stuffed the dirty dishes in the dishwasher. But most of the chairs in the house were draped with shirts, pants, and jackets. Twin stacks of old newspapers and magazines sat near the recycling basket, and a TV tray was strategically positioned in front of the sofa bearing his unbalanced checkbook, some unopened mail, and a half-crushed can of beer.

"Things don't normally look this neat," he said with a smile. "But I was hoping you'd come over."

She smiled back, as if appreciating his irony, and said, "This looks lived-in, but fine."

"You want a drink?"

She shook her head, "No, but I would like to use the bathroom."

As soon as the door was closed, Leal made a frantic dash around, gathering clothes, tossing them in the nearest closet, and closing the doors. He dropped the papers and magazines into the plastic box, and was just carrying the TV tray into the kitchen when she came out.

"Just straightening up a little," he said as she looked at him.

She smiled and leaned forward to kiss him when the sound of a beeper went off. Its intrusion halted both of them, and he reached down to his belt, suddenly realizing it wasn't there. He'd been so preoccupied with Sharon's pending decision that he'd left it on his dresser. After retrieving it, he saw it was Brice's cell phone with a 911 behind it.

Shit, thought Leal. I gotta answer this one.

After explaining to Sharon the significance of the 911, he dialed the number and heard Brice's gruff voice.

"Leal? Where the hell are you? I beeped you about thirty minutes ago. Even tried your house a couple of times."

"I went out to eat. What's up?"

"You alone?"

"Yeah," Leal said, not wishing to get into a discussion about whom he was with. "What's up?"

"We got a line on Nuke. A good one from a reliable source. A buddy of mine in Will County. He's hiding out in a construction site near unincorporated Joliet. I'm gonna need you out here ASAP."

Leal sighed and looked at Sharon.

"How do I get there?" he asked. She smiled at him from across the room.

Brice gave him directions.

"I'll have Murphy meet you at the junction of Route 6 and Farrell Road. There's a diner there. He'll be in the maroon unmarked."

"I know the one."

"Okay," Brice said. "I'm in Joliet now, setting up the raid. Get out here as soon as you can. And that means yesterday. Use tac band only to call Murph. My source says the informant told him Nuke's got all kinds of scanners."

"All right," Leal said. "I'll go pick up Hart and be on my way."

"Negative."

"But, Lieu, I promised her—"

"Yeah, yeah, I know," Brice said, cutting him off. "I already got ahold of her and she told me she'd be on her way. And I need you out here now. So get started immediately. That's an order."

"Okay," Leal said. Something in Brice's tone suggested he was lying. Had he really called Hart, or was this another cop-out? After Brice disconnected Leal dialed Hart's place anyway. The phone rang several times. No answer, not even her machine. Leal glanced at his watch. She's probably at the gym, or something, he thought, remembering that she'd told him Rory was working her harder with the contest so close. His gaze drifted over to Sharon, who was partially eclipsed by the shadows.

After he hung up, Leal went over to her and they embraced.

"Sharon, I—"

She put her fingers to his lips, then kissed him softly.

"You don't have to say it," she said. "I already know how important this case is to you. And your career."

He sighed.

"Thanks, babe. I'll make it up to you, I promise." Christ, he thought. It sounds like we're already married. "You're welcome to stay here, if you want. Or I can call you a cab, or you can drive my car home."

"Your new Firebird?" she said. "Hey, that's for me. Give me those keys."

He grinned, winsomely wishing they'd perhaps ended their dinner a half hour earlier.

"Come by afterward and get it," she said. "Shall I wait up?"

"I'll probably be gone for the duration on this," he said, handing her the keys.

"Then wake me up for breakfast then."

"You've got a deal," he said. "But I need you to do me a favor first."

CHAPTER THIRTY-FIVE
Father Knows Best

The big twisted pink neon sign blinked alternating, ALWAYS OPEN/ 24 HOURS above the well-lit parking lot. As his headlights swung around, bouncing over the big wooden post that marked the entrance to the diner, Leal spotted Murphy's unmarked squad car. He saw Murphy switch the spotlight on and off, signaling him.

As if he doesn't stand out enough, Leal thought. He pulled up next to him and cranked the window down.

"What's the story?"

Murphy's face looked ashen in the pale lighting. He motioned with his head and said, "Get in my car. Brice don't want too many vehicles rolling up on the place."

Leal got out and locked his door, looking around. He'd taken the time to change into a pair of jeans and a dark T-shirt with a lightweight jacket covering his weapon. If this thing drew on into the night, he wanted to be comfortable. He also wanted to be able to move if he had to.

Leal went to the trunk of his car and opened it.

"What are you doing now?" Murphy yelled. "I told you I'm driving."

Leal stared at him briefly, then retrieved his kevlar vest from the trunk and slammed the lid. "Just in case," he said, holding it up. He got into the front seat with Murphy and tossed the vest over his shoulder. Murphy was wearing dark clothing, and being this close to him, Leal noticed the big man's face was wet with sweat. He stunk, too. The kind of stink you can smell when somebody's really scared, Leal thought.

"You ready?" Murphy asked, his hands in a white-knuckle grip on the steering wheel.

"Good to go. Fill me in. Where's Brice?"

"He went on ahead with Will County. Maybe the whole thing'll be over with by the time we get there."

"How far is it?"

"Just up the road a bit," Murphy said. He held his portable radio up to his mouth and said, "We're en route."

As Brice's static-laden reply came over the tac band, a Will County squad car passed them going the other direction. The officer gave them a casual courtesy wave, but Murphy kept both his hands on the wheel.

"Ever read *How to Win Friends and Influence People*, Murphy?" Leal asked.

"Huh?"

"That Will County copper. How come you didn't wave to the guy? Ain't they supposed to be our backup out here?"

Murphy frowned. "Didn't see him, I guess."

They rode the rest of the way in silence. About a quarter mile down the highway, Murphy picked up the radio and advised Brice they were entering the access road.

"Douse your lights," came the response on the radio.

Murphy swerved onto the shoulder and killed the headlights, then crept forward slowly. The right side wheels crunched over the gravel surface. He proceeded about twenty feet, then angled to the right some more, getting on a macadamized road that bisected a grove of trees. About a hundred yards ahead of them Leal could see a fairly well-lit structure perhaps six or seven stories

high. Three vehicles were parked in front of it: a two-ton
truck along the side of the building, Brice's tan unmarked, and a dark blue pickup. Several figures stood between the truck and the car. Murphy pulled around in
front of them.

The building was probably little more than half-
finished. Several Dumpsters, stacks of bricks, lumber, and
cement blocks were scattered around in various places
around the site. Many were covered with heavy plastic
sheets. A long white construction trailer was parked near
the road. As he got out of the car Leal smelled the unmistakable odor of tar and saw the machine sitting on the
bed of the truck nearest the building. A long pipe, with a
thick rope running parallel, went from the roof to the
machine on the truck bed. Most of the bottom floors had
glass windows installed in them, and the big floodlights
installed around the base cast eerie shadows along the
structure.

Murphy got out and quickly jogged over to Brice, who
was wearing black pants and a charcoal gray jacket. Leal
retrieved his vest and began to slip it on as he moved toward them.

"Where's he at?" he whispered. The whole scene was
unfolding so haphazardly that Leal was suddenly worried
that Brice's laxity was going to get someone hurt. "And
where's our Will County backup?"

"Relax," Brice said. "You won't need your vest."

"He's in custody?" Leal asked, and saw two figures moving toward them from the other side of the pickup. One
was a heavyset punk, probably still in his teens in a blue
jean jacket. He wore a navy blue handkerchief tied over
his head, and beneath it a pair of wild-looking eyes stared
at Leal. At least one of the eyes did, anyway. The other
drifted off to the right. The second man was bigger, but
dressed almost identically. His hair was somewhat more

rampant, and a growth of beard covered his face. Massive arms sprung from a sleeveless black T-shirt that said in white block letters across the front: WILD LIFE. In the dusky peripheral lighting Leal saw the big man's head tilt back as his lips split open in a sinister-looking leer.

"What the fuck?" Leal said, reaching for his weapon. But suddenly he saw Brice and Murphy pointing their guns at him. Brice cocked back the hammer of his chrome .357 Magnum and pointed it at Leal's head.

"Put your hands on the car. Now!" He tore the vest off Leal's shoulders and tossed it aside.

"Brice, what's going on?" Leal said, but he already knew, deep down in his gut.

"On the fucking car!" Brice shouted, gesturing wildly with his left hand.

Leal placed his palms on the trunk of Murphy's un-marked.

"Get his piece, Murph," Brice said.

Murphy stuck his gun in his belt and began to pat Leal down. He found the Beretta in the pancake holster along Leal's right hip.

"Brice, what the fuck are you doing?" Leal said. "Are you nuts?"

"Shut up," Brice said, extending the barrel of the Mag-num toward Leal's temple. "Just shut the fuck up, Leal. Not another word, understand?"

Murphy found Leal's cell phone and took that, too. He stepped back, shook his head slightly, and handed both of the items to Brice.

Brice snapped on the safety and stuck the Beretta into his belt. He lowered the Magnum and looked at Nuke.

"I thought I made it clear he wasn't supposed to be in on this," he said, nodding toward the wall-eyed punk.

"He goes where I go," Nuke said. "Right, Moose?"

"Fucking right," Moose said, smirking.

Leal watched the strange scene unfold, wondering what his chances were if he were to try and make a break. Slim to none, he thought, and Slim left town.

"Well, I don't want him here," Brice said, raising his voice. "Max, I want you to get in that truck right now and take off."

"Fuck you," Moose said, his lips peeling back in a sneer.

"Change of plans now, Lieutenant," Nuke said, smiling. "Your little boy's done growed up and become a man of his own."

Brice turned toward Nuke now, and Leal cast a quick glance over his shoulder toward Murphy, who was looking to the side. Pushing backward off the car, Leal whirled and shoved Murphy into Brice, then twisted and began running toward the building. It offered the only decent cover in the wide-open area.

If I can get through it and hide in the woods behind it, Leal thought. But the first round whizzed past him, and the deadly sounding crack followed it. Another one ripped by, wide and to the left, he judged from the feel. He heard Brice yelling at Murphy not to use his own piece.

"I got a drop gun," Brice's voice said.

Those sorry motherfuckers, thought Leal. Then he heard the distinctive roar that could only have been the Magnum. Peripherally, he saw Nuke running at an angle, trying to cut him off. A glance over his shoulder told him that Moose was directly behind him and gaining fast.

"Max! Come back, Max," he heard Brice yell.

Then Leal heard heavy footfalls and breathing up along-side him, and saw Nuke out of the corner of his eye. Leal slowed abruptly, throwing the bigger man off his stride as he tried to compensate, too. Nuke's legs staggered for a moment, and Leal shot out a stiff-arm technique that hit Nuke's shoulder and sent him rolling down in a heap. Leal ran straight into the partially open first-floor entrance, hearing Nuke yelling from behind him, "You made it personal now, cop. And I'm gonna make sure I enjoy it."

Moose was right behind him, only seconds away.

The stairs were gray metal set into rough concrete walls. A hanging stream of orange extension cord was strung up on the walls, providing power to light bulbs secured inside small metal cages. Leal reached the second floor before Moose managed to grab him. Leal landed hard on the cement floor, stirring up a cloud of dust. This area was lit with the same type of metallically encased bulbs strung intermittently from the ceiling.

Leal rolled to his feet, then saw Moose lurching forward, arms outstretched, as though he was going to attempt a bear hug. His right eye was staring straight ahead, the left one gazing off at the stairwell.

Counting on this lack of retinal disparity, Leal feinted with his left, then smashed a right hand straight into Moose's nose. The punch staggered him slightly. Another left feint followed by a second overhand right buckled his knees. Leal stepped back.

Moose, screaming wildly, plodded forward, twin streams of crimson pouring from his nostrils. He gave Leal a hefty push, and Leal went with it, putting some more space between them. His hands brushed the floor as he struggled for balance, and his fingers felt something: a section of three-quarter-inch galvanized pipe about a foot and a half long. Gripping it tightly in his hand, Leal swung the pipe against Moose's left shin, then bounced it off his forearm as well. Moose staggered back, crying out in pain, holding his arms up as Leal whipped the pipe again and again, using it like a short baton. Finally, the pipe cracked the other man on the temple, sending his head rocketing backward. His body followed, doing a drunken roll forward, trying to do a little stutter step to catch himself, and then collapsing and falling pell-mell down the stairs, his head making a plunking sound as it hit each step.

Leal caught a glimpse of Nuke and Brice pushing in through the door and he darted up the staircase.

Brice stopped as he saw Moose lying twisted in the stairwell. He holstered the Magnum and knelt next to him, feeling for a pulse.

"Max," he said. "Oh, Max." He cradled the bloody head against his shoulder.

Nuke grinned as he stepped around them. Glancing down at Brice he said, "Father knows best, huh?" He licked his lips and continued up the stairs.

When Murphy saw Brice carrying someone out of the building, he figured it for Leal, so he didn't move. This wasn't turning out the way he'd figured at all. Helping Brice control a homicide investigation was one thing, but actually killing another copper in cold blood, even a copper like Leal, whom he didn't like, was a whole different animal.

If I had any fucking sense, he thought, I'd get in that fucking car and get the hell outta here.

Brice approached, breathing hard from the effort of carrying the extra weight.

"Gimme a hand," he said.

Murphy went forward and saw that the limp figure wasn't Leal after all.

"Jesus, boss, what's going on?"

"Open the fucking car door," Brice said. Murphy went over and helped Brice lower the still-unconscious Moose into the backseat. Brice thumbed open his son's eyes, looking at the pupils.

"I got to get him to a doctor," he said. "He might have a concussion."

"Boss, where's Leal at?" Murphy asked. He heard the quiver in his own voice and swallowed hard.

Brice straightened up and took several deep breaths. The shoulder of his gray jacket was darkened with blood.

He turned and looked up at the structure. "Murph, just stay here and guard Max till I get back, okay?" He pulled the .357 from his belt and began to walk back across the site toward the building.

"I'll be back," he said over his shoulder.

Murphy looked at Brice's stupid kid lying in the backseat in a fetal position, bleeding all over the interior, the blood dropping down onto the floor mat.

Christ, thought Murphy. How we ever gonna explain all this now?

As he ran up the stairway Leal used the pipe to smash some of the suspended bulbs. He could hear the clunking footsteps on the stairs behind him. There was nowhere to go but up. But up to what? Too late, he realized he'd trapped himself, running up to nowhere while they stalked him with guns.

Then he remembered something: the rope attached to the tar truck. They probably used it to haul the tar up to the roof. If he could reach it from one of the upper floors, he might be able to get back to the ground. And he was pretty sure he'd put Moose down for the count, at least temporarily. That left only the other three, Nuke, Brice, and Murphy. He figured it was Nuke coming up the stairs. Probably with Brice right behind him. That left Murphy on the ground. Yeah, he'd take those odds. If he could get them.

He was at the end of the stairway and ran into the room area. A single bulb hung suspended above his head, but he didn't take the time to try and smash it. Instead he dashed for the wall. This section looked like it'd hardly been touched. Bundles of wires sprung from a rough cement floor that was littered with nails, aluminum piping, and sections of cut sheet metal. Large stacks of lumber and brick sat in various locations under thick sheets of blue plastic. The wind was whipping through the open windows, causing the plastic to rustle and snap.

Good, no glass up here yet, Leal thought.

He ran around the piles of masonry equipment and rolls of black paper, scanning for the rope. Which side of the building had that truck been on? He'd become disoriented when he went inside. Leal got to the window and saw he was about six stories up. The rope extended upward, at least ten feet away from him, but canted on an angle toward the building. He might be able to reach it if he could get up to the top floor. The roof would be better. He sprinted toward the stairs again, but only got halfway before he saw Nuke's huge, tapering silhouette, backlit by the naked bulb in the stairwell.

"Brice is really pissed at what you did to his boy," Nuke said, moving forward. His face had a malicious grin that became suddenly visible in the ambient lighting.

"Probably no more pissed than he is at you," Leal said. He could feel the desperation edging into his tone. "For fucking the kid in the ass." He worked his way to the side as he taunted the bigger man, hoping to maneuver Nuke away from the stairs.

Nuke simply unsnapped a leather pouch on his belt and removed a large buck knife. He was still smiling.

"I ain't stupid, cop," he said. "Far from it."

"So you need a knife to get up your fucking nerve, faggot?"

Nuke snorted. "Like I said, I ain't stupid." His voice was calm as he snapped open the blade to the locked position and began to creep forward. "Think you can bait me, huh? That I'll fall for that kind of shit?"

Leal tried to move diagonally, but Nuke, showing surprising agility for a big man, danced to the side and cut him off.

"Remember, cop, I told you it was personal now." He grinned again. "I'm gonna slit open your belly and hang you upside down so you can watch your guts seep out."

Leal still had the lead pipe, but he didn't think he'd fare

well against a knife. He resigned himself to getting cut. And to fighting as hard as he could. He shifted the pipe to his left hand as his right brushed the tough plastic covering a brick stack. A broken half brick lay on top. Grabbing it, Leal pitched it at Nuke as hard as he could.

The sharp edge bounced off the big, overdeveloped pectoral muscle and tore a gash on Nuke's right cheek. Recovering, Nuke halted and did as Leal had hoped. He paused to wipe at the blood. That's when Leal threw the second brick straight at Nuke's head. He ducked, but it caught him a glancing blow. Leal saw him drop the knife and watched it do a skittering bounce into the shadows.

Before Leal could get another brick, Nuke bellowed and rushed forward. Leal swung the pipe hard, but only managed to smack his large foe on the shoulder. Nuke snared Leal's right wrist in a bone-crushing grip. Leal tried to twist away, but suddenly found himself on his back. He still had the pipe in his hand, but Nuke's big boot slammed downward, grinding Leal's fingers, with the pipe inside, against the solid floor. Pulling quickly, Leal managed to wring his fingers away from the pipe, recoiling as it smashed his nails.

Nuke's right fist swung downward, catching Leal under the chin. It was only an arm punch, but it still sent Leal reeling on the edge of darkness for a moment. Instinctively, he tried to stagger to his feet, but Nuke was there again, driving a knee up into Leal's face, then following up with a couple of sharp punches to his side.

"I told you I was gonna enjoy this, cop," Nuke said, laughing.

Leal reeled to the side, seeing a sawed-off two-by-four on the floor in front of him. Gripping it with his left hand, he lashed out, catching Nuke on the right shin. He whipped another backhand, and heard a plunking sound as it connected against the big man's hip bone.

Nuke danced back a few feet, and Leal managed to straighten up all the way.

"You motherfucker," Nuke said, his voice a snarl.

Leal swung the two-by-four again, but this time Nuke sidestepped the blow and slammed the edge of his fist against Leal's temple. Leal tried to react, but Nuke already had a grip on the board and ripped it from Leal's grasp, leaving his hand bleeding from a rash of splinters.

Nuke hefted the two-by-four clublike, as Leal held up his arms to cover up as best he could. He felt the blows crack into his ribs and back, bringing him sinking downward. A kick sent his head reeling backward, and Leal bounced off a cinder block wall. He felt himself drop to all fours, then roll onto his side, his uncontrolled breathing coming with jagged, searing pain each time his chest moved.

Nuke strode across the floor, smacking the two-by-four into his palm with each step.

I'm not gonna die on my knees, Leal thought, struggling to right himself. His fingers touched the floor for support, causing a stinging sensation. Something was there. The open buck knife.

Leal grasped it tightly, covering his movements by hunching his back, the blade pointing upward. He waited on one knee, his face toward the floor.

Nuke's massive feet and legs suddenly appeared in front of him. Leal lurched forward with the knife, and upward, along Nuke's inseam, driving it into the crotch with all the strength he could muster.

Leal heard the other man scream, then felt a tremendous blow strike the top of his head. He felt the rush of blood streaming down his face seconds later. Somehow Leal managed to rotate the blade, causing yet another scream. He saw the board drop to the floor. Leal felt a sudden surge of strength in his legs, and he pushed upward against Nuke. They slammed into the cinder block wall, Nuke's broad back hitting the gray blocks which suddenly began folding inward behind him. A stupid expression swept over Nuke's face and his big arms fumbled in front of him, grasping first at Leal, and then at the air itself. Leal fell forward, too, but his hands hit the solidness of the floor, and he watched as Nuke seemed temporarily suspended in a black void.

Then he was gone, his scream lasting about two or three seconds. Leal managed to place his palm on the base of the wall where it was still intact and pushed himself away from the opening. As he rolled over on his back, another cinder block fell into the darkness and landed with sodden impact below. Leal looked across the fifteen-foot space and saw the sign in bold block letters: CAUTION — ELEVATOR SHAFT.

He struggled for two rasping breaths before pushing himself farther from the edge. Droplets of blood and sweat splashed the concrete under him.

I gotta get up, he thought. I gotta get up.

He was struggling to rise, fighting the waves of nausea that swept over him, cognizant of the warm rush of blood over his face, the stinging sensation in his hands, the wracking pain every time he tried to move. Put one foot in front of the other, he told himself. Like a drunk intent on getting to his car. One step at a time, and I'll get there, he thought. He reached out to steady himself with a nearby pile of lumber.

"Stand up, Leal," the voice said. "I'll make it quick and clean. I promise."

Brice.

Leal saw him now, through the haze of blood and sweat. He wished the constant ringing inside his skull would stop. Brice was about fifteen feet away, the shiny Magnum hanging loosely in his hand. Leal could still tell, even in the dim light, that the man's face was glistening.

"Stand up, dammit, Leal," Brice said. He swallowed hard. "I'll see you get a hero's funeral."

"Why, Brice?" Leal managed to say. "Why?" He saw Brice lick his lips.

"Blood's thicker than rum," he said. He moved forward half a step and raised the pistol.

Leal's eyes desperately searched the floor for the buck knife.

It must have gone over the edge with Nuke.

Brice looked past him to the elevator shaft. He moved in front of Leal, as if anticipating the motion necessary to kick him over the edge.

"I gotta admit, Leal, I never thought you'd be able to take out a guy like Nuke." He still held the revolver pointed at Leal's head. "But to tell you the truth, I was gonna shoot him after he took care of you anyway."

Small consolation, thought Leal. He tried to summon his remaining strength for one last leap, but his body wouldn't obey. Blood's thicker than rum, he thought as he lowered his head and waited for the bullet, the remembered Catholic school catechism racing through his mind: *Holy Mary, Mother of God, pray for us sinners, now and at the hour of our death. Amen.*

"Sorry, Leal," Brice said. Leal heard the hammer cock. "I'd like to say it's nothing personal, but . . ."

"Hold it, Brice. Drop the fucking gun."

Am I dreaming? Leal wondered. His head twisted to the side and he saw a slim silhouette with blond hair holding a stainless steel revolver in the starkly lit stairwell.

Ollie.

Brice hesitated, did a little half turn, and fired a round at the stairs. Leal saw two bright flashes from the stairs, lighting up the room and sending a half foot of flame shooting toward them. Brice grimaced, did an exaggerated stutter step, and tried to raise his gun again. But his arm just extended out in front of him, while his legs curled in the opposite direction. He folded onto the concrete with a soft thud.

Leal tried to look into Brice's eyes, but he saw they were closed, the man's lips twisted in pain.

"Ollie," he called out, wanting to warn her about Brice's other gun, but the words were all jumbled in his head. Nothing would come out in the right order.

"On your stomach, Brice," Hart called out. "Arms spread-eagle, palms up."

Good, Leal thought. She was still behind the cover of the wall.

"I'm shot, you fucking bitch," Brice said. "Get me an ambulance."

"Get on your stomach, or I'll put the next one right between your eyes," Hart said. "I've got backups with me. It's all over now."

Leal watched Brice's face sag. He released his hold on the Magnum and slowly rolled onto his stomach. Hart was there, suddenly snapping her handcuff over his left wrist, twisting his arm into a hammerlock, and locking the arm with her knees as she bent back his right arm and secured that one also.

Leal tried to tell her about the second gun again, but she'd already found it, pulling up Brice's jacket and removing a snub-nosed .38 from a holster on his belt.

He gathered his strength and managed to say, "Good job, Ollie."

Hart stood up, and Leal took some measure of delight at seeing the darkening puddle spreading out from beneath his former boss. Then he felt Hart cradling his head against her breasts.

"Oh, God, Frank," she said, taking his pulse. Then into her radio, "We've got an officer down on the sixth floor. Get the paramedics. There's a suspect down, too. In custody."

Leal felt a surge of pride as he watched her, the light from the bulb seeming to make a halo around her blond head. He started to tell her she looked like an angel when dark walls pushed closer, sending a swarm of black dots in front of his eyes.

CHAPTER THIRTY-SIX
Cisco and Pancho

The only thing Leal remembered about the ambulance ride, besides the sirens blaring, was the paramedic holding a white plastic bucket under Leal's mouth so he could puke. The dark vomit, mixed with copious amounts of blood, made him wonder if he had internal injuries.

That was one hell of an ass whipping, he thought, then tried to smile as he remembered Brice's whimpering. The fucker was actually crying, he tried to tell the paramedic.

"Just vomit into the bucket, sir," the paramedic said.

When he opened his eyes again, bright lights shone down from above. The numbing pain suddenly felt good, because at least he knew he was still alive. A nurse was swabbing his face with something. Alcohol. She was, he reflected, the most beautiful nurse he'd ever seen. Then her face was replaced by a bearded man in a lab coat, probing him with latex-covered fingers.

Then he saw her. Ollie.

"How you feeling?" she asked.

"I been better," he said.

"You're going to be okay, Frank," she said, touching his face. "I've already called Captain O'Herlieghy and Special Prosecutions."

"Brice?"

"In surgery," she said. "He's expected to live. To stand trial."

Leal nodded.

"What about Murphy?"

"As soon as I showed up with Will County, he boogied," she said. "There's an ISPERN dispatch out on him. It's only a matter of time before he gets spotted."

Leal grunted suddenly as pain shot up his arm.

"I believe your shoulder is dislocated, sir," the bearded guy said. "I know it's painful, but I'm trying to slip it back in. I guess the pain medication hasn't quite kicked in yet."

Leal grunted a response through clenched teeth.

"Ollie, how did you know where?"

"After your lady friend beeped me, I made a couple of calls right away." Her fingers brushed back some of his dark hair. "I was afraid to call your cell if you were on a stakeout. But neither Joliet PD nor Will County knew what I was talking about. I figured they'd have to be in on it, so I started to get worried. I called HQ, and as far as they knew, Brice never checked in with them, either. I figured I'd better get out there."

"Intuition."

She smiled.

"So I got real lucky, then. I followed the directions to the diner that Sharon gave me, and I found a Will County officer finishing up his lunch there."

"In uniform?" Leal asked. "Was he in uniform?"

She nodded.

"The guy Murphy didn't wave to," he said.

She looked down at him with a quizzical expression, then continued. "Anyway, he remembered seeing an unmarked squad take a right down the gravel access road earlier. When I told him I was looking for a construction site, he led me right to it. Then there was Murphy standing there, looking stupid, and Brice's son unconscious and bleeding in the backseat. From the look on Murphy's face,

I knew something was up. I tried to question him, but he got into his car and took off."

"He stunk," Leal said.

"What?"

"He stunk, didn't he?"

She smiled again, and nodded.

"Yeah. So he bolts and the Will County guy and I are just standing there looking at each other. He calls for backups, and I figured that if I could get up to the top of that building, I'd have a better view to look around. Then on the second floor I saw all kinds of blood."

"Mr. Leal," the doctor said, "can you feel this?"

"Feel what?" Leal said. He felt the black lights starting to swarm again.

"Good, the meds are starting to kick in," the doctor said. "I'm going to suture the top of your head. You've got a nasty gash up there. Try to lie still, please."

"I'll do my best," Leal said. "So was that Moose guy really Brice's kid?"

"Uh-huh," Hart said. "A real hardcase, I guess."

"Like father, like son."

"We haven't got the whole story yet," she said. "And Captain O'Herlieghy told us to wait till Special Prosecutions gets here, but apparently Brice got drawn in trying to protect him. We'll know more when we can interview them both."

"And Murphy."

"Right," she said. "And Murphy."

Leal took a deep breath, realized it hurt, and coughed a few times. The doctor told him to be still. Leal said he was sorry, then canted his head slightly toward Hart.

"This is the second time you've saved my life," he said.

"Well," she said, her fingers caressing his face, "since I can't remember the first, how about we just call it even, huh, Cisco?"

"Okay, Pancho," he said, trying to smile. "Ollie?"

She looked at him.

"You're the best partner I've ever had," he said thickly, as he felt a wave of slumber sweep over him.

Richard Connors hadn't heard from Brice in two days, despite numerous attempts to get hold of him. But maybe no news is good news, he thought as he slipped in a Sinatra CD and began listening to "The Best is Yet to Come." He hadn't really appreciated the Chairman of the Board until after he died, but now he'd come to realize the importance of calling all the shots and having your own sense of style.

The doorbell rang as Candy was drying herself off from a session in the jacuzzi. Connors went to the door and looked out the peephole. He could see some blond chick standing there with a paper in her hand. Maybe she was selling something, but he wasn't buying. He began to walk away when a persistent and rather loud knocking commenced.

What the hell? he thought, and was just about to go give her a piece of his mind when he heard a crash and the door flew inward. The blond chick, now looking like some Amazon, burst inside, followed by a slew of uniforms. Before he could say or do anything the bitch pointed a gun in his face and told him to "get on the floor."

"What the hell is this?" he demanded.

"Search warrant, Mr. Connors," she said. "You're also under arrest for conspiracy and the attempted murder of a police officer."

Attempted, he thought. Oh no, that goddamn Brice blew it and now he's flipped on me. In his mind's eye he saw the white chessmen lining up to surround the black king. Mate in two moves, he thought. Game's over.

Richard Connors disappeared completely two days after posting a one hundred thousand dollar cash bond. When

Leal and Hart went to interview Candy, his girlfriend, as to his whereabouts, she would only say that he'd called her the day he got out of jail and said it was over.

"Over?" Hart asked. "Between the two of you, or with everything?"

Candy shrugged. "I don't know. With me, I guess. Ricky always bragged that he had some kind of plan. An escape pod, he called it."

"Did he say where he might be going?" Leal asked. His right hand was still in a cast and his arm in a sling, but he felt very safe with Hart.

"I asked the same thing," she said. "He just told me he was 'going south.' If I had to guess, I'd say it was someplace in the islands." She got a faraway look in her eyes. "Like, one time we went down to this Club Med place in the Caribbean. It was so awesome. You didn't even need to wear a suit on the beach. It was sooooo cool."

Leal and Hart looked at each other.

"Maybe they'll send us down there to pick him up for extradition," he said.

"Be a good chance to work on our tans," she said.

"It's Over," the caption under Sheriff Donald O'Hara's picture proclaimed in the newspaper. The headline had more succinctly summed up his concession speech:

O'HARA: IT'S AN HONOR TO HAVE SERVED.

"Despite having solved the Miriam Walker murder case, as he said he would, incumbent Donald O'Hara went down in flames election day, the victim of the spiraling scandal within the ranks of the Cook County Sheriff's Police Department."

But in the same edition, one quasi-sympathetic editorial asked another pointed question: "Will Michael Shay be any better?"

Leal pondered this and other such imponderables as he folded the paper under his arm and flashed his badge at the security guard. The guard grunted and let them by. He and Sharon proceeded backstage at the Rosemont convention center where the contestants were pumping up for the Women's National Bodybuilding Championships.

"You don't think O'Hara lost because of that commercial I was in, do you?" Leal asked. His hand was now in a more flexible cast, and the sling, reserved for only rare occasions, was in Sharon's purse.

"Of course not. You and Hart looked very distinguished. If anything, it forestalled the inevitable."

They walked down the back hallway to a room that was being used as a staging area. Inside, muscular women flexed and pumped with various weights while their trainers applied copious layers of baby oil.

Some were already posing in front of the large mirrors that had been hung on the walls. Others sat on benches doing concentration curls. Leal saw Hart in the corner, her big biceps muscles dancing under her taut sandy-colored skin as she waved at them. Rory Chalma was on his knees, rubbing both hands over her back.

"Hi," Hart said. "Thanks for coming."

"We wouldn't miss it," Leal said, watching Rory reach around to apply more baby oil over Hart's rippled abdominal muscles, and thought it was too bad he couldn't appreciate the unique opportunities of a job like that.

"Do you think this looks okay?" Hart said, pointing to her black posing bikini.

"More than okay," Leal said, and felt Sharon slap him playfully.

"It looks great, Ollie," Sharon said. "And so do you."

"Yeah, you'll knock 'em dead," Leal said.

"Not if you don't start pumping up," Chalma said.

"Okay," Hart said. "In a minute, Rory." She looked at them and smiled crookedly. "I'll get nervous if you watch me pump."

Leal nodded. "We'll be in the third row. Good luck, kid."

"Thanks. I'd hug you both but I don't want to cover you with baby oil and instant tanning dye." Rory's hands moved around the inside of her thighs. "We'll have ice cream after the contest," Hart called as they were leaving. "My treat."

In the hallway Sharon snared his left arm and brought it around her waist.

"I still think this women's bodybuilding is a little too much," she said.

"Yeah, but she's one helluva a good partner," he said.

"And do you think Sergeant-In-Charge Ryan will let you two go on working together?"

"He'd better," Leal said, grinning, "Or I'll have Ollie kick his butt."

She smiled and leaned her head on his shoulder as they walked. They were coming to the end of the corridor, and the big ballroom was filled with howling fans already screaming and cheering some of the preliminary lighter-weight competitors who were on the stage. Leal saw Sharon looking at them going through the motions of the posedown and shaking her head.

"Well, Hart does look fantastic, in a muscular sort of way," she said. "Do you think she'll win the contest?"

"I don't know," he said as they continued toward their seats. "But she'll always be a champion to me."

SANDRA
RUTTAN

One year ago, a brutal case almost destroyed three cops. Since then they've lost touch with one another, avoiding painful memories, content to go their own ways. Now Nolan is after a serial rapist. Hart is working on a string of arsons. And Tain has been assigned a series of child abductions, a case all too similar to that one. But when the body of one of the abduction victims is found at the site of one of the arsons, it starts to look like maybe these cases are connected after all....

WHAT
BURNS
WITHIN

ISBN 13: 978-0-8439-6074-7

MADAME PRESIDENT

As the first female president of the United States, Carolyn Connor is under constant intense scrutiny. So if anyone discovers that her childhood friend Mike Stanbridge has become her lover, not just her marriage but also her career might be ruined by the scandal.

Their secret could be blown sky-high when a woman close to the president is murdered. Worse yet, Mike is the main suspect. Someone clearly wants Mike to take the fall as more and more evidence seems to point his way. With political assassins trying to kill him and the FBI trying to arrest him, Mike will need to move fast if he wants to stay alive and find the truth behind the lies.

ROB PALMER

EYES OF THE WORLD

ISBN 13: 978-0-8439-5676-4